Collier's *Junior* Classics

Series Editor
Margaret E. Martignoni

Series Titles	*Volume Editors*
A, B, C: GO!	**Rosemary E. Livsey**
ONCE UPON A TIME	**Elizabeth H. Gross**
MAGIC IN THE AIR	**Mary V. Gaver**
JUST AROUND THE CORNER	**Alice Brooks McGuire**
IN YOUR OWN BACKYARD	**Marian C. Young**
HARVEST OF HOLIDAYS	**Ruth Weeden Stewart**
LEGENDS OF LONG AGO	**Jane Darrah**
ROADS TO GREATNESS	**Louise Galloway**
CALL OF ADVENTURE	**Charlemae Rollins**
GIFTS FROM THE PAST	**Elenora Alexander**

in your own backyard

A completely new selection of outstanding children's stories and poems compiled for enrichment reading by a distinguished editorial board of children's librarians.

Series Editor
MARGARET E. MARTIGNONI
Former Superintendent
Work with Children
Brooklyn Public Library

Editor-in-Chief
DR. LOUIS SHORES
Dean, Library School
Florida State University

Managing Editor
HARRY R. SNOWDEN, JR.

Volume Editor
MARIAN C. YOUNG
Chief, Children's Services
Detroit Public Library

Collier's *Junior* Classics Series

THE CROWELL-COLLIER PUBLISHING COMPANY • NEW YORK

In Your Own Backyard

Introduction

Collier's Junior Classics Series

We are children only once, and then only for a few brief years. But these are the most impressionable years of a lifetime. Never again will the world and everything in it be so eternally new, so filled with wonder. Never again will physical, mental, spiritual growth be so natural and unavoidable. During these years, habits become ingrained, tastes are developed, personality takes form. The child's whole being is geared toward learning. He instinctively reaches out for truth and, having no prejudices, seizes upon that which is good, just, beautiful. For these reasons, a child deserves what Walter de la Mare has called "only the rarest kind of best."

What do we mean by "best" in a book for children? Best books reflect universal truths with clarity and artistry. Such books reveal that man is essentially good and that life is infinitely worth living. They do not deny the existence of evil, but rather emphasize man's thrilling struggle against evil through faith, courage, and perseverance. They awaken the young reader's imagination, call forth his laughter as well as his tears, help him to understand and to love his fellow man. The reading of such books constitutes a rich heritage of experience which is every child's birthright.

The librarian-editors of *Collier's Junior Classics* have combed the best children's books of the past and present to assemble in a single series a sampling of the finest literature for boys and girls. High standards have been maintained for the art work also, which in most instances has been taken from the original book. No attempt has been made to cover all fields of knowledge or to include factual material for its own sake. The emphasis here is on good literature, chiefly fiction and biography, folk lore and legend, and some poetry. Special attention is given to the American scene and American democratic ideals, but many selections cover other cultures, geographical areas, and historical periods.

The purpose of *Collier's Junior Classics* is to introduce boys and girls to some of the best books ever written for children, to stimulate young readers to seek for themselves the books from which the selections have been drawn as well as other good books of similar appeal, and to encourage children to become discriminating, thoughtful, life-time readers. Author, title, and publisher are given at the foot of the page on which each selection opens. This enables readers to ask for the complete book at a library or bookstore. When necessary, brief introductions set the scene for the selection, while follow-up recommendations, complete with publishers' names, appear at the end of most stories.

Collier's Junior Classics is a series of ten individually indexed volumes. A, B, C: GO! has been lovingly compiled for the youngest, and consists of nursery rhymes, favorite folk tales, best-loved poems, and stories for reading aloud. Four volumes have been assembled for the intermediate group: ONCE UPON A TIME, a wonderous collection of fables, world folk tales, and modern fairy tales; MAGIC IN THE AIR, selections from great masterpieces of fantasy; JUST AROUND THE CORNER, excerpts from warm-hearted stories of other lands; and IN YOUR OWN BACKYARD, selections from stirring books about our own country. Four additional volumes cater to the interests of more mature boys and girls: GIFTS FROM THE PAST, memorable selections from world classics; LEGENDS OF LONG AGO, selections from great myths, epics, and American tall tales; ROADS TO GREATNESS, excerpts from biographies of some of the greatest men and women of the world; and CALL OF ADVENTURE, selections from action and suspense stories of today and yesterday. Finally, and most unusual of all, is the volume entitled HARVEST OF HOLIDAYS, a feast of stories, poems, documents, and factual material about twenty-two American national and religious holidays. Although perhaps of greatest interest to the intermediate group, HARVEST OF HOLIDAYS will intrigue and delight all ages.

The tables of contents for the ten volumes read like an all-time Who's Who of distinguished writers. A brief mention of only a few of these authors would include such names as Lewis Carroll, Kenneth Grahame, Charles Dickens, Mark Twain, Louisa May Alcott, Pearl Buck, Laura Ingalls Wilder, Eleanor Estes, Genevieve Foster, Robert Louis Stevenson, Robert McCloskey, Valenti Angelo, Carl Sandburg, A. A. Milne, Eleanor Farjeon, Elizabeth Enright, and Margaret Wise Brown. Among the illustrators, many of whom are also authors, are to be found the Petershams, the d'Aulaires, Wanda Gág, Louis Slobodkin, Helen Sewell, Lois Lenski, Roger Duvoisin, Maurice Sendak, Kurt Wiese, Marguerite de Angeli, Steele Savage, Howard Pyle, Lynd Ward, James Daugherty, Arthur Rackham, Fritz Kredel, and Gustave Doré.

Collier's Junior Classics is intended primarily for the home, although libraries will find the series valuable for browsing as well as for introducing children to many different books. Because each book is an individual volume, complete with its own index, it can be shelved where the librarian believes it will be most useful to the children.

No pains have been spared to make the individual volumes a series of stepping stones to all that is best in the magic world of children's books.

Margaret E. Martignoni
SERIES EDITOR

Contents

vii

In Your Own Backyard

Every United States coin carries the phrase, E PLURIBUS UNUM. It means "From many, one"—from many countries, from many backgrounds, from many religions, one nation.

In colonial times settlers poured into the new world from many parts of Europe. After the Revolutionary War, when the United States was formed, more and more people found homes in America. They came from many lands; they followed a variety of religions, they spoke in different languages. Together they tamed a wilderness, built cities, and worked to create a strong and free United States.

America is proud of her people. There are Polish Americans and Puerto Rican Americans; Jewish and Amish Americans; Americans who are brown, others who are white; Americans who are city dwellers, others who live on farms. As individuals, they think and speak, worship and work in their own ways. But as Americans, they are alike in their belief in freedom, in their willingness to help their country, in their respect for the laws of the land.

IN YOUR OWN BACKYARD is a potpourri, a mixture of Americans. It tells stories of young people growing up in the America of yesterday—traveling through the wilderness in covered wagons, pioneering on the plains. It tells stories of young people living in America today—running a paper route, waiting for a new puppy, being a stranger in a new school. IN YOUR OWN BACKYARD tells the story of a democracy through the lives of boys and girls in many parts of the United States.

MARIAN C. YOUNG
Chief, Children's Services,
Detroit Public Library

Laura's family traveled by covered wagon from the little house in the big woods of Wisconsin to the little house on the Kansas prairie. They were never afraid because Pa was always there to protect them.

The Wolf Pack

BY LAURA INGALLS WILDER
Illustrations by Garth Williams

T HE walls are up," Pa was saying to Ma in the morning. "We'd better move in and get along as best we can without a floor or other fixings. I must build the stable as fast as I can, so Pet and Patty can be inside walls, too. Last night I could hear wolves howling from every direction, seemed like, and close, too."

"Well, you have your gun, so I'll not worry," said Ma.

"Yes, and there's Jack. But I'll feel easier in my mind when you and the girls have good solid walls around you."

"Why do you suppose we haven't seen any Indians?" Ma asked.

"Oh, I don't know," Pa replied, carelessly. "I've seen their camping-places among the bluffs. They're away on a hunting-trip now, I guess."

Then Ma called: "Girls! The sun's up!" and Laura and Mary scrambled out of bed and into their clothes.

"Eat your breakfasts quickly," Ma said, putting the last of the rabbit stew on their tin plates. "We're moving into the house today, and all the chips must be out."

So they ate quickly, and hurried to carry all the chips out of the house. They ran back and forth as fast as they could, gathering their skirts full of chips and dumping them in a pile near the fire. But there were still chips on the ground inside the house when Ma began to sweep it with her willow-bough broom.

Ma limped, though her sprained ankle was beginning to get well. But she soon swept the earthen floor, and then Mary and Laura began to help her carry things into the house.

Pa was on top of the walls, stretching the canvas wagon-top over the skeleton roof of saplings. The canvas billowed in the wind, Pa's beard blew wildly and his hair stood up from his head as if it were trying to pull itself out. He held onto the canvas and fought it. Once it jerked so hard that Laura thought he must let go or sail into the air like a bird. But he held tight to the wall with his legs, and tight to the canvas with his hands, and he tied it down.

"There!" he said to it. "Stay where you are, and be—"

"Charles!" Ma said. She stood with her arms full of quilts and looked up at him reprovingly.

"—and be good," Pa said to the canvas. "Why, Caroline, what did you think I was going to say?"

"Oh, Charles!" Ma said. "You scalawag!"

Pa came right down the corner of the house. The ends of the logs stuck out, and he used them for a ladder. He ran his hand through his hair so that it stood up even more wildly, and Ma burst out laughing. Then he hugged her, quilts and all.

Then they looked at the house and Pa said, "How's that for a snug house!"

"I'll be thankful to get into it," said Ma.

There was no door and there were no windows. There was no floor except the ground and no roof except the canvas. But that house had good stout walls, and it would stay where it was. It was not like the wagon, that every morning went on to some other place.

"We're going to do well here, Caroline," Pa said. "This is a great country. This is a country I'll be contented to stay in the rest of my life."

"Even when it's settled up?" Ma asked.

"Even when it's settled up. No matter how thick and close the neighbors get, this country'll never feel crowded. Look at that sky!"

Laura knew what he meant. She liked this place, too. She liked the enormous sky and the winds, and the land that you couldn't see to the end of. Everything was so fresh and clean and big and splendid.

By dinner time the house was in order. The beds were neatly made on the floor. The wagon-seat and two ends of logs were brought in for chairs. Pa's gun lay on its pegs above the doorway. Boxes and bundles were neat against the walls. It was a pleasant house. A soft light came through the canvas roof, wind and sunshine came through the window holes, and every crack in the four walls glowed a little because the sun was overhead.

Only the camp fire stayed where it had been. Pa said

he would build a fireplace in the house as soon as he could. He would hew out slabs to make a solid roof, too, before winter came. He would lay a puncheon floor, and make beds and tables and chairs. But all that work must wait until he had helped Mr. Edwards and had built a stable for Pet and Patty.

"When that's all done," said Ma, "I want a clothes-line."

Pa laughed. "Yes, and I want a well."

After dinner he hitched Pet and Patty to the wagon and he hauled a tubful of water from the creek, so that Ma could do the washing. "You could wash clothes in the creek," he told her. "Indian women do."

"If we wanted to live like Indians, you could make a hole in the roof to let the smoke out, and we'd have the fire on the floor inside the house," said Ma. "Indians do."

That afternoon she washed the clothes in the tub and spread them on the grass to dry.

After supper they sat for a while by the camp fire. That night they would sleep in the house; they would never sleep beside a camp fire again. Pa and Ma talked about the folks in Wisconsin, and Ma wished she could send them a letter. But Independence was forty miles away, and no letter could go until Pa made the long trip to the post-office there.

Back in the Big Woods so far away, Grandpa and Grandma and the aunts and uncles and cousins did not know where Pa and Ma and Laura and Mary and Baby Carrie were. And sitting there by the camp fire, no one knew what might have happened in the Big Woods. There was no way to find out.

"Well, it's bedtime," Ma said. Baby Carrie was already asleep. Ma carried her into the house and undressed her, while Mary unbuttoned Laura's dress and petticoat waist down the back, and Pa hung a quilt over the door hole. The quilt would be better than no door. Then Pa went out to bring Pet and Patty close to the house.

He called back, softly, "Come out here, Caroline, and look at the moon."

Mary and Laura lay in their little bed on the ground inside the new house, and watched the sky through the window hole to the east. The edge of the big, bright moon glittered at the bottom of the window space, and Laura sat up. She looked at the great moon, sailing silently higher in the clear sky.

Its light made silvery lines in all the cracks on that side of the house. The light poured through the window hole and made a square of soft radiance on the floor. It was so bright that Laura saw Ma plainly when she lifted the quilt at the door and came in.

Then Laura very quickly lay down, before Ma saw her naughtily sitting up in bed.

She heard Pet and Patty whinnying softly to Pa. Then
the faint thuds of their feet came into her ear from the
floor. Pet and Patty and Pa were coming toward the
house, and Laura heard Pa singing.

"Sail on, silver moon!
Shed your radiance o'er the sky—"

His voice was like part of the night and the moonlight and the stillness of the prairie. He came to the doorway, singing,

"By the pale, silver light of the moon—"

Softly Ma said, "Hush, Charles. You'll wake the
children."

So Pa came in without a sound. Jack followed at his
heels and lay down across the doorway. Now they were
all inside the stout walls of their new home, and they
were snug and safe. Drowsily Laura heard a long wolf-
howl rising from far away on the prairie, but only a little
shiver went up her backbone and she fell asleep.

All in one day Pa and Mr. Edwards built the stable for
Pet and Patty. They even put the roof on, working so
late that Ma had to keep supper waiting for them.

There was no stable door, but in the moonlight Pa
drove two stout posts well into the ground, one on either
side of the doorway. He put Pet and Patty inside the
stable, and then he laid small, split logs one above another, across the door space. The posts held them, and
they made a solid wall.

"Now!" said Pa. "Let those wolves howl! I'll sleep, tonight."

In the morning, when he lifted the split logs from behind the posts, Laura was amazed. Beside Pet stood a
long-legged, long-eared, wobbly little colt.

When Laura ran toward it, gentle Pet laid back her ears and snapped her teeth at Laura.

"Keep back, Laura!" Pa said, sharply. He said to Pet, "Now, Pet, you know we won't hurt your little colt." Pet answered him with a soft whinny. She would let Pa stroke her colt, but she would not let Laura or Mary come near it. When they even peeked at it through the cracks in the stable wall, Pet rolled the whites of her eyes at them and showed them her teeth. They had never seen a colt with ears so long. Pa said it was a little mule, but Laura said it looked like a jack rabbit. So they named the little colt Bunny.

When Pet was on the picket-line, with Bunny frisking around her and wondering at the big world, Laura must watch Baby Carrie carefully. If anyone but Pa came near Bunny, Pet squealed with rage and dashed to bite that little girl.

Early that Sunday afternoon Pa rode Patty away across
the prairie to see what he should see. There was plenty of
meat in the house, so he did not take his gun.

He rode away through the tall grass, along the rim
of the creek bluffs. Birds flew up before him and circled
and sank into the grasses. Pa was looking down into the
creek bottoms as he rode; perhaps he was watching deer
browsing there. Then Patty broke into a gallop, and
swiftly she and Pa grew smaller. Soon there was only
waving grass where they had been.

Late that afternoon Pa had not come home. Ma stirred
the coals of the fire and laid chips on them, and began
to get supper. Mary was in the house, minding the baby,
and Laura asked Ma, "What's the matter with Jack?"

Jack was walking up and down, looking worried. He
wrinkled his nose at the wind, and the hair rose up on
his neck and lay down, and then rose up again. Pet's
hoofs suddenly thudded. She ran around the circle of her
picket-rope and stood still, whickering a low whicker.
Bunny came close to her.

"What's the matter, Jack?" Ma asked. He looked up at
her, but he couldn't say anything. Ma gazed around the
whole circle of earth and sky. She could not see anything
unusual.

"Likely it isn't anything, Laura," she said. She raked
coals around the coffee-pot and the spider and onto the
top of the bake oven. The prairie hen sizzled in the spider
and the corncakes began to smell good. But all the time
Ma kept glancing at the prairie all around. Jack walked
about restlessly, and Pet did not graze. She faced the
northwest, where Pa had gone, and kept her colt close
beside her.

All at once Patty came running across the prairie. She
was stretched out, running with all her might, and Pa
leaning almost flat on her neck.

She ran right past the stable before Pa could stop her.

He stopped her so hard that she almost sat down. She was trembling all over and her black coat was streaked with sweat and foam. Pa swung off her. He was breathing hard, too.

"What is the matter, Charles?" Ma asked him.

Pa was looking toward the creek, so Ma and Laura looked at it, too. But they could see only the space above the bottom lands, with a few tree-tops in it, and the distant tops of the earthen bluffs under the High Prairie's grasses.

"What is it?" Ma asked again. "Why did you ride Patty like that?"

Pa breathed a long breath. "I was afraid the wolves would beat me here. But I see everything's all right."

"Wolves!" she cried. "What wolves?"

"Everything's all right, Caroline," said Pa. "Let a fellow get his breath."

When he had got some breath, he said, "I didn't ride Patty like that. It was all I could do to hold her at all. Fifty wolves, Caroline, the biggest wolves I ever saw. I wouldn't go through such a thing again, not for a mint of money."

A shadow came over the prairie just then because the sun had gone down, and Pa said, "I'll tell you about it later."

"We'll eat supper in the house," said Ma.

"No need of that," he told her. "Jack will give us warning in plenty of time."

He brought Pet and her colt from the picket-line. He didn't take them and Patty to drink from the creek, as he usually did. He gave them the water in Ma's washtub, which was standing full, ready for the washing the next morning. He rubbed down Patty's sweaty sides and legs and put her in the barn with Pet and Bunny.

Supper was ready. The camp fire made a circle of light in the dark. Laura and Mary stayed close to the fire, and kept Baby Carrie with them. They could feel the dark all around them, and they kept looking behind them at the place where the dark mixed with the edge of the firelight.

Shadows moved there, as if they were alive.

Jack sat on his haunches beside Laura. The edges of his ears were lifted, listening to the dark. Now and then he walked a little way into it. He walked all around the camp fire, and came back to sit beside Laura. The hair lay flat on his thick neck and he did not growl. His teeth showed a little, but that was because he was a bulldog.

Laura and Mary ate their corncakes and the prairie hen's drumsticks, and they listened to Pa while he told Ma about the wolves.

He had found some more neighbors. Settlers were coming in and settling along both sides of the creek. Less than three miles away, in a hollow on the High Prairie, a man and his wife were building a house. Their name was Scott, and Pa said they were nice folks. Six miles beyond them, two bachelors were living in one house. They had taken two farms, and built the house on the line between them. One man's bunk was against one wall of the house, and the other man's bunk was against the other wall. So each man slept on his own farm, although they were in the same house and the house was only eight feet wide. They cooked and ate together in the middle of the house.

Pa had not said anything about the wolves yet. Laura wished he would. But she knew that she must not interrupt when Pa was talking.

He said that these bachelors did not know that anyone else was in the country. They had seen nobody but Indians. So they were glad to see Pa, and he stayed there longer than he had meant to.

Then he rode on, and from a little rise in the prairie he saw a white speck down in the creek bottoms. He thought it was a covered wagon, and it was. When he came to it, he found a man and his wife and five children. They had come from Iowa, and they had camped in the bottoms because one of their horses was sick. The horse was better now, but the bad night air so near the creek had given them fever 'n' ague. The man and his wife and the three oldest children were too sick to stand up. The little boy and girl, no bigger than Mary and Laura, were taking care of them.

So Pa did what he could for them, and then he rode back to tell the bachelors about them. One of them rode right away to fetch that family up on the High Prairie, where they would soon get well in the good air.

One thing had led to another, until Pa was starting home later than he had meant. He took a short cut across the prairie, and as he was loping along on Patty, suddenly out of a little draw came a pack of wolves. They were all around Pa in a moment.

"It was a big pack," Pa said. "All of fifty wolves, and the biggest wolves I ever saw in my life. Must be what they call buffalo wolves. Their leader's a big gray brute that stands three feet at the shoulders, if an inch. I tell you my hair stood straight on end."

"And you didn't have your gun," said Ma.

"I thought of that. But my gun would have been of no use if I'd had it. You can't fight fifty wolves with one gun. And Patty couldn't outrun them."

"What did you do?" Ma asked.

"Nothing," said Pa. "Patty tried to run. I never wanted anything worse than I wanted to get away from there. But I knew if Patty even started, those wolves would be on us in a minute, pulling us down. So I held Patty to a walk."

"Goodness, Charles!" Ma said under her breath.

"Yes. I wouldn't go through such a thing again for any money. Caroline, I never saw such wolves. One big fellow trotted along, right by my stirrup. I could have kicked him in the ribs. They didn't pay any attention to me at all. They must have just made a kill and eaten all they could.

"I tell you, Caroline, those wolves just closed in around Patty and me and trotted along with us. In broad daylight. For all the world like a pack of dogs going along with a horse. They were all around us, trotting along, and jumping and playing and snapping at each other, just like dogs."

"Goodness, Charles!" Ma said again. Laura's heart was thumping fast, and her mouth and her eyes were wide open, staring at Pa.

"Patty was shaking all over, and fighting the bit," said Pa. "Sweat ran off her, she was so scared. I was sweating, too. But I held her down to a walk, and we went walking along among those wolves. They came right along with us, a quarter of a mile or more. That big fellow trotted by my stirrup as if he were there to stay.

"Then we came to the head of a draw, running down into the creek bottoms. The big gray leader went down it, and all the rest of the pack trotted down into it, behind him. As soon as the last one was in the draw, I let Patty go.

"She headed straight for home, across the prairie. And she couldn't have run faster if I'd been cutting into her with a rawhide whip. I was scared the whole way. I thought the wolves might be coming this way and they might be making better time than I was. I was glad you had the gun, Caroline. And glad the house is built. I knew you could keep the wolves out of the house, with the gun. But Pet and the colt were outside."

"You need not have worried, Charles," Ma said. "I guess I would manage to save our horses."

"I was not fully reasonable, at the time," said Pa. "I know you would save the horses, Caroline. Those wolves wouldn't bother you, anyway. If they had been hungry, I wouldn't be here to——"

"Little pitchers have big ears," Ma said. She meant that he must not frighten Mary and Laura.

"Well, all's well that ends well," Pa replied. "And those wolves are miles from here by now."

"What made them act like that?" Laura asked him.

"I don't know, Laura," he said. "I guess they had just eaten all they could hold, and they were on their way to the creek to get a drink. Or perhaps they were out playing on the prairie, and not paying any attention to anything but their play, like little girls do sometimes. Perhaps they saw that I didn't have my gun and couldn't do them any harm. Or perhaps they had never seen a man before and didn't know that men can do them any harm. So they didn't think about me at all."

Pet and Patty were restlessly walking around and around, inside the barn. Jack walked around the camp fire. When he stood still to smell the air and listen, the hair lifted on his neck.

"Bedtime for little girls!" Ma said, cheerfully. Not even Baby Carrie was sleepy yet, but Ma took them all into the house. She told Mary and Laura to go to bed, and she put Baby Carrie's little nightgown on and laid her in the big bed. Then she went outdoors to do the dishes. Laura wanted Pa and Ma in the house. They seemed so far away outside.

Mary and Laura were good and lay still, but Carrie sat up and played by herself in the dark. In the dark Pa's arm came from behind the quilt in the doorway and quietly took away his gun. Out by the camp fire the tin plates rattled. Then a knife scraped the spider. Ma and Pa were talking together and Laura smelled tobacco smoke.

The house was safe, but it did not feel safe because Pa's gun was not over the door and there was no door; there was only the quilt.

After a long time Ma lifted the quilt. Baby Carrie was asleep then. Ma and Pa came in very quietly and very quietly went to bed. Jack lay across the doorway, but his chin was not on his paws. His head was up, listening. Ma breathed softly, Pa breathed heavily, and Mary was asleep, too. But Laura strained her eyes in the dark to watch Jack. She could not tell whether the hair was standing up on his neck.

Suddenly she was sitting straight up in bed. She had been asleep. The dark was gone. Moonlight streamed through the window hole and streaks of moonlight came through every crack in that wall. Pa stood black in the moonlight at the window. He had his gun.

Right in Laura's ear a wolf howled.

She scringed away from the wall. The wolf was on the other side of it. Laura was too scared to make a sound. The cold was not in her backbone only, it was all through her. Mary pulled the quilt over her head. Jack growled and showed his teeth at the quilt in the doorway.

"Be still, Jack," Pa said.

Terrible howls curled all around inside the house, and Laura rose out of bed. She wanted to go to Pa, but she knew better than to bother him now. He turned his head and saw her standing in her nightgown.

"Want to see them, Laura?" he asked, softly. Laura couldn't say anything, but she nodded, and padded across the ground to him. He stood his gun against the wall and lifted her up to the window hole.

There in the moonlight sat half a circle of wolves. They sat on their haunches and looked at Laura in the window, and she looked at them. She had never seen such big wolves. The biggest one was taller than Laura. He was taller even than Mary. He sat in the middle, exactly opposite Laura. Everything about him was big—his pointed ears, and his pointed mouth with the tongue hanging out, and his strong shoulders and legs, and his two paws side by side, and his tail curled around the squatting haunch. His coat was shaggy gray and his eyes were glittering green.

Laura clutched her toes into a crack of the wall and she folded her arms on the window slab, and she looked and looked at that wolf. But she did not put her head through the empty window space into the outdoors where all those wolves sat so near her, shifting their paws and licking their chops. Pa stood firm against her back and kept his arm tight around her middle.

"He's awful big," Laura whispered.

"Yes, and see how his coat shines," Pa whispered into her hair. The moonlight made little glitters in the edges of the shaggy fur, all around the big wolf.

"They are in a ring clear around the house," Pa whispered. Laura pattered beside him to the other window. He leaned his gun against that wall and lifted her up again. There, sure enough, was the other half of the circle of wolves. All their eyes glittered green in the shadow of the house. Laura could hear their breathing. When they saw Pa and Laura looking out, the middle of the circle moved back a little way.

Pet and Patty were squealing and running inside the barn. Their hoofs pounded the ground and crashed against the walls.

After a moment Pa went back to the other window, and Laura went, too. They were just in time to see the big wolf lift his nose till it pointed straight at the sky. His mouth opened, and a long howl rose toward the moon.

Then all around the house the circle of wolves pointed their noses toward the sky and answered him. Their howls shuddered through the house and filled the moonlight and quavered away across the vast silence of the prairie.

"Now go back to bed, little half-pint," Pa said. "Go to sleep. Jack and I will take care of you all."

So Laura went back to bed. But for a long time she did not sleep. She lay and listened to the breathing of the wolves on the other side of the log wall. She heard the scratch of their claws on the ground, and the snuffling of a nose at a crack. She heard the big gray leader howl again, and all the others answering him.

But Pa was walking quietly from one window hole to the other, and Jack did not stop pacing up and down before the quilt that hung in the doorway. The wolves might howl, but they could not get in while Pa and Jack were there. So at last Laura fell asleep.

Little House on the Prairie *is one of Mrs. Wilder's famous "Little House" books, of which* Little House in the Big Woods *is the first. Other titles include* Little Town on the Prairie *and* By the Shores of Silver Lake, *all published by Harper.*

Away Goes Sally

BY ELIZABETH COATSWORTH

Illustrations by Helen Sewell

When Aunt Nannie refused to leave her comfortable home to make the trip to Maine, her brothers built a little house on runners to be pulled by oxen. And away went Sally and her three aunts—over the snow, right through a storm, and headlong into a big adventure!

WILDER and wilder grew the country through which they passed, and farther and farther apart were the settlements, but still the little house went on. One day when Dinah was running along beside the oxen, as she sometimes liked to do for a little while, she was almost carried away by a fox that chased her right in among the oxen's hoofs before sliding off into the woods again like a red shadow. After that, Sally never let Dinah down without walking with her, and Dinah herself kept looking over her black shoulders at the woods.

Sometimes they made long journeys and sometimes short, for it was not so easy now to make sure that the cattle had a barn-roof over them each night.

One morning Sally was walking by herself at the head of the procession. A feeling of early spring was in her bones. They had passed some men sugaring off, boiling the maple syrup in big kettles over a leaping fire, sunk deep the snow. The men called out to them and came to admire the little house and look over the oxen. They insisted that the ladies must take a crock of their syrup and would accept no pay.

"You'll do as much for us some time," said one of them.

Sally walked on, eating a piece of bread and syrup carefully, her eyes on a scolding squirrel in one of the trees. When she looked ahead she saw someone or something coming towards them. For a long time she thought it must be a man with a dog, but when they came nearer she saw that the animal was a black bear-cub on a chain. The little bear shambled along, swinging his head from side to side. His coat was black and shiny except about his nose which was brown. His little eyes looked at her expectantly. When the man who was leading him stopped, the cub sat down and held the chain between his front paws like clumsy hands.

"How do you do?" said Sally, looking from the cub to the man who was with him. He was an Indian, tall and thin, wearing an old coat and hat that had belonged to white men, but his leggings and moccasins were made of fringed buckskin. He smiled at her gravely and she smiled back. She had seen few Indians, but she liked them. She put her hand on the cub's head and he dropped the chain and played with her wrists instead.

Uncle Joseph rode up and pulled in Peacock, who snorted. The oxen stopped, heads low, stamping at the smell of wild life.

"He's a real cute little fellow," said Jehoshaphat Mountain, rubbing the bear's ribs with the end of his pole.

"I wish I could have him, Uncle," said Sally wistfully.

"What would you do when he grew big and cross?" asked Uncle Joseph.

"Let him go back to the woods," said Sally.

"I won't have a dratted bear in the house," called Aunt Nannie from the door. "There's enough of us as it is without cubs, I should think."

Uncle Eben had come up.

"Just what I need to keep me warm in the sleigh," he

said without a twinkle. "I've been wanting a bear-cub for ever and ever so long. Dinah's too small to be any good as a warmer, and Sally keeps in front of the procession. How much, hey?" he went on to the Indian, and in five minutes he had bought the little bear—collar, chain and all—and carried him off to Dorcas and the sleigh, while Aunt Nannie, and Aunt Deborah, and Aunt Esther crowded to the window to watch.

Dorcas soon got used to the smell of bear, though at first she tried to run away, and from that time on Sally spent a good many hours with Uncle Eben in the sleigh. Hannibal, as the little bear was called, was very fond of Sally and would cuddle close to her and lick her cheek. He and Uncle Eben talked together, Hannibal in grunts and whines and Uncle Eben pretending to understand and answer.

"You say it's late, do you, and time to have dinner? Well, you'll just have to wait. You don't like waiting, you say? Well, here's a doughnut Sally will give you if you're polite. Now say 'Thank you.' You won't? And why not? You say one doughnut isn't enough, do you?"

"How can you tell what he's saying, Uncle Eben?" Sally would ask.

"Why, can't *you?*" Uncle Eben seemed surprised. And after a while Sally almost thought she could understand, too.

It took only a few days for the oxen and horses to get used to having Hannibal near them, but the cows never got over lowering their horns at him when he came close. He usually slept beside Jehoshaphat Mountain in one of the barns at night, but it was Sally who gave him warm milk in the morning and the evening at milking time.

One gray afternoon she and the aunts were sitting in Aunt Nannie's house sewing when Aunt Deborah sighed.

"This afternoon seems long," she said. Through the windows endless trees moved slowly by, each tree making room for another tree to take its place. A little snow was falling.

"Let's invite Hannibal for tea," said Aunt Esther.

Aunt Nannie started to protest, but stopped herself. She thought for a moment and then said to Sally:

"Put on your cloak, child, and tell Master Hannibal that Mrs. Dinah would be honored if he would take a dish of milk with her by the stove."

Uncle Eben pretended to grumble.

"Who's going to keep me warm? What's that you say, you rascal? You don't care? You want to go, anyhow? You've never been introduced to Mrs. Dinah, but you've admired her from a distance? Well, go along, then. I suppose I can keep myself warm," and he pulled Dorcas to a halt while Hannibal scrambled to the ground and Sally and he ran off to the house together.

It was the merriest afternoon. The squirrels in the dark trees at the sides of the road and the few crows passing overhead must have been surprised at the peals of laughter ringing out from the go-abroad house. Even the oxen twitched back their stolid ears to listen, and Peacock pranced as he led the cavalcade. In the first place, Dinah looked furious at having another animal come into her world. She backed slowly towards one of the beds, her back up, her tail like a bottle brush, her ears laid close to her head and her eyes sparkling. When she backed into the bed, she thought something had attacked her from behind and spit like a perfect fury. All the time Hannibal stood looking at her, apologetic and worried, until she went out of sight under the bed. Then the cub saluted each of the ladies, as Uncle Eben had taught him, and Sally brought him an apple. From time to time volleys of hisses came from under the bed to remind them that Dinah was still on hand. Sally had to crawl in after her and bring her out by the scruff of the neck, but after

coaxing she finally settled down. When Hannibal's back
was turned to her, she crept up softly and patted him
with her paw. When he swung around, she retreated hissing, but before an hour was up they were lapping milk
out of the same saucer, and by the time the uncles came
in for tea Dinah was asleep on Hannibal's shoulder, her
head almost lost in his warm fur.

"How do you like my bear, Nannie?" asked Uncle Eben,
smacking his lips over his chocolate.

"He's a nice enough little creature," said Aunt Nannie,
and then, feeling that she had relented too far, she added
quickly, "But what good is he to anyone?"

"You wait and see," said Uncle Eben, more wisely than
he knew, for it was not many days before Hannibal
proved his usefulness in a very unexpected way.

"I don't like the feel of the air," said Aunt Deborah
timidly one morning as they were having breakfast.

"What's wrong with it, Debby?" asked Uncle Eben
helping himself to another piece of pie.

"It feels like a storm," said Aunt Deborah shivering. "I
wish, Brother Joseph, you would put up here for another
day."

Sally looked from the window and saw the men bringing the cattle out of the crude log barn in which they had
been crowded together the night before. Beyond them
she saw the settler's cabin, an untidy sort of place in a
clearing ugly with raw stumps sticking through the snow.

They were so near the Penobscot now that she hated the idea of any delay. Aunt Esther hated it, too, Sally could see.

"Better safe than sorry," Aunt Nannie remarked.

"I don't notice anything unusual," said Uncle Joseph. "The wind's northwest and we might get a squall, but nothing to speak of. I'll talk to the man here and see what he says."

Sally watched him consulting with a small bearded man in a raccoon-skin cap. They looked at the sky, wet their fingers and tested the wind. She was glad to see that the yoking of the oxen went on.

"He thinks it's all right, Deborah," said Uncle Joseph, sticking his head through the door, and was off.

Sally loved the start in the morning. All the animals knew now what was expected of them, even Hannibal who clambered into the sleigh by himself and sat among the fur rugs watching everyone with a funny look of pride on his face. Dinah jumped on Sally's lap and looked out, too. Like all cats she was full of curiosity. Then came the fine moment of the morning when Uncle Joseph rode Peacock to the head of the line. Jehoshaphat Mountain and the other men shouted, the oxen heaved forward, the little house gave a lurch as it broke out of its position, and the caravan was off.

The jolt upset Dinah, who retired with a look of irritation for another nap. There was nothing unusual, except that Aunt Deborah still had a worried air. Now they were out of the clearing and in the woods again, going down the narrow rough road between the two endless dark walls of trunks. It was almost dinner time when the snow began. At first it came lightly, and Uncle Eben joked Aunt Deborah, as they ate about the little table.

"Here's your blizzard, Debby," he said affectionately. "Someone's been shaking a feather-bed somewhere."

But Uncle Joseph did not joke. He hurried through his

meal, and soon Sally saw him helping to get the oxen in
line again. In half the usual time they were on the road,
with Jehoshaphat urging on the teams to their greatest
speed. The snow fell heavier, and now most of the windows were covered thick with it and the little house was
dark. Sally, peering through the sheltered top of a window, could no longer see the leaders, but only the backs
of the nearest pair.

Aunt Deborah lit the lamp in silence, and the aunts
knitted quietly together. Sally went to put a stick of
wood on the fire.

"No, child," said Aunt Nannie, looking up. "We had
better save the wood."

Sally sat by the window on the lee side staring out, but
she could not see two feet ahead of her. Several times
she had a shadowy glimpse of Uncle Joseph riding by
on Peacock. Once he tapped on the window, and leaned
out of the saddle so that his face was near the glass. He
looked at her inquiringly, his hair and eyebrows matted
with snow. Sally wanted to cry, but she smiled and nodded at him instead. All was well in the house. He disappeared again into the curtain of snow.

Dinah lay in Sally's lap, but though Sally stroked and
coaxed her, she would not purr. Sometimes she shivered
and burrowed her head against Sally as though she were
trying to get away from something. The room was growing colder, and all the time it seemed to Sally that the
little house was going more and more slowly. Sometimes
it stopped, and she knew an ox had stumbled, but always
it went on again.

"Put the stick on now, child," said Aunt Nannie from
the silence. "The fire mustn't go out."

"I wish we'd followed your advice, Aunt Deborah," said
Sally, as she put a small stick on the embers.

"Tut, my dear," answered Aunt Deborah almost sharply. "There's no use crying over spilled milk."

"Do you think Uncle Eben and Hannibal are safe?" whispered Sally, voicing the fear that had been in her mind for a long time now.

"Of course," said Aunt Nannie, "or Brother Joseph wouldn't go on. But I wish I felt so sure of old Brindle and the cows."

Then there was silence again—only the knitting needles and the clock sounded in the room, and outside the snow fell and fell, and the wearying oxen stumbled forward through the deepening drifts, and the little house still crept slowly onward towards the Penobscot.

It was Dinah who first gave the signal that the storm was over. She jumped down from Sally's lap, yawned, and began washing her paws. Sally, who had been in a sort of trance, looked out and then clapped her hands.

"I can see the trees, Aunt Nannie! Look, Aunt Deborah! Look, Aunt Esther, there are the trees again!" It seemed to her like heaven, just to see the forest beside the road, after the blinding hours they had been through.

The snow was over as quickly as it had come. In another half-hour the last flurry had fallen, and Sally in her red cloak, under a clearing sky, was floundering in the deep drifts, making her way back to Uncle Eben.

"Are the cows all there?" she called to one of the men.

He wiped his mitten across his face and grinned, nodding. The cows were plodding on, their sides heaving with the effort, but the oxen ahead had trampled the path for them and the little house had broken part of the force of the storm.

"Hello!" said a cheerful voice, and, looking up, all her fear melted into one peal of laughter. Two white snow-crusted faces surrounded by snowy fur were turned to her from the sleigh, two pairs of brown eyes looked at her kindly, two fat bodies in bearskins sat side by side.

"I can't tell which is which," Sally said, "but may I come up?"

The bells stopped ringing. In a moment she was tucked in under the rugs between the other two and the sleigh-bells returned to their gay wild song. All the time the caravan moved on.

"It wouldn't be safe to let the beasts stand," explained Uncle Eben. "Joseph will keep them moving so they won't stiffen. Easy does it. There's nothing to worry about now."

He beat his mittened hands against his chest.

"Don't you want to come in and get warm, Uncle Eben?" asked Sally anxiously.

"Can't desert the ship," said Uncle Eben. "Don't worry, my dear, I'm right as rain. But you might take Hannibal in to warm his nose. He hasn't any hair on it, you know."

The world seemed beautiful as Sally and Hannibal made their way forward towards the house. The road was soft and white as the breasts of pigeons, and the dark pine branches were bending under heavy epaulettes of snow. Here and there a birch was doubled almost into an arch, and the thickets were mounded whitenesses. A cow lowed, a man shouted, the sleigh-bells rang cheerfully, and Sally and Hannibal made slow haste through this ermine world to overtake the house moving slowly ahead.

But suddenly Hannibal was pulling sideways at his chain.

"Hurry up," cried Sally, giving it a jerk.

But Hannibal refused to budge.

He had his little beady eyes fixed on something by the side of the road which Sally had not noticed. It looked like a log, almost hidden with snow, which some wood-cutter had left leaning against a pine.

Sally's feet were cold.

"Don't be silly, Hannibal," she exclaimed, tugging with all her might.

But Hannibal would not come. Instead, he began pulling Sally towards the log.

"Drat the bear!" thought Sally to herself, but she had to give in. Better let Hannibal get his idea out of his head, whatever it was. She wondered if there could be a honey tree near by. Here the snow was unbroken, but she managed to struggle after Hannibal.

"What's up?" called Uncle Eben, stopping Dorcas.

"It's Hannibal," Sally called back. "I can't do anything with him."

They had almost reached the stump, and the cub turned and looked at her as though saying, "There, do you see now?"

And Sally, looking closely, did see at last.

"Uncle Eben!" she called. "Oh, Uncle Eben! It's a man!"

"Is he dead?" thought Sally, sitting in a corner of the room with her arms round Hannibal's neck for comfort. The uncles had carried the man in and laid him motion-less on a bed. Between their bodies, leaning over him, Sally caught glimpses of a little man with a stubbly beard

and a face like a friendly monkey's, that had somehow been turned to marble.

"He *is* dead!" said Sally out loud, and began to cry softly.

"Hush!" whispered Aunt Deborah, hurrying by with some blankets. "He's not dead, child."

Sally caught her skirt. "Will he be all right?" she whispered back.

"I don't know." Aunt Deborah spoke low as though the man might overhear her. "Let me go, dear. There's no time to be lost."

Outside all was still, but inside people were hurrying softly and speaking low quick directions. Sally, watching with her heart in her mouth, saw Uncle Eben force the man's mouth open with the top of the rum bottle, and a moment later she was brought to her feet by seeing the stranger's eyes open, in a bright blue stare that made her catch her breath. But she had little time to be relieved for Uncle Joseph just then came in with a pail full of snow. She saw him cutting off the man's shoes with his knife, and now they were all filling their hands with snow and the uncles were rubbing his feet with it and the aunts were rubbing his hands and nose and ears, while the man groaned and stirred.

"Poor man, isn't he cold enough?" thought Sally. "But Uncle Joseph and Aunt Nannie must know."

Hannibal, feeling the trouble all about him, began to whine.

"Oh, stop it, Hannibal," said Sally. "You *must* stop it."

The snow was getting low in the pail, and Sally took another one outdoors to fill. The hired men were walking the horses and oxen and cows up and down slowly while the struggle went on inside.

"How is the poor critter, Miss Sally?" asked Jehoshaphat Mountain, sympathetically.

"He's alive," said Sally. "But it's awful, Jehoshaphat Mountain—everyone's rubbing him with snow."

"So he won't lose his fingers and toes, that is," said Jehoshaphat. "They mustn't warm too quick or they would fall right off. A peddler, I think he is, from the pack we found beside him."

Sally hurried back with the snow. And now even she could see that the circulation was coming back into the man's veins, and his flesh no longer looked so like stone. But he was groaning worse than ever.

"Is he dying, Uncle Eben?" she asked, putting the pail handy.

"Not a bit of it, child," said Uncle Eben. "The blood's coming back, that's all. He'll be all right in two shakes of a lamb's tail. But get more snow, there's a good child. We want to save all of him, if we can."

Sally was out in the snow and back again like a flash. The peddler wasn't groaning so much now and everyone looked more cheerful.

"There, Esther," said Aunt Deborah, "his face is safe, I think. You'd better warm some more blankets now. How are his feet, Brother Joseph?"

"A few minutes more on this left one and his feet will be out of all danger too," Uncle Joseph replied.

The man spoke for the first time, whisperingly. "I'm

sure I'm much obleeged to you all," he said. "Is my pack safe?"

"Safe as can be," answered Aunt Nannie with a kind smile.

"It's my living, ma'am," said the man, and fell soundly to sleep with his mouth open.

Uncle Joseph shook himself. "Well, now," said he, "since the peddler's attended to, poor man, we'd best be getting the cattle on, Eben." And the uncles bundled again into their heavy fur coats and clambered out, and soon the journey was resumed. Meantime, the aunts returned to their knitting, after Aunt Deborah had put some broth on the stove to heat.

"Like as not he'll want something hot when he wakes up," she said. There was an air of relief and satisfaction in the room that one could feel as truly as the heat of the fire.

Sally sat on the little stool, basking in it, with Hannibal blinking drowsily in the warmth. After a long while Dinah appeared from nowhere and climbed into her lap.

"Bad weather for peddling," said Aunt Nannie out of the peaceful silence.

"I suppose, Sister," said Aunt Deborah, "beggars can't be choosers. If he has no place of his own, he must earn his bread winter as well as summer."

"Poor man," said Aunt Esther, "I'm glad we found him in time. Half an hour more and we couldn't have done very much."

"It was Hannibal who found him, wasn't it, Hannibal?" said Sally from her stool.

"You're right, child, we mustn't forget Hannibal," said Aunt Esther, leaning over to rub the cub's head for a moment.

"You think he's good for something *now*, don't you, Aunt Nannie?" went on Sally.

Aunt Nannie looked up.

"Let this teach us all that we can never judge another," she said, solemnly. "Without Hannibal, the poor man would have died in his sleep, still sitting on that stone by the road. All the same," she added with a change of voice, "he smells dreadfully furry with the snow melting off him, my dear."

Late in the afternoon Sally looked up and found the peddler's bright blue eyes upon her. He was looking at them all, wonderingly—at Sally and the cub, at the aunts knitting, at the painting on the wall.

"Now, I call this snug," he said in a voice that sounded suprisingly big and deep for such a small man. "Whar am I? The last I knowed, I was all beat out and almost froze a-trying to git to Nobleboro. Now here I be in bed and yit a-moving-like."

"Drink this broth," said Aunt Deborah, filling a bowl for him, "and Sally, dear, bring the gentleman a piece of bread and butter."

It was Aunt Nannie who told him who they were and how they had found him.

"So it was that thar angel child and her cub-b'ar lighted on me!" he exclaimed, and before anyone could stop him he had swung off the bed, draped in a couple of blankets, and limped over to the corner where his pack lay. He rummaged there for a moment, and drew out a large wooden doll with carnation-pink cheeks and black painted hair, dressed in the latest fashion.

"Here you be, miss," he said, "at your sarvice. As fine a doll as ever I carried, and proud to give her to my pre-sarver. And here's a peppermint stick for the cub-b'ar, and to the ladies, my humble thanks. Mr. Burin is your sarvint, Miss and Miss and Miss," he went on, bowing with absurd dignity in his blankets.

Sally sat with the doll in her arms, for Dinah had jumped down from her lap at the approach of a stranger and slid like a shadow behind the stove. But Sally had

no eye for Dinah, or for Hannibal, holding his peppermint stick between his paws and licking it delightedly. After a breathless thank-you to the peddler, she had given a quick look at Aunt Nannie, but Aunt Nannie was smiling. She might keep this wonderful doll, then! She had never had a doll like this before, only home-made ones that were little more than a billet of wood wrapped in a piece of cloth. But this doll was jointed at the shoulders and body and knees. She had painted hands and real leather shoes and petticoats like a person, and eyebrows arching over the blackest of eyes. Her expression was a little severe, but it did not seem so to Sally.

"Do you think Eunice would be a nice name?" she asked, out of a dream.

"A very nice name," said Aunt Esther.

Meantime, Mr. Burin had gone into the little room at the back to put on some of Uncle Eben's clothes which Aunt Nannie had lent to him, since his own were not dry yet. He came out spry as a cricket, and limped briskly to his pack.

"I'm so lame," he exclaimed cheerfully. "Tree fell on me when I was a boy. Killed my brother, it did. Here's books, pins, needles, black sewing-silk, all colors tape, varses, almanacs, an' sarmons, thread, fine thread for cambric ruffles, here's varses on the pirate that was hung on Boston Common, with a border of coffins atop, and 'Jack the Piper,' 'Whittington's Cat,' 'Pilgrim's Progress,' 'The History of the Devil,' an' a great many other religious books," he went on all in one breath.

The aunts hurried to light a candle—for darkness still came early on gray days—and were soon handling tapes and spools. Sally found the story of Whittington's cat and showed Eunice the pictures. They were all so busy that they did not notice when the house stopped, and looked up in surprise at the uncles' entrance. Mr. Burin had been doing a brisk trade.

"Glad to see you so well, sir," said Uncle Joseph in his friendly way. "We've arrived at Nobleboro and made our arrangements for the night. But I declare, no one here has even noticed we've stopped, you're so taken up with pretties. Why, what's that you've got, Sally?" he asked, seeing Eunice for the first time. "A regular belle, she is. Will you introduce us, my dear?"

Uncle Eben's eyes danced with mischief. "It's Saturday evening after sundown, and the Sabbath has begun, Nannie," he said, delighted at a chance to tease his sister.

Aunt Nannie looked startled, but recovered quickly. "With all these clouds you can't tell for sure if the sun is down or not," she said firmly. "But I declare, we'd best do no more. We're late with our supper as it is. Bring in the milk as soon as you can, Brother, so we can get the chores done and the Sabbath properly begun."

Everyone hurried to finish supper, for it was the custom to have all work out of the way by sundown Saturday night. But the storm and the rescue had delayed everything. It was after seven when the last dish was clean and back in place. Now it was time for farewell.

"That's whar I was a-going, and that's whar I'm now a-getting, thanks to that thar angel child and her cub-b'ar," he said, a gentle look on his wrinkled face. "Whara'r you be, Miss, you know someone is wishing you well. And may that thar Eunice doll remind you sometimes of old Burin, the peddler. Your sarvint, everyone. I have to thank you if I'm alive this night!" And with this the peddler, with tears in his blue eyes, went off to sleep in the house near by, where he was well known.

When he was gone, Uncle Joseph sat wearily down with the big Bible open on his knees.

"May I hold Eunice if I don't play with her, please, Aunt Nannie, just this once?" asked Sally.

Aunt Nannie nodded. "Just this once, mind, child," she said.

All too soon it was eight o'clock, Saturday night bed-time. Uncle Joseph came out of his doze, to make a simple prayer, thanking God for having preserved them through the dangers of that day, and for having permitted them, by the aid of a wild beast of the forest, to save a human life. They all said "Amen" with all their hearts, and Uncle Joseph put on his coat and lit the lantern to take a last look at the tired cattle and the horses. Sally put on her cloak, too, and went with him, wrapping Eunice carefully in a fold of the cloth. Outdoors they stopped, struck by the cold stillness of the night. The trees were black on the silver of the snow, and the barn looked like a cave under its white roof. Over the house where the peddler slept hung the Pleiades, and a tree's bare branches were dark against a dew of stars.

Then a cow lowed and they stepped down into the cold velvet of the snow.

Elizabeth Coatsworth is a born storyteller. You will also enjoy her Alice-All-by-Herself, The Boy with the Parrot, *and* The Cat and the Captain, *all published by Macmillan.*

Waiting for Jeptha

BY BILLY C. CLARK

Illustrations by Veronica Reed

> **To a boy born in the Kentucky mountains, the hunter's horn and a good coon dog are the most important things in the world. That's why when Uncle Jeptha's hound Lucy gave birth to a pup, Jeb waited eagerly for Uncle Jeptha's visit.**

JEB stood by the window and looked down the narrow path winding like a brown snake through the willow saplings on the banks of Catlettscreek. It would be along this path, he knew, Uncle Jeptha would come, his big shoulders pushing the willow limbs out of the path. In front of him, swishing her long tail, would be his small redbone hound, Lucy. Lucy would not be bringing a pup with her this time, according to Jeptha. It would be a while longer. Today, Jeptha had said, he would come to tell Jeb how he was to earn the pup Lucy was going to find.

Every time the wind lifted the willow limbs along the path Jeb caught his breath and waited. He held his breath until the wind died and the willow limbs swayed back in place. Ever since Jeptha had told Jeb about earning the pup, Jeb had done little but think of how he would be asked. Maybe, he thought, Jeptha would ask for money, and there were not many ways a boy could earn money here in the Big Sandy Valley this time of year. From the signs of the sky, Grandma Quildy said the water from the creek would rise over the bank early and flood the bottoms. Ground would be broken late and there would be little work in the bottoms until late spring. By this time, Jeb would be too busy raising the garden at the cabin to work for neighbors. Jeptha would be upriver cutting the tall trees and rafting them to float down to the mouth of the Big Sandy River, and he would not be home to help with the garden. Grandma Quildy was old and could not do much work.

Jeb turned from the window and looked toward the fire grate. Grandma Quildy sat in her rocking chair reading the Bible. The flames from the fire flickered. a light across the wrinkles of her face and down her long, gray hair.

"Grandma Quildy," Jeb said, "do you reckon Uncle Jeptha will sure enough come today?"

"Before dark if the Lord's willing," Grandma Quildy said, placing a pine split between the pages and closing the Book. She looked toward the window and squinted her eyes at the dark clouds hovering over the steep ridge above the cabin.

The clouds came every year at this time. And Jeptha came from the hills every year at this time. And always Jeb stood by the window and waited. Grandma Quildy would always mumble a prayer that Jeptha be guided along the tramroads to the cabin.

Jeptha was a big man and Jeb knew that he knew the hills. He had helped build most of the tramroads. And when the creek swelled early, Jeptha knew the shallow places to cross. A man as smart as Jeptha would be needing little help from a Book, Jeb thought.

There were many things Jeb did not understand about the Bible. When he was younger, Grandma Quildy had told him that this Book had guided his mother and father up the steep hill-path to the ridge to rest a while. And then the Book had sent him to live with her. This Book had placed a cover of earth over his mother and father to shield them from the snows of the winters and from the sun and rains of the summer. One day they were to be brought up from the ground and led to a home beyond the clouds, above the mountains. This Book would guide them.

Once Jeb had asked Grandma Quildy if hound-dogs lived beyond the clouds and she told him that she could not find any print in the Book that said they did. Jeb told her if they did not he didn't believe he would care to go there and she scolded him. He asked Jeptha once about it and was told that Grandma Quildy's eyes were failing with old age and she couldn't see the print in the Book too well. What she couldn't see she made up, Jeptha figured.

"How would you be able to hunt if there were no hound-dogs there?" Jeptha had said.

This had been some time ago and Jeb figured he had learned many things. But he still believed that Jeptha's knowing the signs of the hills would be all he needed to guide him home.

It was dusk when Jeptha came up the path. The black clouds had opened and emptied the rain and when Jeptha came through the door he was soaking wet. He walked to the fire and Grandma Quildy handed him a towel. She told him that she had been worried about his coming home during time of storm.

"Swam the creek with one hand and guided Lucy with the other," Jeptha said, laughing and rubbing the towel through his hair.

The door opened and Lucy stood with her nose just inside. She held her head low and turned her eyes toward Jeptha. Her tail made a thumping noise against the side of the door.

"Come in, Lucy," Jeptha said, looking toward Grandma Quildy, knowing Lucy would track water across the floor and shake more from her hair.

Lucy came farther into the room. Her hair was parted by the rain from her nose to her tail. She was the prettiest hound Jeb thought he had ever seen, even though Grandma Quidly had said Lucy's tail was too long for just one dog. Her hair was the color of the redbird, and her eyes as black as the sparrow's. Her tail was long . . . the longest Jeb had ever seen on just one dog.

Once Jeptha had told Jeb that he could have sold part of Lucy's tail. A man at the timber mill by the name of Chet Potters had asked to buy it. Chet's sister had sent him a bulldog from over in West Virginia and it had come to the hills without a sign of a tail on it. That is, nothing but a short stub.

"Now whoever heard of a dog without a tail on it here in the hills?" Jeptha had said, laughing.

Chet had been kidded so much about the tailless dog that he had offered to buy part of Lucy's; according to Jeptha. He had intended to sew part of it onto the stub of the bulldog's.

"Now whoever heard of a redtailed bulldog here in the hills?" Jeptha had asked. "Worse yet, whoever heard of a bobtailed hound?"

It didn't seem possible, but Jeb had seen his Uncle Jeptha graft limbs to trees and make them grow and he was not sure. If it were true, then he was glad that Jeptha had not sold part of Lucy's tail. A bobtailed hound would look funny, he thought. And a good hound could well be judged by the swish of its tail. This he had heard from Jeptha, and Jeptha knew all there was to know about hound-dogs.

Jeb sat at the table waiting for Jeptha to eat. He was not hungry himself yet he knew he must wait until his Uncle Jeptha had finished before he could ask about the pup. Hound-dog talk had no place at an eating-table, according to Grandma Quildy. But when Jeptha filled his plate again Jeb became restless and said:

"I want to ask you something, Uncle Jeptha."

"Not at the table, Jeb," Grandma Quildy said.

Jeptha finished the plate and pushed it into the center of the table.

"Reckon we'll have to go into the other room to talk," he said.

Jeb followed Jeptha in by the fire grate and when Jeptha sat down in the rocking chair, Jeb squatted on the floor. Jeptha filled his pipe and slid a match over the arm of the chair. He looked toward the other room for Grandma Quildy. He knew if he had been seen striking the match on the arm of the chair he would be scolded.

"I reckon," he said, blowing out a white puff of smoke, "what you want to ask is concerning this pup Lucy is about to find."

"Reckon," Jeb said, scooting closer to the chair.

"Been doing some thinking about this pup," Jeptha said. "It ought to be a powerful pup." Jeptha wrinkled his face and rubbed his chin. "Hound-pup is worth a heap of money here in the hills. A man from the hills has got to have a hound-dog. They all can't have one like Lucy, and I figure this pup to be about as close to her as you can get. Some of the men at the timber mill have asked me a price already. Chet Potters has bid highest so far."

"Maybe he is after the tail," Jeb said, still wondering if it were possible to graft the tail onto the stub of a bull-dog.

"Maybe," Jeptha said. "It's not my concern to ask what he wants the pup for; it's the money he will pay. Once sold, the pup is his."

Jeb looked at Lucy. She was curled close to the fire.

"Grandma Quildy says the creek will rise early this year," Jeb said. "I won't be able to work along the bottoms to earn money. But I am willing to work. I could go back to the hills with you and work until I made enough money to buy the pup."

"Can't do that," Jeptha said. "Got to be someone here to look after Ma and take care of things."

Jeb looked toward the kitchen where Grandma Quildy was washing dishes. He was thinking that if he had to stay home to work, then by rights Grandma Quildy should help him talk for the pup. But then, he thought, she had not been concerned about his getting the pup. Whenever he tried to talk to her about it, she would say that hound-dogs were men talk.

Jeb looked toward the fire, toward where Lucy lay. He knew he could not bid with Chet Potters in money. If he could not work for it then there was little hope of his ever getting the pup.

"There might be a way, though," Jeptha said. "Money is good to have, but it is not the only thing. Good, hard work goes a long way with me." Jeptha filled his pipe again and slid another match across the chair-arm. This time he did not look up, as if not concerned about what Grandma Quildy would say. "By the time I come again the creek will be swollen over the bottoms. Carp will be swimming upcreek, and you know how I like to take a spell at catching a mess. Bait is the only thing that slows me down."

"I could get the bait," Jeb said. "Lots of it." Jeb was thinking this might be the way Jeptha had decided for him to earn the pup. "I could get red worms. I know where they live." Jeb was thinking of the rich dirt beside the barn, kept warm and soft by the bedding hay he put there during the winter.

"Not worms," Jeptha said. "Worms will not be carp bait. When water covers the bottoms, worms are brought to the top, out of the ground, and the carp get all they want. They get independent when it comes to worms. But . . . say a man was to have some doodlebugs. That would be real carp bait."

Jeb thought of the doodlebugs. They were small, white worms similar to a grubworm in many ways. Their home was underground, and there was only one way they could be caught. With a straw. Like the crawdad, they dug into the ground and left an opening. Once you had found a hole you poked a straw into it and twisted the straw around carefully. If the doodlebug was there he would move the straw and try to push it out of his hole. If you pulled gently on the straw you could draw him to the top and grab him. If you twisted too hard you would push the straw through the tender skin of the doodlebug and kill it.

But the ground had to be warmed by the sun before the doodlebug would stir, and it was early in the year.

The sun was still slow breaking through the leafless oaks on top of the ridge.

"How many doodlebugs?" Jeb said, thinking of the few he had caught last year.

"Maybe twelve," Jeptha said. "Not many doodlebugs for Lucy's pup."

"That's a lot of doodlebugs," Jeb said, "with the ground still thawing."

"The pup will be a lot of hound too," Jeptha said. "Of course it might be too much work for you. Bids are in at the mill. I figure Chet to stay high. Maybe it's the tail, and maybe not."

Jeb thought of the twelve doodlebugs he would have to catch. And then he thought of the hound-pup walking around at the timber mill to be laughed at because its tail was gone.

"I can catch the doodlebugs," he said.

"Think about it tonight," Jeptha said. "If at daylight,

when I leave, you still believe it is not too much work to
catch them, you can have a chance to earn the pup."

At daylight Jeb was more determined than ever to
catch the doodlebugs. Grandma Quildy looked toward
the spotted sycamore that stood at the edge of the yard.
Jeb knew she was judging the wind by the sway of the
naked limbs. And by judging the wind she could know
how soon the rain would come. Jeptha looked toward
the sycamore and then toward Grandma Quildy.

"I will be at the mill ahead of the rain," he said.

Jeb walked as far as the willow grove with Jeptha,
talking about the pup all the way.

"I'm depending on you, Jeb," Jeptha said, "to watch
after Grandma Quildy. She is getting old and you will
have to do most of the work. These doodlebugs will have
to be on your own time."

Jeb stood until Jeptha and Lucy were out of sight and
then he turned toward the cabin. Grandma Quildy sat
in the rocking chair reading the Bible.

"A dozen doodlebugs are not very many, are they,
Grandma Quildy?" Jeb said.

"Poor doodlebugs," Grandma Quildy said. "Taken from
the ground to be skinned on a hook."

Jeb didn't think Grandma Quildy wanted to talk about
the doodlebugs and so he walked to the creek to gather
driftwood. He sat most of the day under the willows
listening to the creek water. The sun was disappearing
from the slopes and the birds had begun to chatter. Jeb
wondered if the birds chattered because the sound of
the water over the rocks kept them awake. They flew
from limb to limb, as restless as the wind.

Once Jeb had thought if he listened long enough he
would be able to know what the birds were saying. But
now that he had grown older he knew that he never
would. Nor would he ever understand the talk of the
water. Jeptha did not know yet, and he knew all the

signs and sounds of the hills. Jeb knew that there were many things about the dark hills that he would never learn.

The sound of the water running over the rocks, Jeb thought, was the prettiest of all the sounds of the hills. It was even prettier than the hum of the wind through the trees and it would put you to sleep if you listened long enough. Sometimes the water was loud, and sometimes so low that Jeb had to bend his ear close to hear it. But it was always there. And it was company to Jeb. Sometimes it was lonely at the cabin with just Grandma Quildy.

Sometimes Jeb caught himself mumbling back at the water. And now he was saying "poor doodlebugs," thinking of what Grandma Quildy had said. As if it were wrong to take them from the ground, according to the Book. He knew he could talk free here at the creek and the words would not be repeated.

A week passed before the rainy weather broke. The clouds disappeared and the sun began to sift early through the oaks and shellbark hickory of the ridge. But it had been a cold winter and the ground was frozen deep. It would take a lot of sun to draw the coldness from the ground. The black loam along the creek would be the first to warm; it would take the sun longer to break through the clay on the hillside.

But Jeb knew that he would not be able to doodle for the doodlebugs in the black loam because of the rising water. The thawing of the frozen ground and the heavy rains had already begun to push the creek over the bottoms. His chance for the doodlebugs would have to come from the hillside. The garden patch would be his only chance. Made soft by the plow of last year, it would not be as hard as the clay never before turned.

So Jeb began to work the hillside above the cabin, clearing the ground. And while he grubbed the ground

of sawbriars, crabgrass, and wild honeysuckle he looked
for doodlebug holes. When he found a hole he lay his
grubbing hoe aside and squatted to the ground, holding
his straw. Slowly he twisted and moved the straw. But
the only movement came from the slow wind moving
down the ridge, weaving the straw back and forth. The
holes that he found were smooth and level on top and
he knew that these were old holes and that the doodlebugs had left them with the coming of the snows of last
winter. A new hole would have a fresh mound of dirt
around it where the doodlebug had shoved it out in dig-
ging the hole. But there would be little time and he
knew that he must try every hole if he was to catch
twelve before Jeptha came.

A week passed before Jeb spotted the first fresh hole.
It had been dug close to the roots of a tall black oak that
stood at the edge of the garden patch. Jeb stretched on
his stomach and eased a straw into the hole. He twisted
slowly and waited. The wind moved the straw and Jeb
jumped. For a minute he was mad. And he took a deep
breath. He knew that he was too anxious and had been
fooled by the wind.

The next time he cupped one hand in back of the
straw to shield it from the wind, twisted the straw and
waited. The straw moved. Jeb eased the straw toward
the top of the ground. He could feel the weight of the
doodlebug and his heart beat fast. He spotted the head
of the doodlebug above the hole and moved his hand
fast to cup it. The doodlebug let go of the straw and slid
back into the hole. Jeb had grabbed too fast, not letting
the doodlebug come out far enough. Now the doodlebug
would be wise and harder to fool. But Jeb knew he had
to have him.

He eased the straw into the hole again, twisted and
waited. But it did not move. He twisted again and
waited. Again there was no movement. Maybe, Jeb

thought, the end of the straw had split and could not reach the bottom of the hole. He was sure that the doodlebug would be at the very bottom. He pulled the straw out and looked at the end. The end of the straw was feathered and it was wet. Jeb felt the straw and wrinkled his forehead. He had been too anxious. The straw had been pushed through the tender skin of the doodlebug and now it could never be brought out. He thought of the doodlebug lying dead at the bottom of the hole, picked up the grubbing hoe and moved it slowly over the tough pods of crabgrass. It seemed as though he would never catch the doodlebugs.

The next day Jeb's hopes were higher; he spotted another fresh hole. This time he moved slowly and brought the doodlebug out. He fumbled it in his hand and looked at it for a long time. It was like holding a piece of money, and Jeb thought it had been harder to earn.

When evening came he took the doodlebug home, put it in a box of black dirt and sneaked it into his room, hiding it under the eaves of the roof. And when darkness came he lay awake and listened to the sparrows chatter outside the eaves. He could not sleep. He thought there was a chance the sparrows knew the doodlebug was in the box and that when he was asleep they would find a way into the eaves and get it.

Jeb found the next doodlebug hole under a pod of crabgrass. He had started to grub the crabgrass away when he spotted the fresh mound of dirt. He lifted the blades of grass and eased in the straw. And up came the doodlebug. Before the sun set below the oaks Jeb had caught four. This gave him five. There would be seven more to go.

In three days Jeb would have to turn the ground to plant seed, and there would be no doodling holes left to spot; only the long, red furrows. Away from the garden patch the ground would still be hard, not loosed by plow, and there would still be some coldness under the hard crust. There were not likely to be new holes in that kind of earth. But Jeb could not shun his work, because Jeptha had said the doodling must come on his own time. Grandma Quildy was depending on the garden and so the seed had to be planted in time.

Jeb sneaked the four doodlebugs to the box in his room. And he went to bed early. Tomorrow he would have to have keen eyes and watch closer than ever for new holes.

At daylight Jeb stood along the slope of the hill and watched the sun sift through the limbs of the oak. He bent over the hoe, scanning the ground closely, until his back ached. When he came to a large pod of grass or honeysuckle he stopped and lifted the leaves aside searching for a hole. At the end of the day he had found one. And from this hole he coaxed a doodlebug almost too small to cover a hook. He put the doodlebug in his hand, covered it with dirt and walked toward the cabin. Before he was off the slope he could see Grandma Quildy standing in the yard, looking toward him.

"Jeb," she said, "I'm ashamed of you, putting doodlebugs in your room. The house is no place for worms. Something just told me to look close to the eaves when I cleaned the room."

"But Grandma Quildy," Jeb said, "the doodlebugs are in a box and they can't climb out. Doodlebugs can't climb like fishing worms."

"The house is no place for them," she said. "And you will have to take them out. I'm not going to touch a box of worms."

"Where can I put them?" Jeb said. "I got to watch them. Uncle Jeptha will be here any day now and I don't have time to catch more."

"You don't have to watch a box of doodlebugs," Grandma Quildy said. "I never heard of a person stealing doodlebugs. Either out they go or the chickens get them. I won't sleep another night in there with the thought of worms crawling around."

Jeb took the box of doodlebugs from his room and walked into the yard. He looked for a safe place to hide them. If he put them very far from the house he wouldn't be able to watch them. And if he kept them too close, Grandma Quildy was apt to feed them to the chickens. He looked toward the woodpile under the big sycamore. He could see this woodpile from the window of his room. This seemed to him to be the only place. During the day he could take the doodlebugs to the slope with him, and during the nights when the moon was bright he could watch them from the window. On dark nights he would have to take a chance.

Jeb made a flat place on the woodpile and placed the box. He laid a flat board over the box to shield the doodlebugs from rain that might come without warning. And while he placed the box, Grandma Quildy's rooster scratched in the dirt below the woodpile, turning its head sideways and watching Jeb. Jeb threw a stick at it and it ran around to the other side of the house.

"You get my doodlebugs," Jeb said, "and Uncle Jeptha will be stringing chicken on a hook when he comes."

When night came Jeb could not sleep. The moon was gone and cold winds crawled down the high slopes and shook the limbs of the sycamore. Jeb looked from the window but he could not see the box. He thought about Grandma Quildy saying something had told her the doodlebugs were in his room. He wondered if it could have been something she had seen in the print of the Book. He wondered if the Book had the great powers she often spoke of. Uncle Jeptha *had* always made it from the hills, and at times the weather had been bad. There was a chance the prayers Grandma Quildy said for him had something to do with guiding him.

If Jeb lost the doodlebugs, he lost the pup. If there was any chance at all in the power of the Book it was worth a try. So Jeb knelt beside his bed.

"Lord," he said, "I don't rightly know if it was You who told about the doodlebugs being in my room or not. And I wouldn't be caring if there was a moon tonight and I could see to the woodpile. You must know, I reckon, that they are out there. Grandma Quildy says You know everything. What I'm wanting to ask is that You help me watch the doodlebugs until Uncle Jeptha comes. I can watch them myself during the day, and if You can sorta keep an eye on them at nights for me I'd be obliged. In case You don't know everything like Grandma Quildy says, I want to tell You that I think the danger is in that rooster of Grandma Quildy's. He knows the doodlebugs are there. No matter how hard I try I can't see the woodpile tonight. Amen."

Jeb was at the woodpile when daylight broke. In front, lying on the ground, was the box. The black dirt was scattered over the red clay of the yard and the doodlebugs were gone. There were chicken tracks in the dirt. Jeb looked around the yard. The big rooster flapped its wings beside the house. Jeb grabbed a stick and ran after him. The rooster squawked and Grandma Quildy came out of the house.

"What are you doing to that rooster, Jeb?" Grandma Quildy said.

"He got my doodlebugs!" Jeb said. "He watched me put them on the woodpile and waited until I was asleep. You knew all the time if I was to put them there the rooster would get them. You never wanted me to have the pup!"

"Lord help me if I knew the rooster would get the doodlebugs," Grandma Quildy said, wringing her hands.

"Lord didn't help me last night when I asked Him to help me," Jeb said.

"The good Lord had nothing to do with the doodlebugs, Jeb," she said.

"He had nothing to do with guiding Uncle Jeptha home, either," Jeb said. "I asked Him to help me and He helped the rooster. It was a high climb to the woodpile and the rooster couldn't have made it himself without a light to see. Chickens are blind in the dark."

"You have no faith, Jeb," Grandma Quildy said, wiping her forehead with her apron. "If you had had, perhaps you wouldn't have needed the doodlebugs in the first place. You pretended to have faith last night, but you can't fool the Lord."

"And I don't have time to fool twelve doodlebugs," Jeb said. "How will I ever get the pup?"

"Maybe it is not too late for faith," Grandma Quildy said. "But you would have to believe with all your heart. Last night you prayed for the Lord to watch the doodlebugs and then you got up in the night and went to the woodpile to see about them. I heard you. You didn't have faith that the Lord could watch them."

"I'll never get the pup," Jeb said.

"I will search the print," Grandma Quildy said. "You search for faith. Strange things are written in that Book."

On the weekend Jeptha came. Jeb was on the hill and it was not until he came down and saw Lucy that he knew Jeptha was there. He ran to the house.

"Did you bring the pup?" Jeb said, catching his breath.

"Bring me the doodlebugs," Jeptha said, in a slow voice.

Jeb looked toward Grandma Quildy and she lowered her head.

"I reckon," Jeb said, "there is something I ought to tell you about them doodlebugs."

"Don't have to," Jeptha said. "Just bring them to me so I can count them."

"I don't have the doodlebugs," Jeb said. "Grandma Quildy's rooster went to the woodpile where I was hiding them and ate them."

It was hard for Jeb not to cry. Yet he didn't want Jeptha to see the tears. Tears were not the mark of a man, or of a boy the size of Jeb. But he had worked hard and had not shunned his work. The doodlebugs had been caught. Grandma Quildy just sat with her eyes lowered. There was nothing Jeb had to offer for the pup. Nothing except maybe this faith that Grandma Quildy had spoken of. And this seemed very small compared to the box of doodlebugs. Yet it was the only chance.

"Grandma Quildy said," he said, "that faith could be counted same as the doodlebugs."

"Perhaps . . ." Jeptha said. "Perhaps that's what it was."

Jeb looked down at Jeptha and then toward Grandma Quildy. Grandma Quildy had raised her eyes and looked toward Jeptha.

"Coming through the hills this morning I had the funniest feeling," Jeptha said. "As if something was calling my name. I thought it was the wind through the trees. You know how the wind will sometimes catch in the knothole of a tree and make a sound that you can reason to be a voice. But Lucy began to whimper and she hung her long tail between her hind legs and crouched close to me. I tried to make out the sound and for some reason I got to thinking of the doodlebugs. I thought of the work that had been left here to do while I was away at the mill.

"Surely, I figured, this feeling is only from the sound of the wind, and so I looked up into the tall hickories where this sound seemed to be coming from. I found a knothole in the tallest tree and waited for the wind to catch it again. It did. But somehow it didn't sound like the wind. I've never been as keen on this faith as

I ought to be, but I have sense enough to know I've
been guided along the tramroads for years without asking. Maybe if I had started earlier the trips would have
been shorter and I wouldn't have had to lean on Ma's
faith all this time. Faith is a better bait than a doodlebug, Jeb, and I reckon the pup is yours."

Jeb's heart beat so loudly that he was sure it could
be heard across the room. Grandma Quildy laughed
and wiped her eyes. And Jeptha walked to the other
room and came back holding the small, red pup. He
handed it to Jeb.

Jeb looked at the pup. The pup had one eye as black
as the sparrow's; the other eye was as white as the bark
of the sycamore. Jeb looked at the broad head and long
ears. And then he looked at the tail.

"Look!" he said, pointing to the stub. "Uncle Jeptha
has sold the pup's tail."

"Wait a minute," Jeptha said. "How can you sell a tail
when there was no tail to sell?"

"There was a tail," Jeb said. "All hound-dogs have tails.
There is a part of it left. Its eyes are not even the same
color. They both ought to be as black as the sparrow's,
like Lucy's."

"Don't you know what that white eye is, Jeb?" Jeptha
said. "That's the mark of the moon. You don't find it in
a thousand dogs."

Jeptha slid a match over the arm of the chair and
Grandma Quildy scolded him.

"I learned it years ago," Jeptha said, "from an old hunter
that lived as close to the mountains as the black oak.
Do you know why it is, he said, a hound-dog howls
from the ridge at night when it is not treed? And why
it will set all night and bark at the moon, first on the
flat, then up the slope, and then from the highest peak?
Not many men would know the dog is chasing the
moon; the dog is trying to find a pup. They know the

moon is the sign of the night and if they can catch it
the moon will mark the pup with the signs. Not many
dogs catch it. Most of the hounds give up and settle
for an ordinary pup. Lucy didn't quit, Jeb. She trailed
night after night. And that bulldog of Chet Potter's went
with her. Sometimes I would catch a glimpse of her
along the steep ridge and hear her deep voice along
the slopes. She must have climbed the tallest mountain
and sunk her teeth in the moon.

"Now, I figure that Lucy pulled the moon close enough
to the peak for the bulldog to grab ahold. The moon
marked her pup with the signs of the night; a mooneye,
the old hunter called it.

"Now as for the tail, it was in all rights that the moon
give the bulldog something if he sunk his teeth in. And
I figure it was the stubtail, like the one he had. A mooneyed hound is one in a thousand."

"Maybe we could graft a tail on the pup," Jeb said.

"The pup will be stronger with the stub," Jeptha said.
"The fewer limbs a tree has, the more powerful the
trunk. It ought to work the same on a hound-dog. That's
going to be a powerful pup."

"Grandma Quildy," Jeb said, "I think you have good
eyes to see the print in the Book with."

"What made you think my eyes were bad, Jeb?" Grandma Quildy said.

"If I was you, Jeb," Jeptha said, "I believe I'd take the
pup to bed. It is small and will need lots of rest for the
trails it will run."

"Come on, Mooneye," Jeb said, picking up the small
pup in his arms. Lucy followed behind, whimpering
and wagging her long tail.

Jeb tucked the covers over the pup and placed its
head on the bed beside his. Lucy curled up at the foot.
The pup whimpered.

There was no need for the pup to be afraid, Jeb

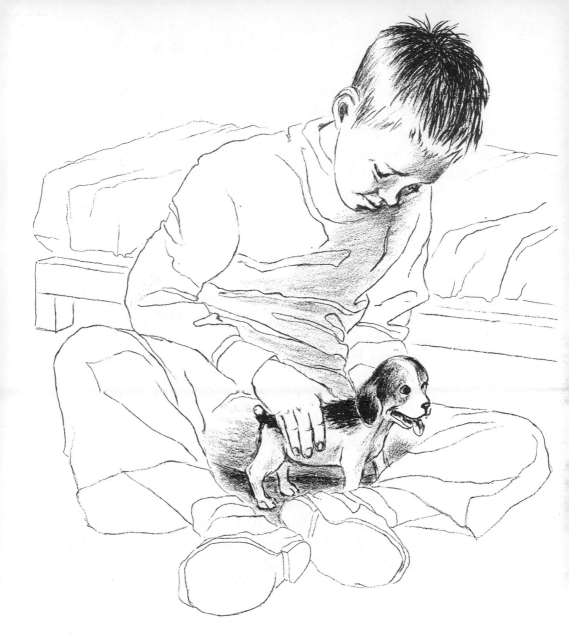

thought as he rubbed the pup's hair. What it heard was only the wind in the sycamore. Jeb looked toward the sycamore. Then he looked up the steep slope, toward the ridge. Way above the ridge he could see the moon.

But Jeb could not sleep. During the night the wind became stronger and the pup began to whine. Lucy kept moving from the foot of the bed to look at the pup. Each time Jeb scolded her and she went back to the foot of the bed. Each time he had to wait until she circled around and around before lying down. Lucy always circled before lying down and Jeb thought of the night on the dark ridge that Uncle Jeptha had told him the reason.

Dogs had learned this from the foxes and wolves, according to Jeptha. They circled so that if a hound struck their trail while they slept, and got close, they could move on. And the hound would circle and circle when he came to their bedding place, trying to work out the trail. This would give the fox or wolf time to place distance between them.

The wolf was no longer on the mountains, but Jeb had watched foxes circle and lie down. But he didn't see why Lucy had to circle and keep him awake. There was nothing after her.

It seemed to Jeb that he had just fallen asleep when Lucy sprang from the bed and woke him. And in the dim light he could see her cross the floor, wagging her long tail. The pup tried to follow and Jeb held it with one hand and rubbed his eyes with the other. He squinted and looked toward the door.

He could see the tall shadow of Jeptha standing in the doorway. He patted Lucy and walked toward the bed. Jeb could see that he carried something in his hand.

"Are you awake, Jeb?" he said.

"Yes," Jeb said, sitting up straighter, still rubbing his eyes.

"The wind is high in the trees," Jeptha said. "I am going to go early to beat the rain. I brought you something to keep while I am away."

He held out his hand.

Jeb rubbed his eyes again to be sure that the little light from the gray rain clouds was not fooling his sight. He could hardly believe what he saw. But there it was. A horn. A hunter's horn.

"If you are going to train the pup," Jeptha said, "he must be trained to the horn."

Jeb reached and took the horn. He raised it to his lips and blew as hard as he could. He didn't worry about waking Grandma Quildy if she was still asleep. He was too happy.

But the horn didn't blow. "I can't blow it," he said, trying again and again. "Neither can the pup follow a trail yet," Jeptha said. "The horn can be blown only by a hunter. But you are like the pup, Jeb. You have not followed many trails, so you will have to train like the pup. And when you are able to blow the horn, the pup will have learned to trail."

Jeptha spoke to Lucy and turned toward the door. Lucy stopped when she heard the pup whine and Jeptha spoke to her again. She whimpered back at the pup and then turned, stopping at the edge of the door. Jeb could see Lucy, her head low, looking back at the pup. She wagged her long tail and turned out the door.

Jeb gripped the horn tight. He let his fingers run over the smooth horn and up the rawhide that was tied to both ends so that the horn could be slung across the shoulder. He thought of the sweet music of the horn, music that was inside it. It was a sound that he hadn't forgotten since the first time he had heard Jeptha use it to call Lucy from the trail. Never before had Jeptha offered to let Jeb blow the horn. Jeptha had always kept the horn as close to him as Lucy.

And now Jeb could hardly believe that he held the horn in his own hands.

"The horn can be blown only by a hunter"—Jeb kept thinking these words that Jeptha had said. And he wondered how long it would be until he would blow the music of the horn through the tall trees over the ridges and into the deep valleys. He could see himself standing on the slopes with the horn to his lips. And he could imagine Mooneye fighting his way through the heavy underbrush, coming in to the sound.

A hound always comes to the sound of a horn—that is, a good hound. A horn is the only thing that will break a good hound from a trail, even if he is in sight of the game. Only the horn. And once trained to the horn, the voice cannot call him in.

Lucy was a hound, and one blast of the horn made her turn. And so might Mooneye, Jeb thought. He was Lucy's pup. He was a hound, and according to Jeptha, one hound in a thousand. Not even Lucy had a moon-eye and she was the best in the Kentucky hills.

Jeb was so happy about the horn that he had forgotten to walk to the willows with Jeptha. He looked through the window, now, but there was not enough light to see down the path. He laid the horn beside him and pulled up the covers. The horn was nearly as big as the pup. Jeb watched the pup curl into the curve of the horn and lie still.

Mr. Clark has continued writing about the Kentucky mountains in The Mooneyed Hound, published by G. P. Putnam's Sons. If you wish to read about other types of dogs you will enjoy Clarence, The TV Dog, by Patricia Lauber published by Coward-McCann, Inc., and Beano, Circus Dog, published by Farrar, Strauss and Cudahy.

A Friend in Need

BY SYDNEY TAYLOR

Illustrations by Mary Stevens

Have you ever stayed out late without permission from Mother and Dad? When Ella does Papa becomes angry, and the funniest things happen.

B UT why do I have to go to bed so early?" Henny kept insisting.

"Why, why! Always why!" replied Papa. "I've answered that question so many times already. A girl your age needs lots of sleep if she wants to be healthy. If you don't get your rest, you won't do your lessons right. You have trouble enough as it is, keeping up your marks in school."

"But nine thirty is awful early!" Henny protested. "You let Ella stay out till ten thirty."

"For Heaven's sake!" Ella exploded. "Ten thirty is early enough for a girl nearly sixteen years old without your trying to spoil it!"

"Aw, heck!" muttered Henny. "Not a single one of my friends has to be home that early. You treat me like a baby."

"Never you mind about your friends. Their parents will worry about them," Papa answered sharply.

"But it's Saturday night. There's no school tomorrow."

"I know very well what night it is."

"Couldn't you make it ten o'clock, at least?"

Papa shook his head. "No, Henny. I've been very patient with you up till now, no matter how many times you were late before. Now my patience is at an end. I expect you home by nine thirty."

"Nine forty-five, Papa, please!"

"Henny! I said nine thirty, and not one minute more!" Papa was getting angry. He shook his finger at Henny threateningly. "And if you're late this time, you'll get a licking for sure!"

Charlotte couldn't understand why Henny was making such a fuss. "Gertie and I like to go to bed early," she remarked. "We have so much fun."

"Yes," Gertie agreed. "Charlotte makes up such wonderful stories. All about two naughty girls, even better than the Katzenjammer kids; and every night she tells me another chapter. The stories are so exciting that sometimes I just can't wait till it's bedtime!"

Sarah sighed. "Ella and I used to have lots of fun too. Remember, Ella, how we used to fix up our make-believe house? Now most times I have to go to sleep all by myself. When Ella creeps into bed, she puts her cold feet right on top of my warm feet and it wakes me up. But by that time I'm so sleepy I don't feel like talking any more."

Ella put her arm around Sarah's shoulder. "Tell you what," she said consolingly, "my whole crowd's getting together right after supper. I promised I'd be there, but I'll get home real early. Like old times. Okay?"

"Oh yes!" Sarah replied, giving her sister a hug.

"That marcel-waved Jules going to be there tonight?" Henny inquired mischievously.

Ella replied unthinkingly. "No, he won't. He has to stay home and study for exams."

"I thought so!" Henny laughed. "No wonder you're so big-hearted all of a sudden!"

Ella didn't bother to answer.

It was nine thirty. Charlie lay asleep in his bed, like a small angel. In the girls' room, Gertie and Charlotte had ceased to giggle and whisper in the dark, but Ella and Sarah were still wide awake planning the decoration of a room in blue. In the kitchen Mama and Papa sat reading.

At nine forty-five Papa laid down his newspaper. "The child must be taught a lesson," he fumed. He turned to Mama. "No need for both of us to wait up. Why don't you go to bed? I know you must be tired."

Mama pressed her finger tips against her weary eyes. "I am, a little," she admitted. "But what's the use? I won't be able to sleep till Henny gets home."

"Lie down, anyway," Papa urged. "At least that way you'll get some rest."

"All right, Papa." Mama started for the bedroom. Hand on the doorknob, she hesitated. "You won't be too hard on her? You know how children are. They get to talking, they don't realize the time."

On the kitchen shelf, the clock loudly ticked the minutes away. Ten o'clock! Papa's fingers strummed anxiously on the table. So once again Henny had disobeyed him. Despite everything he had said. Well, tonight she'd get what she deserved! It was long overdue! He stood up, slipped the bolt in the kitchen door shut, turned out the light, and went to bed.

Tonight all of Henny's friends had congregated in Fanny's house. Fanny could play the latest songs on the piano, and the girls gathered around and sang. Most of them could waltz pretty well, too; but they didn't any of them know how to do the new dance called the foxtrot. Fanny's big sister and her boy friend, who were very good dancers, showed it to them. The girls were entranced; everyone wanted to learn. Fanny grew awfully

tired thumping out the same tune over and over while each girl had her turn at a dancing lesson.

Afterwards, everyone felt hot and thirsty. "Let's go to Mrs. Blumberg's and buy a penny chocolate soda," suggested Henny. Down in the candy store they stood around sipping the sweet drink slowly, talking and laughing. Before they knew it, Mrs. Blumberg was shooing them out. "Go— go on home already! I gotta close up."

In a flash Henny remembered. She'd given Papa her word! "Is it nine thirty yet?" she inquired anxiously.

"Nine thirty it wouldn't be any more tonight," Mrs. Blumberg replied. "It's ten o'clock."

"Ten o'clock!" There were exclamations of dismay. "Oh, am I late!" "I gotta get home!" "So long, everybody!" All the girls made a rush for the door.

Henny caught hold of Fanny's arm as they ran. "Some

friend you are!" she said reproachfully. "Why didn't you remind me? I told you I promised my Papa I'd be home by nine thirty. Boy, will I catch it!"

"What do you think I am, an alarm clock?" Fanny replied.

Henny was worried. "Maybe it won't be so bad. I'm only a half hour late." Papa hardly ever spanked the children. Still, she doubted if she'd be able to escape a licking tonight, especially after she argued about the time. Papa had certainly sounded as if he meant what he said. She reached about desperately for a solution. All at once she had a thought.

"Listen, Fanny, how about coming up to my house?"

"Right now? Are you crazy?"

"Oh, I don't mean to stay. Just come upstairs with me."

"I can't. I have to be home, too. I'm late enough as it is."

"Oh, come on. It'll only be for a few minutes."

"What difference would it make if I came along?"

"Well, Papa wouldn't spank me in front of a stranger—I don't think. Then we could sort of explain what happened, and maybe he wouldn't be so angry."

"Well—" Fanny debated with herself for a moment and finally gave in. "All right. But I must go home right away."

The hall lay in utter darkness. The two girls had to grope their way up the stairs. No light streaked through at the sill of the kitchen door, either. "Everybody's asleep already," Henny said in an undertone. Stealthily she turned the knob, her knee pressing against the door. It did not yield. "How do you like that!" she whispered fiercely, "I'm locked out! Now I'll have to bang on the door and wake everybody up."

"Gee, that'll make your Papa madder than ever. I'm going!" Fanny started toward the stairs.

Henny pulled her back. "You can't leave me now," she begged. "You promised! Anyway, I've got an idea."

"What?"

"Ella's and Sarah's bed is right up alongside the wall. I'll knock on the wall for a signal. When Ella hears, she'll understand. She'll open the door for me, and I'll creep into bed without Papa even knowing."

"Do you think she'll hear?"

"Sure!" She felt along the wall till she reached the spot where she imagined the bed to be. "Well, here goes," she murmured, tapping out a signal. "Ta ta—ta ta—ta ta ta ta." She paused, then tapped a second time. With her mouth against the wall, she called softly, "Ella! Ella!" The girls held their breath for a moment, waiting.

The door unlatched and opened. A strong arm reached out into the darkness. Without a word, Papa turned his captive over his knee. Whack! Whack! Whack!

"Papa! Please, Papa, stop!" Henny yelled.

Papa went right on with his spanking. Once, twice, three times more. A hand tugged at his sleeve. "Papa! You're hitting the wrong girl. I'm Henny. That's Fanny you've got there!"

Papa's hand stopped in mid-air.

Fanny had been too terrified to utter a sound. Now she started to bawl at the top of her lungs. A light went on in the kitchen, and Mama appeared. "What's going on?" she demanded. She looked down at the bawling Fanny. "And what happened to you?"

Abashed, Papa tried to explain. "It was dark, Mama. I was giving Henny a spanking—"

Mama looked around, puzzled. "Then why is Fanny crying?"

"Well, you see, Mama," Papa stuttered—"I couldn't see—it was a mistake—and—"

"He whacked Fanny instead of me," Henny finished for him.

Mama gathered the weeping Fanny into her arms. "Oh, you poor child!"

Papa tried to smile. "You'll have to excuse me, Fanny, dear child. I made a bad mistake. I didn't mean—"

Henny walked over to Fanny and took her hand. She felt awfully guilty, but somehow the whole thing suddenly seemed very funny. She felt a fit of giggles coming on. She tried to control herself, but it was no use. She just doubled over with laughter. In another moment, Fanny's screwed-up face changed to a smiling one. A moment more, and both Papa and Mama were laughing so hard they couldn't stop.

The sounds of such unusual merriment brought the sisters running, their startled eyes blinking at the light. Mama shooed them in. "Back to your beds! It's late!"

"But why is everyone laughing?" sleepy Gertie asked.

"It's your Papa. Such a way to carry on! He'll have

good cause to remember this night. I'll tell you all about it in the morning. Into bed now, every one of you!"

Henny needed no urging. No sense hanging around to remind Papa that he still owed her a licking. "Thanks loads, Fanny," she whispered quickly and skedaddled off to bed.

"Go right home, Fanny," Mama went on. "Your folks must be anxious."

Papa locked the door with what sounded like a sigh of relief.

"Oh, Papa!" Mama shook her head at him in comic distress. "How am I ever going to explain to Fanny's mother?"

For a delightful reading experience don't miss Sydney Taylor's first book about this family, All-of-a-kind Family, published by the Follett Publishing Company, which won the Charles W. Follett award for 1951. And be sure you read the rest of the stories in More All-of-a-kind Family.

The Yellow Shop

BY RACHEL FIELD

Illustrations by Adrienne Adams

Have you ever wanted to earn your own spending money? The twins found a way to go into business and have lots of fun at the same time.

ALL her neighbors on Cranberry Common advised Miss Roxanna Robbins against adopting the twins.

"You're not so young as you were," Miss Peters, who lived next door, told her, "and two children will eat you out of house and home."

"Oh, I guess not," said Miss Roxanna. "Besides they're my brother's children and I don't want they should go to strangers."

"How old are they?" asked Mrs. Winterbottom, the Doctor's wife. When Miss Roxanna said they were going on nine, she shook her head very knowingly. "Just the age to get mumps and measles and chicken pox and whooping cough," she added.

"But they've had all those already," said Miss Roxanna. "It says so in this letter."

"I don't believe it for a minute," said Mrs. Winterbottom, "but even if it's true, you ought to have your roof mended first."

"It won't leak any worse because two more are under it," Miss Roxanna told her, "and they're coming day after to-morrow."

So Will and Rebecca came.

They had been living with her nearly a year. The roof still leaked, but they all knew just where the rain was likely to come in. They took turns sleeping in the room with the biggest leak. There was an old umbrella always kept within reach that could be set up at the first drop on the pillow.

Although they were twins they did not look at all alike. Will had blue eyes and sandy hair and freckles and he could whistle more tunes than any other boy in the brick schoolhouse. Rebecca had dark eyes and brown hair and she could make boats and birds and wind-mills out of paper quick as a wink. Miss Roxanna liked the tunes and paper birds and boats very much indeed, but all the neighbors said something useful would be more to the point. It was overhearing Miss Peters saying this to Mrs. Winterbottom that made the children decide to open the little yellow shop.

It stood down by Miss Roxanna's gate and it had been boarded up for so many years that only a few people remembered that it had once done a thriving business.

"Why don't we keep store?" they said to each other as they walked home from their last day of school.

So the next morning they were up early and at work. Will pried the boards off the door and window and they went inside. It was just the way Miss Roxanna's brother Timothy had left it years before.

"It's just the right size for us," said Rebecca.

"Yes," agreed Will, "and that's as nice a counter as I ever saw and those drawers behind will hold a lot."

All that morning they worked away on it, Rebecca with the broom and dustpan, and Will with pail and scrubbing brush. It was spick and span by noon when they called their Aunt out to see. Although it was so small, it had drawers and shelves and a small rusty black iron stove with a chimney that stuck out of the roof. Best of all, on one shelf they found a box half full of clay pipes, an old china teapot, and two blue glass jars. On still another there was a bolt of red-and-white checked gingham.

"Well," said Miss Roxanna when they showed her, "I'd forgotten all about that teapot and the jars. Timothy used to keep molasses drops and peppermint sticks in them, and that gingham looks as good as new."

That was how the store started, though if it had not been for Silas Bean there would have been very few customers. Silas Bean lived down the road all by himself, and everyone said he was the handiest man for miles around. That very evening after supper Will and Rebecca went to see him and tell him all about their plan.

"But the trouble is," explained Rebecca, "that people won't come to a store 'way off on a back road."

"That's so," said Silas Bean, puffing at his pipe.

"If we could just get our shop moved over to the sign-post on the Turnpike," Will went on, "lots of cars would be sure to stop."

"That's so," said Silas, nodding his head.

"You moved Jones's ice-house half a mile away and it's five times as big," Will reminded him. "Besides, we've got an old cart with blue wheels to hoist our shop on."

"That's so," said Silas Bean again, but this time he uncrossed his legs and put away his pipe. "Well, I'll be over in the morning and see what I can do about it."

When Silas Bean said he would see what he could do about anything, it always meant business, so in a day or two the neighbors were startled to see the little yellow shop mounted on blue wheels and creaking down the road behind Silas Bean's white horse.

"Sakes alive!" cried Miss Peters, who had dropped in to chat with Mrs. Winterbottom. "Do you see what's going by?"

"Well, I never!" exclaimed Mrs. Winterbottom. "Next thing we know the meeting house will change places with the county jail and then where'll we be?"

"It's all those children's devilment," agreed Miss Peters, "and I think Roxanna Robbins might be more considerate of her neighbors. But then what can you expect, adopting two young ones at her age?"

Just before the Turnpike reached Cranberry Common four roads met. Where they crossed there was a small three-cornered island of grass holding a signpost. The letters on the signboards were not very clear. People often found it hard to know which road to take. It was here that Will and Rebecca had decided to set up shop.

"You see," Will told Silas Bean, "they 'most always stop to ask the way and if we're right here they may buy something too."

"That's so," said Silas Bean, backing the horse in neatly.

The yellow shop with its two big blue wheels just fitted in comfortably with enough grass to spare all round and the signpost rising above it like a tree. Silas Bean had promised not to send any bill for moving them till the end of the season, so they had been able to invest in tea, lemons, sugar, peppermint sticks, and lemon drops. Besides this they had bought a geranium for the window. It just matched the red in the curtains and Rebecca's apron, which Miss Roxanna had made out of the bolt of checked gingham.

She had made them molasses drops just like the kind her brother Timothy had sold, and a batch of sugar cookies. Will had picked cherries off their tree to go in the little paper boxes Rebecca had made and lined with rhubarb leaves.

After the blue glass jars were filled, they squeezed lemons and made a big pail of lemonade with a piece of ice floating in it and a dipper all ready for their first customer.

Then they sat down in the open door and waited for business to begin. It seemed a long time before any of the scudding cars slowed down, but at last one did. It was a very big green and black one with a driver in front and a lady sitting behind with a little dog beside her. They wanted to know which road went to Oldport. Will told them as politely as he could. Then he summoned up his courage and said,

"You wouldn't like anything to-day, would you? We have very nice candy and lemonade and cookies."

"And everything's home-made," added Rebecca.

The Lady smiled and her little dog put out his pink tongue as if he had understood.

"Well," she said, "it's a little early in the morning for me, but Sandy here would like a drink of water and a cookie."

So Rebecca went in to get the cookie and Will dipped out some water from the pail he had carried down from their well. Sandy seemed to enjoy it very much and the Lady said they would surely stop again soon.

"Look," said Will, staring down at the dime in his hand, "she gave us the same as if it had been tea or lemonade."

Rebecca laughed.

"I never thought our first customer would be a dog," she said.

It happened that Fourth of July came along during their very first week. This was fortunate and they both felt relieved when fine weather was predicted. By noon on the third, cars were spinning along at such a rate that

Will and Rebecca decided to invest most of the three dollars and fifty-seven cents they had cleared so far in a large supply of lemons and bottles of ginger ale, root beer, and sarsaparilla. They added more molasses drops and peppermints, till the old glass jars were full to the top, and their Aunt Roxanna had made an extra large batch of cookies. These, with the last of the cherries, carefully arranged in the paper boxes, made them feel ready for any number of customers next day.

They were up almost before the sun rose over Tumble-down Mountain, and breakfast and chores were done before the dew had dried off the grass in the dooryard. Off they set with their pails and bundles. Soon they were hard at it. Rebecca squeezed lemons and set out their wares on a little table by the door while Will went over to the store for a piece of ice. Even before he was back with it cars were beginning to stop and ask directions. Soon he and Rebecca were so busy filling glasses and answering questions they hadn't time to notice how hot it was getting. Sometimes they heard distant pops from the direction of the town, and they knew that meant that many of their schoolmates were setting off torpedoes and fire-crackers.

"They're making a big noise on the Common," Will remarked after one very loud burst, "but I'd lots rather be doing this, wouldn't you?"

"Oh, my, yes," Rebecca said. "How much money have we taken in so far?"

"Two dollars and five cents," Will told her proudly. "And it's not twelve o'clock yet. I shouldn't wonder if we made as much as five by to-night."

Just then they saw a cloud of dust and in the middle of it a Motorcycle Policeman, keeping an eye out for speeding cars. The sight of his uniform made the children feel a little sober, even though they felt sure he wouldn't be interested in a shop that stayed perfectly still in one place.

"There he comes again," said Will, pointing.

"He must be pretty hot chasing around in the sun after cars," said Rebecca. "Maybe we ought to give him some lemonade."

"I guess he'd drink it, all right," Will said, "and we give some to Old Man Jenkins 'most every time he goes by with the mail."

The Motorcycle Policeman seemed very glad to stop a few moments. He had a pleasant smile and looked much less old and terrifying when he took off his goggles.

"Well," he said looking the little Yellow Shop and its owners over, "nice place you've got here. Business good?"

"Oh, yes," they told him, "we've had lots of customers already."

"I have to go chasing after my customers," he explained with a grin.

"Have you arrested lots?" Will couldn't help being curious.

"I've done pretty well so far, and this afternoon I expect to do better."

Presently, with the pleased feeling that they were on speaking terms with a person of great importance on the road, they watched him ride away.

Besides all the cars heading out into the country, a great many were bound for Oldport, where that afternoon there was to be a big celebration. This was in honor of the town's founding and the Governor was to make a speech. When the Motorcycle Policeman came by an hour or so later he called:

"Better watch out for the Governor's car. I've had word to patrol this road, for he's on his way now."

"Oh, I wish he'd stop," said Rebecca.

"But his driver will be sure to know the way," Will reminded her, "and I don't suppose they'd want any lemonade."

"I tell you what we could do," Rebecca said after a minute or two. "We could pick some flowers for him."

So Rebecca went across the road and picked daisies and some blue chicory. Then she sacrificed the biggest flower on their geranium plant and tied them into a little bunch with grass for string. It made just the right size to go in a buttonhole.

"See, it's red, white, and blue for Fourth of July," she explained to Will. "Oh, I do hope they won't go by so fast they won't see us."

Fortunately for them their own Motorcycle Policeman rode ahead of the three cars that were taking the Governor and his staff to Oldport. The two children stood as close to the road as they could get and made such frantic motions that no one could help seeing they wanted something very much. So their friend slowed down and motioned the others behind him to do the same.

"He'll be in the middle car," cried Will.

And sure enough he was, smiling and waving his hat as the car drew up alongside the signpost.

Rebecca held out the flowers and the Governor leaned over and took them right out of her hands.

"They're red, white, and blue for your buttonhole!" Will told him, his own face nearly as scarlet as the geranium.

Another smile and wave and he was out of sight.

"He's wearing them, Will!" cried Rebecca.

"Yes, and he's stopped here and we've talked to him." Will was saying, "Wonder if they'll be going back this way."

But that was a little too much to expect even on the Fourth of July. Besides they had sold all their stock of food and drink by six o'clock and their cash box was heavy with five dollars and eighty-seven cents.

"If we keep on at this rate," Will and Rebecca told each other as they closed the Shop door and started home again, "we'll be almost rich by September."

But September is a long way from July. A good many things can happen in between, as they soon discovered. In fact it was the very next day that unpleasant rumors began to reach them.

Old Man Jenkins was the first to give them any warning. He stopped as usual on his way out with the mail.

His dog Nellie sat beside him on the front seat of his dilapidated Ford car, with the Rural Free Delivery mail bags piled behind. Nellie was one of their best dog customers and Old Man Jenkins was glad to stop and chat on his way coming and going. It was from him that Will and Rebecca learned how Tony, the Hot-Dog-Stand-Man, was feeling about them.

"Yes, sir," he told them the morning after the Fourth, "Tony's got it in for you two, all right."

"What—what's the matter?" asked Will and Rebecca together.

"You've run off with all his trade, that's what," Old Man Jenkins explained between gulps of lemonade. "He says you catch all the cars 'fore they get to his stand on the Bridge."

"He's mad because we thought of coming here first," said Will. "He could have put his stand here long ago if he'd wanted to."

"Oh, he's mad, all right." Old Man Jenkins wagged his head and helped himself to another cookie. "Swears he's goin' to get you out of here."

"But he couldn't do that, could he?" asked Rebecca with a little worried frown.

"Well,"—Old Man Jenkins wiped his moustache thoughtfully with his blue spotted handkerchief—"I don't say as he could, and then again I don't say as he couldn't. He's tricky, Tony is, and mean, so you watch yourselves, that's all I've got to say."

Will and Rebecca were rather sober after he drove off, but they had a good many customers, because it was a very warm day and lemonade was in demand. They squeezed more lemons and ladled it out into glasses carefully, but their thoughts were busy with wondering whatever they would do if Tony, the Hot-Dog-Stand-Man, started to make trouble. They were both very much relieved when towards noon they saw their friend the Motorcycle Policeman coming along the road.

"Hello!" he sang out with a wide grin. "How's business to-day?"

"Fine," they said. "How's yours?"

"Not nearly so good as Fourth of July. I've only stopped three cars this whole morning."

"That's too bad," said Rebecca sympathetically, "for you, I mean. I guess the people in the cars don't mind."

"I guess they don't!" he laughed, and took the glass of lemonade that Will brought him.

"We want to ask you something," Will began with a look at Rebecca. "You know all about roads and—and everything."

"Maybe not quite everything," their customer put in. "But ask me anyway."

"People couldn't put us off this place, could they?" Will went on. "I mean if someone didn't like our being right here by this signpost he couldn't make trouble for us, do you think?"

"Why, there's nothing in this world someone couldn't trouble about," the Motorcycle Policeman told them. "But don't let it bother you. I'll say a good word for you in court."

They were too upset by his last word to notice the friendly wink he gave as he rode off.

"I do wish he hadn't said that about 'court,'" sighed Rebecca to Will. "I don't know what Aunt Roxanna will say when we tell her."

Miss Roxanna Robbins said a great many things when she heard about it from them that night. But she had also heard about Tony and his threats from Miss Peters and Mrs. Winterbottom earlier in the day.

"They say he's going to the Selectmen about it," she

told them, "and he claims he can put you off because that little piece of land the signpost stands on is public property."

"Well, the Motorcycle Policeman said he'd say a good word for us in court," Will told her.

But that only made matters worse.

"Oh, dear me!" his Aunt cried. "I don't know what I'd do if anything like that happened to you. Your Grandfather Robbins would turn right over in his grave if you landed in court. We must remember he brought the brig *Rebecca* three times around the Horn, and it wouldn't do to disgrace him now."

"Oh, no," said Rebecca, "especially with me named after the brig."

"And me after him," added Will, not wishing to be left out.

"Mrs. Winterbottom even said," Miss Roxanna went on soberly, "that people could be fined large sums of money for selling things on public property. I'm sure I won't be able to sleep to-night for thinking of us all in court and maybe fined as much as a hundred dollars."

They were very quiet for a long while after that, and none of them ate much supper or slept very well that night.

Next morning Will was very thoughtful and Rebecca's eyes looked as if she had been crying.

"You ask Silas Bean when he goes by if he'll come and move us back after his supper to-night," Will said without looking at his Aunt's face.

"Well, I guess that's the best thing to do," she answered with a sigh. "It seems a pity with you and the Yellow Shop all fixed there so nice. Still, we can't afford to have any trouble and maybe we can find some other way to get the roof mended."

It was beginning to rain by the time the twins reached the crossroads, but they felt too miserable to remember that this would mean fewer customers.

They opened the Shop door and began watering the geranium and set about their duties for the last time.

Old Man Jenkins came by presently and looked sympathetic when they told him.

"Well, now, that's too bad," he said, "but I can see how your Aunt feels about it. She don't want to get in no hot water with the law."

"That's it," nodded Rebecca, and she and Will gave him extra cookies because it was the last time.

After he had gone they sat indoors by the window and watched cars scudding by in the rain.

"Let's light the fire and make some tea," said Rebecca at last. "It looks so nice to see the smoke coming out of the chimney and perhaps someone would like a cup."

Just as they had the tea steaming and ready to pour out of the china teapot, they heard a car stopping.

"It looks like that big green one with the Lady and

Sandy in it," Will said, peering through the rain-splashed window.

Sure enough when he opened the door, there they were.

"Good-afternoon," said the Lady from the back of the car. "Sandy would like another cookie. But no water," she added with a laugh, "there's too much coming down already." She spoke to the driver before she turned to Will again. "And I think if you have room for us Sandy and I will come in and wait in your shop while John takes the car to the nearest garage. We've been having some trouble with it since we left home."

So presently the little Yellow Shop was as full as it could be, with Rebecca pouring out tea on the counter for them all. The Lady sat on the one chair, drinking hers out of their only cup and saucer, and admiring the curtains and the blue glass jars. In fact all the time she talked about other things her eyes kept going back to the shelf where they stood.

Sandy could sit up and beg and "speak" for bits of cookie, and this pleased Will and Rebecca so much they almost forgot their own troubles. It was only when the Lady said what a very nice shop they had that they remembered it would not be there very much longer.

"It won't be here after to-day maybe," Will told her.

"No," explained Rebecca passing the cookies, "we've got to go because Tony, the Hot-Dog-Stand-Man at the Bridge, is going to make trouble."

"It's a pity, too," Will added, "for there's no place on the road as good as this and we were going to make enough money to get the roof sh—." He stopped just in time, knowing that Aunt Roxanna would not like them to mention such a thing before strangers.

"I'm very sorry to hear it," said their visitor, setting her cup down on the counter, "especially when I can't remember ever having a better cup of tea." Then, after she had looked at the shelf for a long time, she continued. "I wonder if you'd let me have a look at those blue glass jars?"

Rebecca reached them down from the shelf and stood them on the counter beside her. Their customer took each one up carefully, turning it slowly this way and that in her hands.

"They look like very old ones," she said.

"Yes, they are," Will told her. "They belonged to Aunt Roxanna's brother Timothy and he's been dead for years and years."

But the Lady kept rubbing the glass with her handkerchief and the children watched her curiously. After a while she looked up and smiled at them.

"Do you know," she said, "I've been looking for just such a pair of blue glass jars for more years than you two are old? Do you think your Aunt would let me buy them?"

Will and Rebecca had to go behind the counter to talk this over in whispers.

"What do you think?" Rebecca asked Will. "Maybe she wouldn't like for us to sell Uncle Timothy's glass jars."

"Still," Will reminded her, "you know she'd forgotten all about them till we opened the Shop."

"Do you think we'd dare ask as much as a dollar apiece for them?"

"Let's ask her," decided Will.

The Lady did not think a dollar apiece was too much. In fact she opened her bag and took two right out. Then she began to write something on a slip of paper with her fountain pen.

"I want you to give this to your Aunt, please," she told them when she had finished and folded it. "She will know what to do with it."

Just then John came back with the car and soon she

and Sandy and the two glass jars were inside, driving away down the Turnpike.

"Well, we've made almost as much money as if it had been a pleasant day," Will told Rebecca.

They were quite happy for a few moments till they recollected it was their last day under the signpost.

"Oh, dear," sighed Rebecca for the twentieth time that day. "I do wish something would happen to make things all right again."

"So do I," Will answered, just as he had every other time she had said it.

Just as the last spark had died out of the fire and they were gathering up their things to go home, they heard the sound of wheels and a voice calling.

It was Silas Bean and their hearts sank, for this must mean that he had come to move them back.

He stood in the door looking very tall in his rubber boots and sou'wester.

"No, I ain't come to move you to-day," he told them. "Get in the wagon and I'll drive you home."

"But—but didn't Aunt Roxanna tell you?" they questioned him as they jogged along behind his white horse under the big yellow umbrella Silas Bean always put up when it rained.

"Let's see," said Silas Bean, "seems to me she did say something 'bout it when I drove by this noon."

"About Tony, the Hot-Dog-Stand-Man," Rebecca prompted, "and how he's going to make trouble?"

"Why, yes, that was what she said." Silas shook the water off the reins before he went on: "But I told her not to bother her head over it."

"But he's going to complain to the Selectmen," said Will.

"Well, let him," said Silas Bean. "I just come from makin' a little call on the head Selectman myself."

"You did!" The twins both stared up at him in amazement.

"Yes, sir, him and me used to go to school together down in the brick schoolhouse. So he's glad to do me a good turn every now and then."

"And you asked him to let us stay by the signpost all the rest of the summer?" they both asked him in the same breath.

"That's right, and he said there wouldn't be no trouble from Tony, leastways if there is, they'll tell him he can't have his stand by the Bridge, for that's public property, too."

"Why, so it is!" exclaimed Will. "I never thought about that."

Miss Roxanna was beaming when she met them at the door. She had made a new batch of molasses cookies and she invited Silas Bean to stay for supper.

"Well, I don't mind if I do," he agreed and went off to put the horse in the barn.

It wasn't till they were all through and the dishes done that Rebecca remembered about Uncle Timothy's glass jars and the slip of paper the Lady had given them, which was still in Will's pocket. When Miss Roxanna put on her spectacles and read what was written on it her cheeks grew very red.

"Oh, my," she said, "I guess there must be some mistake. Nobody could possibly pay as much as all that for two old glass jars."

"Let's see," said Silas Bean. He turned the slip of paper over several times, scrutinizing every letter carefully. "Looks all right to me," he said at last, "and I guess fifty dollars will come in sort of handy to you right now. Want me to buy some shingles and start in on your roof to-morrow?"

"Oh, yes," cried Will and Rebecca, "because we'll have lots more by the end of the summer."

Only Miss Roxanna hesitated.

"I hope it's all right to take it," she said a little doubtfully. "I don't believe your Grandfather and Uncle Timothy would mind, but I don't know what Miss Peters and Mrs. Winterbottom will say."

"I know," said Rebecca. "They'll say, 'This is what comes of taking two children at your age, Roxanna Robbins!'"

"That's so," said Silas Bean.

If you have enjoyed reading **The Yellow Shop,** *you will want to read* **Patchwork Plays,** *as well as the other stories in* **The Rachel Field Story Book,** *both published by.* **Doubleday & Company, Inc.**

The Covered Bridge

BY CORNELIA MEIGS

Illustrations by Marguerite de Angeli

> *Connie learned that a covered bridge is built high and roofed over so rain can't rot the floor. It should last a hundred years, unless. . . .*

ANIMALS usually know when people are trying to help them. The big bull, Nicodemus, stopped plunging and struggling as Connie slid down toward him, and stood watching her steadily, his eyes rolling with terror.

"Poor Nicodemus, good Nicodemus," she said, although she was breathless and the words came unsteadily. She was holding tight to Sarah with one hand, and found it awkward to try to slip the rope through the ring of Nicodemus' halter, with only one hand to spare. She tried, slipped, caught herself and tried again. The end of the rope slid through the ring and she scrambled up, holding to Sarah, holding to Peter, catching at the trunk of the tree. Peter pulled up the rope, holding both ends in his hand, so that he had a steady pull on Nicodemus' halter.

They set themselves firmly, Peter with his knees against the tree. "Be ready to pull when I say three," he directed. "One—two—three—"

No tug of war for a school championship was ever pulled more stoutly. Even Tim lent a hand, although most of what he did was to jump up and down. Nicodemus seemed to have waited for the signal, too. At the first tug on his halter he heaved himself up for a terrific

effort, his eyes wide, his nostrils blowing out great snorting clouds. His hoofs cut through the ice in one place, failed to crack the hard crust in another. But the pull on his halter was just enough to steady him and he came lurching up the hill, slipping, catching himself, slipping again, but at last, with a fearful heaving and snorting, getting himself safely on the level ground. He stood with his head hanging, his great breaths blowing the trampled snow away, and his sides heaving.

They all patted him and comforted him, "Poor fellow, good fellow."

Peter said, "He was almost done for."

Peter led him down the hill finally, with Jock walking beside, to see that the rescue he and Tim had begun so well was safely carried to its end. Then Tim ran away home to tell the other Guyer children what an adventure they had missed.

Connie sat opposite the fire that evening. She was pleasantly tired, and comfortably satisfied with a full day's work, a successful adventure, a good supper and a long peaceful evening. She thought of her mother and father every day, she had thought of them so much that they seemed part of all this that was around her. She had just finished a long letter to them on which she worked every evening, a very pleasant sort of writing lesson. Peter with papers spread out on the table was doing a sum in arithmetic, one that was not in any of the books: "If four calves eat a bushel of grain in two days—they would have to be worth by spring—" He knitted his brows, the problem was a hard one. But whatever Peter did he did with all his might, and he was not only going to calculate how much the calves should be worth by spring, but was going to see that they would actually be worth it. Jock got up from his place on the hearth, because he was too hot, and came over to lie down with a thump beside Connie. He was getting to be a big dog.

He loved her, he loved Peter, he seemed to love red-haired Tim almost as much. Connie was thinking of the Guyer children and she was moved to ask a question which had come into her mind a hundred times but which had always been pushed away by something else.

"How can it be," she said to Sarah, "that there are six children at the Guyer house and three of them are eleven years old and two of them are nine? And I asked Tim when his birthday was and he said he didn't know. So I asked Mrs. Guyer—and what do you think, she didn't know either!"

"She couldn't know," Sarah answered," because she isn't their mother. The biggest girl and Tim are sister and brother, but the others don't even belong to each other. Hereabouts, when children have no homes and no parents, someone takes them in and all the people in the neighborhood help to pay for their living. Cousin Cephas is the selectman who has charge of such things, and he says Mrs. Guyer is the best person in the world to have them. They have come to her house so young they don't remember anything else. But her hands are very full and she can't be expected, really, to keep track of birthdays."

Connie sat thinking for a long time. "Sarah," she proposed at last, "couldn't we give them a birthday party, just pick out one birthday for them all and bake them a cake? Mrs. Guyer has so much to do; and you and I have a lot to do too, but couldn't we find time for that, Sarah?"

"We could indeed," Sarah answered heartily. "Not just at once perhaps. A birthday party is not so nice in the winter as in the spring. How would a day toward the end of April do? That will give us a good long time to be making presents for all six of them. Then when the time comes I will bake a grand cake. I have a pan big enough, but you and Peter will have to help me stir it."

Cold weather had not really come, even yet, and bright autumn days still followed, one after another. While

Sarah and Constance were busy in the house hanging up strings of onions and corn to dry, boiling down apple butter and pickling eggs, Peter was toiling even harder than they to get ready for winter. Early every morning and for the short time after school that it was still light, and through all of the long Saturdays, he worked over in the woods, cutting winter fuel. Cousin Cephas, in part exchange for the rent of the pasture, had sent up a man to chop down the trees that had been chosen, and to help Peter saw up the big trunks. Now they must be cut smaller and split, and, since there was a great amount of it, the wood was being exchanged for all the things they needed.

On top of the hill above them lived old Mr. Sam Breen, "a smart farmer" as everyone described him, who had raised on his high acres more corn and hay and apples than he needed, but who did not have any broad stretch of woods in which to cut fuel. He was exchanging with Peter, therefore, and had already brought them onions and apples, pumpkins, corn and hay, for which Peter was to bring him loads of wood as they were ready. He drove rather sharp bargains, Sarah said, but all he gave in exchange was fair and good. Cousin Cephas was also getting wood from Peter and had lent his oxcart and the big pair of black and white oxen to haul it. Peter was to keep them in Sarah's barn until the wood was all cut and carried.

Constance used to bring his lunch to him Saturdays, across the side of the hill to the farthest edge of the farm. Jock would go leaping and jumping ahead of her, and their feet would slip a little on the smooth brown grass, sometimes with the frost on it still, even at high noon. The valley below would look very distant and quiet, half hidden in the faint autumn haze, and the noise of Peter's ax would come very loud to their ears, through the still air.

Connie wondered sometimes if she would really know when winter came, but certainly there was no doubt of it when it actually arrived. Every morning when she opened her eyes she could see the great shoulder of the mountain beyond her window. There had been traces of autumn red in the woods that covered it, when she first came; then it was bare and brown with darker patches where the pine trees grew. And now, one morning, she suddenly awoke to see it smooth and white, with all the roughness of rocks and hollows buried and only the dark shapes of the stretches of pine woods still distinct in the midst of the snow. She sat up and looked and looked. Something within told her that she was not to see it rugged and brown again until spring.

It was exciting to come out into the sharp cold, with the snow squeaking underfoot as she and Peter set off to school. Jock scampered and barked and rolled over on the hard surface, but Peter came tramping along behind them both, looking serious. "The snow is earlier than usual," he said. "It's going to be a long winter. And we haven't got all the wood in yet." It seemed that the first day of winter gave one a great deal to think about. But Connie did not think much further than how beautiful it was.

School had been going on long enough now for them all to be fairly well settled down at their work. Connie found, a good deal to her surprise, that she did not read as well as some of the others, and that her writing was not the best in school either. But in geography she easily led them all. To have a dear father coming home at the end of months of absence to tell her all about the places he had been, to Spain and Portugal, to the ports of North Africa, even on one long voyage that she thought would never end, to China—all that had taught her much. His letters, too, and her mother's, told her about the islands and cities of the West Indies, so that she could tell them all that Santo Domingo and Haiti were on one big island, that there were miles and miles of sugar plantations in Cuba, and that fierce Indians and runaway slaves lived on some of the little islands of the Lesser Antilles. She could even explain about the Trade Wind which was always blowing, and which had given the name to the Windward and the Leeward Islands. She must have known how to make it all very clear, for all the classes stopped studying when Constance Anderson stood up to recite her geography.

She was in the middle of the lesson on morning and was standing in front of the big map pointing to the chief cities of England, when she stopped suddenly; for there was a stranger at the door. Very, very seldom did visitors come to the little school, and this one was unlike anybody she had ever seen before.

He was very tall, taller than anyone she had ever known, and had great broad shoulders and a big chin and twinkling blue eyes. When he stepped over the threshold, he moved stiffly, as though the years had been hard on his joints; but as he came into the room he looked like some great rugged tree, so big he was and so powerful, the kind of tree which has stood against half a hundred storms and will stand against many more. He was bare-headed in spite of the cold, and he wore a leather jacket.

"Go on, little lady," he said to Connie who had stopped in the middle of a word. "Go on. It is good to hear of London as just a name on a map, not as the place where King George used to sit among his councilors and deal out what he called justice to the rebels in America."

"Indeed, sir, the lesson was just finished," Connie said. She did not feel afraid of him at all, big and strange as he was. His broad smile, which was like a mischievous boy's, would make any person feel at ease.

The man came striding down the aisle between the benches and came up on the little platform where the master's desk stood. "Now bless you, Jonathan Ennis, I've been of a mind, this long time, to visit this school of yours." He went straight to the blackboard, rubbed out all the neat figures which the schoolmaster had set out upon it, took up the chalk and wrote in big letters:

TODAY IS A HOLIDAY

He looked first at the children with a beaming smile and then turned a questioning glance at the schoolmaster to see how he would take it. But Mr. Jonathan Ennis was all smiles also. "There is no one else in the world who could come into my school and declare a holiday, no one but you, Ethan Allen," he said. "You can have your way wherever you go, for every person in Vermont owes you a debt of gratitude."

The big man thrust his great hand through his hair and made it stand out in all directions.

"When I was a boy," he said, "and used to sit in school with my legs too long for the bench and the lesson too hard for my wandering wits, I used to dream of how someone might, just possibly might, come by and step in the door and say to the schoolmaster, 'This is a holiday.' I know you like your school," he finished, turning to the rows of excited faces above the desks, "for you have a good schoolmaster, but no school is ever the worse for a little change and diversion, so I propose that we have it. Since it is near noontime, we will all have our lunch first. Let's see what you have. Can any of you give a wandering stranger a bite of what you have brought?"

They could indeed. Out came all the boxes and bags, with crusty bread and jam, with apple butter, and brown nutty cakes, sections of pie and rounds of maple sugar. The fire was built up and they all gathered in a circle about it. When they were all settled and the flutter of surprise and delight had died down, Mr. Jonathan Ennis made a little speech.

"This my young friends, is Mr. Ethan Allen, the man who has given Vermont—given her everything she has. He has stood for her rights against those who would have oppressed her on every side. In the war which set America free from England, he has fought with courage. He has been a friend of Washington. He has been a prisoner of war. And I am very proud to say that he has long been a friend of mine, and that he can have anything for which he asks me."

Ethan Allen spoke after him. "I ask no more than that these children should have just such a day as I longed for myself, when the spelling book and the arithmetic became too much for me. Now, my friends, draw up to the fire and set your cheese to toasting and put your apples down to roast. We have everything here which should make a feast for a king, for an even better one than King George. And I have a pocketful of chestnuts to roast among the apples."

It was a feast indeed, bountiful through generous sharing, varied with cookery before the fire which Ethan Allen had learned in soldiers' camps, spiced by such gay talk as kept them all in gales of laughter. When they had finished eating, he began telling them tales of Vermont when it was a young settlement, not yet a state, and claimed by both New York and New Hampshire as part of their domain. Connie had heard from Sarah and Peter about the Green Mountain Boys, the band of young men whose leader was Ethan Allen, how they had defended the rights of Vermont and then, when the war of the Revolution began, had marched away to defend America's freedom. She had come to understand that this great rugged man of the frontier had been more than a soldier, more than a helper and friend to George Washington; that he had been wise in the plans for Vermont's future, that he had advised patience when she would have quarreled with the other states, that he had brought her into union with the other sister colonies at last. She looked at him, sitting there on a stool before the fire, long and lean and weather-beaten, an elderly man but still brave and wise and full of spirits.

The boys gathered around him but the girls had kept a little apart, surprised and wondering and whispering questions among themselves. But Connie crept nearer and nearer to hear what he was saying, to listen to the story that he was pouring out to the boys who hearkened almost without breathing, so afraid were they that they would miss a word.

"It was one of the times that the Green Mountain Boys had not had the best of luck, and they were slipping away into the hills so that the king's men should not catch them. But the redcoats were marching in on every side, and presently we found ourselves between two bands, one coming up the road before us and another marching from the other direction round the curve of the hill. We crept into the covered bridge and lay there in the dark, seven of us, waiting and wondering what would come next. One band of soldiers went into camp and we saw them putting up their tents and kindling their fires. But we could still hear the others coming, tramp, tramp— away off along the road. We knew for certain that by and by they would come across the bridge."

"Was it—was it—our covered bridge?" Connie asked breathlessly.

"That very bridge you cross every day to come to school. We lay there in the dark and we whispered together about what to do. I was leaning back against the wall, and I felt one of the boards give, for some man who worked on building it had been in haste and had not driven the pegs that fastened those boards deep enough. It gave a creak in the quiet and we held our breath wondering if the redcoats would hear, but they did not. And it gave us an idea."

He stopped for a moment to look at the intent faces in the circle around him. Even the girls were, every one, pressing close now, to hear.

"We pushed the board free—gently, oh, so gently—so that it did not make a sound. Then we pried at another, stopping to hold our breath when it creaked, but the soldiers in the camp never heard. When we made an opening, we slipped through it, one after another, and dropped into the stream below. The pool is deep and we made little sound, not much more than a fish jumping. We were crouching on the bank below when we heard the second band of soldiers come across the bridge, tramp, tramp, tramp. One of the riders carried a lantern and we saw it flash through the opening. He stopped and looked a little puzzled and said to his comrades that these Yankees were bad builders, look at this great gap they had left in the wall, a man might stumble through it in the dark. Then they joined the others and doubtless all told each other what a rousing fight they would give the Green Mountain Boys—when they found them. Our clothes were wet and so were our guns, so we could only slip away over the mountain and wait for a day of better fortune."

The time had passed very quickly, so that now it was three o'clock and time for school to close. Mr. Ethan Allen got up and buttoned his deerskin jacket. He shook hands with every boy and girl in the school. "I am glad to have had a little talk with you," he said. "Now that all the hard work is done and Vermont is a peaceful state at last, I like to see the young Vermonters and to wonder what they will do. Peter Macomber, I will walk across the bridge with you and Miss Constance, for I am going your way."

They went slowly, Ethan Allen leading his big black horse, so that they could talk as they went along. It seemed that he often made these journeys through Vermont, stopping to talk to all the people he knew. "I was always a restless boy," he said, "and life has not made me any less so. And I know every inch of the Green Mountains from north to south, and I like to pass over them now and again just to find peace in knowing that they are always the same."

He asked them many questions about Sarah Macomber, whom he knew, it seemed, and esteemed highly. "A fine woman and a brave one," he remarked. "And with

the pair of you to help her, she will make good this plan
of living on her farm again. But it is a struggle the first
year; wind and snow, fire and water—how a farmer's
heart goes over and over them as the months and years go
by; for they can serve him well or they can destroy the
good of all his work. Remember that, you two, for it is
the whole wisdom of a farmer when he has learned how
to meet them."

"Are you a farmer, sir?" Constance asked.

"Bless you, everyone in Vermont is a farmer," he answered. "That is how we all live in a new state, for Vermont is still new and has most of her great affairs before
her. And no person has ever come to live here who does
not love the land."

He stopped then, for they had crossed the bridge and
reached the foot of the lane. "Give my highest respects
and regards to Sarah Macomber," he said, "and tell her
that I am glad to see that the spirit of adventure is still
alive in her heart and those of her two stout helpers. Give
her all the aid you can. By spring you will know whether
you are winning to success or whether the task has been
too hard. I pray it may not be."

It was on one of the early days of April that Constance
stood on the doorstep and actually watched spring come.
At least so it seemed. There had been four days of rain,
a Thursday and Friday so stormy that none of the children could go to school, a Saturday and Sunday when
the whole valley was still hidden behind the heavy dark
curtain of the downpour. But early on Monday morning
the weather had begun to clear, and now the storm was
rolling up and up, leaving the valley visible, then the
sides of the mountain and at last their bold, rocky tops.
Connie saw that in those four days the spring had arrived. The long slope before her was green with new

grass, the hillsides, which had been dark and gray all the winter, when they were not white, were now strange colors, faintly pink and reddish and yellow shading to green, as the trees budded and changed their dead color to a living one. A sound came up to her ears such as she had never heard before, a deep, steady, singing sound, that lifted and dropped as the puffs of warm wind carried it up the hill. "What is that?" she asked Peter, who had come out to stand beside her.

"That is Hebron Brook," he said. "The ice has broken; you will hear its voice all summer. But I have never heard it so loud as this."

When they crossed the bridge that morning Connie stopped to look down, through one of the cracks between the boards, to watch the water hurrying past. Such haste, such tumbling and foaming and leaping over the great stones in a whirl of foam! It seemed strange to stand still and quietly above it and see all that furious hurrying, hurrying, hurrying go on below her, and not hurry some-where too. Where did it all come from, that there was always so much always hastening away to make room for more? She watched and listened till her eyes were fairly dizzy with the whirl below her, and her ears re-echoed with the sound. She could hear it still loud in her ears that night as she fell asleep. She loved it, wondered about it, listened for it. Somehow it seemed to her that she would dream of that plunging water every night forever. But she slept without dreams, as a little girl who has had a busy day is bound to do.

It was on the next afternoon, when she and Peter were turning their faces up the hill to go home from school that they heard a sound which had not come to their ears for months, the deep rumble of coach wheels on the covered bridge. The stagecoach was making its first trip of the season, and the driver on his tall seat flourished his whip in greeting. That indeed was a sign of spring.

The chickens were laying eggs fast now, the calves

were impatient in the barn, and scampered and kicked up their heels when Peter let them out. How big they had grown, what fine young creatures they were. Peter walked behind them looking very old and dignified, so proud was he of what his animals had accomplished. Cousin Cephas came up to see them and he and Peter stood for a long time, leaning over the barnyard fence and talking grown-up farmer talk about this thing and that. Peter's face beamed as he came in later; evidently Cousin Cephas had praised him for what he had succeeded in doing. That was the day, too, when Connie baked a whole batch of bread by herself, a row of four beautiful, perfect loaves, that came out of the brick oven the exactly proper shade of gold shading to brown, with a fragrance that can be compared to nothing else, for freshly baked bread smells better than any other thing in the world. As least so Connie thought.

As she was studying that evening with her books spread out on the table and Peter bent over his arithmetic opposite, she found, suddenly, that the reading lesson was easy, that she could go through it without any trouble. And yet, so she remembered, she had glanced ahead at that particular lesson weeks ago and thought how fearfully hard it looked and had wondered what she would do when they came to it. And now, because she had worked so hard and tried so earnestly to read as well as the others, it was not difficult at all. Even Peter had said it was a hard lesson. Why, this meant that she could read almost as well as Peter. She had not realized how much she was learning. She sat thinking for a little while, until Peter looked across at her and grinned broadly. His face was thinner than in the autumn and his freckles had faded, although they still showed. He was taller, too, Connie noticed all of a sudden. And, how queer, she was taller herself. Last autumn she had rested her feet on the top rung of the chair as she sat to study, and now she had them on the lower one.

"What are you thinking about, Connie?" Peter asked. He did not often interrupt his lessons to speak to her, but plowed through them to the end and then tossed his book into the air with a delighted whoop. But the look of pondering on Connie's face seemed too much for him tonight and he said again, "You have an idea, Connie. What is it?"

"Why," answered Connie slowly, "I was just thinking that—that," she ended quickly, for she had found the words to it at last, "that the thing that makes spring so exciting is seeing, all of a sudden, what the winter has accomplished."

Sarah, in her chair by the fire, put down her sewing. "You are becoming a wise girl, Connie. And that is another thing that a winter on a farm brings about. People learn to think." She got up to cover the fire, for it was time for them all to go to bed. Peter closed his books and yawned. Studying had a tendency to wear Peter out, he put so much effort into it.

"Don't you think, Sarah," Constance asked as she put her papers together, "that it's almost time for the Guyer children's birthday party, for that great enormous cake you said you were going to bake?"

"I do," said Sarah promptly. "I have been thinking of it for several days. Suppose we have them come next Friday. But, mercy, I have little enough left in the store-room after all this long winter. You must stop and ask Cousin Cephas on your way home from school if he won't bring us up some bacon and flour and sugar from the village, and let me exchange it for the wood we have left. What we got from Sam Breen wasn't enough, and we are even short of grain for the calves and chickens. And see if Margaret has any dried currants left, a birthday cake must have something gay in it. I believe the cake will just take the last flour we have."

When the Guyer children came past to go to school

next day the great invitation was issued. They were dumb with astonishment at first. A birthday for all of them? Not just a birthday cake, but a birthday! Mrs. Guyer had been very good to them and gave them everything they needed, but she had never thought of their needing birthdays. Timmy let forth a high squeal of delight. They all went scampering down the hill, chattering like sparrows. The Guyer children, too, had a message for Cousin Cephas. In their house also the food was running low. Would Cousin Cephas, as part of his duty as selectman, please see that there was some more sent to them from the village of Hebron?

They all stopped after school and told him about it. Because the cold and snow had begun so early and lasted so long, no one up here on the mountain slope had a great deal left. Cousin Cephas was going down to the village in a few days on business, and would have to be away all night, but by Saturday morning he would come back with all that they would need and would bring it up the hill on his big cart. Would that be early enough? When Connie brought back his answer Sarah nodded. Yes, that would do very well. They would be out of flour after the cake was baked, but they would have enough bread anyway and need not bake again until Saturday. But they would not have much of anything else.

It seemed like a long week, even though preparations began on Wednesday. They had to stone the currants and sift the flour and sugar and go out to find the eggs. A whole basketful of eggs it would take, but the chickens did their generous best. It was after Connie and Peter got home from school on Thursday evening that they mixed the cake. Just breaking the eggs was a task in itself. And, gracious, what a great bowl of batter Sarah had put together. Sarah stirred, Connie stirred until her arms ached, Peter stirred until even he had to confess he was too tired to lift the big wooden spoon for one more stroke, then Sarah stirred again. It was all light and yellow and fluffy at last, and was poured into the big pan which Sarah got down from the top shelf. It had indeed taken all their flour and sugar, it had practically swept the cupboard clean. It was long after bedtime when they got it into the oven. Sarah sat up to take it out when it was baked and Connie and Peter stumbled sleepily upstairs.

Next morning mild Mr. Ennis, the schoolmaster, seemed to feel that there was some unusual excitement in the air; for the whole school was quivering with it. Some of the Guyer children got their lessons far better than usual, some could not get them at all, since excitement affects different people in different ways. Connie, it had to be admitted, was very poor in hers. Only Peter kept a steady head and recited calmly and without mistakes. It was a whole hour earlier than usual when Mr. Ennis rang his bell.

"Whatever is the matter with you today, you are of no use to the world as scholars," he said. "So I think the best thing to do is just to send you all home." His eyes twinkled as he said it. Evidently he had caught the magic word as it passed from one to another and knew that this was not any usual birthday party. "And besides," he added as they filed out, "I think there is going to be rain again before evening. I want to make sure you all get home safe and dry." He stood in the doorway, watching them troop away. Connie looked back as they turned the corner of the path to cross the bridge. He was still watching, perhaps anxious to make sure that they went straight homeward and wasted no time. She waved her hand to him and he waved in return. She was to see him and know him for a long time afterwards, but she was never to see him again just as he was then, standing framed in the log doorway of the stout little schoolhouse.

There was probably not a step of real walking done all the way up to the house. As they turned into the road near the head of the bridge Cousin Cephas' wife Margaret called to them a message for Sarah and Mrs. Guyer.

"Tell them that Cephas has gone to town and will be back tomorrow with everything they need. And good luck to the birthday party."

The brownies all skipped at the very mention of the magic word and their feet went pattering over the old board floor of the bridge. Even Connie for once had scarcely time to stop even for a second to look at the white water whirling past below.

Sarah was all ready for them. On the big table in the middle of the kitchen was a pile of presents. Sarah and Connie and Peter had been making them for weeks, a wooden doll, a carved chain—for Peter was good at wood carving—a sunbonnet, a pair of knitted stockings, a gay flowered apron, a doll's patchwork quilt, treasures over which the brownies shrieked in shrill excitement and delight. Then the supper was spread with cold chicken and currant jelly, the last jar, and hot rolls—such a wealth of good things for lusty appetites. One would never have guessed that this was the final end of a long hard winter and that the shelves of the storeroom were as bare as after spring house cleaning. At last came the cake, with the room darkened and the candles lighted and the fire leaping on the hearth. Oh, what a cake! The brownies could not even squeal now, they were so full of supper and of happiness.

"Is it really ours, just for us, for our birthdays?" Tim asked, in anxious doubt.

Connie wondered what he would say if he knew that most children are used to having a birthday apiece and not a sixth share of one. But the cake was big enough to do credit to a dozen birthdays, so vast and white it was outside, so yellow and rich within. Connie had stood up to cut it and Peter was helping her to bear down upon the knife when she stopped suddenly to listen.

It was Sarah who spoke, "Hark, it's beginning to rain."

It was not merely rain, but the roar of wind, something like the voice of Hebron Brook only louder, much louder, coming nearer and nearer. Sometimes it rose high, then it dropped to a hoarse bellow, the voice of the gale that was sweeping across the mountainside.

When people hear a storm coming they must always run quickly and do something, no matter what. Peter dashed out of the door to the barn, to make sure the calves would be safe. Connie and the brownies scurried up the stairs to fasten the wooden shutters, and Sarah

rushed about below to make fast all the windows and to
bar the front door. Connie, from her bedroom, could
see the storm coming, a great black cloud that blotted
out the valley, then the stream and the bridge, then the
hillside, and suddenly was upon the house. The rain
drummed and rattled the shuttered windows, the wind
rose and fell. Connie pressed her nose to a pane at the
back of the house, but, although the shutter was a crack
open she could see nothing but blackness outside, as
though it were midnight instead of six o'clock in the
afternoon. She turned back to the room. The brownies
were sitting at the table, round-eyed and waiting.

Sarah had taken up the knife and was gravely cutting
the next slice. "Even if the wind is high it won't spoil our
cake," she declared. "Hold your plate, Tim; this slice was
baked just exactly for you."

The birthday supper went on, even though the candles
fluttered in the drafts, and the fire dwindled and then
leaped up the chimney as the tempest rose and fell. They
all ate, laughed, got up finally and played games about
the kitchen. It was a gay birthday, no matter what was
the darkness and noise and wind and rain outside.

"It will blow itself out," Sarah said finally. "We have
only to wait. The Guyer children will get home a little
late, but Mr. and Mrs. Guyer will know where they are."

It was indeed just as Sarah had said, and the storm
with a final roar swept across the hill and was gone. The
rain fell less heavily and finally stopped. Connie opened
a window and the fresh, sweet, wet smell of spring came
in, and with it a new sound.

"That Hebron Brook," Peter said beside her, tugging
at the shutter fastening. "Did you ever hear it sound so
loud?"

No, not even Sarah had ever heard the brook roar
like that.

The clouds were carried clean away and the sky was

clear, with stars coming out. Sarah lighted the lantern
and they all put on their cloaks. She and Connie and
Peter were going to see the brownies home. As they
climbed the hill they saw the marks of the wind everywhere, great branches snapped off the butternut trees,
twigs strewing the ground, places indeed where the path
was still deep in running water and they had to scramble
over the rocks at the sides. At the Guyer house, which was
so high up the hill that it had been even harder struck
by the storm, the pigpen had been blown over but, fortunately, not before the pig family had been safely driven
into the barn. But there was a whole dozen of round
spotted pig babies who had been soaked and chilled and
were being warmed before the fire in the summer kitch-
en. Mr. Guyer, an old man, went limping about giving
directions, lamenting and worrying. Mrs. Guyer was
calmer, but she looked anxious and tired.

"I'm glad the storm passed quickly," she said. "I hope
it won't interfere with Cephas getting back from the
village with all the things we need. I'm blessed if I have
more than three meals worth more in the cupboard. I've
never known a winter to last so long."

The three came down the hill again. The night was
growing lighter, for the moon was coming up. The path
was difficult to follow, in some places it was quite washed
away. A tiny stream, which usually came trickling and
murmuring down beside the path, was now a plunging
brook, pouring over its stones, sweeping around curves
with a loud tumult of hurrying waters.

"Let's go down the lane," Constance proposed as they
came near their own house. "I want to see how the water
is in Hebron Brook."

Even from there it was possible to hear with what a
new voice the brook was shouting below. It sounded
angry now instead of being loud and hurried as they
had heard it for days. The others wanted to see it as much

as Connie, so they walked onward down the hill, the moon above them growing brighter and brighter as they went.

Not one of them was prepared for what they saw when they reached Hebron Brook. Sarah herself had never known such a thing in all the years she had lived on the mountain and Hebron Brook had flowed under the covered bridge. It was beaten into yellow foam and was rolling in great heaving waves that went pouring down the bed of the stream. The water was so high it filled the whole rocky bed; the water had come up and up, so that the wide tossing level of beaten foam was almost on a level with the floor of the bridge. Branches and whole trees, torn up by the roots further above, came drifting down and caught against the beams; for the stream was so high that they could not pass beneath. A great muddy tangle began to gather and hang against the upper wall of the bridge. It grew larger and larger even as they watched.

They stood staring until Peter said, speaking loud to be heard above the noisy water, "The stream has risen even since we were standing here. It is going to be over the floor of the bridge in a very little while."

"But what will all the sticks and tree trunks do?" Connie asked. "They can't float away."

Sarah spoke, raising her voice as Peter had done. "They will carry the bridge away. See how they are battering against it now. If the water comes up even a few inches more, they will sweep the bridge downstream, boards and beams and everything together. There is nothing that can save it."

"There must be," Peter cried. "There has to be a way to save it."

Sarah answered hopelessly, "Once, a long time ago, my husband saw some such thing was going to happen and he went out to the middle and knocked off some of the boards, to make a place for the water to sweep through. He knew it in time, and he managed to save it. But it is too late for anything like that now."

The water began to rise more quickly. Peter stood thinking and staring in the moonlight, saying nothing. Then suddenly he exclaimed in a hard, clear voice that was almost like a man's, "It's not too late." He turned away and went dashing up the hill.

"Peter, come back," Sarah cried. "There's nothing you can do now."

Even Connie felt that it was hopeless. But she stood there, watching, unable to take her eyes away. To see the bridge shiver into pieces and go whirling downstream, what a strange, what a terrible sight. If Cousin Cephas were there, could he have done anything? Perhaps not. And Cousin Cephas was far away. Had Peter gone to call old Mr. Guyer? He could scarcely be of any help. But Peter was back, even as she began to wonder. He carried a coil of rope, a crow bar, the ax from the woodblock and the little sharp hatchet.

"You can help, Connie," he said. "There isn't much danger for a minute or two yet." He ran out on the bridge to the middle. Sarah did not protest, but followed him with Connie close beside. Constance was afraid Sarah would order them back, but she did not. The look on her face was exactly like the look on Peter's. They would both dare anything to save the covered bridge.

Peter, Constance and Sarah all worked together desperately, and as though they were one person. The voice of the waters made a queer hollow echoing as they stood in the tunnel of the bridge, very different from the wild free sound they listened to outside. It was Sarah who gave directions, for she had seen the bridge saved once and knew what must be done now that it was threatened again. But it was Peter who was sure that they could save it.

"Take the lower side, the wall that faces downstream," Sarah directed. "It will be easy to knock a hole in the boards there, then we can try the other."

A bridge that has stood twenty years, and is built to stand a hundred more, is hard to tear to pieces. But Ethan Allen had made an opening in it once, and Peter could do it again. And if human hands could save it, saved it should be.

Peter chopped, with great swinging blows of the ax, trying to cut through the big wooden pins which held the wall boards in place on the downstream side. Connie was chopping too with the hatchet. Whenever a board cracked under Peter's ax he would move forward and leave her and Sarah to thrust the iron bar under it and wrench it free. One plank gave way and then another. Peter climbed up a slanting beam, steadied himself on one of the cross timbers and knocked the boards free at the top. They dropped one by one and were whirled away like matches, leaving a great gaping hole on the lower side.

"Now the other." Peter was breathless now, as he climbed down and turned to strike with all his might at the opposite wall. He chopped steadily, never wildly, knowing just where each blow should be put. There was a loud crack, and another, the boards were giving way. But the task was no easy one, the very force of the water held the planks in place. Peter chopped, the other two strained and struggled. Connie felt something cold about her feet and looked down to see that the water was trickling over the floor.

Peter had stopped to draw a breath. "They are free at the bottom, I have to climb up now and knock them off at the top." He looked down at the water coming up around their feet and said steadily, "There's still time, there's plenty of time."

Sarah nodded. It still could be done if he were quick.

Sarah took Constance firmly by the hand and led her toward the shore. "We can't help him now," she said.

She still held Connie's hand as they turned about to watch. Just as they stepped off the bridge a deep ripple washed over it and wet Connie's ankles, but she scarcely felt it.

How she wished she were Peter, as he scrambled up a beam, braced himself on two cross timbers and began to swing his ax. "Crack, crack,crack," it sounded above the roar of the water. The instant the boards were loosened the stream began to snatch at them; they fell one after another and went whirling away. There was a wide opening and the brook was running through, a foaming torrent all across the floor where they had just been standing, and with Peter bold and trimphant perched on the strong framework above. He left the ax on a beam and came scrambling toward them. Connie could see how he was grinning with relief and she heard Sarah breathe a "Thank God" that was almost a sob. He had almost reached the shore, and was climbing down, when his hand slipped and he fell. A curl of water came washing all around him. He struggled for a second. It was Connie, holding to a beam and catching at his arm, who held him firm, so that he got to his feet, and came splashing to dry ground.

They all stood watching for a minute, fifteen minutes, half an hour. Was it true that the water had dropped a little? It had. The bridge had been a dam, an obstacle that the stream would not endure. Now that its waters could run free again, the stream spread out to flow more smoothly and evenly. It was not angry now. Hebron Brook was no longer determined to destroy the covered bridge.

For a long time the three could not drag themselves away. It was as though a spell were upon them and as though the bridge was only safe as long as they watched it, black and clear in the moonlight, with water glittering silver as it flowed over the floor. Then at last Sarah spoke sharply.

"Why in the world do we stand here gaping, and Peter wet through?" They turned and went up the hill, but Connie looked back again and again to make sure, absolutely sure, that the bridge was still standing.

They opened the door of the house and went in, all of them wet, Peter still dripping. Connie stopped in surprise. It seemed so long ago that they had left it, that she hardly knew what this thing meant, the big, half-cut cake on the table and the burnt-out candles. Peter cut himself a slice and ate it. Sarah was building up the fire.

"It is good that we all like birthday cake," she observed. "There's very little else we'll have to eat in this house until Cephas comes up to us. And if the bridge had gone, heaven only knows when we would have got anything, either for ourselves or the poor beasts in the barn. But the water will go down now, and Cephas will get to us before tomorrow is over. Now drink a cup of hot milk, both of you, and get to your beds."

When Connie came downstairs next morning, Sarah was making milk porridge before the fire, but Peter had gone out first to see to the calves and then to race down the hill to look at Hebron Brook. It was running more quietly, he reported, although the floor of the bridge was still flooded. The bridge was standing safe.

"We could get to school if the water is only as deep as that," Peter suggested conscientiously, but he grinned at Sarah's prompt answer:

"I may let you wade in ice-cold water when I must, but once in twenty-four hours is enough, I think. Sit down and eat your porridge now. We're not in any real danger of starving, but I'll be glad when Cephas comes. And there's still some birthday cake."

People have a way of feeling hungrier than usual when

there is not much food in sight. Connie felt that she could have eaten two breakfasts the size of that one, and that birthday cake in the morning was rather surprising fare. There was some skimmed milk to give to the chickens. As for the calves, there was a little new grass for them to nibble, although it was not long enough for them to get more than one good bite of a tuft here and there that had grown tall in the sun. But they were delighted to be let loose, to run and kick and jump into the air until it made Constance laugh aloud to watch them.

Sarah seemed to be pondering as to how to make the most of this day when Connie was free from school. "I've certainly precious little cooking to do," she observed. "Of course we could do some house cleaning, but there, the first days of spring come and go so quickly and are like nothing else in the world. Suppose we go up the hill to look for wild flowers. The hepaticas will be out."

They went up the long slope, all three together, with Jock galloping ahead. The little hill brook was pouring down noisily. They crossed it on stepping stones. How warm the sun felt on their backs and how bright the sky was! Little yellow flowers were showing here and there in the grass, and even the silvery green cushions of mullein leaves were beginning to appear. They came to where a spur of woods stretched out into the pasture. There was no snow between the big trunks now, but the wood was clean and open with the bushes bare and the twisting vines still leafless. Some little red berries of wintergreen were left from last autumn, among the delicate green tufts of new moss.

At first Connie could not see any flowers, but Sarah told her to look again. Then she began to catch sight of them in the open places where the sun fell warm and clear, making bright patches on the dark leaves. There, opening to the warmth and brightness, were the hepatica flowers, their bluish-white cups spreading wide to let the sunshine into their very hearts, their dark brittle leaves brown among the brown of those which had fallen from the maple trees to keep them warm all winter. Connie began picking them, coming across frail pointed blood-root flowers here and there also, but everywhere discovering more and more of the pale, delicate blossoms of the hepaticas. She had a great bunch presently, and so had Sarah, when Peter told them firmly it was past noon and they must go home.

"He wants to explain to the calves why they aren't getting any grain today," Sarah declared.

Constance came slowly down the slope, looking at all the green and blue and the brightness everywhere about her. The floor of the valley was spread below her feet; the squares of the fields were all different shades and colors, where they had been plowed or planted or where the green of new grass was covering the pasture lots. The mountains looked big and near; the blue of the distant ones was deep and brilliant, cutting sharply into the paler blue of the sky. Faintly, very faintly, there came up to her ears, even here, the song of Hebron Brook. She stood still, looking and looking, not thinking, but only feeling. If her half-finished thoughts could possibly have been put into words it would have been something like this—

"What a pity it is that all the people in the world don't know how beautiful it is just here." And this was what living on a farm was, all this work, all these adventures, all this beauty. What a great deal for just four words to say, "Living on a farm." But she would always know what they really meant.

They came into the house and Sarah managed to get a few things together so that they sat down to something like a meal. "We won't have many dishes to wash," Peter suggested cheerfully.

But Sarah's face was grave and she said more than once, "Mrs. Guyer said she had three meals left, didn't she? Then the brownies aren't hungry yet. I wish Cephas would come."

After the work was all done, Constance sat down in the big cushioned chair in a bright pool of sunshine beside the window. She was pleasantly sleepy and so comfortable. How much they had done the night before, how late they had all been up! Why, it must have been— Her eyes closed. She was awakened by the creak of wheels and by the sound of Sarah's flinging open the door and exclaiming, "Cephas, God bless you. How good that you are here."

Connie ran out to see Cousin Cephas with the big cart and the pair of black and white oxen. A heavy task it was even for them, to pull that laden cart up the hill; for it was piled high with sacks of flour and sugar, with sides of bacon and bags of coffee. It looked as though no one could be hungry for a year with all that food unloaded at the door.

Peter helped to lift down the bags and bundles, and Sarah and Connie carried them in to set them on the storeroom shelves. What a different feeling it gave one to see the place piled up with supplies again, a safe, happy, powerful feeling as though there would never be need to be anxious about anything again. Then Peter and Cousin Cephas and the oxen went creaking off up the hill to carry the Guyers their share. Presently they came down again and loaded the cart with wood, of which Sarah still had a greater pile than she needed, and then Cousin Cephas suggested to Connie, "Perhaps you would like to come down with us and see what the storm has done. It's going to surprise you."

Had something happened to the bridge after all? Connie wondered in a second of panic. But no, that couldn't be, or Cousin Cephas would not have got up to them. They went down all together, the oxen, with their big careful feet, stepping sedately down the lane, Peter driving them as he loved to do, holding a stick before their noses to signal whether they were to go slowly or faster, saying "Gee" and "Haw" when they were to turn right or left. As they came near the brook Cousin Cephas declared that the water had fallen even since he came up the hill. Was it really only last night that they had fought with the angry stream and kept it from devouring the bridge? The water was flowing now, in thin, clear ripples across the floor, not half an inch deep. Jock went rushing through it, throwing out a great spray on each side. Peter and Cousin Cephas splashed across, dry in their big boots; the oxen trod cautiously but seemed rather to like it. Connie rode over on the cart.

"Now," said Cousin Cephas suddenly as they halted on the other side. "Just look there at the schoolhouse."

"But what's happened," Connie cried. "It isn't there."

A pile of boards and logs and broken window frames was all that was left of the schoolhouse. A few hours ago Mr. Ennis was standing in the door, wishing them good luck for the birthday, and now he could never stand just there again. He was safe in his own house when the storm broke. It was the wind, and not Hebron Brook which had brought the building down. It was just as well that they had all gone home early to the birthday party.

"But where will we go to school now?" Connie asked blankly.

"School's very nearly over," Cousin Cephas told her. "Here in the country it has to end early so that the children can help with the spring planting. That's a time when a farm needs every pair of hands it can get. And I've been thinking that, since more than half of you live up the hill, you might as well have school in Sarah's big kitchen if she's of a mind to let you."

They went on to Cousin Cephas' barnyard where he and Peter unloaded the wood and piled the cart with a great mound of hay which Cousin Cephas had thrown down from the loft. "The cattle have been in the barn too much this long winter and I'm going to turn them out. They're wild to get to the new grass. There isn't quite enough to feed them yet, but I'm taking up some loads of hay so they won't go hungry."

Therefore when they went out of the gate and rumbled across the bridge again, there was a long procession trailing out behind them. Nicodemus the great bull walked just behind, his big black head so close to Connie's knee, as she sat in the back of the cart, that she could reach out and pat him when the oxen went slower. Behind him came the cows, the nearly grown calves, the whole herd trudging quietly and properly behind the big leader.

But when they had mounted the hill, when Peter and Cousin Cephas had let down the pasture bars to turn the cattle in on the new grass, what running there was, what flirting of heels, what tossing of black heads and rolling of great eyes, what rocking-horse galloping across the slopes. Jock ran and barked and swung them this way and that. He was a very proud dog now, this was his real duty, this was the herd which would be under his charge as long as he could drive cattle. The calves raced and skipped sideways, even Nicodemus dropped his head and began pawing the ground in his excitement. Then they all scattered over the hill, snatching mouthfuls of grass, looking and snuffing here and there, exploring their old feeding ground, glad beyond the power of dumb beasts' telling, to be out on the free, wild mountain again.

Connie sat on the edge of the cart thinking how gay and strong and happy they were until suddenly Cousin Cephas' voice broke in upon her.

"I declare, I clean forgot to give you your letter. The coach couldn't get over the bridge yesterday and so left your mail at my house. I've had it in my pocket for you since I set out up the hill."

Constance took it slowly and broke the seal. She was always slow with letters from her father and mother, to make them last longer. She read—how easily she could read now—and suddenly was slow no more. Her eyes raced down the page hardly taking in the words, news of a ship coming in, of a long voyage ended, of dear ones coming home at last. The final words, above her father's name, said:

"I'm coming up to get you by the first coach I can manage to take."

She jumped down from the cart. Oxen were not fast enough to carry a little girl with such news within her.

"Sarah," she shouted even when she was a long way off, "Sarah, they've come home again. He's coming for me."

She stood still, having got the words out, and waited until Peter, with a very sober face, came tramping up the hill. "Did you hear, Peter? Aren't you glad?"

"Yes, I'm glad," he agreed, "but—you will go away, Connie."

That was true, she would go away. All that glorious broad valley, that long mountain slope, the low house against the side of the hill, the pasture and the cattle dotted over it, Sarah's dear kind face, Peter's slow smile, when would she ever see them again?

Her voice sounded choked as she said, "Yes, Peter, I'm going away, but surely you and Sarah will let me come back."

Peter's serious face brightened into his own glad smile. "Oh, Connie, think what fun to see the coach stop and watch you jump out and come running up the hill. Promise me that you will surely come. Cousin Cephas is going to buy two of the calves, but the other one will be full grown then and we will have our own crop of corn and apples." He and Sarah were never going to leave the farm now, it was theirs to keep and to make prosper for the rest of their lives.

A few days went by, while the bright spring seemed to grow warmer and greener almost with every hour. They did indeed have school in Sarah's big kitchen, with the brownies sitting in rows on the new benches and Sarah coming in with a big pitcher of milk and a mountain of cookies, "just to break up the long morning." Mr. Ennis seemed to be quite as glad to have it broken as any of the rest of them.

The schoolmaster had saved a few things from the wreck of the schoolhouse, one of them being the big map which hung now upon Sarah's wall. On the last morning Connie stood up before them all and traced on it the course of her father's ship north from the West Indies, homeward bound.

It was the very next afternoon that the coach stopped below the hill and the guard blew his horn, with that deep sweet note that meant someone was arriving. As Connie rushed out to see, there was a tall figure striding up the hill, a broad-shouldered man with a sunburned face and with his arms stretched wide for Connie to run into them. It was her father.

The coach would not come back for two days, two beautiful days in which she could show him everything, tell him all about everything, while Sarah watched them both with her quietly happy face that reflected the joy on Connie's.

"Yes, we've made a good winter of it," Constance heard her telling Captain Anderson. "We've taken care of the farm between us and we know that we can go on with it. Peter and I can manage, we are certain of that now. I will be getting older all the time, to be sure, but then, so will he. But I don't know how we could have succeeded, either of us, in this hard winter without Constance to help. She will surely come back to us another year, in the summer. You must promise that she will."

The moment for going came, the carpet bag was packed, the coach came rolling up and stopped for them to climb in. The horses started; their hoofs sounded hollow on the covered bridge and the walls echoed the sound of the wheels.

"That's the hole Peter made," Connie told her father as they rumbled through. Long slivers of sunlight fell through the cracks in the wall, ran across Connie's face. She was leaning out, so that as soon as they were clear of the bridge she could look back up the hill. There they were above, Sarah waving her apron, Peter standing so tall beside her, both arms lifted in a last signal of good-by. He was bigger and broader than old Peter, but his dark figure against the sky looked once more like the Peter on the wall of the kitchen where Connie first heard about him, like the Peter printed on the snow she had seen on the night of her coming.

Cousin Cephas was at his gate to wave his hat and there at the next crossroads was a tall figure on a big black horse, both splashed with mud.

"Look, look!" she cried to her father. "It's Mr. Ethan Allen."

Not many little girls could have one of the great men of America's history to wave her good-by. A mile further and she saw a little gray house on a hillside, with a plowed field below it and a tall youth going back and forth sowing grain. That must be Dick McGowan, he had come up the hill once to show Peter the colt he had bought. He stopped to shade his eyes and watch the coach roll by.

Yes, certainly she would come back to all this. She settled back on the seat with a happy sigh. You could always think about coming back to a farm. That was the last beautiful thing to think about, that the valley and the mountains and the long slope of the hill would always be there, would always be the same.

Other good stories of pioneer days by Cornelia Meigs are Willow Whistle *and* Fair Wind to Virginia, *both published by Macmillan.*

Little Navajo Bluebird

BY ANN NOLAN CLARK

Illustrations by Paul Lantz

> *Mother always said: "Follow your trail as the bluebird flies." Doli, a modern Navajo Indian girl living in Utah, found that the trail led to much happiness.*

DOLI peeped shyly from the deep folds of her mother's wide skirts. Her black eyes shone.

Here was no home hogan, no rounded mud-plastered walls, no friendly center fire on which the supper mutton stew slowly bubbled and steamed. This place was the Trading Post, a great room of boarded walls with corners. The walls were lined with ladderlike shelves filled with hard things and soft things. At one end were Navajo blankets of many numbers, folded and stacked in piles of colors. On the side in back of the counter were cans on cans of foods. Some of the cans were covered with papers the colors of sunset and others were beautiful with pictures of green growing things.

Doli's mouth watered for the good food the cans held; she could almost taste their goodness.

Father was looking at the glass case full of silver rings and bracelets, coral and shell necklaces, and strings of turquoise. Father stood there, not talking, not moving, just looking at those things within the case.

Mother had come to the Post to sell a blanket of her weaving and to buy cans of tomatoes and peaches, sacks of wheat flour and cane sugar, bags of salt and coffee. If

the day was a lucky one and Mother received many of
the round, silver money pieces for her blanket, she would
buy more things, perhaps candy, lard, baking powder.

Doli could not remember that she had been to this
Trading Post before, although her mother said she had.
Hobah, the elder sister, had told her of it many times as
they sat together in the shade of the twisted juniper and
lazily watched Sun-Carrier going on his day-long journey through the blue above them.

Doli was afraid, but very curious. Soon she ventured
out from the shelter of her mother's many skirts and
found a better place between the knees of her tall father
where he stood looking at the turquoise and silver.

She leaned far out from the gateway of his knees, her
stiffly gathered yellow-brown calico skirts petaled flower-
like above her bare brown feet. Turquoise earbobs swung
gently against her thin brown cheeks. Her velvet blouse
was the color of a bluebird's wing, for she was a Bluebird
child of the yellow sand country. Her thick black hair
was smoothed back in a fat queue and tied with strings
of white yarn, for she was a woman child and must look
and act like Mother and like Elder Sister, Hobah.

Doli thought to herself, "This is a great place, this
Trading Post." Her heart sang, "Beautiful. Beautiful.
Things here are beautiful."

Flies buzzed in and out the doorway. Mother looked
at many things and marked in her mind those it was
good that she should buy. Doli watched her mother as
she bought, one by one, the things she needed.

Through the open door she could see Navajo men
squatting in the sand. Slowly, slowly, step by step, Doli
went over to see what they were doing. They were playing a game. They drew a circle in the sand and placed
small stones around its line. Two sticks made a little door
in the circle of stones. Doli peeked around the side of the
Trading Post door. There was Uncle! He was playing

with the other men. He had three chips which were painted black on one side. Uncle tossed the chips and they came down with the unpainted side showing. That gave him one mark for each chip so he could place his little stick three stones from the door of the circle. The men spoke little. Their game was silent and swift. Doli liked watching them, but she was afraid to stay long for fear she might miss something else exciting.

She went around the wall, back to where her mother was buying things from the Trader's shelves and bins. Doli stood on tiptoe with her big eyes just above the counter. Mother's shopping was a game, too. Mother put a bag of cornmeal to one side and gave the Trader some silver pieces from the small pile which he had given her for the blanket. Mother waited a long time, looking and thinking. Then she put a box of matches beside the cornmeal and paid the Trader some more round money, this time a little piece.

Mother pulled her blanket closer about her. She went outside to the wagon to get another blanket in which to carry the things she bought. Doli went with her. They did not hurry. Going to the Trading Post was not an everyday happening. It was a day that had been looked forward to and planned for and it must be enjoyed slowly. Doli and her mother did not intend to treat it lightly or hurriedly. Buying things was fun enough and important enough to take a long time to finish.

They did not seem to be looking, but they saw the men who were still playing their game. Uncle was tossing the chips again. This time all the black sides came up. Each black chip gave three marks, so Uncle moved his little stick nine stones around the circle. Uncle was good at tossing chips. His little stick was way ahead. He was winning.

Mother went into the store to unfold her blanket on the counter and put into it her bundles and bags. This done, she bought a bag of coffee and looked longingly at some bright velvet.

Doli watched her father. He was not talking to the Trader. He was not looking at the Trader, but the Trader was looking at him. The Trader was looking at the new bracelet Father was wearing. Father had just finished it this morning before they had started for the Post. He had made it to sell, but now he acted as if he had forgotten that he had it. Doli looked up at him. His eyes were still. Suddenly she knew something. Father was playing a game, too. He was playing that he did not want to sell his bracelet.

The Trader was very busy. When he was not taking round silver money from Mother's pile for the things she bought, he was trying to make Father want to sell his bracelet. Doli ducked her head. She had to put her hand over her mouth to hide a smile. At last Father said, Yes, he would sell the bracelet and the Trader gave him four round silver money pieces for it. Father took also, for good measure, some little brown papers and a bag of tobacco for the cigarettes which he liked to smoke.

The Trader gave Father a square of paper with black marks on it. He said it was a letter from Big Brother in the far-distant School land where he had gone so long ago. The Trader made the paper talk for Father, saying words of greeting from Big Brother to his home people.

Doli suddenly had a great longing for the home hogan and for tall, laughing Big Brother, who used to bring her gifts of bluebird feathers and colored stones. But that was long ago before he had gone to the School. Only once since then had he returned to visit them.

Doli took the candy which the Trader gave her, but the wonders of the Trading Post were gone. She no longer saw the cans of food, the blankets, the silver-trimmed saddles, the beautiful blue kettles and pans. She wanted to go home to her sheepskin bed by the friendly center fire. She was tired. She was hungry, so hungry that she could almost smell the hot, woolly smell of the supper mutton stew. She remembered the first supper with Big Brother the time he had come back to visit. There was mutton stew that night, but he had not eaten. He had sat in the shadows of the darkening hogan, not laughing, but quiet with a kind of anger that was frightening. When he spoke at all it was of a table and dishes and chairs and beds. Doli had not understood. What were these things of which he talked, she wondered. Why did he want them for this home place which always had felt so right?

Big Brother's second going had been in the season of the corn-growing-large. Corn-growing-large time had come again, but Big Brother had not returned.

Doli looked up. She had forgotten that she was here at the Trading Post. The Trader was looking down at her. He had given her candy. Father spoke to her in Navajo. He said in his low kind voice, "This White Man likes children, I think."

Little Bluebird pushed against her father's knees. In English she said to the Trader, "Big Brother." It was all the English she knew. Big Brother, himself, had taught her Navajo tongue to say it. "Big Brother," she repeated softly, shyly, but with great courage to show him that she was pleased with his gift of candy.

Tall Father moved toward the door. Doli went with him. He lifted her into the wagon and untied his horses from the bar. By and by Mother finished shopping and came out with her blanket bundle. She, too, climbed into the wagon. She pulled her blanket high up around her head and from within its shelter she looked out at the wagons and horses and people around the Trading Post. Doli pulled up her blanket but she, too, saw the happenings around her.

Navajos sitting in the door shade looked up from their

game and nodded. Navajos standing by the watering trough looked back and nodded. Father said to them. "The People speak as they pass. My way lies in this direction."

It was sun-hot time of day. Far away a whirlwind danced across the sand. Doli held the bag of candy tightly in her thin brown hand. Father called to the horses a high-pitched, long-drawn "A-ya-an-na."

They started toward home. The horses moved slowly along the sandy ruts. Yucca bloomed by the side of the road. A road-runner ran a race with the wagon. A prairie dog sat by his front door and watched their passing. A jackrabbit loped across the road.

Father sang as he drove along. Doli was sleepy. Her head nodded to her father's singing and to the lurchings of the wagon.

It had been a long day. It had been a good day, but now the journey to the Trading Post was over.

Home hogan was a rounded, mud-plastered house with a blanket-covered door facing eastward. There were no windows. The chimney was a hole in the middle of the rounded, mud-plastered roof. The floor was clean yellow sand. Sheepskins were the beds; boxes were the chairs, and the stove was a hollowed place in the sandy floor. A brushed-clean place beside the stove was used for table.

This was the family hogan, their house, their home, a friendly, happy place for Doli.

When Doli and her mother and her father reached home hogan from the Trading Post, day had come to cool time. Red rocks were sending out their long gray shadows to the edges of the sandwash near by.

Elder Sister, Hobah, had been out all day with the flocks, but now she was home again. She had turned the sheep and the goats into the night corral among the piñons. She had carried water from the well. She had chopped wood at the woodpile and now smoke from the newly made supper fire filled the hogan door. Hobah was beautiful, tall for her age, slender, and strong. She did whatever work there was to do, quietly and well, as her mother had taught her.

Now she came out to the wagon to carry her mother's blanket bundle into the hogan. Mother went to milk the goats and Doli stumbled sleepily to sit on her sheepskin bed beside the fire. She told Hobah of the happenings of the day. She told her about Uncle's winning the game that he played with the men and about Father's selling the bracelet to the Trader. She told about the things she had done and had seen and had heard, but she did not say Big Brother's name. One said with words those things that the eyes saw, but even with Hobah one guarded the whisperings of the heart.

Father came in. He had unhitched his horses and had hobbled them for the night grazing. Hobah hastened to serve him with food. Mother's blanket had been full of good things. Tonight the family had store bread and canned peaches to eat with the mutton stew. Tonight the strong black coffee was sweetened with sugar and colored creamy brown with milk from a can.

Fiery clouds of sunset covered the sky and changed the yellow sands of the drywash to purple and rose. Hobah moved quietly about the hogan, serving Father with food and helping Mother end the work of the day.

Doli was sleepy but not yet was she ready to let sleep come. She sat in the door of the hogan and let the little night winds wash her face with their cooling fingers. Far away, far off, in the thickening shadows, she heard singing. Some stranger singing. At first it was just a singing sound, but little by little, as the rider came nearer, the singing sound grew into words of song, into words of the hogan song. Clearly they came across the gray shadows, the words of the hogan song:

> "My hogan,
> My hogan,
> My happy hogan,
> My blessed hogan,
> Hogan.
> My hogan."

So sang the far rider as he urged his tired horse homeward. Father came to stand in the hogan doorway. He took up the chant. He sent his singing out into the coming night to meet the tired rider to sing him home. Father sang:

> "Look!
> Yonder the hogan,
> The beautiful hogan,
> The precious hogan."

Doli gathered her skirts close around her. She hugged her knees in delight. Father's singing wrapped her in a blanket of happiness.

"My hogan,
Hogan,"

sang Father, and the rider answered:

"Hogan beautiful,
My hogan."

Doli turned toward the fire-lighted hogan. She watch Hobah's blue shadow moving along the wall. It made her think of Turquoise Woman on her way to the Western Waters.

"Uncle must tell us again of Turquoise Woman," she said to herself; "I will ask him to tell us when next he comes to my mother's hogan."

"Hogan, my hogan, my hogan blessed," sang the far rider.

Darkness came swiftly into the desert. Night came upon the People there.

The family moved their sheepskins out under the stars. One pelt alone was left inside, not used, not needed. It lay to one side, partly unrolled, wholly neg-lected. It was Big Brother's bed waiting for him to come home.

Outside, the night was clear and the stars hung low. Mother moved quietly, unrolling the sheepskins, tuck-ing in the blankets. Doli lay upon her pelt in the soft, warm sand, in the warm, still night. Mother's hand found her hand in the darkness, softly, lightly, swiftly brushing it, like a raindrop, almost. Doli slept.

The next morning, after sunup, after breakfast, after Hobah had taken the flocks to graze, Uncle came riding around the red rocks and up through the sandwash. Un-cle came riding, his arms held stiffly, elbows pointing outward, and jerking up and down with the pony's trot-ting. Doli stood by her mother's loom under the juniper tree, watching him coming. She stood still, waiting, feel-ing happy to see him. Uncle was young, almost as young as Big Brother. He was gay-acting and gay-looking. He wore tight blue jeans and a bright red shirt and a big black hat. His hair was long like Father's and he wore it tied in a fat queue wrapped with long white cord.

Mother was beginning a new blanket. She was stringing her loom. She was letting Doli help her. Mother's yarn that she had sheared from her sheep, had spun and dyed, was rolled neatly into balls and was piled on the sheepskin beside them. Mother saw Uncle trotting his pony through the sandwash. She smiled at Doli. She was pleased to see her younger brother coming.

Father was making a silver ring. His workbench was a cottonwood stump. His tools were a hammer, a sandstone mold, and leather bellows. He sat cross-legged on the ground with his head bent low over his work, but he heard Uncle come riding around the red rocks.

Work stopped. They waited for Uncle.

Uncle lifted his pony into a run until they were just beyond the clearing of the juniper tree. Then Uncle made him stop with stiffened legs in a cloud of flying sand. It made Doli laugh to see Uncle's pony stop so quickly that it almost sat down.

Now that he had arrived in a dashing way, Uncle felt that he could take his time. So he sat there, looking at the waiting family. Then he got off slowly, throwing his pony's reins to the ground so it would not stray. He walked slowly to the shade of the hogan wall. He sat down slowly, saying not a word. His pony, reins dragging, began to graze on the sparse clumps of green.

Now all was stillness where but a time before was swift-moving action. Father came over to the hogan shade. He sat down by Uncle. He rolled himself a cigarette. He gave Uncle a little brown paper and his bag of tobacco and a match. He nodded to Uncle, meaning, "You may smoke." Uncle rolled a cigarette. He lit it, using the match that Father used and putting his own

match carefully in the pocket of his bright red shirt. Now both men puffed their tobacco. Smoke came. Two blue lines curled upward.

Then Father spoke gravely to Uncle. "Greetings, Younger Brother," he said. Uncle answered gravely, "Greetings, Elder Brother."

Doli went near them. She stood shyly by her father, looking away from the loved Uncle whom she wanted so badly to see. "Greetings, Small One." Uncle spoke softly, looking straight ahead. He did not want to frighten the little Bluebird.

Doli, still not looking, put the bag of candy down where Uncle could reach it. She said to her father, "It is a gift for him."

Uncle picked up the limp bag of squeezed and melted candy. He looked at his pony. He said, "I, too, have a gift to offer."

Uncle took from inside his shirt a small brown bundle. He handed it to Father. Mother left her weaving and came over to look at the brown paper package. Everyone looked at it. Then Father untied the string. Two deerskin moccasins with silver buttons on the sides stood proudly in the crumpled paper. Father took Doli in his arms and put the moccasins on her small brown feet. Doli looked at them. They were beautiful. She felt them. They were soft to the touch.

Presently Mother went to the well for water. She carried a large bucket. Her yellow-brown skirts swished softly as she walked through the sand. Doli went with her. Her yellow-brown skirts swished softly. She carried a little bucket. The loose sands slid into the tiny footprints the moccasins made.

Mother filled her pail with water at the well. Doli filled hers. Water splashed on her foot. She saw it, but she did not feel it. She pushed her foot out from the flounces of her skirts and poured more water on it. She watched the water flashing silver on its way down, but when it touched her foot she felt neither cold nor wetness.

Doli looked up at her mother. Her eyes were big with surprise. The moccasins were shelters. They were like little houses for her feet. They were good. They must like her small brown feet!

She and Mother walked back through the sand to the hogan. They went inside. The hogan was clean and cool and quiet. Sunlight came in at the doorway and lay like a bright blanket on the sand of the floor. Mutton cooked over the coals in a big black pot. The hogan cat washed its face and shook out its whiskers to dry. Far away came the tinkle of the bell goat with the flock that Hobah herded slowly to the waterhole. Doli looked up at her mother. They smiled together, a quick little understanding smile that said, "We are glad to be together in this hogan because it is beautiful and good."

Other stories in this book tell about camping out at night, herding sheep, and gathering peaches. The author has also written a beautiful story about the Pueblo Indians entitled In My Mother's House, *published by Viking.*

. . . And Now Miguel

BY JOSEPH KRUMGOLD

Illustrations by Jean Charlot

> Miguel Chavez is a real boy who lives near
> Taos, New Mexico, on his parents' sheep-
> raising farm. He has a secret yearning to go
> with the men of his family to the Sangre de
> Cristo Mountains, for Miguel wants very
> much to prove himself a man.

I AM Miguel. For most people it does not make so much difference that I am Miguel. But for me, often, it is a very great trouble.

It would be different if I were Pedro. He is my younger brother, only seven years old. For Pedro everything is simple. Almost all the things that Pedro wants, he has —without much worry.

I wanted to find out how it was with him one day when we were in our private place near the Rio Pueblo, the river that goes through our farm. I asked him, "Pedro, suppose you could have anything you want. Is there anything you want?"

"Ai, of course." He looked up from reaching below a rock in the river. In this way we catch trout, slowly feeling around in the quiet places beneath big stones. If the fish comes by, sliding soft against your hand, you can catch him. Pedro was just learning to fish like this. He looked up, not wishing to talk. "Of course, sure I want something."

"Like what?"

"Like not so much school."

From . . . *And Now Miguel,* by Joseph Krumgold, copyright 1953 by Joseph Krumgold. Published by Thomas Y. Crowell Company.

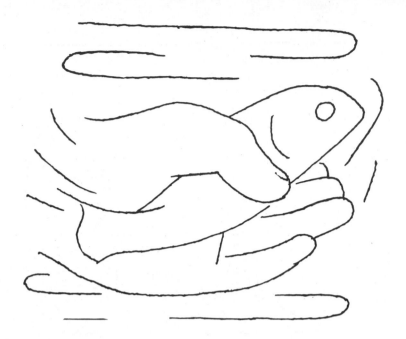

"School—yes. But that is something that you do *not* want."

"Like I say—not so much."

"Then what is it that you *do* want?"

"Shh!" He closed his eyes, moving his hand slowly, slowly in the water, holding his breath, with his tongue between his teeth.

Of a sudden he grabbed, splashing. He made a big commotion in the water. It was no good. Even before he took his hand out of the water, I knew it was empty.

"A good big trout, that's what I do want." Pedro looked at me like he was mad at me, like I spoiled his chance for the fish. "A good one, six inches big!"

He was mad. He took a stone and threw it into the water with all his might.

So I caught him a trout. It is not so hard. You lay down with your hand in the water, in a place where there are shadows below the bank. You leave your hand there for a long time, until the fish see that it is nothing strange. Until they come by, even touching you. Until you can touch them, even rub them very lightly. They seem to like this, the fish, for you to rub them this way. Then when you feel them coming through your fingers, slowly

you hold on to them, slowly but tight. Without any sudden move. And that's that.

I gave the fish to Pedro. It was almost six inches. He was happy with me again.

That's the way it is with Pedro. One such fish, not too big after all, and he is happy.

It is enough for him for everything to be like it is.

When the sun shines hot and dry and he can go swimming in the pool where the river goes around the farm of my Uncle Eli, that for Pedro is enough.

And when it rains, that too is enough. He is a great artist, Pedro. He sits in the kitchen when there is thunder outside, and all the pictures in his book he turns yellow and red and blue with his crayons.

If there is a ball, he will play ball. And if there is not, he will roll an old tire. No matter which, he is content.

It would be good to be Pedro. But how long can you stay seven years old? The trouble with me is that I am Miguel.

It would be good to be Gabriel. He is also my brother, and he is nineteen years old. Next to my Grandfather, and my Uncle Bonifacio, and my Uncle Eli, and next to

my father who is called Old Blas, and my biggest brother
who is called Young Blas and who wears a badge and
drives the school bus, Gabriel is the greatest man in the
world.

Everything that Gabriel wants, he can get. He explained this to me one Friday last winter.

All week long Gabriel goes to the high school in Taos,
which is a very big town eight miles away, of one thousand people and many stores that sell marshmallow
candy. This year Gabriel will graduate from high school.
And that will be too bad for the basketball team and the
baseball team as well as for the Future Farmers of America, a club of which he is president. From Monday to
Friday Gabriel goes to school and wins the games there
and is a president. But on Friday he forgets all these
things and helps my uncles and my father with the sheep.

In our family there is always one thing, and that is the
sheep. The summer passes and the winter comes and
soon it is Easter and the time for spring; but all the time,
no matter when, there is the sheep. In our house we may
be very happy. Like the time my littlest sister, Faustina,
was born. Or very sad. Like when Young Blas was hurt
by the mowing machine. But these things they come and
go. Everything comes and goes. Except one thing. The
sheep.

For that is the work of our family, to raise sheep. In
our country, wherever you find a man from the Chavez
family, with him will be a flock of sheep. It has been this
way for many years, even hundreds, my grandfather told
me. Long before the Americans came to New Mexico,
long before there was any such thing here called the
United States, there was a Chavez family in this place
with sheep. It was even so in Spain where our family
began. It is even so today.

And so when Gabriel finishes school for the week, on
Friday, he goes out to the sheep camp. There he takes

the place of one of my uncles or my father, and the older man can come home for a day or two.

In the winter we pasture our sheep on the big mesa that stretches from the cliffs on the other side of our river, far, far north, flat and straight almost into Colorado. This wide plain spreads out to the west to the Rio Grande river where there is a deep arroyo, a great canyon that goes down, down into the earth to where the big river flows. The land is owned by the Indians of the Taos Pueblo and my father pays the war chief of these Indians ten cents every month for each sheep that we pasture. We are very good friends with the Indians. It was not always so, my father tells me, but now we are good friends.

The sheep camp is built into a wagon, so that it can be moved as the sheep are driven from where they have eaten to new pasture. It has a bed built in, and shelves, and a stove. No matter how hard it snows or how cold it gets, inside the sheep wagon it is always tight against the wind and dry and warm.

On this Friday the wagon was in place very near to the Rio Grande canyon, almost twelve miles from our house. Gabriel went there with the pick-up truck, and he took me along. Driving the truck is very hard. There are no roads. You drive right across the mesa through the mesquite bushes, keeping away from the big holes and the big rocks. It is wise to drive slow and be careful.

But Gabriel did not drive slow, yet he was still careful. He swung the big truck from side to side like it was a little stick, and all the time he sang a beautiful song about a red flower.

"Miguel," he turned to me after he had finished with the song, "what's up with you? You haven't opened your mouth since we left the house."

"Me?" I stopped looking at the bushes and the rocks. "As for me, I've been thinking."

"About what?"

"About how easy it is for you—." Gabriel swung the wheel, and the truck skidded in the snow away from a big hole. "Well, how easy it is for you—to be Gabriel."

Gabriel laughed. "Easier for me than anyone else in the world. After all, that's who I am."

"But it is not so easy for me—to be Miguel."

"Maybe not." Gabriel smiled, watching the snow ahead. "It takes a little time. Wait a year or two, and it'll be easier."

"Only to wait? Isn't there something else I can do? Like—practice?"

"Being Miguel—it's not like playing basketball. No, it's a hard thing to train for."

The truck was going faster. Gabriel was looking through the windshield, his eyes a little closed and tight, like he was looking into the wind. But now that we were talking about such important things, there was much that I wanted to know.

"There must be a secret! Some kind of a special secret, isn't there?"

"For what?" It was hard to talk now, the truck was roaring so much because we were going so fast.

"How to get to be a president." I had to yell. "So easy. And when you want a deer, you take a horse and in a day or two you come back with a deer. And the house?"

"What house?" Gabriel yelled back at me.

"The house by the cottonwood tree. You're going to build such a house of adobe?"

"Sure. Someday."

"And you're going to become an engineer? At the college?"

"Uh-huh."

"How?" I had to shout real loud. "How is all this done —so easy—to get what you wish?" I took him by the arm because he didn't seem to be hearing. "How?"

"Mike!" He shoved me away, back into the corner of the seat. "Lay off. Coyote."

I looked off to one side where Gabriel nodded with his head. And there it was, racing away for the edge of the mesa, no bigger than a dog, than our sheep dog Cyclone. He was just a speck, the coyote, moving against the snow. They are terrible animals for the sheep. Every year they kill many lambs, sometimes more than two dozen. They are smart and they are faster than a bird.

But with Gabriel driving we were getting closer. There was no more time to be careful. Into holes and over rocks we went, and I held on or else I would hit the ceiling of the truck with my head. We pulled closer. I could watch the coyote, moving like a fist that opens and closes quicker than you can blink your eyes. A shadow sliding across the snow.

"Reach down," Gabriel spoke quick. "In back of the seat."

I got the rifle that was there and held it. At just the right moment, Gabriel stamped on the brakes. Before the car even stopped skidding in the snow, Gabriel had pulled off one of his gloves, grabbed the gun and was sighting it. I hardly knew he'd taken it out of my hands before I heard it crack.

The coyote stopped in the middle of a leap. As if a tight wire was stretched in his path and caught him. But when he dropped he continued on his way, not so fast but he still kept going.

Gabriel took his time, carefully holding the animal in the sights of the rifle. He actually hummed the song about the red flower as he took his time. He tightened his finger on the trigger.

The second bullet stopped the coyote for good. And Gabriel laughed. It was good to kill a coyote. With two bullets, many lambs were saved. Gabriel laughed because it was good and because it was so easy.

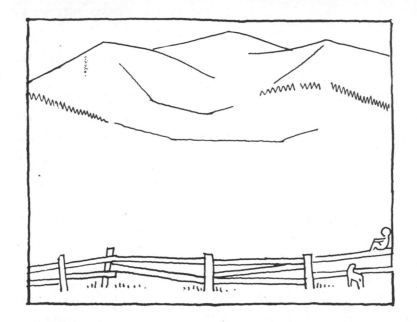

That's the way it was with Gabriel. Everything that he wants he can get. With Pedro, it is the opposite. Everything that he has is enough.

Both of them, they are happy.

But to be in between, not so little anymore and not yet nineteen years, to be me, Miguel, and to have a great wish—that is hard.

I had such a wish. It was a secret and yet not a secret. For how secret can you keep high mountains that one can see for hundreds of miles around, mountains that face me when I first open my eyes every morning and are the last thing I see in the night.

This was my wish, to go up there—into those mountains that are called the Mountains of the Sangre de Cristo.

"I am here! Here. The time has come and I am here! I am here!"

The last thing I heard was the clock in the kitchen going nine, ten, eleven times. So now it must be midnight or maybe even after. That's when I heard it. The cry of the first lamb of the New Year. I heard it coming in through the window of the bedroom, from far away off on the prairie, a little sound all alone in the wide night that was bright with the moon.

"Look what's happened," the lamb cried. "Me."

It didn't speak the words, of course. It didn't even sound like the words. The cry of the lamb sounded like my friend Juby, at school, when he tries to yell far away and at the same time he keeps coughing. Not like words. But it stands to reason. What else could a new lamb, especially the first lamb born in the whole flock, once he got to his feet and opened his mouth to baa—what else would he say?

"Me! I'm here."

Without taking my head from the pillow, I listened until I was sure. Then I folded back the comforter, and slipped my feet out from Pedro's legs, and took away his arm from around my neck. One would think that Pedro, who sleeps with me in the same bed, was training to be a wrestling champion, the way he sleeps.

Without opening his eyes, Pedro said, "Right away," for this is how he wakes up every morning. When he says "right away" it means that right away he'll get up and have breakfast and go to school.

But he never does. And even though no one believes him any longer, he still says "right away" when he wakes up, as if it were his morning prayers. The truth is, to get Pedro out of bed it is necessary to pull him by the feet, and let him fall on the floor, and then bend the mattress in half so there's no more bed anymore he can get back into.

Faustina, who sleeps on the other side of our bedroom, she heard me too.

"Miguel?"

"Yes."

"I'm thirsty."

"Down here there is no water." I was underneath the bed looking for my shoes.

"Where d'you think you're going?" Pedro looked down at me from over the side of the bed. He was actually awake.

"It's started. The lambing. I just heard it—the first lamb. I'm going to go and have a look."

"Yah!" Faustina hiccuped and giggled. "He's gonna go look."

"That's what you think," said Pedro.

"Now's bedtime." The way Faustina laughed 'way high up, you'd think this was one big joke.

"In order to grow, we gotta stay in bed," said Pedro. "You know that."

"For you, yes." I didn't even wait to get dressed. I started out with my arms filled with clothes. "I've had enough growing."

I was the first one out of the house, where only my mother and big sisters slept these nights. The men stayed with the flock out in the fields and in the corrals, sleeping in the sheep wagon and around camp fires, waiting for many nights now for the lambs to start. And now, surely, it had begun. Out on the veranda where I finished to dress myself, I heard it even more clearly.

"Baa. Aah. It's me. I'm here."

"Mickey. What are you doing?" It was my sister Tomasita. She was all wrapped around with a bathrobe. "It's not allowed. Go back."

"I know." I was trying to put one leg in my pants, while balancing, and without looking. "I know—but that was last year. Now could be different."

"No, Miquito. Go back!" Tomasita hurried down the path, through the wooden gate to the corrals. And the screen door behind me banged again. I couldn't see who it was because my head was all caught in my jersey, because I was trying to get dressed so fast.

"You'd better watch out, Mike, Mother's coming." It was Leocadia, who is next to my biggest sister.

"Maybe she'll let me."

"Maybe." Leocadia helped me to push my head through the hole in the top of the jersey. "But I don't think so. She'll say you must wait."

"A whole year more?"

"Until morning." Leocadia pulled the jersey down in the back. "You can see the new lamb in the morning." And she was off after Tomasita.

It was not a question of morning, to wait until morning. But to be with the others from the very start this time. That might make all the difference.

I was putting on the second shoe when my mother came out.

"Miguelito!" My mother was surprised to see me, yet she spoke softly for no one to hear, even though there was no one around who could listen. Only Cyclone, the dog, who was tied to the fence. He started to bark.

"If you will let me tell you something, there is something I have to tell you," I told her. "Like the way I worked hard all the winter. And at school. There was no day in which there was not a new star in my book. You yourself said no one worked harder at the ditching."

This had happened only the week before, the ditching. That is the time at the end of the winter when all the

families who live along the same irrigation ditch come
together to clean up the ditch. This is in order to make
everything ready for when the fields are plowed and the
seed is planted. Then to get water coming down the ditch
and onto the fields, it is best to have all the rocks and
bushes and mud from the winter out of the ditch.

There are many families on our ditch, more than a
dozen, stretching from where we live to our village of
Los Cordovas. But concerning the ditch, everyone listens
to Mr. Martinez, who is of my mother's family, for he
is the *Mayor Domo* of the ditch. In English this means
he is the ditch boss, and among us a new one is elected
every year to tell each family what to do, and how many
days of water each can have, and what days he can let
the water into his own fields.

At ditching time each family is supposed to bring so
many men to work for so many days. And my father let
me stay home from school in order that I, too, could go
along to help. Mr. Martinez said I could count for a half
a man, which is not too great a thing, and I asked my
father to speak with Mr. Martinez in order that I should
be counted three quarters of a man at least. But when
he did so, everyone laughed, including my father, because at ditching time everyone does laugh most of the
time, and there is a lot of singing as well as wine and
other things to drink.

The question though was settled fine. It was agreed
that even though I would remain one half a man, since
the next day was Saturday and I didn't have to go to
school, I would be allowed to work two full days. So
that I did end up being counted as one whole man. This
was perfect for me, and better for everyone since frac-
tions are hard to keep straight anyway.

To prove it was no mistake I worked as good as I could,
using only the biggest shovels and the biggest pickaxes.
So that my mother that night made me eat a third mutton

chop, just like the older men, because I had worked so hard. And I ate it, too, easily.

And now, when I reminded her, she remembered it all.

"I know," she said. "You already have become one whole man, Miguel. But even a whole man must learn to wait until his time comes. He can work, and he can prepare, but he must know how to wait, too."

"I've learned how to wait. In twelve years, I've learned."

"Is it so hard, then, to wait until morning?"

"Another year. That's how long it will be. This time comes just once every year."

"Miguel!" My mother stopped me. She held me by the chin, tight. She wiped her apron at my eyes. "I have watched you using all your strength to open the gate to the barnyard, the one from which the big stone hangs. But this is not like a gate. To become something different from what you are, it takes more than being strong. Even a little time is needed as well. No, no!" She wouldn't let me speak. "Go back with the others, with Faustina and Pedro."

"They will be glad to see me!" I kicked off one of my shoes. Not hard. Just enough to hit the door a good bang.

"Back to bed or we'll see about this!" When my mother says, we'll see about this, sometimes it can hurt. I picked up my shoe and started into the house. When I looked back she was untying Cyclone, who was barking, so that even he could go.

Everybody, even the dog, got out that night to see the first lamb.

"And you," said Pedro. He was waiting for me with a smile on his face. "Did you get a good look?"

I didn't answer. With my shoe, I took aim at the floor and let it go. First one, then the other. What difference how much noise I made?

"Okay!" yelled Faustina. "Okay. Okeydokee!" Every

few days Faustina learns a new word, and then that's the only word she uses. It doesn't mean anything.

"It's sure nice when someone grows enough." Pedro kept talking behind my back. I sat on the edge of the bed, pulling off my clothes, and he kept talking and laughing. "Everything's sure nice. They get up in the middle of the night. Just like that. Go where they want. Whoopee!" He lay on his back and kicked his feet in the air.

"Okeydokee!" Faustina squealed till she had no more breath.

"Shut up!" I gave a shout, louder than both of them. When they quieted down, I pointed out the window. "You see out there, far, far away out there." They both crawled across their beds and looked out in the night.

"What is?" asked Faustina.

"You mean the mountains?" said Pedro looking where I was pointing.

"Yes. The Mountains. The Sangre de Cristo. You know what's in those mountains?"

"Clouds," said Faustina.

"Don't be crazy," Pedro told her. "Clouds in the mountains! Clouds are in the sky."

"They come from the mountains. I see them every day, every day, every day."

"You're crazy every day." Pedro tried to stop her.

I stopped Pedro. "I'll tell you what's in those mountains. The biggest fish anywhere, and when they're cooked they taste like the best salted peanuts together with roasted marshmallows. And the best hunting, wild turkeys and bears to shoot at. And camping out every day. And every night getting up whenever you feel like it. And cooking whatever you want to eat."

"*Sopaipillas* with jelly?" These were sort of a puffed-up kind of biscuits and they were what Faustina liked best.

"Yes," I told her.

"What else?" she asked.

"Up there are pools to swim in, with waterfalls coming down that you can slide in like a sled going down hill in the winter. Only to slide down in the water into a big pool is forty times better. Up there is never hot in the summer. On the very top of each mountain there is snow, like it was a big bunch of ice cream piled up."

"What flavor?" asked Faustina. "Chocolate?"

"No flavor."

"How does it taste then?"

"It tastes cool."

"That's all?"

"That's all."

"Okay," said Faustina.

"What else?" said Pedro.

"And up there are no mountains higher than where you are. When you look up, all you see is the sky. And the air is so clear every breath makes you fill up like a balloon. And when you look down you see everything. The whole Rio Grande Valley, almost the whole of all of New Mexico. No one can see more, or feel better than up there."

Faustina and Pedro kept looking at me even though

I stopped talking and the only noise was Cyclone barking, out there where the family was with the new lamb.

"What else?" said Pedro.

"What else can there be? That's everything."

"So?" Pedro looked at me. "What's about it?"

Now was the time. For many years it had been a
secret that I kept only to myself. A secret of only one
person after a while gets too hard to keep. To make it
real you have to tell someone else, even though they
laugh at you, you've got to tell. Otherwise, all you got
left is just one small, dried-up secret that's not worth
anything.

"I'm going up there."

"To the Sangre de Cristo?"

"Yes."

"Okay," said Faustina. And she started to crawl back
to her pillow.

"Sure," said Pedro. "Someday. We all go."

"Not someday. I go with the others this year. This here
year!"

They both stopped from getting under the covers and
looked at me. They didn't laugh.

"How do you know?" asked Faustina.

"I will arrange it myself."

"Arrange. That's not the way." Pedro shook his head.
"First you got to know how to do everything. Then when
you get into high school, or sometime like that, then it
happens."

"Sure," said Faustina as if she knew what was all about.

"It never happens when anyone is so little like us,"
Pedro said.

"Like who?"

"Us."

"That's you," I told him. "Us—that's not me. You and
Faustina are us. But me—I'm Miguel. And what I say is
this. I'm going."

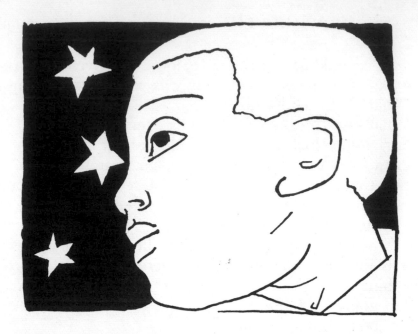

"How?"

What could I say? I said, "I have made a plan."

This was a big surprise to them both. They looked at me like I just grew wings.

"Your own plan?" Pedro crawled back to the side of the bed. I nodded my head, yes. "Like what?"

What could I say? I said, "A first-class plan. But I can't tell you about it. You'll see how it works."

"When?" yelled Faustina. "How soon? When can we see?"

"It starts tomorrow."

"Tomorrow!" Pedro yelled, too. With no one in the house, there was no reason not to make noise. "Tomorrow begins the plan? And you know how it all works, everything?"

"Everything."

"Wango!" Pedro made like he was throwing rocks all over the bedroom, he was so excited. "This is better than anything. This is as good like when we got the new tractor!"

"Okay," Faustina squealed. "Okeydokee!"

I laughed and yelled, too. It got so I thought I did have a plan, a real, good one. And everything was fixed

so it would be all right now. We had a good time making
a lot of noise. Pedro climbed up the back of the bed, the
iron part where there are bumps and flowers.

"Look at me! I'm Miguel. I'm way up high. Miguel
standing right on top of the mountains."

"I just remembered," yelled Faustina.

"What?"

"I'm thirsty."

I went and got her a glass of water from the kitchen.
Then I put out the lights and undressed and got into bed.

In the quiet, I remembered. I didn't have any plan.
In the quiet I heard them beyond the corral, Cyclone
barking and the lamb making its kind of noise and the
ewe making her kind of noise. All I could do was listen.

But even so, it was good. I had explained the secret.
I had come out, like from behind the bushes when we
play The Bandits Robbing Schaeffer's Drugstore, which
is a drugstore in Taos and a game we play at school.
I had come out from behind the bushes and that meant,
at least, that something had begun. And now that it had
begun, I took one good look at the mountains through
the window and then I went to sleep.

*Joseph Krumgold's . . . And Now Miguel
won the 1954 Newbery Medal. Another fine
book by Mr. Krumgold is Onion John, the
story of the friendship of a twelve-year old
boy for a European-born vegetable peddler.
Also published by Thomas Y. Crowell, this
book won the 1960 Newbery Medal.*

Experiment 13

BY ROBERT McCLOSKEY

Illustrations by the author

> *When Dulcy Dooner inherited a jar of seeds instead of the ninety thousand dollars he expected, it was a big disappointment. But Dulcy was not a man to give up easily.*

THE Centerburg courthouse clock was just striking eight as Homer rode into the town square. He parked his bike in front of the barbershop, poked his finger into a crack in the wooden barberpole, and pulled out a key. After unlocking the door and putting up the shades, Homer swept the floor.

By quarter of nine Homer had finished with all of his opening-up chores. He started looking through the stack of old magazines, the same magazines that had been there last Saturday and the Saturday before, the same magazines that had been in the barbershop since Homer started working there. Homer had looked at them all a hundred times, so he just sat looking out of the window, waiting for the barber to arrive at nine o'clock.

Through the barbershop window he watched the sheriff walk across the square at ten minutes to nine, as usual, and go into Uncle Ulysses' lunchroom for breakfast.

He watched the mayor drive up and go into the town hall at five minutes of nine, as usual.

The courthouse clock struck nine, and Homer yawned. Just for variety he looked in the mirror, so that he could see the town square backwards. Then, by sitting in the barber chair and leaning way back, he looked in the mirror and saw the town square *upside down* and backwards. Homer smiled as he watched the barber come out of the lunchroom upside down.

Boosting himself out of the barber chair, Homer looked at the clock and thought, "He's a little bit late, as usual!" Then he said, "Gosh!" to nobody in particular. "Everything is so *usual* around here. Seems as though nothing ever happens here any more."

"Morning, Homer," the barber said as he came in. "I see we are open and ready for business." It was the same thing that the barber said every Saturday morning.

"Good morning, Mr. Biggs," said Homer, watching the barber take off his coat and hat and hang them on the same hook he always hung them on.

"Now he will put on his eyeshade," thought Homer, "and his white jacket with the two buttons missing. Next he will take his razor from the little white cabinet marked sterilizer and began to strop it."

While the barber was stropping his razor the door opened and Homer knew exactly who it would be. He said, "Hello, Sheriff!" without even having to look.

"Good morning, everybody," the sheriff greeted and sat down in the barber chair to be shaved.

Just as the barber finished shaving the sheriff and Homer finished shining the sheriff's shoes, Uncle Ulysses arrived right on schedule and just as usual.

"Anything new?" asked Uncle Ulysses.

Homer shook his head, and the barber said, "Nope."

"Things are mighty slow," said the sheriff with a yawn.

"No new magazines?" asked Uncle Ulysses hopefully, looking through the same old stack. Then he glanced up and said, "Uhowh!" and the sheriff, the barber, Homer, and Uncle Ulysses moved over to the window to look.

Dulcy Dooner and Lawyer Stobbs were hurrying across the square just as fast as they could go.

"Something's up!" said the barber.

"Where are they going?" mused Uncle Ulysses.

"Looks like they're beaded for the hank—I mean head-ed for the bank!" said the sheriff.

"The bank doesn't open until nine-thirty," said Homer.

Clear across the square they heard Dulcy bang on the door of the bank and shout, "Open up! Open the door, I say!" And they saw the door of the bank open two min-utes before nine-thirty and Dulcy and Lawyer Stobbs go inside.

"First time the bank ever let anybody in before nine-thirty for as long as I can remember," said Uncle Ulysses.

"Dulcy is sure excited about something," said the sher-iff. "Usually he isn't even up this time of day."

"Say, Homer," said the barber, looking in the cash drawer, "I seem to be running out of change. You take these two dollars and run over to the bank and get me some nickels."

"All right, Mr. Biggs," Homer agreed, and the sheriff and the barber and Uncle Ulysses stood by the open door while he ran across the square and into the bank.

"Sh-h, listen!" said Uncle Ulysses. "I can hear Dulcy shoutin'."

"He just yelled 'ninety grand,'" whispered the barber.

"No, he didn't," Uncle Ulysses disagreed. "He said 'I demand.'"

"Here comes Homer," said the sheriff. "We'll soon know what the fuss is all about. What's goin' on, son?" he asked.

"Has Dulcy got ninety grand?" asked the barber, reaching for his two dollars' worth of nickels.

"What's he demanding?" asked Uncle Ulysses.

"Dulcy is demanding and *maybe* he's got ninety grand. That's what he's demanding to find out," said Homer. "Dulcy's uncle Durpee Dooner died of fever over in Africa and left everything to Dulcy."

"That's nothing to be so mad about," said Uncle Ulysses.

"Naw," the barber agreed, "Dulcy will be a rich man."

"Havin' money should make him easier to get along with," said the sheriff.

"Well, Dulcy hasn't got any money, not yet anyway," said Homer. "All he's got so far is that old greenhouse and ten acres of land where Durpee Dooner used to run his seed business before he got to be so famous."

"Why, Durpee Dooner must have made lots of money," said the barber.

"Sure!" agreed the sheriff. "Bein' such a samous fientist —I mean famous scientist—and goin' on expeditions all over the world!"

"Well, Dulcy and Lawyer Stobbs can't find any money. They have looked everywhere and gone through all of the papers. There were no bank books, or stocks, or bonds, or anything. All they found was a key to a safe deposit box, and that must be where all the money is. Dulcy is so mad because they are making him sign a lot of papers before they let him go in the vault and unlock the box."

"It sounds like things have calmed down over there," said Uncle Ulysses, cocking an ear. "I think I'll just walk across and cash a small check."

"I been needin' a new blotter, so I'll just come along," said the sheriff.

The barber went along to get some more change, and Homer ran along behind to take the sheriff his coat. No telling, the sheriff might need his badge.

As they went into the bank the banker was just opening the heavy door of the vault.

"Just step inside, Mr. Dooner," he said. "Here is the deposit box, number one hundred and thirteen."

"It's about time," growled Dulcy, jabbing his key into the lock.

The sheriff, the barber, Uncle Ulysses, and Homer all

crowded up to the counter and peered through the bars to watch.

Dulcy turned the key and pulled out the box. His hands shook so much with excitement that he had trouble opening the lid. He managed to get it open and then let out a wild howl!

"What kinda joke is this?" he yelled, and he jumped around something awful, banging the vault, bumping the banker, and bumping the lawyer.

"Take care, Mr. Dooner! You'll break it!" shouted the banker, grabbing Dulcy by the arm before he could throw the something that was in the box.

"Calm down, Dulcy," the lawyer demanded. "Let's be sensible and take it out in the light and examine it."

"Of all the lousy tricks!" growled Dulcy, holding a small glass jar up to the light.

"What's in it?" Uncle Ulysses demanded through the paying teller window.

"Aw, nuts!" said Dulcy, giving the jar a shake.

"Did you say nuts?" asked the sheriff.

"No!" yelled Dulcy. "It's a lousy jar of *seeds!*"

"A most unusual place for keeping seeds," said the banker.

"Maybe they are unusual seeds," Homer suggested.

"Yes, Dulcy, they are no doubt very valuable seeds," said the lawyer. "That little glass jar might be worth a fortune. Why else would Durpee Dooner keep it locked up in the bank? Look here, there's a label that says *Experiment 13.*"

The thought of owning a jar of valuable seeds made Dulcy less mad, but he was far from happy. He shook his head sadly and said, "People inherit money every day, and I have to be the one that inherits a jar of seeds—an experiment at that!"

"What are you going to do with your seeds, Dulcy?" asked Homer.

"Well," said Dulcy, rubbing his chin and frowning at the jar, "I'll plant some of them, I guess." He crammed the jar of seeds into his pocket and started for the door.

"Just a minute, Dulcy," the lawyer cautioned. "Better keep them locked up here in the bank and take out some of them when you are ready to plant."

"Yes, by all means, Mr. Dooner," advised the banker. "The seeds are apparently very valuable, and you must protect them."

Dulcy thought for a minute and then did as the lawyer and the banker suggested. He locked the jar of seeds up in the deposit box and went off to his greenhouse to prepare a place to plant.

"Too bad Dulcy didn't find a nice stack of government savings bonds in the deposit box," said Uncle Ulysses when they had arrived back at the barbershop.

"Yup!" said the sheriff. "With savings bonds you know just what's what."

"Dulcy's Uncle Durpee was a great scientist," reminded the barber, "and that jar of seeds might be worth millions."

"Durpee was a great hand at breeding new plants and improving old ones," said Uncle Ulysses. "He was an up-and-coming fellow for his generation—far ahead of his time."

"Remember the giant squash he developed?" asked the barber.

"Yup," said the sheriff, "and remember the Durpee Tremadous Tomentoes—I mean Tremendous Tomatoes?"

"The Strawberry Tree was the best thing, I always thought," said Homer.

"But the Durpee Dooner Honey Onion was the most remarkable plant he ever bred," Uncle Ulysses asserted. "Looked just like any old onion but tasted just like honey. A Honey Onion pie with meringue on top is one of the world's best foods. Durpee Dooner was a genius, no doubt about it!"

"Well, what do you think Dulcy's seeds will grow into?" asked the barber.

"They were little bitsy things like grass seed," said Homer.

"Something rare that old Durpee brought back from one of his expeditions to Asia or Africa, no doubt," said Uncle Ulysses.

"No," said Homer, "the jar was labeled *Experiment 13*, so the seeds must be for some sort of plants that he developed himself."

."*Farmer's Almanac* says a mild spring," said the sheriff.

"Time to start planting next month," said the barber.

"It'll still be a long time though before we find out what Dulcy's seeds grow into," said the sheriff.

"Dulcy's got a greenhouse," reminded Uncle Ulysses.

"Golly," said Homer, "Dulcy can plant *today!*"

And Dulcy did plant that same day. By eleven o'clock he was back downtown with a truck, buying fertilizer and vitamin plant food. And he was back at the bank again before noon to get some seeds. He carefully counted out twelve seeds, and one more for good measure, into an envelope. Once more he locked up the glass jar in his safe deposit box and rushed off in the direction of his greenhouse.

By four o'clock, when Homer stopped by the greenhouse, there was Dulcy inside admiring the thirteen damp mounds of earth where he had planted his seeds.

"Hello, Mr. Dooner," said Homer.

"Hello, Homer," said Dulcy. "I'm pretty tired, and my back is sore from haulin' fertilizer and from spadin'."

"You need some help," Homer suggested. "School is out next month, and Freddy and I could help out doing hoeing and spraying—that is, if the seeds grow into anything."

"You're hired, Homer, and Freddy too!" said Dulcy. "They'll grow all right," he added confidently. "I put two bushels of vitamin plant food around each seed."

"Whe-e-ew!" whistled Homer. "What kind of plants do you think they will be, Dulcy?"

"I dunno," said Dulcy. "But whatever they are, they'll be the biggest and the best."

Sunday afternoon Homer called Freddy on the phone and said, "Hi, Freddy. Have you heard about Dulcy's seeds?"

"Gosh, yes, Homer! Everybody in Centerburg's heard about Dulcy's seeds," said Freddy. "Everybody's talking about them. The minister even preached about them this morning. *If that's what you sow, that's what you reap.*"

"Dulcy's already planted thirteen of them," said Homer.

"Yeah, I know," Freddy said. "And the jar said *Experiment 13.* My grandmother says no good can come of that."

"That's just superstition," said Homer. "You're not superstitious, are you, Freddy? Because Dulcy's going to give us a job watering, weeding and taking care of the plants when school's out."

"Oh, gosh, Homer, that'll be swell. Mebbe they will be Strawberry Trees!"

"Nobody knows," said Homer. "But working for Dulcy we'll find out as soon as anybody. We'll stop at Dulcy's tomorrow after school and see what's happening."

"Okay, Homer," said Freddy. "Good-by."

"Good-by, Freddy," said Homer. "See you tomorrow."

Homer and Freddy stopped at the greenhouse the next day after school; they stopped every day all week, and nothing exciting was going on. The seeds had not come up. Dulcy was getting more and more restless and complaining about his back. Along about Friday he started complaining about a stiff neck from watching so steadily for the seeds to come up.

On Saturday morning Homer was late getting to the barbershop. He rushed in and shouted, "They're up!"

"What's up, son?" asked the sheriff.

"Dulcy's plants! Dulcy's plants are up, all thirteen of them!" Homer said.

"Let's go look!" said Uncle Ulysses, throwing down his magazine.

And the barber and Homer and Uncle Ulysses went over to the greenhouse with the sheriff in his car.

"Look!" said Dulcy, proudly displaying the thirteen tender green shoots.

"Healthy-looking plants," said the barber.

"You can almost see them grow!" said Uncle Ulysses.

"You *can* see them grow, if you look closely," said Dulcy, and he started scooping vitamin plant food out of a bag and sprinkling it generously around the plants.

Even with a truckload of vitamin plant food to help out, the plants took weeks to get as high as Homer's head. The tallest one of the thirteen plants came just to the bottom of his ear on the day school was out and Homer and Freddy started working at the greenhouse.

They sprinkled the plants with vitamin plant food and they sprinkled them with water. They carried bags of fertilizer and they listened to Dulcy complain about his back.

"Gosh, Homer, it seems like it takes forever for a plant to grow anything but stems and leaves," Freddy complained. "Why can't these things make a few berries or squashes or something, so we'll know what they are?"

"They have got a lot of stems and leaves," Homer agreed. "Sometimes when I look at them I think they'll be bushes, and other times they remind me of vines."

"They're growing faster now that the weather is warmer," said Freddy. "Look, Homer, this one has grown almost a foot today!"

Sure enough, when Homer stood next to the plant the

top reached way above his ear; it was way above his *head.*

The next morning when Homer and Freddy arrived at Dulcy's the tops of the plants were right up touching the glass roof of the greenhouse.

"We have to break out some sections of the roof and give them room to grow," shouted Dulcy.

"Gosh, Dulcy, they're going to be trees!" Freddy exclaimed.

"They're really a-growin' now, son!" said Dulcy with a happy chuckle. "You boys grab a couple of hammers and start knockin' some openings in the roof. You want to be careful," he cautioned, "when you break the glass, that it doesn't hurt the plants."

While Dulcy went off downtown to get another truckload of vitamin plant food, Homer and Freddy climbed around on the roof knocking out openings for the plants to grow through.

Freddy swung his hammer, and a pane of glass went out with a loud crash! and a few small pieces slid tinkle-tinkle down the slant of the roof.

"This is the most fun we've had on this job yet, Freddy," shouted Homer with a laugh.

"Yeah, Homer, but there will be a lot of"—*crash*-tinkle-tinkle—"pieces to pick up," said Freddy as he swung his hammer down.

"That's the sort of job that hurts Dulcy's back," said Homer, stopping to rest. "Holy smoke, Freddy! Look at 'em grow!"

"Wow!" said Freddy, and he dropped his hammer.

The plants were pushing right up through the holes in the glass. It seemed as though they were glad to be out in the warm summer sunshine. Homer peered through the glass and saw a large stalk pushing against the roof. He bashed out a hole and the plant popped through, spread its leaves, and seemed so grateful that

Homer politely said, "You're welcome," without thinking.

By the time Dulcy returned with the vitamin plant food every single stalk was through the roof, pushing its way into the sunshine, the new green leaves rustling in the summer breeze. Dulcy went right to work, spreading vitamin plant food around the bases of the stalks, while Homer and Freddy picked up the glass.

As stories of how Dulcy's plants were growing spread through Centerburg, people began to come out to have a look. Dulcy charged fifty cents admission to the greenhouse and made fifty-nine dollars the first afternoon. By the end of the week, however, business was bad. Not that the plants stopped growing, or that people stopped coming out to look. The plants grew faster than ever— that was the trouble. There was three times as much plant *outside* as there was *inside* the greenhouse. Large crowds gathered on the road every day to watch them grow. Dulcy reduced the price of admission to ten cents but still not many came inside. He was pretty mad about it, but there was not a thing he could do.

"After all, you can't keep people from lookin' at a forest in the middle of a ten-acre lot," said Uncle Ulysses, and that's just about what Dulcy's plants looked like.

One day the rumor went around that there were melons eight feet across inside the greenhouse. Business improved, but not for long, because there were no melons, not even little ones. There were no berries or fruit of any kind, no vegetables, not even a suggestion of a blossom.

"They ain't very pretty plants," said the sheriff, who was on hand every day to handle the traffic problem.

"They're pretty enough," said Dulcy, taking offense, "and bigger than anything you will ever grow!"

"The plants have a familiar shape," said Homer, "and it seems as though I ought to recognize the leaves."

"Maybe they're potatoes, and under the ground," Freddy suggested.

"If they're potatoes, Dulcy," said the sheriff with a chuckle, "you'll have to find a sheam stovel—I mean steam shovel—to dig 'em out."

"Just you wait and see!" Dulcy shouted. "These plants will grow the biggest—the biggest—well, the biggest *somethings* ever grown," and he stamped into his greenhouse to spread on more vitamin plant food.

Two whole weeks went by and Dulcy's plants were producing nothing more remarkable than leaves and stems, but leaves and stems they produced like mad. The plants had become the most important feature of the Centerburg skyline, towering way above the Centerburg courthouse and the smokestack of the Enders Products Company.

"I don't think they're going to bear anything," the barber said one day at lunch in Uncle Ulysses' lunchroom. "They're using up all their strength putting out shoots and leaves. Dulcy should have pruned them down."

"It'll be a big disappointment to Dulcy," said Uncle Ulysses. "He's worked harder on those plants of his than he has since he put up the street signs out at Enders Heights."

"He can try again next year and keep 'em pruned," said the sheriff, brushing a doughnut crumb from his mustache. "He's got plenty more seeds locked up in the bank."

The door opened and, in no special hurry, Homer walked in and sat down at the counter.

"Hello, Homer," said Uncle Ulysses. "Have a doughnut, fresh from the machine."

"No, thank you, Uncle Ulysses," Homer replied, and he sat quietly at the counter, watching the automatic doughnut machine make doughnuts.

"You not feeling well?" Uncle Ulysses inquired.

"I'm feeling all right," Homer replied. Then he announced, "I know what Dulcy's plants are."

"You do?" asked Uncle Ulysses, and everyone rushed to the lunchroom window and looked across the square to where Dulcy's plants rose high above the trees and buildings on the far side.

"You can just make them out from here," said Homer. "There are thousands and thousands of buds on top."

"They look familiar," said the barber.

"That's what I've thought for weeks," said Homer. "It's the size that fools you. Hold your hand so as to cover the trees and buildings and pretend for a minute that the plants are ordinary size."

Everybody did as Homer suggested; then one of the customers began to giggle, then another, and finally all the people in the lunchroom began to laugh.

"Poor Dulcy!" laughed the barber, holding his sides.

"He'll never get over this," chuckled Uncle Ulysses. "The town will never stop teasing him. Dulcy's plants are just giant-size *weeds!*"

"Yes, but what kind of weeds?" Homer asked without laughing.

Everybody looked again. This time nobody laughed.

"Jiminy Zeus!" cried Uncle Ulysses.

The barber gulped and said, "I'll have to leave town!"
"So will I!" said another customer.
"Me too, I'm leaving today!" said another.
"Dad gum!" the sheriff said. "Now who'd ever thought them plants was *wagreed!*"
"They're ragweed, all right," said Homer, "and I expect they'll blossom in a few days."
"We'd better get the mayor and go see Dulcy," Uncle Ulysses suggested, and the sober little group from the lunchroom started for the town hall. The dentist and several patients came out to see what was going on, and they joined the group. So did the plumber, the jeweler, the printer, and the druggist.
"I have a feeling," said the barber, taking leave of the gathering crowd, "that Dulcy will be in one of his arguing moods. I'm going right home and pack my bag. Just the thought of those things makes me sne-sn-s-*hahuruschooh!*—sneeze."
"An awful lot of folk are troubled with hay fever," said the druggist. "Reminds me I had better order a carload of paper handkerchiefs."
"When all those thousands of buds open up and start filling the air with pollen, this place is going to look like the dust bowl," said the dentist.
Uncle Ulysses and the sheriff went on into the mayor's office, while the others waited outside.
Almost at once the mayor came rushing out of the town hall. He shaded his eyes with his hand, looked solemnly up and across the square at Dulcy's thirteen colossal ragweeds silhouetted against the afternoon sky.
Everybody knew that the mayor was susceptible to hay fever, so they were not surprised when he pulled out his handkerchief, just from force of habit. For a minute it looked as if the mayor might start running; but he tucked away his handkerchief, squared his shoulders, and started walking grimly toward Dulcy's.

The crowd followed along behind him.

Dulcy came running out to meet them. "They're budding!" he shouted. "They got thousands and thousands of buds! Howdy, Mayor," he greeted. "I was just about to come see you. I wanted to ask you, would you please send the Fire Department out here so's I can cut off a few sprigs of buds to exhibit? My ladder is too small to reach the lowest branches."

The mayor was slightly taken aback by Dulcy's request and couldn't think of what to say or how to begin.

"I could cut off a few sprigs for you, Mayor," said Dulcy generously, to help the mayor decide. "They'll look mighty nice in a vase in your office when the blossoms come out."

"Dulcy, I—I—" the mayor began and could not continue.

Dulcy Dooner looked around at the solemn faces of the crowd. "What's the matter? This is a big thing for Centerburg! Don't you frown at me, Sheriff, I'm bein' a good citizen. My plants will put this town on the map. I'm doin' a lot for this town, so how about loanin' me the town hook and ladder?"

"Dulcy, I—ah—we—" began the mayor unhappily. "As mayor of Centerburg, I am sorry to inform you that your plants are *ragweeds.*"

Dulcy swallowed hard and craned his neck to look up at his tremendous weeds. In the unhappy silence the gay singing of the birds seemed out of place, and the slight rustle of the giant ragweed leaves suddenly sounded ominous in the summer afternoon.

"Ragweeds? Why, durned if they ain't!" said Dulcy. He seemed disappointed that there would be no fruit or berries to sell, but then he smiled and said, "Well, anyway, I got the biggest dang ragweeds in the world! That'll make Centerburg famous! So look, Mayor, how about the ladder?" he asked.

"See here, Dulcy," said the mayor, "ragweed pollen gives people hay fever!"

Dulcy looked around at the worried faces. "Shucks! Don't you trouble yourselves about me. I'll be all right. I never get hay fever."

"In the interest of public health and pursuit of happiness, for the best interest of the town of Centerburg, I ask you as a good citizen to cut down your ragweeds," said the mayor.

"Cut 'em down?" cried Dulcy. "Cut my ragweeds?" he asked as though he could not believe his ears. "No!" he shouted. "No, I won't cut 'em down." And the citizens watched Dulcy turn on his heel, stamp into his greenhouse, and slam the door.

"Didn't argue much," said the sheriff tartly.

The mayor glanced uneasily up at the thousands of giant ragweed buds swaying innocently in the breeze.

"Sword of Damocles!" Uncle Ulysses exclaimed softly. "In a matter of hours the buds will open, the pollen will —I hate to think of it!"

"Time is important," said the mayor. "We must hold a special town meeting this very evening and decide what to do. Everyone come to the town hall at seven-thirty. Until then, I'll be at my desk, and I will welcome any and all suggestions," he added humbly, "of how to deal with this, the greatest and gravest threat our town has ever known."

"Homer," Freddy said on the way back to town, "my grandmother was right—*Experiment 13*, thirteen plants."

"Superstitious!" Homer replied. "Let's go along with Uncle Ulysses and see what's going to happen."

Uncle Ulysses, the sheriff, the dentist, the printer, Homer, and Freddy found the barber, suitcase in hand, tucking the key to his shop into the crack of the barberpole. They persuaded him to wait over and attend the town meeting that evening, so he opened his shop and invited them all in.

"If ordinary ragweed gives some people hay fever," the

printer reasoned, "then these things will be enough to affect everybody!"

"This town will sneeze itself plumb out of the state of Ohio!" the sheriff declared.

"They're growing just west of town too," the dentist said. "The prevailing winds blow all the pollen smack down our throats."

"Ulysses, you're a man of ideas," said the barber. "What are we going to do?"

Uncle Ulysses was thinking hard. He paced the floor and said, "We could air-condition the town, but it would cost a lot. Not enough time either. Then again, we might drop dry ice in the clouds from an airplane and make it rain. That would keep down the pollen."

"What clouds?" the barber asked gloomily, looking out at the clear blue sky.

"Dulcy might change his mind," said the printer.

"Not Dulcy," said the sheriff. "We might as well decide to take what's comin' and all go to bed with a big supply of haper pandkerchiefs—I mean perper kerpanchiefs—chaper handkepips—dad gum! You know what I mean—tensing clissues!"

Nobody knew what to do. There was a long line of people waiting to buy tickets at the railroad station. Just like the barber, other businessmen, the plumber, the hardware dealer, the jeweler, even Lawyer Stobbs, were closing their shops and offices and hanging out cards saying:

OUT OF TOWN
REOPENING
SHORTLY AFTER
THE FIRST FROST

But everybody stayed in town to attend the town meeting as a last hope.

Toward seven o'clock Centerburg was a town of

gloom. As the sun dropped lower in the sky, groups of residents gathered in the square, and as the sun dropped lower the shadows lengthened. The longest shadow by far was the shadow of Dulcy's thirteen giant ragweeds; and the people watched them extend across and darken the square and ease slowly up and darken Uncle Ulysses' lunchroom, up and darken the movie theater, and last of all the steeple of the Methodist church.

From one corner of the square there came angry shouts, "Let's chop 'em down! Burn 'em! Spray 'em with weed killer! Spray Dulcy too!"

But the sheriff was right on the job. "Hold on, boys!" he shouted. "You can't destroy private property in this town. Let's get on into the meeting and solve this thing regular!" And he headed the disturbers into the town hall along with everybody else.

Everybody was there, yes, everybody. Dulcy came too. He walked into the hall at the very last minute, and all eyes were turned to the rear where Dulcy stood with the people who could not find seats.

Seeing that his fellow citizens expected him to say something, Dulcy cleared his throat and said, "I been thinkin'. We could solve this problem the democratic way just as easy as that!" He snapped his fingers, and a murmur of hope sounded through the hall.

"Yeah," said Dulcy, gathering courage, "Centerburg doesn't need no crop o' ragweed!"

At this the murmur grew louder, and someone shouted, "Good boy, Dulcy!"

"This town doesn't need ragweeds," he repeated. Then he took a deep breath and said, "When the government decides the country doesn't need cotton, the government pays the farmer to plow it under. When the government decides there's too many potatoes, the government pays to have 'em destroyed. Now, I reckon, since Centerburg doesn't need no ragweeds—well, I reckon the town ought to pay me so's they can get rid of 'em. I figger a thousand dollars and expenses, paid in cash, ought to be a fair price."

Another murmur went through the hall. The printer rose from his seat and addressed the mayor. "Mr. Mayor, a thousand dollars seems a big price for a crop of rag- weed."

"These are big ragweeds, Your Honor," said Dulcy modestly.

"This sum should be paid by the national government and not by the town of Centerburg," said Lawyer Stobbs.

At this the county agent jumped to his feet and cried, "I make a motion that the town pay Dulcy. By the time that we filled out all the papers and sent them to Wash- ington, it would be too late."

"I second that motion!" the barber spoke up.

Over the whispering of the audience the mayor called for silence and said, "A motion has been made and sec- onded that the town pay Dulcy Dooner one thousand dollars and expenses in cash for his ragweed plants. Be- cause time is short and at any hour the plants may break into bloom, we will have an oral vote. All those in favor say 'aye.'"

"Aye!" said everyone.

"Anyone against?" asked the mayor. No one spoke.

"Majority rule," said Dulcy. "It's nice we could solve this problem so democratic like."

Then he made his way to the front of the hall and handed the mayor a paper listing his expenses:

70 bags of vitamin plant food @ $4.00 a bag $280.00
2 assistants @ $13.00 each   26.00
Rubbing alcohol for lame back   7.13
                                              _____
        Total expenses $313.13

The mayor read this aloud and then said, "Added on to the thousand dollars, the total amount due to Mr.

Dooner is thirteen hundred and thirteen dollars and thirteen cents."

"Homer," whispered Freddy, "there're those numbers again. That means more trouble—"

"Sh-h, Freddy," said Homer. "Look, the town treasurer and the banker are leaving to get the cash for Dulcy."

When the treasurer returned from the bank he carefully counted out thirteen hundred and thirteen dollars in bills into Dulcy's eager hand, and then just as carefully he counted out the dime and one, two, three pennies.

Dulcy stuffed the money into his pockets, and the mayor announced that after the meeting the Fire Department, and any men who might care to volunteer, would cut down the giant ragweeds and attend to the burning of the trunks and stems and blossoms.

The people applauded and cheered with relief, now that the threat had been dealt with. Life in Centerburg would not come to a sneezing halt, and business could be resumed as usual.

The mayor held up his hand for silence. "Now that we are all assembled, is there anything else that should be brought before the meeting?" he asked.

"Yes," said the town treasurer. "This business has left the town finances pretty low. We ought to discuss how to raise thirteen hundred and thirteen dollars and thirteen cents to make the budget come out right."

"We could have some new taxes!" Dulcy suggested happily. "An extra penny on ice-cream cones, a tax on movies, a penny tax here and there, and nobody'd hardly notice it."

"That's impractical," said the banker. "Think of the bookkeeping trying to keep track of a penny here and there. Borrow the money from the bank and take ten years to pay it back in easy installments."

"Oh, don't do that!" Dulcy cautioned. "The town can't be payin' for *this* year's ragweed *next* year. Ya see, I got lots more seed locked up in the bank, and next year I'm countin' on a bumper crop o' giant ragweed, maybe a hundred times as much!"

"Homer," whispered Freddy, "how much is a hundred times thirteen hundred and thirteen dollars and thirteen cents?" And the whisper sounded loud over the troubled silence.

"Seems as if our troubles are never over," the mayor said sadly.

Dulcy Dooner seemed to be the only happy person in the whole population of Centerburg. "Say!" he suggested brightly. "How about a tax on doughnuts, say, twenty-five cents a dozen?"

"No!" shouted Uncle Ulysses. "You can't get away with that, Dulcy Dooner! It's preposterous to think that the doughnut eaters of Centerburg are going to pay for your ragweed growing!"

"No need to get mad, Ulysses," said Dulcy. "Let's do this thing democratic."

Uncle Ulysses called out, "Mr. Mayor, I move that we put a tax of twenty-five cents on a dozen ragweed seed!"

"I second that motion," said the printer over Dulcy's shouts of "No! No!"

When the mayor called for a vote the "ayes" won, and only one person voted "no."

"Mr. Mayor," said the banker, "I move that this tax be collected immediately, in cash!"

"I second that motion," said the dentist with a chuckle.

There was plenty of chuckling and laughing throughout the hall now and everybody gleefully voted "aye."

Everybody except Dulcy Dooner. He voted "NO—O!"

"Mr. Dooner!" chuckled the mayor, "majority rule, remember? Let's be a good citizen about this!"

"You're steppin' on the minority's toes!" Dulcy shouted, but no one seemed to take notice.

The mayor appointed Uncle Ulysses Ragweed Seed Counter and made him chairman of a committee to count the seeds and collect the tax from Dulcy.

Then at last the meeting was over. The people were in a celebrating mood, the fire bell jangled merrily, and the Fire Department took over the rush job of disposing of Dulcy's plants. Groups of singing people were soon clustered about fires of burning ragweed, and it made a pretty sight, what with spotlights of the fire truck alternating red and white flashes. There was the sound of axes and saws, and then the excited cry of "Timbe-e-er!" followed by the earth trembling *crash* as a stalk of giant ragweed hit the ground.

"There goes the thirteenth ragweed plant," said Freddy with relief.

"You still worried about numbers, Freddy?" Homer asked. Then he said, "Let's go back to the bank and see how Uncle Ulysses is getting on counting ragweed seeds."

Homer and Freddy peeked through the window of the bank; it was closed up tight, and Uncle Ulysses and his committee were not inside counting seeds. Then they looked in the barbershop; the mayor, the sheriff, the barber, and Lawyer Stobbs were playing rummy, but Uncle Ulysses and his committee were not there. They finally found the seed counters in the lunchroom. Uncle Ulysses was hunched over, squinting through a magnifying glass, counting the tiny giant ragweed seeds. Every time Uncle Ulysses counted twelve, the jeweler put down a mark, and the banker, who excelled at arithmetic, was multiplying the number of marks by twenty-five cents to find out how much the tax of twenty-five cents a dozen on ragweed seeds was mounting up to.

And Dulcy—Dulcy was there, watching like a hawk to see that nobody made mistakes in his counting or marking or multiplying. All four were so intent upon their job that they did not notice when Homer and Freddy arrived.

"Three thousand nine hundred and ninety-nine," said the jeweler.

"One, two, three, four, five, six, seven, eight, nine, ten, eleven, twelve," counted Uncle Ulysses.

"Four thousand dozen," said the jeweler.

"Four thousand dozen times twenty-five cents is one thousand dollars' tax," said the banker, "and we still have several thousand dozen seeds inside the jar to count!"

"Looks like the town is going to make money on this tax," said the jeweler.

"No, it ain't!" cried Dulcy. "Not from me it ain't!" He counted out a thousand dollars and slammed the money down on the table. "There's your durned thousand, and I'm keeping my expenses!" Then he headed for the door.

"Just a minute, Dulcy!" called Uncle Ulysses. "There are a lot more o' yer seeds to count and tax."

"My seeds, my eye!" shouted Dulcy. "You can shove 'em all in your shoe! I never want to look at another seed!" And he slammed the door of the lunchroom on his way out.

"What are you going to do with the seeds, Uncle Ulysses?" asked Homer.

"Oh, hello, boys," Uncle Ulysses said. "You're just the fellows we need here. Homer, Freddy, you finish countin' these things. It's pretty fine work and takes a young, sharp eye. We old fellows are pretty tired, and besides, we better go across to the barbershop and report to the mayor."

Homer and Freddy started counting and the committee went off to make its report.

"Gosh, Homer," Freddy complained, "there's still thousands of seeds here to count and it will take all night! I don't see why they have to be counted anyway. Dulcy isn't going to pay any more tax on them."

"It's important to count them, though," said Homer. "You know something, Freddy, counting and keeping track of every single one of these seeds is just about the most important job in Centerburg."

"More important than being mayor?" asked Freddy.

"Sure," said Homer, "because if one single seed got lost, it might grow into a giant-size ragweed."

"Just one giant-size ragweed might not make every-body sneeze so bad, Homer," said Freddy.

"Yes, it would too," Homer said. "If the pollen from one giant ragweed mixed itself with all the common wild ragweed hereabouts, then the next year there would be hybrid ragweed every place."

"Gosh, Homer, just like hybrid corn. The hybrid rag-weeds would be bigger than ever!" said Freddy.

Homer nodded his head gravely. "Just supposing somebody subversive, like an enemy, was to capture these seeds, Freddy, and plant them some night right next to the White House and the Capitol!"

"And the President and the senators and representa-tives all started sneezing with hay fever!" Freddy said.

"Yup," said Homer. "The President couldn't hold press conferences and the senators couldn't make speeches, and I just guess the government would come to a stop. Everything would get tangled up and disrupt the coun-try. You see, counting these seeds is super important!" And he picked up the magnifying glass and started to count giant ragweed seeds.

Over across the town square in the barbershop, Uncle Ulysses and the committee had joined the game of rum-my, after they had reported to the mayor.

"It's your turn to draw a card, Ulysses," said the sheriff.

"Queen of seeds," said Uncle Ulysses, turning over a card. "Zeus!" he said. "I keep seein' those things in front o' my eyes. Reminds me, I better call up the lunchroom and see how Homer and Freddy are gettin' along." He picked up the phone and gave the number. "Hello, Ho-mer? How're you makin' out? Still have a lot to count, eh?" Uncle Ulysses listened for a minute and then he said, "We thought we'd just lock 'em up in the bank again. Nobody would ever think of plantin' a crop of ragweeds—except Dulcy, that is. If they knew what they was plantin', they wouldn't." Uncle Ulysses listened again and stopped smiling; then he looked worried. "Homer," he said, trying to control his voice, "you just keep right on countin' and be extra careful not to lose a single seed. Don't you worry, son, we'll talk it over and think of a way to get rid of 'em somehow." Uncle Ulysses hung up the receiver and went back to the rummy game with terror in his eyes and fear in his heart.

"Men," said Uncle Ulysses gravely, "we've got to think hard or this country will be one big sneeze clear from the Atlantic to the Pacific coast! Why, one single enemy plane could sow those seeds from New York to San Francisco in a couple of hours!"

"What are you raving about, Ulysses?" asked the barber.

"It's the strain of counting all those little seeds that's got him upset, I guess," said the banker.

"I'm not ravin'!" said Uncle Ulysses, glaring wildly at the rummy players. "You men put down your cards and listen to me. We have to think and think fast of a way to get rid of those seeds. If the wrong kind of people were to get hold of 'em, it would mean the ruin of this country!"

"Shucks, Ulysses, we're going to lock 'em up again in the safe deposit vault, so stop worrying and let's get on with the game!" said the printer.

"Stop being so—so—so complacent," Uncle Ulysses sputtered. "Banks get robbed almost every day and you know it." Then he looked over his shoulder and leaned way over close and whispered hoarsely, "And the kind of people I mean wouldn't stop at nothing."

"I'll lock them ragweed seeds in the jail," said the sheriff triumphantly. "That'll stop 'em!"

"Rubbish," said Uncle Ulysses. "As many as twenty people have broken out of your jail, Sheriff, and it's a durned sight easier to break in. Besides, the jail has got mice. Suppose some mouse was to take some of those seeds home to a hole in the ground to feed his family? Then where'd we be? Right back where we were with Dulcy, only this time we might not act in time." Uncle Ulysses was excited now and he shouted, "Bees and bugs! We'll have to get rid of 'em so they won't find 'em! I tell ya, men, if the pollen from just one of these giant ragweeds gets loose and mixes with our wild ragweeds, we'll have hybrid ragweeds bigger even than the giant ragweeds."

All the men finally realized the seriousness of the situation, and they sat glancing uneasily at one another. The mayor was the first to move; he dashed over to the window and looked across the deserted square at the lunchroom.

"There's no use worrying those two boys about this," he said. "But we had better post a guard outside while they finish their counting. Sheriff," he ordered, "you take your gun and cover the front entrance. And Biggs," he said, handing the barber his keys, "you'll find a revolver in the upper right-hand drawer of my desk. You guard the back entrance. The rest of us will stay here and try to dope out a solution to this problem. In case of trouble, fire a shot into the air and we'll be right over to help out."

The sheriff and the barber went out the door, and the rest of the men drew their chairs up close together for a conference.

"Now then," said the mayor, "let's decide what to do."

Nobody said anything for some minutes. They all sat thinking. Then Uncle Ulysses said, "Well, let's decide."

"I've heard tell that birds sometimes plant seeds in out-of-the-way places," said the banker.

"Yeh, birds and mice and bugs. We have to dispose of them some way so they won't get at them," said Uncle Ulysses.

"The most important thing is to keep these ragweed

seeds from falling into the hands of enemy agents," said Lawyer Stobbs. "Sneezing could seriously impair the functioning of the executive and the judicial as well as the legislative branches of our federal government."

"What can we do with them? Where can we put them? How can we get rid of them so not one seed can fall into the hands of some enemy agent? Or mouse? Or bird? Or bug?" asked Uncle Ulysses, pacing up and down.

"The bank wouldn't be safe," said the banker.

"It wouldn't be safe to bury the seeds," said the printer.

"If we hid them inside a mattress, the mice would find them," said the mayor.

"I was thinking, if we were to hide them up at the very top of the courthouse tower it might be a good place, but the—"

"Pigeons!" everybody said at once.

"Of course," said Uncle Ulysses, "if we had the time, we could have a special burglar-bug-bird-and-mouse-proof container made to order, something like the Time Capsule that they buried at the World's Fair. That would take months, and it would be a tremendous responsibility to guard those seeds day and night until then."

"I'm for calling in the FBI right now," said the banker. "There isn't a single place under the earth, on the earth, or a steeple over the earth that's a safe place to hide those seeds."

"The ocean!" shouted Uncle Ulysses. "The Atlantic Ocean! The sheriff could take the seeds to Atlantic City and hire a boat to take him to a nice deep spot. Then he could toss the ragweed seeds overboard, and that would be that."

"That's it, Ulysses," said the mayor. "There's a train for the East that goes through here at twelve-forty tonight. We'll send the sheriff to Atlantic City to sink those seeds!"

"I've got a metal cashbox with a lock and a nice

handle," said the banker. "The sheriff could carry the seeds in that and handcuff it to his wrist, so nobody could steal it on the train."

"And I've got some heavy lead type to put in the box just to make sure it'll sink," said the printer.

"Fine," said the mayor. "You two fellows get the box and weight it with type, and Lawyer Stobbs, you relieve the sheriff at the front of the lunchroom, so he can go home and pack. Ulysses and myself will call the station and make reservations for the sheriff on the twelve-forty."

In shortly less than half an hour the box was ready and back at the barbershop; and five minutes later the sheriff came in carrying his bag, all packed and ready to go. He pulled out a pair of handcuffs, and one side he fastened to his wrist and the other he snapped through the handle of the box.

"You mustn't forget to unfasten yourself before you toss the box, Sheriff," said the printer with a smile.

"This is no time for joking," said the mayor severely. "Now, Sheriff, you realize how much depends on you. Don't speak to strangers on the train," he cautioned, "and as soon as you get to Atlantic City, hire a boat and go out and sink the seeds."

"You can depend on me, Mayor!" promised the sheriff.

"All right," said the mayor, "let's go over to the lunchroom and pick up the seeds."

The mayor led the way across the town square, followed by Uncle Ulysses, the sheriff, the banker, and the printer. Lawyer Stobbs, gun in hand, met them at the door of the lunchroom.

"Everything all right inside?" Uncle Ulysses asked in a whisper.

"Yes," whispered the lawyer, "I think they're all finished with counting. Sh-h! What's that!" he said, pointing his gun out into the shadows of the square.

After a tense moment of waiting, the postmaster's dog came up wagging his tail. Everybody relaxed and Uncle Ulysses chuckled, "That dog can smell doughnuts cookin' a mile away! Come on. Let's go inside and pack up the seeds and get something to eat. I'm hungry." He opened the door and went in, followed by all the men and the postmaster's dog.

"Hello, boys. All through counting, I see," said the mayor.

"Ah-h!" exclaimed Uncle Ulysses. "Very thoughtful of you, Homer, to make some doughnuts. The sheriff can take some with him for a snack on the train, and we're all pretty hungry right this minute." He paused to admire his automatic doughnut machine make doughnuts. And as he watched, the machine stopped.

Uncle Ulysses, who had started passing out the hot doughnuts, said, "You didn't mix up enough batter. You should have made more."

"But, Uncle Ulysses, we only meant to make a dozen," said Homer.

"Yeah," said Freddy, who had been counting the doughnuts as they came out of the machine. "We only meant to make a dozen." Then he added miserably, "But it turned out to be thirteen!"

"Well, there's enough to go around, so help yourselves, everybody," Uncle Ulysses offered.

"But Uncle Ulysses—" said Homer.

"Freddy, you go to the back door and call the barber," Uncle Ulysses said, suddenly remembering that the barber was still guarding the rear.

"Uncle Ulysses—" Homer started to say.

"Let's get the seeds in the box and locked up," said the mayor, taking a bite of doughnut, "and then I'd like a cup of coffee."

Freddy came back with the barber, and Uncle Ulysses handed him a doughnut. Then he turned to Homer. "Get the ragweed seeds, son, and put them in that box the sheriff's got danglin' from his wrist."

"But, Uncle Ulysses," said Homer, "that's what I've been trying to tell you!" Then he asked, "Have you ever heard of a berry growing into a berry bush after it had once been cooked into a pie?"

Uncle Ulysses had his mouth full of doughnut and so did all the other men, so they all shook their heads "no."

"Have you ever heard of a nut growing into a nut tree after being baked into a cookie?" Homer asked.

And again all the men nodded their heads, because they were chewing doughnuts and trying to swallow.

"Popcorn won't grow after it's been popped either," said Freddy, "because I tried it once."

Uncle Ulysses gulped and said, "Homer, you're a good boy, it's gettin' late, and you and Freddy run along home now."

After Homer and Freddy had gone the mayor fed the rest of his doughnut to the postmaster's dog. So did Uncle Ulysses and the barber and the jeweler, the printer, the banker, the sheriff, and Lawyer Stobbs. Then they fed him the rest of the doughnuts and watched silently while he ate up every last crumb. As the last crumb disappeared the sheriff said, "There goes my trip to Atlantic City."

And the barber said, "From now on, every time I look at that dog or even mail a letter, I'll probably have to sn-sn-s-s-ss*harah-choowh!*"

For more hilarious stories about Homer and his unusual friends, read Homer Price, *by the same author. It is also published by Viking.*

The Hundred Dresses

BY ELEANOR ESTES

Illustrations by Louis Slobodkin

*Everybody laughed and nobody believed
Wanda Petronski when she said she had one
hundred dresses hanging up in her closet at
home, for Wanda wore the same faded blue
dress to school every day.*

TODAY, Monday, Wanda Petronski was not in her
seat. But nobody, not even Peggy and Madeline, the
girls who started all the fun, noticed her absence.

Usually Wanda sat in the next to the last seat in the
last row in Room 13. She sat in the corner of the room
where the rough boys who did not make good marks on
their report cards sat; the corner of the room where
there was most scuffling of feet, most roars of laughter
when anything funny was said, and most mud and dirt
on the floor.

Wanda did not sit there because she was rough and
noisy. On the contrary she was very quiet and rarely said
anything at all. And nobody had ever heard her laugh
out loud. Sometimes she twisted her mouth into a
crooked sort of smile, but that was all.

Nobody knew exactly why Wanda sat in that seat unless it was because she came all the way from Boggins
Heights, and her feet were usually caked with dry mud
that she picked up coming down the country roads.
Maybe the teacher liked to keep all the children who
were apt to come in with dirty shoes in one corner of
the room. But no one really thought much about Wanda

Petronski once she was in the classroom. The time they thought about her was outside of school hours, at noon-time when they were coming back to school, or in the morning early before school began, when groups of two or three or even more would be talking and laughing on their way to the school yard.

Then sometimes they waited for Wanda—to have fun with her.

The next day, Tuesday, Wanda was not in school either. And nobody noticed her absence again, except the teacher and probably big Bill Byron, who sat in the seat behind Wanda's and who could now put his long legs around her empty desk, one on each side, and sit there like a frog, to the great entertainment of all in his corner of the room.

But on Wednesday, Peggy and Maddie, who sat in the front row along with other children who got good marks and didn't track in a whole lot of mud, did notice that Wanda wasn't there. Peggy was the most popular

girl in school. She was pretty; she had many pretty
clothes and her auburn hair was curly. Maddie was her
closest friend.

The reason Peggy and Maddie noticed Wanda's absence was because Wanda had made them late to school.
They had waited and waited for Wanda—to have some
fun with her—and she just hadn't come. They kept thinking she'd come any minute. They saw Jack Beggles running to school, his necktie askew and his cap at a pre-
carious tilt. They knew it must be late, for he always
managed to slide into his chair exactly when the bell
rang as though he were making a touchdown. Still they
waited one minute more and one minute more, hoping
she'd come. But finally they had to race off without seeing her.

The two girls reached their classroom after the doors
had been closed. The children were reciting in unison
the Gettysburg Address, for that was the way Miss
Mason always began the session. Peggy and Maddie
slipped into their seats just as the class was saying the
last lines . . . "that these dead shall not have died in
vain; that the nation shall, under God, have a new birth
of freedom, and that government of the people, by the
people, for the people, shall not perish from the earth."

After Peggy and Maddie stopped feeling like intrud-
ers in a class that had already begun, they looked across
the room and noticed that Wanda was not in her seat.
Furthermore her desk was dusty and looked as though
she hadn't been there yesterday either. Come to think
of it, they hadn't seen her yesterday. They had waited
for her a little while but had forgotten about her when
they reached school.

They often waited for Wanda Petronski—to have fun
with her.

Wanda lived way up on Boggins Heights, and Boggins Heights was no place to live. It was a good place to

go and pick wild flowers in the summer, but you always held your breath till you got safely past old man Svenson's yellow house. People in the town said old man Svenson was no good. He didn't work and, worse still, his house and yard were disgracefully dirty, with rusty tin cans strewn about and even an old straw hat. He lived alone with his dog and his cat. No wonder, said the people of the town. Who would live with him? And many stories circulated about him and the stories were the kind that made people scurry past his house even in broad daylight and hope not to meet him.

Beyond Svenson's there were a few small scattered frame houses, and in one of these Wanda Petronski lived with her father and her brother Jake.

Wanda Petronski. Most of the children in Room 13 didn't have names like that. They had names easy to say, like Thomas, Smith, or Allen. There was one boy named Bounce, Willie Bounce, and people thought that was funny but not funny in the same way that Petronski was.

Wanda didn't have any friends. She came to school alone and went home alone. She always wore a faded blue dress that didn't hang right. It was clean, but it looked as though it had never been ironed properly. She didn't have any friends, but a lot of girls talked to her. They waited for her under the maple trees on the corner of Oliver Street. Or they surrounded her in the school yard as she stood watching some little girls play hopscotch on the worn hard ground.

"Wanda," Peggy would say in a most courteous manner, as though she were talking to Miss Mason or to the principal perhaps. "Wanda," she'd say, giving one of her friends a nudge, "tell us. How many dresses did you say you had hanging up in your closet?"

"A hundred," said Wanda.

"A hundred!" exclaimed all the girls incredulously, and the little girls would stop playing hopscotch and listen.

"Yeah, a hundred, all lined up," said Wanda. Then her thin lips drew together in silence.

"What are they like? All silk, I bet," said Peggy.

"Yeah, all silk, all colors."

"Velvet too?"

"Yeah, velvet too. A hundred dresses," repeated Wanda stolidly. "All lined up in my closet."

Then they'd let her go. And then before she'd gone very far, they couldn't help bursting into shrieks and peals of laughter.

A hundred dresses! Obviously the only dress Wanda had was the blue one she wore every day. So what did she say she had a hundred for? What a story! And the girls laughed derisively, while Wanda moved over to the sunny place by the ivy-covered brick wall of the school building where she usually stood and waited for the bell to ring.

But if the girls had met her at the corner of Oliver Street, they'd carry her along with them for a way, stopping every few feet for more incredulous questions. And it wasn't always dresses they talked about. Sometimes it was hats, or coats, or even shoes.

"How many shoes did you say you had?"

"Sixty."

"Sixty! Sixty pairs or sixty shoes?"

"Sixty pairs. All lined up in my closet."

"Yesterday you said fifty."

"Now I got sixty."

Cries of exaggerated politeness greeted this.

"All alike?" said the girls.

"Oh, no. Every pair is different. All colors. All lined up." And Wanda would shift her eyes quickly from Peggy to a distant spot, as though she were looking far ahead, looking but not seeing anything.

Then the outer fringe of the crowd of girls would break away gradually, laughing, and little by little, in pairs, the group would disperse. Peggy, who had thought up this game, and Maddie, her inseparable friend, were always the last to leave. And finally Wanda would move up the street, her eyes dull and her mouth closed tight, hitching her left shoulder every now and then in the funny way she had, finishing the walk to school alone.

Peggy was not really cruel. She protected small children from bullies. And she cried for hours if she saw an animal mistreated. If anybody had said to her, "Don't you think that is a cruel way to treat Wanda?" she would have been very surprised. Cruel? What did the girl want to go and say she had a hundred dresses for? Anybody could tell that was a lie. Why did she want to lie? And she wasn't just an ordinary person, else why would she have a name like that? Anyway, they never made her cry.

As for Maddie, this business of asking Wanda every day how many dresses and how many hats and how many this and that she had was bothering her. Maddie was poor herself. She usually wore somebody's hand-me-down clothes. Thank goodness, she didn't live up on Boggins Heights or have a funny name. And her forehead didn't shine the way Wanda's round one did. What did she use on it? Sapolio? That's what all the girls wanted to know.

Sometimes when Peggy was asking Wanda those questions in that mock polite voice, Maddie felt embarrassed and studied the marbles in the palm of her hand, rolling them around and saying nothing herself. Not that she felt sorry for Wanda exactly. She would never have paid any attention to Wanda if Peggy hadn't invented the dresses game. But suppose Peggy and all the others started in on her next! She wasn't as poor as Wanda perhaps, but she was poor. Of course she would have more sense than to say a hundred dresses. Still she would not like them to begin on her. Not at all! Oh, dear! She did wish Peggy would stop teasing Wanda Petronski.

Somehow Maddie could not buckle down to work.

She sharpened her pencil, turning it around carefully in the little red sharpener, letting the shavings fall in a neat heap on a piece of scrap paper, and trying not to get any of the dust from the lead on her clean arithmetic paper.

A slight frown puckered her forehead. In the first place she didn't like being late to school. And in the second place she kept thinking about Wanda. Somehow Wanda's desk, though empty, seemed to be the only thing she saw when she looked over to that side of the room.

How had the hundred dresses game begun in the first place, she asked herself impatiently. It was hard to remember the time when they hadn't played that game with Wanda; hard to think all the way back from now, when the hundred dresses was like the daily dozen, to then, when everything seemed much nicer. Oh, yes. She remembered. It had begun that day when Cecile first wore her new red dress. Suddenly the whole scene flashed swiftly and vividly before Maddie's eyes.

It was a bright blue day in September. No, it must have been October, because when she and Peggy were coming to school, arms around each other and singing, Peggy had said, "You know what? This must be the kind of day they mean when they say, 'October's bright blue weather.'"

Maddie remembered that because afterwards it didn't seem like bright blue weather any more, although the weather had not changed in the slightest.

As they turned from shady Oliver Street into Maple, they both blinked. For now the morning sun shone straight in their eyes. Besides that, bright flashes of color came from a group of a half-dozen or more girls across the street. Their sweaters and jackets and dresses, blues and golds and reds, and one crimson one in particular, caught the sun's rays like bright pieces of glass.

A crisp, fresh wind was blowing, swishing their skirts and blowing their hair in their eyes. The girls were all exclaiming and shouting and each one was trying to talk louder than the others. Maddie and Peggy joined the group, and the laughing, and the talking.

"Hi, Peg! Hi, Maddie!" they were greeted warmly. "Look at Cecile!"

What they were all exclaiming about was the dress that Cecile had on—a crimson dress with cap and socks to match. It was a bright new dress and very pretty. Everyone was admiring it and admiring Cecile. For long, slender Cecile was a toe-dancer and wore fancier clothes than most of them. And she had her black satin bag with her precious white satin ballet slippers slung over her shoulders. Today was the day for her dancing lesson.

Maddie sat down on the granite curbstone to tie her shoelaces. She listened happily to what they were saying. They all seemed especially jolly today, probably because it was such a bright day. Everything sparkled. Way down at the end of the street the sun shimmered and

turned to silver the blue water of the bay. Maddie picked up a piece of broken mirror and flashed a small circle of light edged with rainbow colors onto the houses, the trees, and the top of the telegraph pole.

And it was then that Wanda had come along with her brother Jake.

They didn't often come to school together. Jake had to get to school very early because he helped old Mr. Heany, the school janitor, with the furnace, or raking up the dry leaves, or other odd jobs before school opened. Today he must be late.

Even Wanda looked pretty in this sunshine, and her pale blue dress looked like a piece of the sky in summer; and that old gray toboggan cap she wore—it must be something Jake had found—looked almost jaunty. Maddie watched them absent-mindedly as she flashed her piece of broken mirror here and there. And only absent-mindedly she noticed Wanda stop short when they reached the crowd of laughing and shouting girls.

"Come on," Maddie heard Jake say. "I gotta hurry. I gotta get the doors open and ring the bell."

"You go the rest of the way," said Wanda. "I want to stay here."

Jake shrugged and went on up Maple Street. Wanda slowly approached the group of girls. With each step forward, before she put her foot down she seemed to hesitate for a long, long time. She approached the group as a timid animal might, ready to run if anything alarmed it.

Even so, Wanda's mouth was twisted into the vaguest suggestion of a smile. She must feel happy too because everybody must feel happy on such a day.

As Wanda joined the outside fringe of girls, Maddie stood up too and went over close to Peggy to get a good look at Cecile's new dress herself. She forgot about Wanda, and more girls kept coming up, enlarging the group and all exclaiming about Cecile's new dress.

"Isn't it lovely!" said one.

"Yeah, I have a new blue dress, but it's not as pretty as that," said another.

"My mother just bought me a plaid, one of the Stuart plaids."

"I got a new dress for dancing school."

"I'm gonna make my mother get me one just like Cecile's."

Everyone was talking to everyone else. Nobody said anything to Wanda, but there she was, a part of the crowd. The girls closed in a tighter circle around Cecile, still talking all at once and admiring her, and Wanda was somehow enveloped in the group. Nobody talked to Wanda, but nobody even thought about her being there.

Maybe, thought Maddie, remembering what had happened next, maybe she figured all she'd have to do was say something and she'd really be one of the girls. And this would be an easy thing to do because all they were doing was talking about dresses.

Maddie was standing next to Peggy. Wanda was standing next to Peggy on the other side. All of a sudden, Wanda impulsively touched Peggy's arm and said something. Her light blue eyes were shining and she looked excited like the rest of the girls.

"What?" asked Peggy. For Wanda had spoken very softly.

Wanda hesitated a moment and then she repeated her words firmly.

"I got a hundred dresses home."

"That's what I thought you said. A hundred dresses. A hundred!" Peggy's voice raised itself higher and higher.

"Hey, kids!" she yelled. "This girl's got a hundred dresses."

Silence greeted this, and the crowd which had centered around Cecile and her new finery now centered curiously around Wanda and Peggy. The girls eyed Wanda, first incredulously, then suspiciously.

"A hundred dresses?" they said. "Nobody could have a hundred dresses."

"I have though."

"Wanda has a hundred dresses."

"Where are they then?"

"In my closet."

"Oh, you don't wear them to school."

"No. For parties."

"Oh, you mean you don't have any everyday dresses."

"Yes, I have all kinds of dresses."

"Why don't you wear them to school?"

For a moment Wanda was silent to this. Her lips drew together. Then she repeated stolidly as though it were a lesson learned in school, "A hundred of them. All lined up in my closet."

"Oh, I see," said Peggy, talking like a grown-up person. "The child has a hundred dresses, but she wouldn't wear them to school. Perhaps she's worried of getting ink or chalk on them."

With this everybody fell to laughing and talking at once. Wanda looked stolidly at them, pursing her lips together, wrinkling her forehead up so that the grey toboggan cap slipped way down to her brow. Suddenly from down the street the school gong rang its first warning.

"Oh, come on, hurry," said Maddie, relieved. "We'll be late."

"Good-by, Wanda," said Peggy. "Your hundred dresses sound bee-you-tiful."

More shouts of laughter greeted this, and off the girls ran, laughing and talking and forgetting Wanda and her hundred dresses. Forgetting until tomorrow and the next day and the next, when Peggy, seeing her coming to school, would remember and ask her about the hundred dresses. For now Peggy seemed to think a day was lost if she had not had some fun with Wanda, winning the approving laughter of the girls.

Yes, that was the way it had all begun, the game of

the hundred dresses. It all happened so suddenly and un-
expectedly, with everybody falling right in, that even
if you felt uncomfortable as Maddie had there wasn't
anything you could do about it. Maddie wagged her
head up and down. Yes, she repeated to herself, that was
the way it began, that day, that bright blue day.

And she wrapped up her shavings and went to the
front of the room to empty them in the teacher's basket.

Now today, even though she and Peggy had been late
to school, Maddie was glad she had not had to make fun

of Wanda. She worked her arithmetic problems absent-mindedly. Eight times eight . . . let's see . . . nothing she could do about making fun of Wanda. She wished she had the nerve to write Peggy a note, because she knew she'd never have the courage to speak right out to Peggy, to say, "Hey, Peg, let's stop asking Wanda how many dresses she has."

When she finished her arithmetic, she did start a note to Peggy. Suddenly she paused and shuddered. She pictured herself in the school yard, a new target for Peggy and the girls. Peggy might ask her where she got the dress she had on, and Maddie would have to say that it was one of Peggy's old ones that Maddie's mother had tried to disguise with new trimmings so that no one in Room 13 would recognize it.

If only Peggy would decide of her own accord to stop having fun with Wanda. Oh, well! Maddie ran her hand through her short blonde hair as though to push the uncomfortable thoughts away. What difference did it make? Slowly Maddie tore the note she had started into bits. She was Peggy's best friend, and Peggy was the best-liked girl in the whole room. Peggy could not possibly do anything that was really wrong, she thought.

As for Wanda, she was just some girl who lived up on Boggins Heights and stood alone in the school yard. Nobody in the room thought about Wanda at all except when it was her turn to stand up for oral reading. Then they all hoped she would hurry up and finish and sit down, because it took her forever to read a paragraph. Sometimes she stood up and just looked at her book and couldn't, or wouldn't, read at all. The teacher tried to help her, but she'd just stand there until the teacher told her to sit down. Was she dumb or what? Maybe she was just timid. The only time she talked was in the school yard about her hundred dresses. Maddie remembered her telling about one of her dresses, a pale blue one with cerise-colored trimmings. And she remembered another that was brilliant jungle green with a red sash. "You'd look like a Christmas tree in that," the girls had said in pretended admiration.

Thinking about Wanda and her hundred dresses all lined up in the closet, Maddie began to wonder who was going to win the drawing and color contest. For girls, this contest consisted of designing dresses, and for boys, of designing motor boats. Probably Peggy would win the girls' medal. Peggy drew better than anyone else in the room. At least that's what everybody thought.

You should see the way she could copy a picture in a magazine or some film star's head. You could almost tell who it was. Oh, Maddie did hope Peggy would win. Hope so? She was sure Peggy would win. Well, tomorrow the teacher was going to announce the winners. Then they'd know.

Thoughts of Wanda sank further and further from Maddie's mind, and by the time the history lesson began she had forgotten all about her.

The next day it was drizzling. Maddie and Peggy hurried to school under Peggy's umbrella. Naturally on a day like this they didn't wait for Wanda Petronski on the corner of Oliver Street, the street that far, far away, under the railroad tracks and up the hill, led to Boggins Heights. Anyway they weren't taking chances on being late today, because today was important.

"Do you think Miss Mason will surely announce the winners today?" asked Peggy.

"Oh, I hope so, the minute we get in," said Maddie, and added, "Of course you'll win, Peg."

"Hope so," said Peggy eagerly.

The minute they entered the classroom they stopped short and gasped. There were drawings all over the room, on every ledge and window sill, tacked to the tops of the blackboards, spread over the bird charts, dazzling colors and brilliant lavish designs, all drawn on great sheets of wrapping paper.

There must have been a hundred of them all lined up!

These must be the drawings for the contest. They were! Everybody stopped and whistled or murmured admiringly.

As soon as the class had assembled Miss Mason announced the winners. Jack Beggles had won for the boys, she said, and his design of an outboard motor boat

was on exhibition in Room 12, along with the sketches
by all the other boys.

"As for the girls," she said, "although just one or two
sketches were submitted by most, one girl—and Room
13 should be very proud of her—this one girl actually
drew one hundred designs—all different and all beautiful. In the opinion of the judges, any one of her drawings is worthy of winning the prize. I am happy to say
that Wanda Petronski is the winner of the girls' medal.
Unfortunately Wanda has been absent from school for
some days and is not here to receive the applause that
is due her. Let us hope she will be back tomorrow. Now,
class, you may file around the room quietly and look at
her exquisite drawings."

The children burst into applause, and even the boys
were glad to have a chance to stamp on the floor, put
their fingers in their mouths and whistle, though they
were not interested in the dresses. Maddie and Peggy
were among the first to reach the blackboard to look at
the drawings.

"Look, Peg," whispered Maddie, "there's that blue one
she told us about. Isn't it beautiful?"

"Yeah," said Peggy, "and here's that green one. Boy,
and I thought I could draw!"

While the class was circling the room, the monitor
from the principal's office brought Miss Mason a note.
Miss Mason read it several times and studied it thoughtfully for a while. Then she clapped her hands and said,
"Attention, class. Everyone back to his seat."

When the shuffling of feet had stopped and the room
was still and quiet, Miss Mason said, "I have a letter
from Wanda's father that I want to read to you."

Miss Mason stood there a moment and the silence in
the room grew tense and expectant. The teacher ad-
justed her glasses slowly and deliberately. Her manner
indicated that what was coming—this letter from Wan-

da's father—was a matter of great importance. Everybody listened closely as Miss Mason read the brief note:

"Dear teacher: My Wanda will not come to your school any more. Jake also. Now we move away to big city. No more holler Polack. No more ask why funny name. Plenty of funny names in the big city. Yours truly,

Jan Petronski."

A deep silence met the reading of this letter. Miss Mason took her glasses off, blew on them and wiped them on her soft white handkerchief. Then she put them on again and looked at the class. When she spoke her voice was very low.

"I am sure none of my boys and girls in Room 13 would purposely and deliberately hurt anyone's feelings because his name happened to be a long unfamiliar one. I prefer to think that what was said was said in thoughtlessness. I know that all of you feel the way I do, that this is a very unfortunate thing to have happen. Unfortunate and sad, both. And I want you all to think about it."

The first period was a study period. Maddie tried to prepare her lessons, but she could not put her mind on her work. She had a very sick feeling in the bottom of her stomach. True, she had not enjoyed listening to Peggy ask Wanda how many dresses she had in her closet, but she had said nothing. She had stood by silently, and that was just as bad as what Peggy had done. Worse. She was a coward. At least Peggy hadn't considered they were being mean, but she, Maddie, had thought they were doing wrong. She had thought, supposing she was the one being made fun of. She could put herself in Wanda's shoes. But she had done just as much as Peggy to make life miserable for Wanda by simply standing by and saying nothing. She had helped to make

someone so unhappy that she had had to move away
from town.

Goodness! Wasn't there anything she could do? If
only she could tell Wanda she hadn't meant to hurt her
feelings. She turned around and stole a glance at Peggy,
but Peggy did not look up. She seemed to be studying
hard.

Well, whether Peggy felt badly or not, she, Maddie,
had to do something. She had to find Wanda Petronski.
Maybe she had not yet moved away. Maybe Peggy
would climb the Heights with her and they would tell
Wanda she had won the contest. And that they thought
she was smart and the hundred dresses were beautiful.

When school was dismissed in the afternoon, Peggy
said with pretended casualness, "Hey, let's go and see
if that kid has left town or not."

So Peggy had had the same idea as Maddie had had!
Maddie glowed. Peggy was really all right, just as she
always thought. Peg was really all right. She was o.k.

The two girls hurried out of the building, up the
street toward Boggins Heights, the part of town that
wore such a forbidding air on this kind of a November
afternoon, drizzly, damp, and dismal.

"Well, at least," said Peggy gruffly, "I never did call
her a foreigner or make fun of her name. I never thought
she had the sense to know we were making fun of her
anyway. I thought she was too dumb. And gee, look how
she can draw! And I thought I could draw."

Maddie could say nothing. All she hoped was that
they would find Wanda. Just so she'd be able to tell her
they were sorry they had all picked on her. And just to
say how wonderful the whole school thought she was,
and please not to move away and everybody would be
nice. She and Peggy would fight anybody who was not
nice.

Maddie fell to imagining a story in which she and

Peggy assailed any bully who might be going to pick on Wanda. "Petronski—Onski!" somebody would yell, and she and Peggy would pounce on the guilty one. For a time Maddie consoled herself with these thoughts, but they soon vanished and again she felt unhappy and wished everything could be nice the way it was before any of them had made fun of Wanda.

Br-r-r! How drab and cold and cheerless it was up here on the Heights! In the summer time the woods, the sumac, and the ferns that grew along the brook on the side of the road were lush and made this a beautiful walk on Sunday afternoons. But now it did not seem beautiful. The brook had shrunk to the merest trickle, and today's drizzle sharpened the outlines of the rusty tin cans, old shoes, and forlorn remnants of a big black umbrella in the bed of the brook.

The two girls hurried on. They hoped to get to the top of the hill before dark. Otherwise they were not certain they could find Wanda's house. At last, puffing and panting, they rounded the top of the hill. The first house, that old rickety one, belonged to old man Svenson. Peggy and Maddie hurried past it almost on tiptoe. Somebody said once that old man Svenson had shot a man. Others said "Nonsense! He's an old good-for-nothing. Wouldn't hurt a flea."

But, false or true, the girls breathed more freely as they rounded the corner. It was too cold and drizzly for old man Svenson to be in his customary chair tilted against the house, chewing and spitting tobacco juice. Even his dog was nowhere in sight and had not barked at the girls from wherever he might be.

"I think that's where the Petronskis live," said Maddie, pointing to a little white house with lots of chicken coops at the side of it. Wisps of old grass stuck up here and there along the pathway like thin wet kittens. The house and its sparse little yard looked shabby but clean.

It reminded Maddie of Wanda's one dress, her faded blue cotton dress, shabby but clean.

There was not a sign of life about the house except for a yellow cat, half grown, crouching on the one small step close to the front door. It leapt timidly with a small cry half way up a tree when the girls came into the yard. Peggy knocked firmly on the door, but there was no answer. She and Maddie went around to the back yard and knocked there. Still there was no answer.

"Wanda!" called Peggy. They listened sharply, but only a deep silence pressed against their eardrums. There was no doubt about it. The Petronskis were gone.

"Maybe they just went away for a little while and haven't really left with their furniture yet," suggested Maddie hopefully. Maddie was beginning to wonder how she could bear the hard fact that Wanda had actually gone and that she might never be able to make amends.

"Well," said Peggy, "let's see if the door is open."

They cautiously turned the knob of the front door. It opened easily, for it was a light thing and looked as though it furnished but frail protection against the cold winds that blew up here in the winter time. The little square room that the door opened into was empty. There was absolutely nothing left in it, and in the corner a closet with its door wide open was empty too. Maddie wondered what it had held before the Petronskis moved out. And she thought of Wanda saying, "Sure, a hundred dresses . . . all lined up in the closet."

Well, anyway, real and imaginary dresses alike were gone. The Petronskis were gone. And now how could she and Peggy tell Wanda anything? Maybe the teacher knew where she had moved to. Maybe old man Svenson knew. They might knock on his door and ask on the way down. Or the post office might know. If they wrote a letter, Wanda might get it because the post office might forward it. Feeling very downcast and discouraged, the girls closed the door and started for home. Coming down the road, way, way off in the distance, through the drizzle they could see the water of the bay, gray and cold.

"Do you suppose that was their cat and they forgot her?" asked Peggy. But the cat wasn't anywhere around now, and as the girls turned the bend they saw her crouching under the dilapidated wooden chair in front of old man Svenson's house. So perhaps the cat belonged

to him. They lost their courage about knocking on his
door and asking when the Petronskis had left and anyway, goodness! here was old man Svenson himself coming up the road. Everything about Svenson was yellow;
his house, his cat, his trousers, his drooping mustache
and tangled hair, his hound loping behind him, and the
long streams of tobacco juice he expertly shot from between his scattered yellow teeth. The two girls drew
over to the side of the path as they hurried by. When
they were a good way past, they stopped.

"Hey, Mr. Svenson!" yelled Peggy. "When did the
Petronskis move?"

Old man Svenson turned around, but said nothing. Finally he did answer, but his words were unintelligible,
and the two girls turned and ran down the hill as fast as
they could. Old man Svenson looked after them for a
moment and then went on up the hill, muttering to himself and scratching his head.

When they were back down on Oliver Street again,
the girls stopped running. They still felt disconsolate,
and Maddie wondered if she were going to be unhappy
about Wanda and the hundred dresses forever. Nothing
would ever seem good to her again, because just when
she was about to enjoy something—like going for a hike
with Peggy to look for bayberries or sliding down Barley
Hill—she'd bump right smack into the thought that she
had made Wanda Petronski move away.

"Well, anyway," said Peggy, "she's gone now, so what
can we do? Besides, when I was asking her about all of
her dresses she probably was getting good ideas for her
drawings. She might not even have won the contest
otherwise."

Maddie carefully turned this idea over in her head,
for if there were anything in it she would not have to
feel so bad. But that night she could not get to sleep.
She thought about Wanda and her faded blue dress and

the little house she had lived in; and old man Svenson
living a few steps away. And she thought of the glowing
picture those hundred dresses made—all lined up in the
classroom.

At last Maddie sat up in bed and pressed her forehead tight in her hands and really thought. This was the
hardest thinking she had ever done. After a long, long
time she reached an important conclusion.

She was never going to stand by and say nothing
again.

If she ever heard anybody picking on someone because they were funny looking or because they had
strange names, she'd speak up. Even if it meant losing
Peggy's friendship. She had no way of making things
right with Wanda, but from now on she would never
make anybody else so unhappy again. Finally, all tired
out, Maddie fell asleep.

On Saturday Maddie spent the afternoon with Peggy.
They were writing a letter to Wanda Petronski.

It was just a friendly letter telling about the contest
and telling Wanda she had won. They told her how
pretty her drawings were, and that now they were
studying about Winfield Scott in school. And they asked
her if she liked where she was living now and if she
liked her new teacher. They had meant to say they were
sorry, but it ended up with their just writing a friendly

letter, the kind they would have written to any good friend, and they signed it with lots of X's for love.

They mailed the letter to Boggins Heights, writing "Please Forward" on the envelope. The teacher had not known where Wanda had moved to, so their only hope was that the post office knew. The minute they dropped the letter in the mail box they both felt happier and more carefree.

Days passed and there was no answer, but the letter did not come back so maybe Wanda had received it. Perhaps she was so hurt and angry she was not going to answer. You could not blame her. And Maddie remembered the way she hitched her left shoulder up as she walked off to school alone, and how the girls always said, "Why does her dress always hang funny like that, and why does she wear those queer, high, laced shoes?"

They knew she didn't have any mother, but they hadn't thought about it. They hadn't thought she had to do her own washing and ironing. She had only one dress and she must have had to wash and iron it overnight. Maybe sometimes it wasn't dry when it was time to put it on in the morning. But it was always clean.

Several weeks went by and still Wanda did not answer. Peggy had begun to forget the whole business, and Maddie put herself to sleep at night making speeches about Wanda, defending her from great crowds of girls who were trying to tease her with, "How many dresses have you got?" Before Wanda could press her lips together in a tight line the way she did before answering, Maddie would cry out, "Stop! This girl is just a girl just like you are . . . " And then everybody would feel ashamed the way she used to feel. Sometimes she rescued Wanda from a sinking ship or the hoofs of a runaway horse. "Oh, that's all right," she'd say when Wanda thanked her with dull pained eyes.

Now it was Christmas time and there was snow on the ground. Christmas bells and a small tree decorated the

classroom. And on one narrow blackboard Jack Beggles
had drawn a jolly fat Santa Claus in red and white chalk.
On the last day of school before the holidays, the children in Peggy's and Maddie's class had a Christmas
party. The teacher's desk was rolled back and a piano
rolled in. First the children had acted the story of Tiny
Tim. Then they had sung songs and Cecile had done
some dances in different costumes. The dance called the
"Passing of Autumn" in which she whirled and spun like
a red and golden autumn leaf was the favorite.

After the party the teacher said she had a surprise,
and she showed the class a letter she had received that
morning.

"Guess who this is from," she said. "You remember
Wanda Petronski? The bright little artist who won the
drawing contest? Well, she has written me and I am
glad to know where she lives because now I can send
her medal. And I hope it gets there for Christmas. I
want to read her letter to you."

The class sat up with a sudden interest, and listened
intently to Miss Mason as she read the letter.

"Dear Miss Mason: How are you and Room 13? Please
tell the girls they can keep those hundred dresses because in my new house I have a hundred new ones all
lined up in my closet. I'd like that girl Peggy to have the
drawing of the green dress with the red trimming and
her friend Maddie to have the blue one. For Christmas.
I miss that school and my new teacher does not equalize
with you. Merry Christmas to you and everybody. Yours
truly, Wanda Petronski."

The teacher passed the letter around the room for
everybody to see. It was pretty, decorated with a picture
of a Christmas tree lighted up in the night in a park surrounded by high buildings.

On the way home from school Maddie and Peggy held
their drawings very carefully. They had stayed late to
help straighten up after the play and it was getting dark.

The houses looked warm and inviting with wreaths and holly and lighted trees in their windows. Outside the grocery store hundreds of Christmas trees were stacked, and in the window candy peppermint canes and cornucopias of shiny bright transparent paper were strung. The air smelled like Christmas and bright lights everywhere reflected different colors on the snow.

"The colors are like the colors in Wanda's hundred dresses," said Maddie.

"Yes," said Peggy, holding her drawing out to look at it under the street lamp. "And boy! This shows she really liked us. It shows she got our letter and this is her way of saying that everything's all right. And that's that," she said with finality.

Peggy felt happy and relieved. It was Christmas and everything was fine.

"I hope so," said Maddie sadly. She felt sad because she knew she would never see the little tight-lipped Polish girl again and couldn't ever really make things right between them.

She went home and she pinned her drawing over a torn place in the pink-flowered wall-paper in the bedroom. The shabby room came alive from the brilliancy of the colors. Maddie sat down on the edge of her bed and looked at the drawing. She had stood by and said nothing, but Wanda had been nice to her anyway.

Tears blurred her eyes and she gazed for a long time at the picture. Then hastily she rubbed her eyes and studied it intently. The colors in the dress were so vivid she had scarcely noticed the face and head of the drawing. But it looked like her, Maddie! It really did. The same short blonde hair, blue eyes, and wide straight mouth. Why, it really looked like her own self! Wanda had really drawn this for her. Wanda had drawn her! In excitement she ran over to Peggy's.

"Peg!" she said. "Let me see your picture."

"What's the matter?" asked Peggy as they clattered up the stairs to her room, where Wanda's drawing was lying face down on the bed. Maddie carefully lifted it up.

"Look! She drew you. That's you!" she exclaimed. And the head and face of this picture did look like the auburn-haired Peggy.

"What did I say!" said Peggy. "She must have really liked us anyway."

"Yes, she must have," agreed Maddie, and she blinked away the tears that came every time she thought of Wanda standing alone in that sunny spot in the school yard close to the wall, looking stolidly over at the group of laughing girls after she had walked off, after she had said, "Sure, a hundred of them—all lined up . . ."

You'll love reading Eleanor Estes' amusing tale The Witch Family, as well as her other books, The Moffats and Middle Moffat, all published by Harcourt, Brace & World.

The Great Balloon Ascension

BY KEITH ROBERTSON

Illustrations by Robert McCloskey

> Henry Reed, son of the United States consul in Naples, has come from Italy to spend the summer with his aunt and uncle in New Jersey. His teacher in the American school in Naples asked him to write a record of his experiences and to "do something that can be used to illustrate free enterprise." So Henry and Margaret Glass, the girl next door, founded HENRY REED, INC.

Tuesday, August 20th

I WENT to the library today and read everything that I could find on balloons. It seems the Army and Navy and Air Force and the weather service all use a lot of balloons. One of their troubles is that if they send a balloon up with instruments, such as thermometers and barometers, half the time they never get the balloon or the instruments back. Sometimes they send up bigger balloons with all sorts of complicated radio equipment which automatically sends back information. These are very expensive and if there's much of a wind they often lose these too. Then of course there are the biggest balloons, which go up with a gondola that will carry a man. Naturally they always take a lot of precautions with these because the men who go up want to come back in one piece. They object to being lost with the balloon.

I've thought quite a bit about it and I've decided

that I could do everybody a great service if I could
develop a medium-size balloon, say about the size of my
big plastic silage bag, that would be very cheap but
would carry some instruments which would always get
back. I have what I think is a brilliant idea. I can send
up homing pigeons in the balloon and they can fly back.
Of course a pigeon wouldn't be able to carry a very
heavy instrument, so any thermometers or barometers
that were sent up with the balloon would have to be
small enough to be strapped to the pigeon's leg, but
if I can work out all the other details the armed forces
ought to be able to figure out how to make small instruments.

A real trained homing pigeon would be best, naturally,
but all pigeons tend to find their way back home. I don't
intend to waste time finding just the right pigeon because I haven't got much time. I have to fly back to
Naples next week. Uncle Al got the ticket today. There'll
be just time enough for me to finish my experiments
in space research with my plastic balloon. If my idea
works, Henry Reed, Inc., should really be on the map.
I expect I'll be made a lieutenant in the Army and
Navy and at least a general in the Air Force.

I asked Uncle Al about the pigeons again at dinner
tonight. He says they are all part homing or racing
pigeons and probably would be able to find their way
home from quite a distance. Anyhow, I'm sure they'll
do and I'm going to slip over as soon as it gets dark
and catch a good healthy one.

Wednesday, August 21st

I told Midge about my idea today and she thinks it sounds wonderful. She was a little doubtful at first that we would be able to work out all the details but before the day was over we had practically everything figured out. In fact, I think we should be able to send up our balloon tomorrow.

We did some of the preliminary work today. We took the pigeon that I caught last night and went down the road half a mile with it, carrying it in a basket. Then we let it out. It flew straight back home. I'd put a red leg band around it so there wasn't any mistake. There it was sitting on top of the barn. If I can, I'll catch the same pigeon again tonight.

We found a round wicker basket in Midge's basement which Mrs. Glass gave to us. This afternoon I built a small slotted cage for the pigeon. It has a little door that slides up and down. The problem of how to release the pigeon after he has been up in the air for a while was a tough one. And for a while I didn't think we could solve it. Midge gave me the idea.

"We'll have to put the pigeon to sleep somehow," she said. "Then we can send an alarm clock up in the basket with him to wake him up after he's been up for say half an hour."

Of course she was just kidding but it gave me an idea. Aunt Mabel has an old-fashioned round alarm clock upstairs in the guest room. She didn't want to part with it at first but I offered to buy it and finally she gave it to me. When the alarm goes off, the little thumb screw or handle on the back that you use to wind the alarm goes around and around. I fastened a wire to this and a string to the wire. When the alarm goes off it winds up the string. The string runs over a pulley and is attached to the little door of my pigeon cage and it grad-

ually raises the door. It looks sort of complicated and homemade but it works. Midge and I tried it three or four times and it opened the door every time. We are all set and tomorrow is the great day.

Thursday, August 22nd

We had the great balloon ascension today. The balloon went up and it came down. I don't know whether you would call it a success or not because it didn't work out exactly as Midge and I had planned. I don't think we will be as famous as I had hoped, but it isn't really our fault. Still I'm going to write to the Air Force and tell them my scheme. Maybe they can try it out in the middle of a desert someplace where they won't be bothered by all the complications that we ran into. I guess the best way to explain just why the experiment wasn't completely successful is to tell everything that happened today.

It took us much longer to get the balloon ready than

we had expected. There was considerable work and also we had some interruptions. We spent a good part of the morning chasing Mr. Baines's sheep. Mr. Baines had turned about thirty sheep into the pasture out back of my lot. They found a hole in the fence someplace. At least, eight of them did. We were busy working on the balloon, trying to attach the basket to the plastic bag, when suddenly these sheep walked through the woods and stood there staring at us. We thought we would chase them back where they came from but when I went to look I couldn't find the hole. Maybe they jumped the fence, I don't know.

They weren't bothering us so we let them graze a while on the lot, but then they wandered out toward the road. Three of them started across just as a big green sedan came by. Grover's Corner is such a little place it isn't really a town at all, and a lot of people don't even slow down when they go through. This man must have been going sixty miles an hour and he missed those sheep by inches. He swerved and there was a screech of tires and his car rocked back and forth. He managed to get it under control again but it was certainly close.

We went across the street to Midge's house and tried to call Mr. Baines but no one answered the phone. I don't know whether he was away or out in the fields.

We went back to the lot to see what had happened to the sheep but when we arrived they had disappeared. We thought they had gone back where they came from but a few minutes later we heard a "baa."

"They're over at Apple's," said Midge. "I bet he loves that." The thought of it tickled her so much that she sat down and laughed about it.

I wanted to see exactly what he would do when he discovered the sheep and we took time out to go over by the hedge. The sheep weren't in the front yard so we went on back to where we could look into the back part of his lot. There were the sheep, all eight of them, inside the wire enclosure or pen that Mr. Apple had built. The gate had evidently been left open and they had simply walked in.

"I wonder why he hasn't noticed them," I said. "Usually he's out here with a cannon if a sparrow lands on the place."

"I know," said Midge. "They aren't home. I saw them driving out in their car right after breakfast this morning. She was all dressed up so I suppose they went to New York or Philadelphia or someplace to go shopping."

"If those sheep do wander into the front yard they'll eat all her flowers," I said. "Maybe I ought to slip over and close that gate. They can't do any harm in there."

"That's not a bad idea," said Midge, "but I think we ought to do it for Mr. Baines rather than for Mr. Apple. It will keep his sheep from getting killed on the highway."

I slipped through a hole in the hedge, walked across the lawn, and closed the gate to the wire pen. The sheep were busily eating and didn't bother to look up.

About eleven o'clock Midge went over to her house for something and she called Mr. Baines again. This time Mrs. Baines answered. Mr. Baines had gone with his hired man to some auction sale where he hoped to buy some dairy cows, and would not be back until later. She said he would be over in his truck to get the sheep as soon as he got home. That was settled, so we forgot about the sheep and went back to our balloon.

There's no use going into all the details with the troubles we had getting the basket attached and getting my pigeon cage rigged up just right. We spent most of the morning at it and so it was after lunch before we went to get the cylinder of gas. This was too heavy to handle and I had to go back and get Uncle Al's tractor and cart.

We had quite a time getting the balloon inflated. I
had read enough to know that you don't inflate a balloon
all the way so that it's nice and fat like a sausage. Instead
it should be only half full and look sort of limp. Then
as it goes higher and higher the gas expands and the
balloon fills out.

It took us half an hour to locate a hose to attach to
the cylinder to use for inflating the plastic bag. Finally

we managed it. About three-thirty we had the balloon inflated just right and it was tugging at the ropes. Everything looked promising.

I'd caught the same pigeon the night before and I got him and put him in the little slotted cage. I hooked up the alarm clock and set the alarm to go off in about fifteen minutes. I didn't have any instruments to strap to the pigeon's leg, but since this was just an experimental run we figured that wasn't necessary. The main idea was to prove that it would work. From the way the balloon kept tugging at that anchor rope there wasn't much doubt that it would work.

"What if it goes up too fast?" Midge asked.

"How can it go up too fast?" I said.

"Well, then, too far," she said. "Supposing it goes up so far that the pigeon can't breathe. Doesn't the air get thinner the higher you go?"

I had to admit that it did but I doubted if our balloon would get up that high. However, Midge kept worrying about it.

"Well, I'll tell you what we'll do," I said. "We'll put a couple of bricks in the gondola to add a little weight. We can let it go up a way on a rope to get an idea how far and how fast it will go up."

The trouble was that we didn't have a long rope. The balloon was tied with a piece of clothesline and that was only a few feet long. "A really good strong twine would do the trick," I said. "Do you suppose you could find a ball?"

"I think so," Midge said and started to go across the street to her house. She had gone only a few feet when she turned around and said, "What about witnesses?"

"What do you mean, witnesses?"

"We ought to have someone who sees all this and can swear to it afterwards. Even the Wright brothers had a few people watching."

I had to admit that she had a good point. The only trouble was that if we invited a lot of people over to see our great experiment and then it flopped, we would feel foolish, just as we had when they discovered that our oil well wasn't an oil well at all. I certainly thought it would work, but so did all those Air Force scientists when they fired their first rockets down in Florida. Instead they blew up. I didn't know what to do.

"I know," said Midge. "We can take pictures."

That was a wonderful idea, and we both decided to get our cameras.

It was about twenty minutes to four when I walked into the kitchen. Aunt Mabel had just taken some cookies out of the oven but I was so excited that I didn't wait to get one of them. I rushed upstairs, got my camera, and hurried back toward the lot. Midge was crossing the street as I approached and we reached the barn together. Agony as usual was tagging along with me.

We had tied the balloon out in the middle of the lot where it would be clear of the trees when it started up. There was a big stump there and I had driven a spike into this. There was a loop in our anchor rope and this had been slipped over the end of the spike. The wicker basket was about six inches off the ground, suspended by four ropes from the bottom of the plastic bag.

We stopped and took pictures of our balloon from several angles and then I found several bricks. Since I had put the pigeon in his cage, all we had to do was put the bricks in the basket and let it make an experimental flight tied to Midge's string. We walked up to it, neither of us suspecting a thing, and so we were both flabbergasted when we looked inside. There sitting in the basket was Siegfried, the Apples' white cat. He had knocked over the alarm clock, upset the cage, managed to get the door open somehow, and had killed the pigeon. When he saw us he glared at us and started waving his tail back and forth as though daring us to take the pigeon away from him.

I've never seen anybody as mad as Midge was. She was so mad she couldn't say a word, which means that she was as mad as she can possibly get. She sputtered and stuttered and jumped up and down. I looked around for a stick. In the first place Siegfried is a big cat and I didn't want to tangle with him with my bare hands. And secondly I wanted the stick to give him a couple of good swats, but before I could find one Midge thought of something else.

"I hope you go up so high you never come back," she said, and she reached out and grabbed the rope. Just at that moment Agony either smelled the cat, or saw him, or heard him, or found out somehow what was going on. He came rushing up from behind me and made a leap. He landed in the wicker basket just as Midge pulled the anchor rope off the spike. Midge said later that she was in such a rage she didn't realize for a minute that Agony had jumped into the basket. By the time she did it was too late.

With both the cat and the dog, and of course the dead pigeon, in the basket, the balloon didn't go up very fast. There is really no excuse for my not having caught the anchor rope. I guess I didn't understand what Midge had done for a minute. By this time the balloon was quite a way up in the air. I rushed over and made a leap for the end of the rope but just missed it.

"Agony's in there!" I said to Midge.

Midge nodded dumbly. "Yes I know he is," she said.

We both stood there like a couple of idiots while the balloon kept getting higher and higher. We were sort of hypnotized and we stood watching as it kept moving on toward the tops of the trees.

I doubt if either Agony or Siegfried knew what was happening for the first minute or two. As the balloon

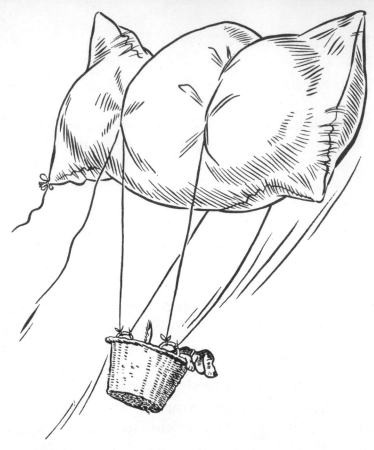

drifted upward, for a while I could hear Siegfried spitting. Then he let out an angry yowl and a minute later there was a yip from Agony. I suppose Siegfried scratched him. Then Siegfried's head appeared above the edge of the basket. I think he was about to jump out but suddenly he saw he was up in the air and couldn't, and after that I guess he was just too terrified to fight Agony any more.

"What are we going to do?" Midge asked in a scared voice.

"I don't know," I admitted.

The balloon reached the level of the treetops and began drifting slowly over toward Apple's. Midge and I traipsed along after it. I don't know what we planned to do but I felt I had to trail that balloon and get Agony down somehow.

The balloon just missed the big oak tree and then went over above Mr. Apple's lawn. Midge and I followed as far as the hedge and stood looking through it. There was scarcely any breeze and the balloon moved very slowly. If Agony hadn't been in the basket it would have been a beautiful sight and I would have been proud of it. As it was I was just plain scared.

It drifted on with the basket swinging back and forth gently beneath the big plastic bag. Then it passed directly over the Apples' house. As it did Siegfried poked his head over the edge of the wicker basket and saw his chance. I'll have to admit that he is a pretty smart cat. He didn't hesitate but jumped. The basket was about eight feet above the roof but of course that was no jump at all for Siegfried. The roof is a steep, gabled slate affair and certainly not a very good place for a landing field. Only a cat could have done it without slipping down and over the edge. As it was, Siegfried very nearly lost his hold. He managed to get one paw over the peak as he landed. Somehow he pulled himself up and crouched there. He was too scared to stir.

I suppose Agony wondered what had become of the cat and he poked his head over the edge. It was the first time I'd seen him since he'd jumped in the basket and I imagine it was the first time he realized that he was up in the air. I would like to have seen the expression on his face. At the time, however, all I was worried about was that he might become panicky and jump.

"Stay in there, Agony," I shouted. "We'll get you down."

I didn't know how I was going to get him down but I was hoping. Up until this time Midge and I had followed along like a couple of big oafs, fascinated by that sight of that balloon up in the air, and not really thinking at all. Slowly we began to come out of it.

"Well, I might as well take some pictures," Midge said. "I guess Agony's on his way out into the great blue yonder. Maybe I can win a prize with my picture."

"I'm going to go see if somebody can't help us," I said.

For the first time I halfway wished that Agony's original owner would appear and want his dog. I would have been glad to see anyone who would help me get Agony back down to earth again. But no one did appear and I started running for home. At least I could ask Aunt Mabel for advice.

About halfway home I saw Mr. Ainsworth standing in his yard, looking up in the sky with a puzzled expression on his face.

"Is that contraption something of yours?" he asked.

I nodded. "It's a balloon, but my dog got in the basket by mistake and I've got to get him down!"

"Your beagle's in there?" Mr. Ainsworth asked.

Again I nodded. "Who do you think I should call? The state police? Do you suppose they could help me?"

"Maybe you'd better call out the Army and they could shoot it down." Then suddenly he grinned. "That's it," he said. "That isn't up so high. Maybe I can shoot it down for you. Come on."

We hurried to his house where he got out a .22 rifle. Then we got in his car and drove down the road. Midge was back by the road by this time and we picked her up too.

The balloon had drifted on and was over the middle of a big pasture beyond the Apples'. We got out of the car and hurried into the pasture a short distance. Mr. Ainsworth looked around carefully and then up at the balloon. "A twenty-two long will carry about a mile," he said. "I want to be sure where the bullet is going to land before I go firing up in the air."

I wasn't too keen on the idea of his firing that .22 in Agony's direction. "Are you sure you can hit the balloon without hitting the basket?" I asked.

Mr. Ainsworth looked at me and snorted. "Son, I've hunted ducks for forty-five years. I may be sixty-seven years old but my hand's still pretty steady. If I can't hit

that balloon without killing your dog, then I'll take up knitting."

He raised his gun and fired. He waited a second and fired twice more.

"The trouble with this set-up is you can't tell whether you hit it or not. I think I've hit that bag but I'll give it a couple of more shots and then we'll wait and see what happens."

The balloon was still rising slowly and was probably another twenty-five or thirty feet higher than when it had passed over Mr. Apple's house. It was also drifting very gradually across the field. We followed a short distance behind. Mr. Ainsworth fired three times more before we reached the fence.

"That's got at least four or five holes in it," he said. "The trouble is that there isn't much pressure inside the bag to force the gas out."

"If the holes are up near the top, the gas will leak out," I said. "Of course it may take quite a while through little holes like that."

"All right, we'll make sure there's some near the top," he said, and he fired another three shots.

We all stood at the fence for several minutes, watching the balloon closely. When it had drifted almost to the far side of the next field, I climbed over the fence to go after it.

"I think it's settling a little," said Mr. Ainsworth. "It's certainly not rising any more. You go on ahead and follow it. I'll go get in the car and drive around and down Maple Road. That's straight ahead about three fields over. By the time it reaches that we should be able to tell what it's doing."

Mr. Ainsworth was right. It was fifteen minutes later before we were positive the balloon was settling, and I had to follow it about half a mile beyond Maple Road, but it did settle. Toward the last it came down rather fast and for a few minutes I was scared it would come down too fast and that Agony would be hurt. The basket landed with a bump but Agony jumped out uninjured. He was really glad to see me.

Mr. Ainsworth came up and together we examined the plastic bag. It was full of holes. I think almost every shot he fired must have hit.

"I'm certainly glad I found you," I said. "You saved Agony's life."

"I enjoyed doing it," said Mr. Ainsworth. "It isn't every day that a man gets to shoot down a balloon carrying a beagle."

Mr. Ainsworth dropped us off at the barn. There wasn't much left of all our equipment. The balloon was full of holes, the pigeon was dead, the alarm clock didn't seem to work any more, and the wicker basket hadn't been much good to begin with. Both Midge and I felt pretty discouraged.

"Some day I'll kill that cat," Midge said.

"Hey, what about the cat?" I asked. "Do you suppose he's still up there on the roof?"

We hurried over to the hedge and looked through. Siegfried was still clinging to the peak of the roof. He knew better than to move because those slates were slippery.

"How do you suppose the Apples are going to get him down from there?"

"I think they should get him down the same way we got Agony down," Midge said. "Shoot him down."

"The Apples still aren't home," I said, looking at their empty garage.

"They'll have a nice pleasant surprise when they do get

back," Midge said and started laughing. "I'll bet that will keep Mr. Apple busy for a while—figuring out how that cat got up there."

It was a funny idea and we both sat down and laughed about it for a while. There just wasn't any possible way that cat could have gotten up there except by being dropped from an airplane or balloon.

"Don't worry," said Midge. "They'll blame us anyhow. Mrs. Apple will claim that you picked up the cat by the tail and threw him up there."

"I wonder how soon they'll be back," I said. "Sooner or later that cat will either try to make a move or he'll get so tired he can't hang on any longer. If he falls he'll be killed."

"Well, I'm not going to go over and hold a net and wait for him," Midge said. "I don't feel a bit sorry for him."

She did though, and we both got more and more worried. There was a big tree toward the front of the house and I had the idea that if the cat could be coaxed up in that direction he might be able to make a leap into the tree. Midge and I walked out to the road to take a look. When we got there we saw that it would be a pretty long leap.

"They might stay out to dinner for all we know," I said. "They've been gone since early this morning."

"All right," Midge said finally. "I suppose we'd better call the Fire Department. I'll do it but I'm not going to say who I am, because whatever happens the Apples are going to be sore."

The hook-and-ladder truck arrived at about quarter to five, just when people began returning from work. Everyone thought there was a fire and stopped. People are naturally curious and I guess they would as soon see a cat rescued as watch a fire. Anyhow, inside of fifteen minutes there must have been thirty cars parked beside the road and there was a whole group gathered on Mr.

Apple's lawn. Among them was Mr. Glass and my Uncle Al, but Midge and I stayed very carefully on our side of the hedge. We didn't see how anyone could connect us with that cat being on the roof, and we wanted to keep it that way.

The firemen got the ladder up and a man was halfway up to the edge of the roof when the Apples came home. Mr. Apple was too scared to be nasty at first. I suppose he thought his house was on fire. They got out of the car and one of the firemen told Mrs. Apple the cause of all the excitement. She looked up, and when she saw Siegfried on the peak of the roof she very nearly fainted. Mr. Apple and a fireman helped her over to a garden bench where she sat down.

"How do you suppose that cat got up there?" one of the firemen asked.

Mr. Apple just shook his head. We could hear everyone talking from where we stood at the hedge and they all seemed to be puzzled.

After the fireman reached the edge of the roof he still had to put up another short ladder and hook it over the peak in order to get to Siegfried. He finally did it, though, and Siegfried was so glad to get down that he didn't scratch the fireman.

Everything had gone very well up to this point. The Apples were acting almost human. Mrs. Apple was full of thanks to the firemen and Mr. Apple hadn't screamed at anybody for being on his lawn. A tall, sandy-haired man who had appeared with the Apples stood over by a lilac bush watching everything and saying nothing. Just when it appeared that all the excitement was over there were a couple of loud baas from the big back yard beyond the hedge. Midge and I looked at each other in surprise. Mr. Baines still hadn't come for his sheep.

Mr. Apple was surprised too, and then he was suspicious. He hurried over to the hedge and looked through the opening. From the bellow he gave you would have thought he was being murdered. He jumped up and down and shouted something that I couldn't understand, and he looked as though he were going to have apoplexy. I guess everybody else thought the same thing and they all hurried over to find out what was the matter. Of course none of them understood why he was so mad and after they had looked through the hedge they still didn't know anything more than they had before. Midge and I hurried back to see what he would do. We arrived just in time to see him open the gate and rush inside his wire fence. He screamed and shouted and waved his arms. Of course the poor sheep were scared half out of their wits. They all rushed through the gate and went running out through the gap in the hedge into the front yard.

There wasn't much left of the grass inside the fence. After all, eight sheep had been there all day and they had had nothing to do but eat. It was cropped down almost to the roots. They had made a very thorough and very clean job of it. It wouldn't need mowing for a long time. Apple pointed at the ground, dancing up and down, and I wasn't certain whether he was going to cry or blow up. The sandy-haired man walked over, went through the gate, and stood talking with Apple for several minutes. Mr. Apple calmed down a little bit but he was still quite excited. The sheep went baaing off down the road but, as I said to Midge, I thought we had done our duty by them. It wasn't our fault if Mr. Apple let them out on the road to be killed.

Some of the people stood around a few minutes longer, wondering what in the world had happened to Mr. Apple. However, there wasn't anything else to see. The fire truck drove away and soon everyone had gone home. It was dinner time so Midge and I went home too.

Aunt Mabel was home when I got there but she had been up to the road a few minutes earlier, watching Siegfried's rescue. Uncle Al didn't appear for another ten minutes.

"Well, that was quite a lot of excitement," Aunt Mabel said as we sat down to dinner. "How on earth do you suppose that cat got up there?"

"No one seems to know," Uncle Al said, looking at me. "However I was talking to Mr. Ainsworth just before I came in."

I could tell from Uncle Al's expression that he suspected something. After all it wasn't my fault that Siegfried had jumped in the basket and there was no reason why I shouldn't tell them what had happened, so I did. All the time that I was explaining things Uncle Al kept running his hand over his face.

"If I hadn't grown up with your mother I would swear all this was a dream," he said when I finished.

"What on earth was Mr. Apple screaming about there at the last?" Aunt Mabel asked.

"Oh, that," Uncle Al said. "That is the explanation of our little mystery about all his objections to trespassing. That tall fellow in the brown suit was Jim Weber. He used to be county agent around here years ago, and now he's with a seed company in Philadelphia. I thought I recognized him and later on I went over and talked to him. That's why I was a little late getting back. It seems that Mr. Apple has developed some new kind of grass. Or at least he thinks he has. Now, this may sound ridiculous, but his grass is supposed to grow in a sort of a spiral. It's a curly grass and doesn't need mowing very often. He's got some idea that it's immensely valuable and it may be, although Weber says that such discoveries or developments never make a great deal of money. Anyhow, Apple has been working on four or five strains of grass and this is the one he considers to be the final answer. He thinks it will make him famous. He planted a plot in the back yard behind that hedge and put up a wire enclosure around it. According to Weber he's been so secretive and mysterious about it that it's ridiculous.

I guess he was afraid someone would steal his secret. Anyhow, after a lot of negotiations and fiddle-faddle, he arranged for a seed company to send a representative up to see this great discovery. Jim Weber was the man they sent. The trouble is that when he did get out to look at it they found that some sheep had been locked up inside the enclosure and had eaten practically all the grass."

Uncle Al paused and looked at me. "How did those sheep get in there?" he asked.

I guess Uncle Al must be what they call psychic because there wasn't any possible way that he could know that I had anything to do with those sheep being in Mr. Apple's enclosure. "They got through a hole in the fence at the back of our lot," I explained. "Midge and I chased them and they went through the hedge into Mr. Apple's place. Of course that *would* be the only time that he ever left the gate open to his grass plot. I guess that grass must be good. The sheep went right in there and started eating it. I slipped over and closed the gate and Midge called Mr. Baines. We forgot all about them until we heard Mr. Apple scream. Besides we didn't know that was special grass."

"Well, Mr. Apple is very disappointed," said Uncle Al, "and I can't say that I blame him, but after all if he hadn't been so mysterious you'd have known that he was anxious to protect that grass and would have chased the sheep out instead of locking them in. Anyhow, Jim Weber told him this would be a good test of the grass. If it comes back it will be proof that it's tough."

Keith Robertson has also written a number of intriguing mystery stories which you will want to read. Among these are The Phantom Rider, The Mystery of Burnt Hill, *and* Three Stuffed Owls, *all published by Viking.*

The Girl in Pink

BY VIRGINIA SORENSEN

Illustrations by Charles Geer

Ten-year-old Esther is a daughter of the Amish people and has always been taught her lessons at home. Now the State of Pennsylvania has decided she must go to a regular school. Esther's father does not approve because he is afraid his daughter will become dissatisfied with the simple life of her Amish people.

RUTH would be married the first Tuesday in November. Even before school started, a week after Hans' light had come into the window, the house was humming with work and plans. Esther was so busy and excited she almost forgot about school. But, of course, never entirely. In the middle of gathering eggs or putting away dishes or peeling potatoes, she would suddenly think: *"Next week I am going to school!"*

What a mixup her feelings were! She was glad and she was curious. But she was worried too. From going to town and even to the Fair, she knew how it was going to be in many ways. She could not show more if she wore a dress the color of a cardinal. Only in a crowd of dark dresses exactly alike, and white bonnets and black shoes and white aprons, was she hidden. At the Fair, where hundreds of people wore different styles and colors, she had been absolutely clear and alone among them, like one black bird against the sky. At school she would show every day, every hour.

At the Fair, in a little booth, there had been a wooden bird held up for men to shoot with guns. She would be held up like that, alone, at school.

The time came closer and closer. Friday. Saturday. Sunday. It was not until they had come home from meeting Sunday night that Father mentioned what was going to happen the next morning.

Mother said, as usual, "Esther, it is time for bed."

Father reached out and touched her as she passed him, and said, "Sit down at the table for a little. There is something we must talk about. Besides—" he looked at Mother and nodded toward the cupboard where the books were kept. "If you will bring the Book, I have something to read."

Esther sat down. Ruth sat down too, with her knitting. Mother brought the Bible and set it in front of Father, sitting down beside him, then, with her hands folded on her lap.

"Tomorrow, Esther, you must begin at the school," Father said.

Esther's fingers wanted to move on her lap, but she held them quiet. Only her toes stirred in her high shoes, wiggling and wiggling.

"Later we will try to have a school of our own here," he said, "but now they say you must go to this one for a while." He looked steadily at her. "The children at this school are different."

She looked down at her quiet fingers.

"You will see many different things," Father said. He glanced at Mother and seemed to wait for her to add something.

So she said, "Esther has seen some of those different things already. On the streets and in the town."

"But not in the same room!" Father said. And he turned to the worn big book before him. He knew this book so well that it did not take him long to find what he wanted, and Esther knew from what he chose to read that he too had been thinking of The First Step Away.

"'Behold,'" he read, "'we put bits in the horses' mouths, that they may obey us; and we turn about their whole body.' You see the meaning of this, Esther? A small thing may seem smaller than it really is."

This was true. Mother sat nodding.

"'Behold also the ships, which though they be so great, and are driven of fierce winds, yet are they turned about with a very small helm . . .'"

She had never seen a ship, but she had heard of them. Mother had seen ships near Philadelphia; she often told of them with wonder.

"'Even so, the tongue is a little member, and boasteth great things. Behold, how great a matter a little fire kindleth!'" He looked closely at her. "Esther, I only tell you these things so you will understand why it is you will remain by yourself. Though we have learned always to love our enemies, and so never fight . . ."

Ruth gave a little gasp at his words and he looked at her. She blushed and said nothing, though he was looking a question. Mother said quickly, "Ruth means the children in the school are not enemies."

"I did not finish," Father said. "I meant only to say they were not her friends. Esther will look at the teacher and do as the teacher says, unless it is something she is told never to do, here at home. But I do not expect her to look at the children."

Ruth looked closely at her knitting and pretended to count. Mother said anxiously, "Except—"

"Except to keep from falling over them!" Father said, and smiled. Mother smiled too, then, and Ruth.

Esther was glad they smiled.

"Now," Father said in a gentle voice, "you may go to bed."

Esther wanted to tell Father what she had been

thinking lately, and that she would never, never go away. But she could not find the words to say it with. Even the next morning when only the two of them rode in the wagon, out of the yard and down the road toward the school, she could find no words. One reason she could not say it, of course, was that she could think of no way to do so without mentioning the name of Dan. Even if school had been Away for Dan, it need not be Away for her. What Father had read was good to remember. If you did not kindle a little fire in the first place, you would never have a big one that you could not manage to put out.

The bell rang as they turned the last great bend in the road and saw the school on its little hill. Esther jumped, and Father said, "It is only the first bell. There are always two, one five minutes early so slow scholars will hurry."

She had known this, for Dan had told her. She had jumped because of the exciting thought that the bell was ringing now for *her*. But she did not say so.

Father helped her down outside the school. He handed her the lunch-basket and said, "I will be here waiting for you when school is over at three o'clock."

Suddenly she realized how many hours it was going to be. She turned to say this to him, but he drove away without looking back, and she was alone.

She stood still. For the life of her she could not stir off the road and over the bridge and onto the school-lot where children were running in every direction. Nobody seemed to notice her at all.

Then the bell rang again. A woman appeared in the doorway at the top of two wide stone steps. She called something and the children began to run toward her. When they stood in a long crooked line, one behind the other, she stood aside and they marched in.

Esther looked down the road where Father had dis-

appeared. But then she heard the teacher calling from the door again. "Hello! Aren't you coming in?"

Esther had to move now, she knew it. She took a deep trembling breath and crossed the bridge. She did not look up at all, but only at the path and at the steps and then at the teacher's white shoes fastened with a neat row of buttons on either foot.

"Your name is Esther Lapp?" the teacher asked.

Esther nodded.

"We are glad to see you," the teacher said, and took Esther's hand. Inside she led the way down an aisle between two long rows of seats. What a noise! Everywhere were laughing and whispering, like a thousand starlings in a tree.

"You will sit here," the teacher said, and Esther felt the

good strong seat under her. She sat looking at the desk. The wooden top was covered with scribbles she could not read very well and with pictures of things she did not recognize. The teacher went to the front of the room and rapped with a little stick and the noise gradually died away.

Things began to move by. Hands went up. The teacher talked and called out one name and another. Pencils were passed in long boxes. Paper came in sheets, some colored, just as Dan had said. There was a small pair of scissors and a large box of crayons. And then there were books, lovely, lovely books with pictures of more things than Esther had ever seen. Looking at the pictures she did not have to look at the children, and presently she began to breathe deeply again.

At noon she sat still when the others went outside. Her lunch-basket lay under her desk, but she did not feel at all hungry. The teacher came to her and said in a kind voice, "Would you rather eat here today? Don't you want to go outside in the sun?"

She shook her head.

The teacher went back to her own big desk and ate a lunch from a paper bag. She had a long blue container, too, that had milk in it, and a small red cup for a cap. She did not say anything, but when she saw Esther eating slowly and looking at the cup, she smiled. Presently she went again to ring the bell.

The very first person to come in was a girl dressed all in pink. When she appeared, Esther was looking at the door, but dropped her eyes so quickly she saw only a kind of pink cloud, really, like the heart of a sunset.

The pink cloud came down the aisle and stopped beside the desk in front of Esther's. Now Esther remembered seeing the pink dress before, over her book.

"Hello," said the pink cloud, and Esther looked up. "Are you Amish?"

Esther nodded. The girl sat down but twisted herself about in the seat and smiled. "I'm *glad* I sit by you," she said.

Suddenly, though she did not know why the girl was glad, Esther felt glad too. She did not say so, but only sat looking at her desk and then, once more, at the wonderful books. The children all came in, filling the room with noise and motion, until the teacher rapped, again, with her stick.

It was still very bad, for Esther felt squeezed into her desk and into the room and into the crowd of children and even her heart felt tight and her stomach a little sick. But it was not as bad as it had been that morning. Over her book, over her pencil and paper, somehow between Esther and all of the others, was the girl in pink.

Twice during the afternoon she turned with a smile.

Never in her life had Esther dreamed how wonderful it could be to see Father sitting in the buggy, after school finally ended, waiting for her to come. He sat very straight, looking neither to the right nor to the left, even when the teacher called, "Good afternoon!"

As they drove off down the road toward home, Esther looked back once and saw the girl in pink lift her hand to wave good-by. But of course she did not lift her hand to answer, or even so much as glance back again. Father did not mention the school. He did not even ask her how the day had been, but began to tell her of all the things that had happened at home during the day.

For days the school made Esther feel so tight and so terrible that she could scarcely wait until it ended and she could hurry outside where Father sat patiently in the buggy, waiting behind the patient horses, whose names she knew. Each day she could not wait to pat them and speak to them.

The teacher was kind enough. She wore colored shirts and was pleasant to look at when she sat still at her desk. But when she got up she was entirely too thin. Her bones looked uncomfortable, showing at the base of her neck in hard wing-points, like the wings of a plucked chicken, when she wrote on the blackboard. Her voice stretched and broke in two when the boys made her cross. For a few days they did it on purpose, many many times. Esther felt ashamed for them and looked at the floor when it happened. But the boys did not seem in the least ashamed.

Esther did as Father had told her and never looked at the children—at least when they were looking at her. But almost every time she glanced up, somebody was looking. They laughed too. Jumpy laughter. All of a sudden one of them would burst out and then everybody else joined in. It made Esther want to laugh too, so her throat ached with laughter. But then she learned that the laughter was unkind.

She knew this because the teacher scolded about it. "Now we *won't* have this silly laughing!" she said, and pounded on the desk with her little stick.

But they did have it, anyhow, whether she said *Yes* or *No*, and no matter how hard she pounded.

Esther didn't know the laughing was at *her* until the girl in pink said it. She was sitting directly in front of Esther, and did not laugh. Instead, she turned around suddenly one day and said, *"I'm* not laughing at you! I wouldn't!"

Esther looked at her in surprise. Of course it was good to know she *wouldn't,* but it was not good to know the others *were.* She felt her face begin to burn.

"I like you!" said the girl in pink. "My name is Mary."

Mary was the most beautiful and important name in the world for a girl. Esther had always thought so. This Mary, her skin as rosy as her dress, had hair that fell in little golden curls like wisps of silk. Sometimes a curl almost went into Esther's ink-bottle. It never quite went in, but brushed over. Esther reached out once and moved the curl away. It was exactly like the silk in a milkweed pod. It felt like a downy feather. It was so beautiful it made a shiver go through her fingers, and her heart suddenly beat very fast.

Father would not like her to be friends with Mary, or even to look at her. If anybody in the world was really different from Esther herself and all her people, that one was Mary. She wore pink one day and blue the next and then yellow, but Esther liked pink the best. She laughed a good deal. She tossed her hair when the boys chased her in the games at recess, and squealed when they caught her. All the other girls wanted to walk by her side and whisper with her, back and forth. Even when she did not wear the pink dress, Esther still thought of her as The Pink Girl. This was because of her pretty skin and her hands, on which she wore two small rings. Then her knees were pink and her plump legs, which were bare from her little socks upward until they vanished in her fluffy skirt. Mary was like the pretty girls made of glass in shop windows.

"How beautiful you are!" Esther thought many times a day.

One morning Mary turned around with a smile during the writing exercise. "I'm writing you a letter," she said. "Why don't you write one to me?"

Esther looked at the pencil in her hand. She had been making great A's and B's and C's and all the other letters in perfect rows. She knew how to put some of them together; she could make a great many words. But she knew she should not think about writing a letter to Mary. Father had said, "You will not look at the other children," and already she looked at Mary all the time, as much as possible. Writing a letter would be worse than looking, she knew that without being told. She went on making A's and B's and C's in perfect rows.

Soon Mary turned around again. She slipped a folded paper onto Esther's desk.

"Haven't you written mine yet?" she whispered.

Esther's mouth felt dry and she swallowed deeply before she could answer. "Not yet," she said.

It was like a promise. She had not meant it to be, but it was. Mary smiled and said, "It gets easier and easier to write. You'll learn soon. Letters are good practice." She turned back to her desk.

The folded note lay on Esther's desk. She looked at it for a long time before she touched it. Was receiving a letter as bad as writing one? Father received letters from seed companies and from the school officials and many others who lived outside the neighborhood. After all, if

somebody sent you a letter, it wasn't your fault, was it?
She thought of Dan here in the schoolroom year after
year. Did somebody in pink send letters to Dan? Or
maybe somebody with buttons on his coat? All the boys
had buttons on their coats.

She picked up the letter and unfolded it. In very tall
wriggly letters, Mary had written:

> Dear Friend Esther:
> I like you. I think your dress is pretty. Your apron
> is cute too. And your little hat.
> Your friend,
> Mary.

She sat still. What a good letter it was! How could
Mary think such a dark dress was pretty? The white
apron was very common and plain, yet Mary thought it
was cute. A nice little word—cute! cute! cute! It was like
a canary singing. She lifted her hand to her bonnet, tied
securely under her chin with her hair tucked under. It
was possible that her own hair would make curls, she
thought. When she took out the braids and combed it
at night, it fell in wide waves over her shoulders.

Even the Bible said, "If a woman have long hair, it is
a glory to her. . . ."

Suddenly she felt happy, the way she sometimes felt
when she woke and the sun was shining in her window.
Mary turned to see whether the letter had been opened,
and smiled.

Esther must say something, she knew. Not to say something would be unkind, and she was taught always to
return one kindness with another. Or perhaps even with
two. "Thank you very much," she said. "It is a beautiful
letter."

"As soon as you can, write one to me," Mary said. Then,
"Do you play jump-the-rope? Would you like to jump
with me at recess?"

Esther caught her breath. She had watched the girls
jumping every day but never even thought of jumping
herself. "I don't know how," she said.

Mary looked surprised. "It's easy," she said. "I'll teach
you. Except—maybe—do you think your skirt will get in
the way?"

The teacher rapped sharply with her little stick. "No
whispering!" she said. "Mary, have you finished the
exercise?"

"No, ma'am," Mary said.

"Then work, don't visit," the teacher said. "It's almost time for recess."

Mary gave a quick little glance at Esther, and winked an eye! She had not finished her exercise because she had written a letter. It was their secret. She began to write very fast on the exercise. Esther could watch the motion of her pretty pink elbow as she wrote.

Esther tucked the letter inside her desk. She could look at it every day at school, she thought. Every day she could know again that Mary thought her dress was pretty, that her apron was cute, and so was her little hat. "I wish I could show Mary my long hair!" she thought.

Suddenly, then, she thought about Vanity. Hair was tucked away under bonnets so there would be no thinking about brushing and curling. A cold wind seemed to blow through her very soul. Could Mary's letter—such a kind thing!—be The First Step Away? It was impossible. . . .

The bell rang. Instantly, like a sudden burst of water, the children began to flow out of the room.

"Don't push," the teacher said. "In order now! The third grade is first out today. Harry—take your turn. Kenneth—"

Mary rose in front of Esther and they waited for their turn to march. In the most natural way in the world, Mary took Esther's hand in her own. Her hand was soft and warm, as kind as her letter. Esther felt the turn of her fingers. "*I* know!" Mary said. "We'll play jacks instead of jump-the-rope. Just you and I. We don't *want* to jump!"

"I've never played jacks either," Esther said.

"You haven't? Well, I'll show you. It's as easy as fun," Mary said.

Always, her whole life, Esther had learned what kind-

ness was. It was to think of others before yourself. It was
to think of their comfort before your own. This Mary
had thought of how hard it would be to jump in a long
dress with high shoes and heavy stockings. A long skirt
would switch and catch in the rope. But jacks—Esther
had never played, but she had watched the others play
at recess several times. It was simple, bouncing a little
ball and picking up first one jack, then two, until you
swept up all eight at the same time.

Mary kept her hand. "We speak for the step!" she cried
the minute they were outside. "Esther and I get the
step!"

The others looked at them in surprise, the two of them
together.

"You jump," Mary said to the girls who usually played
with her. "I've promised to show Esther how to play
jacks. Then we'll all have a game."

So she managed to get them out of the way. They
wouldn't be standing around watching while Esther was
clumsy, as she was learning. The step was sunny and
warm and the maples around the schoolyard were
changing color. The air was golden because of the
leaves. Tossing the ball and picking up the clever little
jackstones was a beautiful thing to be doing. One—two
—three! She felt them sweep into her hand together.

"Good! Good!" Mary said.

When the bell rang she said, "Next time you'll be able
to get them all."

Oh, it was lovely to march beside Mary, proudly into
the school again. Nobody laughed. It was as if Esther
was just like all the rest.

Sometimes Father was so busy that he came later
than the school bus. Esther had never wondered why
she shouldn't go in the bus with the others and save her
father the trouble of leaving his work to come for her.
She knew the reason: Plain People did not ride in ma-

chines. That day it seemed foolish to her for the first time. She remembered Dan coming along the road in the car with the boys. "I always wondered . . ." he had said. "Now I know."

Mary waved to her from the window of the bus. "See you Monday, Esther!" she called. "See you Monday!" For it was Friday today.

Esther had always been glad when it was Friday before. Now she was sorry. There was all that quiet sitting in church between Friday and Monday. No pink girl would be sitting in front of her, but only children in black and gray and purple and dark brown. Her own Sunday dress was the color of dead leaves that had lain under snow all winter long.

She sat on the step to wait, exactly where she had sat at recess a while before. The leaves glowed brighter as the sun lowered. And there seemed to be another glow besides, where Mary had sat bouncing the ball. Being kind. There were kind good people, then, who wore pink. And blue. And red. All colors . . .

She stood up as she heard the buggy coming. Her heart beat fast as if she had been discovered at a mischief. Or with something she had stolen and must hide away.

This story won the 1956 Children's Book Award, given annually by the Child Study Association of America. The author's Miracles on Maple Hill, *published by Harcourt, Brace & World, won the 1957 Newbery Medal.*

Pony Penning Day

BY MARGUERITE HENRY

Illustrations by Wesley Dennis

> *Long ago, when a Spanish galleon was wrecked near the island of Assateague, just off the Virginia coast, the cargo of ponies swam ashore. Paul and his sister Maureen, who live on the neighboring island of Chincoteague, have set their hearts on capturing two of the freedom-loving ponies descended from the survivors of the wreck.*

PONY Penning Day always comes on the last Thursday in July. For weeks before, every member of the Volunteer Fire Department is busy getting the grounds in readiness, and the boys are allowed to help.

"I'll do your chores at home, Paul," offered Maureen, "so's you can see that the pony pens are good and stout."

Paul spent long days at the pony penning grounds. Yet he could not have told how or by whom the tents were rigged up. He hardly noticed when the chutes for the bronco busting were built. He did not know who pounded the race track into condition. All he knew was that the pens for the wild ponies must be made fast. Once the Phantom was captured, she must not escape. Nothing else mattered.

The night before the roundup, he and Maureen made last-minute plans in Phantom's stall. "First thing in the morning," Paul told Maureen, "you lay a clean bed of dried sea grass. Then fill the manger with plenty of marsh grass to make Phantom feel at home."

"Oh, I will, Paul. And I've got some ear corn and some

'lasses to coax her appetite, and Grandma gave me a bunch of tiny new carrots and some rutabagas, and I've been saving up sugar until I have a little sackful."

In the midst of their talk, Grandpa, looking as if he had a surprise, joined them.

"I hain't rode on a roundup to Assateague for two year," he smiled, hiding one hand behind his back, "but I recommember we allus had a chaw and a goody after the ponies was rounded up and afore we swimmed 'em across the channel. Here, Paul," he said, with a strange huskiness, "here's a choclit bar fer ye to take along." And he pressed the slightly squashed candy into Paul's hand.

It was dark and still when Paul awoke the next morning. He lay quiet a moment to gather his wits. Suddenly he shot out of bed.

Today was Pony Penning Day!

His clothes lay on the chair beside his bed. Hurriedly he pulled on his shirt and pants and thudded barefoot down to the kitchen where Grandma stood over the stove, frying ham and making coffee for him as if he were man-grown!

He flung out his chest, sniffing the rich smells, bursting with excitement.

Grandma glanced around proudly. "I picked the first ripe figs of the year fer ye," she exclaimed. "They're chuckful of goodness. Now sit down, Paul, and eat a breakfast fit for a roundup man!"

Paul sat on the edge of his chair. With one eye on the clock he tried to eat the delicious figs and ham, but the food seemed to lump in his throat. Luckily Grandpa and Maureen came downstairs just then and helped clean his plate when Grandma was busy testing her cornbread in the oven with a long wisp of straw.

"I got to go now," Paul swallowed, as he ran out the door. He mounted Watch Eyes, a dependable pony that

Grandpa had never been able to sell because of his white eyes. Locking his bare feet around the pony's sides, he jogged out of the yard.

Maureen came running to see him off.

"Whatever happens," Paul called back over his shoulder, "you be at Old Dominion Point at ten o'clock on a fresh pony."

"I'll be there, Paul!"

"And you, Paul," yelled Grandpa. "Obey yer leader. No matter what!"

Day was breaking. A light golden mist came up out

of the sea. It touched the prim white houses and the white picket fences with an unearthly light. Paul loped along slowly to save his mount's strength. He studied each house with a new interest. Here lived the woman who paid Maureen three dollars for hoeing her potato patch. There lived Kim Horsepepper, the clamdigger they had worked for. Mr. Horsepepper was riding out of his lane now, catching up with Paul. All along the road, men were turning out of their gates.

"Where do you reckon you'll do most good, Bub?" taunted a lean sapling of a man who, on other days, was an oysterman. He guffawed loudly, then winked at the rest of the group.

Paul's hand tightened on the reins. "Reckon I'll do most good where the leader tells me to go," he said, blushing hotly.

The day promised to be sultry. The marsh grass that usually billowed and waved stood motionless. The water of Assateague Channel glared like quicksilver.

Now the cavalcade was thundering over a small bridge

that linked Chincoteague Island to little Piney Island. At the far end of the bridge a scow with a rail fence around it stood at anchor.

In spite of light talk, the faces of the men were drawn tight with excitement as they led their mounts onto the scow. The horses felt the excitement, too. Their nostrils quivered, and their ears swiveled this way and that, listening to the throb of the motor. Now the scow began to nose its way across the narrow channel. Paul watched the White Hills of Assateague loom near. He watched the old lighthouse grow sharp and sharper against the sky. In a few minutes the ride was over. The gangway was being lowered. The horses were clattering down, each man taking his own.

All eyes were on Wyle Maddox, the leader.

"Split in three bunches," Wyle clipped out the directions loud and sharp. "North, south, and east. Me and Kim and the Beebe boy will head east, Wimbrow and Quillen goes north, and Harvey and Rodgers south. We'll all meet at Tom's Point."

At the first sound of Wyle's steam-whistle voice, the sea birds rose with a wild clatter.

"They're like scouts," Paul said to himself. "They're going to warn the wild ponies that the enemy has landed."

"Gee-up!" shouted Wyle as he whirled his horse and motioned Kim and Paul to follow.

Paul touched his bare heels into Watch Eye's side. *They were off!* The boy's eyes were fastened on Wyle Maddox. He and Kim Horsepepper were following their leader like the wake of a ship.

As they rode on, Paul could feel the soft sand give way to hard meadowland, then to pine-laden trails. There were no paths to follow, only openings to skin through—openings that led to water holes or grazing grounds. The three horses thrashed through underbrush, jumped fallen trees, waded brackish pools and narrow, winding streams.

Suddenly Paul saw Wyle Maddox' horse rear into the air. He heard him neigh loudly as a band of wild ponies darted into an open grazing stretch some twenty yards ahead, then vanished among the black tree trunks.

The woods came alive with thundering hooves and frantic horse calls. Through bush and brier and bog and hard marshland the wild ponies flew. Behind them galloped the three riders, whooping at the top of their lungs. For whole seconds at a time the wild band would be swallowed up by the forest gloom. Then it would reappear far ahead—nothing but a flash of flying tails and manes.

Suddenly Wyle Maddox was waving Paul to ride close. "A straggler!" he shouted, pointing off to the left. "He went that-a-way! Git him!" And with a burst of speed Wyle Maddox and Kim Horsepepper were after the band.

Paul was alone. His face reddened with anger. They

wanted to be rid of him. That's what they wanted. Sent after a straggler! He was not interested in rounding up a straggler that couldn't even keep up with the herd! He wanted the Phantom. Then Grandpa's words flashed across his mind. "Obey yer leader. No matter what!"

He wheeled his pony and headed blindly in the direction Wyle had indicated. He rode deeper into the pine thicket, trying to avoid snapping twigs, yet watching ahead for the slightest motion of leaf or bush. He'd show the men, if it took him all day! His thin shirt clung to him damply and his body was wet with sweat. A cobweb veiled itself across his face. With one hand he tried to wipe it off, but suddenly he was almost unseated. Watch Eyes was dancing on his hind legs, his nose high in the air. Paul stared into the sun-dappled forest until his eyes burned in his head. At last, far away and deep in the shadow of the pines, he saw a blur of motion. With the distance that lay between them, it might have been anything. A deer. Or even a squirrel. Whatever it was, he was after it!

Watch Eyes plunged on. There was a kind of glory in pursuit that made Paul and the horse one. They were trailing nothing but swaying bushes. They were giving chase to a mirage. Always it moved on and on, showing itself only in quivering leaves or moving shadows.

What was that? In the clump of myrtle bushes just ahead? Paul reined in. He could scarcely breathe for the wild beating of his heart. There it was again! A silver flash. It looked like mist with the sun on it. And just beyond the mist, he caught sight of a long tail of mingled copper and silver.

He gazed awestruck. "It could be the Phantom's tail," he breathed. "It is! It is! It is! And the silver flash—it's not mist at all, but a brand-new colt, too little to keep up with the band."

The blood pounded in his ears. No wonder the Phan-

tom was a straggler! No wonder she let herself be caught.
"She's got a baby colt!" he murmured.

He glanced about him helplessly. If only he could
think! How could he drive the Phantom and her colt to
Tom's Point?

Warily he approached the myrtle thicket, then
stopped as a hot wave of guilt swept over him. Phantom
and her colt did not want to be rounded up by men. He

could set them free. No one had brought the Phantom in before. No one need ever know.

Just then the colt let out a high, frightened whinny. In that little second Paul knew that he wanted more than anything in the world to keep the mother and the colt together. Shivers of joy raced up and down his spine. His breath came faster. He made a firm resolution. "I'll buy you both!" he promised.

But how far had he come? Was it ten miles to Tom's Point or two? Would it be best to drive them down the beach? Or through the woods? As if in answer a loud bugle rang through the woods. It was the Pied Piper! And unmistakably his voice came from the direction of Tom's Point.

The Phantom pricked her ears. She wheeled around and almost collided with Watch Eyes in her haste to find the band. She wanted the Pied Piper for protection. Behind her trotted the foal, all shining and clean with its newness.

Paul laughed weakly. *He* was not driving the Phantom after all! She and her colt were leading him. They were leading him to Tom's Point!

Tom's Point was a protected piece of land where the marsh was hard and the grass especially sweet. About seventy wild ponies, exhausted by their morning's run, stood browsing quietly, as if they were in a corral. Only occasionally they looked up at their captors. The good meadow and their own weariness kept them peaceful prisoners.

At a watchful distance the roundup men rested their mounts and relaxed. It was like the lull in the midst of a storm. All was quiet on the surface. Yet there was an undercurrent of tension. You could tell it in the narrowed eyes of the men, their subdued voices and their too easy laughter.

Suddenly the laughter stilled. Mouths gaped in disbelief. Eyes rounded. For a few seconds no one spoke at all. Then a shout that was half wonder and half admiration went up from the men. Paul Beebe was bringing in *the Phantom and a colt!*

Even the wild herds grew excited. As one horse, they stopped grazing. Every head jerked high, to see and to smell the newcomers. The Pied Piper whirled out and gathered the mare and her colt into his band. He sniffed them all over as if to make sure that nothing had harmed them. Then he snorted at Phantom, as much as to say, "You cause me more trouble than all the rest of my mares put together!"

The roundup men were swarming around Paul, buzzing with questions.

"How'd you *do* it, Paul?" Wyle Maddox called over the excited hubbub.

"Where'd you find 'em?" shouted Kim Horsepepper.

Paul made no answer. The questions floated around and above him like voices in a dream. He went hot and cold by turns. Did he do the right thing by bringing the Phantom and her foal in? Miserably he watched the Phantom's head droop. There was no wild sweep to her mane and her tail now. The free wild thing was caught like a butterfly in a net. She was webbed in by men, yelling and laughing.

"Beats all!" he heard someone say. "For two years we been trying to round up the Phantom and along comes a spindling youngster to show us up."

"'Twas the little colt that hindered her."

"'Course it was."

"It's the newest colt in the bunch; may not stand the swim."

"If we lose only one colt, it'll still be a good day's work."

"Jumpin' Jupiter, but it's hot!"

The men accepted Paul as one of them now—a real roundup man. They were clapping him on the shoulder and offering him candy bars. Suddenly he remembered the bar Grandpa had pressed into his hand. He took off the wrapper and ate—not because he was hungry, but because he wanted to seem one of the men. They were trying to get him to talk. "Ain't they a shaggy-lookin' bunch?" Kim Horsepepper asked.

"Except for Misty," Paul said, pointing toward the Phantom's colt. "Her coat is silky." The mere thought of touching it sent shivers through him. "Misty," he thought to himself wonderingly. "Why, I've named her!"

The little foal was nursing greedily. Paul's eyes never strayed from the two of them. It was as if they might disappear into the mist of the morning, leaving only the sorrels and the bays and the blacks behind.

Only once he looked out across the water. Two lines of boats were forming a pony-way across the channel. He saw the cluster of people and the mounts waiting on the shores of Chincoteague and he knew that somewhere among them was Maureen. It was like a relay race. Soon she would carry on.

"Could I swim my mount across the channel alongside the Phantom?" Paul asked Wyle Maddox anxiously.

Wyle shook his head. "Watch Eyes is all tuckered out," he said. "Besides, there's a kind of tradition in the way things is handled on Pony Penning Day. There's mounted men for the roundup and there's boatmen to herd 'em across the channel," he explained.

"Tide's out!" he called in clipped tones. "Current is slack. Time for the ponies to be swimmed across. Let's go!"

Suddenly the beach was wild with commotion. From three sides the roundup men came rushing at the ponies, their hoarse cries whipping the animals into action. They plunged into the water, the stallions leading, the mares following, neighing encouragement to their colts.

"They're off!" shouted Wyle Maddox, and everyone felt the relief and triumph in his words.

Kim thumped Paul on the back as they boarded the scow for the ride back. "Don't fret about yer prize," he said brusquely. "You've got the Phantom sure this time. Once in the water she can't turn back."

But he was wrong!

On the shores of Chincoteague the people pressed forward, their faces strained to stiffness, as they watched Assateague Beach.

"Here they come!" The cry broke from every throat.

Maureen, wedged in between Grandpa Beebe on one side and a volunteer fireman on the other, stood on her mount's back. Her arms paddled the air as if she were swimming and struggling with the wild ponies.

Suddenly a fisherman, looking through binoculars, began shouting in a hoarse voice, "A new-borned colt is afeared to swim! It's knee-deep in the water, and won't go no further."

The crowds yelled their advice. "What's the matter with the roundup men?" "Why don't they heft it into deep water—it'll swim all right!" "Why don't they hist it on the scow?"

The fisherman was trying to get a better view. He was crawling out over the water on a wall of piling. It seemed a long time before he put his binoculars to his eyes again. The people waited breathlessly. A small boy began crying.

"Sh!" quieted his mother. "Listen to the man with the four eyes."

"The colt's too little to swim," the fisherman bawled out. "Wait! A wild pony is breaking out from the mob. Swimming around the mob! Escaping!"

An awed murmur stirred the crowds. Maureen dug her toes in her mount's back. She strained her eyes to see the fugitive, but all she could make out was a milling mass of dark blobs on the water.

The fisherman leaned far out over the water. He made a megaphone of one hand. "Them addle-brained boatmen can't stop the pony," his voice rasped. "It's outsmarting 'em all."

Maureen's mind raced back to other Pony Pennings. The Phantom upsetting a boat. The Phantom fleeing through the woods. Always escaping. Always free. She clutched the neck of her blouse. She felt gaspy, like a fish flapping about on dry land. Why was the man with the binoculars so slow? Why didn't he say, "It's the Phantom!" Who else could it be?

Now he was waving one arm wildly. He looked like a straw in the wind. He teetered. He lost his balance. He almost fell into the water in his excitement.

"It's the Phantom!" he screamed at last. "I can see the white map on her shoulders!"

The people took up the cry, echoing it over and over. "It's the Phantom! She's escaped again!"

Maureen felt tears on her cheek, and impatiently brushed them away.

Again the fisherman was waving for quiet.

"Hush!" bellowed Grandpa Beebe.

The people fell silent. They were like listeners around

a microphone. "It's the *Phantom's* colt that won't swim!" he called out in a voice so hoarse it cracked. "The Phantom got separated from a bran'-fire new colt. She's gone back to get it!"

The people whooped and hollered at the news. "The Phantom's got a colt," they sang out. "The Phantom's got a new colt!"

Again the fisherman was waving for silence.

"She's reached her colt!" he crowed. "But the roundup men are closing in on her! They're making her shove the colt in the water. She's makin' it swim!"

Grandpa Beebe cupped his hands around his mouth. "Can the little feller make it?" he boomed.

The crowd stilled, waiting for the hoarse voice. For long seconds no answer came. The fisherman remained as fixed as the piling he stood on. Wave after wave of fear swept over Maureen. She felt as if she were drowning. And just when she could stand the silence no longer, the fisherman began reporting in short, nervous sentences.

"They're half-ways across. Jumpin' Jupiter! The colt! It's bein' sucked down in a whirlpool. I can't see it now. My soul and body! A boy's jumped off the scow. He's swimming out to help the colt."

The onlookers did not need the fisherman with the binoculars any more. They could see for themselves. A boy swimming against the current. A boy holding a colt's head above the swirling water.

Maureen gulped great lungfuls of air. "It's Paul!" she screamed. "It's Paul!"

On all sides the shouts went up. "Why, it's Paul!"
"Paul Beebe!"

Grandpa leaped up on his mount's back as nimbly as a boy. He stood with his arms upraised, his fists clenched.

"God help ye, Paul!" his words carried out over the water. "Yer almost home!"

Grandpa's voice was as strong as a tow rope. Paul was swimming steadily toward it, holding the small silver face of the colt above the water. He was almost there. He *was* there!

Maureen slid down from her mount, clutching a handful of mane. "You made it, Paul! You made it!" she cried.

The air was wild with whinnies and snorts as the ponies touched the hard sand, then scrambled up the shore, their wet bodies gleaming in the sun. Paul half-carried the little colt up the steep bank; then suddenly it found its own legs.

Shouts between triumph and relief escaped every throat as the little filly tottered up the bank. Almost to the top, her feet went scooting out from under her and she was down on the sand, her sides heaving.

Maureen felt a new stab of fear.

If only the big ponies would not crush her! That

tender white body among all those thrashing hooves. What chance had she? What chance with the wild wind for a mother?

But all the wildness seemed to have ebbed out of the Phantom. She picked her forefeet high. Then she carefully straddled her colt, and fenced in the small white body with her own slender legs.

For a brief second Paul's and Maureen's eyes met above the crowds. It was as if they and the mare and her foal were the only creatures on the island. They were unaware of the great jostling and fighting as the stallions sorted out their own mares and colts. They were unaware of everything but a sharp ecstasy. Soon the Phantom and her colt would belong to them. Never to be sold.

The Pied Piper wheeled around Paul. He peered at the dripping boy from under his matted forelock. Then he trumpeted as if to say: "This sopping creature is no mare of mine!" And he pushed Paul out of the way while the crowds laughed hysterically.

Dodging horses and people, Grandpa Beebe made his way over to Paul.

"Paul, boy," he said, his voice unsteady, "I swimmed the hull way with you. Yer the most wonderful and the craziest young'un in the world. Now git home right smart quick," he added, trying to sound very stern. "Yer about done up, and Grandma's expectin' ye. Maureen and I'll see to it that the Phantom and her colt reach the pony pens."

Other exciting horse stories by Marguerite Henry are King of the Wind *and* Justin Morgan Had a Horse, *both published by Rand McNally.*

A Different World

BY MINA LEWITON

Illustrations by Howard Simon

> *Candita had always lived in Puerto Rico. Now all she had to remind her of home was a carved rabbit that her friend Renaldo had given her. She and Mama had flown to New York to join Papa in their new house. Everything was strange—the noise, the subway, and the people. The first night Candita was so tired that she fell asleep right in the middle of a party.*

CANDITA opened her eyes. Nothing looked familiar. Pink and blue crepe paper decorated the ceiling. Then she remembered the airplane. And the subway. And the new family. This is my new house, she thought. I am in New York.

The flowers and the chocolates and the striped candies had disappeared. The two little girls, in white dresses, were playing on a blanket on the floor.

It was Papa's voice: "When I have brought Candita to school, I can go to work. Then Margarita will take you, Rosita, and the little ones, also, to see the school, and to get Candita at the hour of lunch. The time to be at the school is twelve o'clock. As soon as Candita awakes we will go to the school."

Candita sat up, "I am awake," she said.

All the tiredness was gone. She was anxious to see the new school.

Last night, although she had been half-asleep, she had asked Papa to set Renaldo's rabbit on a shelf. There it

263

was, looking down at her. It now seemed an old friend who had come along from Mayagüez.

Candita put on her dress with the design of red flowers, and put on her sneakers. Mama combed Candita's hair smoothly flat, and as they were leaving, Margarita slipped over Candita's shoulders the pink coat that belonged to Fernanda.

"You must wear this coat," Margarita said, opening the window and looking out on the street below. "Everyone is wearing a warm coat today. It is winter once more." Margarita looked at Candita. "It is true this coat is a little large for you." She turned back the cuffs once, and a second time, and Candita's hands were seen again.

Papa and Candita walked downstairs and toward a wide street into which they turned.

"It is Broadway," said Papa. "That is the name of this street."

On either side, the store windows were brimming with color and crowded with remarkable things. Ladies in flower-splashed summer dresses stood stiffly in one window. Candita stared.

"These ladies are artificial ones," said Papa.

Another store window was heaped high with vegetables and green bananas in huge bunches. Dainty high-heeled shoes were arranged in rows in another window, and in still another there were big and little lamps, brightly lighted even though it was daytime.

Candita could not understand a word of what people said to each other as they passed. These people looked different from the people of Mayagüez. They wore dark, more severe clothing. The children, too, did not look or speak like the children of Mayagüez.

"Are they speaking English?"

"It is English. And in a short time you will speak as well as I speak. Even better, perhaps," said Papa modestly. "The school will teach you. You have never seen such a school as the one we are going to."

When they turned the corner they saw it. It was a new school, made, it seemed to Candita, entirely of glass.

The glass doors were as tall as those of a cathedral. Candita and Papa walked through them and came into a sunlit hall. They seated themselves on a bench.

Almost at once, from behind closed doors, they heard an orchestra begin to play. A parade of children of all sizes came walking in pairs down the hall, passing Papa and Candita.

Candita had never seen so many children. The youngest was no larger than Josefina, and the oldest was taller than she was. They looked curiously at her as they passed, and some whispered and laughed.

It was because of her too-large pink coat, she thought. She slipped out of it and put it on the bench beside Papa.

"This school," whispered Papa, "is not too much like the school of Mayagüez."

"No," she whispered back, "it is not too much like my old school."

The children all disappeared through another set of doors.

Papa said, "We shall have to ask how one begins to go to this school." But he continued to sit beside her in the lonely hall.

A door opened and a tall lady came toward them.

"Excuse me," said Papa, "is it possible for Candita to become a pupil of this school? If so, I will give you the information."

Candita was proud of Papa for speaking English so well. Although she did not understand a word of what he said, the lady of the school did.

"How do you do, Candita," she said in Spanish. To Papa she said, "It does not matter that Candita does not speak English. That is, in fact, a good reason for coming to school. Come into my office, please."

Papa answered all the questions. When there were no more questions to answer, he said good-by. To Candita, pressing her hand as if he were leaving to go on a long journey, Papa said softly, "I leave you now. In this school it is necessary to listen carefully." After he had gone a few steps, Papa came back. "And to try to learn English."

The lady of the school took Candita upstairs. Together they went into a classroom.

Four boys and two girls were writing at a table. They stopped writing and stared at Candita.

"This is Miss Singer," the first lady of the school told Candita. "She is your teacher."

To Miss Singer, seated at her desk and facing the children, she said, "This is Candita."

"I am very glad to meet you, Candita." Miss Singer, too, spoke Spanish.

Candita looked long at Miss Singer. Miss Singer's hair was short, and golden as sunlight, and her eyes were the color of the sea. The most beautiful of all were Miss Singer's eyeglasses, which had tiny diamonds around their rims.

Miss Singer said, "Candita, please sit in the chair beside Alvaro. Alvaro, raise your hand."

The boy next to Alvaro raised Alvaro's hand for him.

When Candita had been sitting for a while in the chair beside Alvaro, Miss Singer came to her and said to her alone, and in a low voice, "We are going to be good friends, Candita."

Candita looked up at Miss Singer's beautiful smiling face and could not think of what to say. She nodded instead, rapidly, happily.

"Candita," Miss Singer said, going to the front of the room once more, "as you are going to be in this class from now on, we will explain what we do here. We read and write and learn a little more English each day. For today, Candita, see what the others do. That is enough for this day which is your first."

Miss Singer spoke slow and careful Spanish as if she, Miss Singer, were a little girl in a Mayagüez school beginning to read out of a Spanish book.

"Now Candita, I will present you to Linda and to Carmen. And to Rafael and Barnabe and Alvaro and Luis."

As soon as possible, she would tell Miss Singer about the little school of Mayagüez and about the mango trees of Mayagüez. She would tell her about the edge of the beach and the color of the ocean and the stars of the Puerto Rican night that sparkled like the diamonds of Miss Singer's eyeglasses. She would tell Miss Singer everything.

Miss Singer spoke in English to her class of seven that now included Candita Rivera.

Then Miss Singer said, "Candita, I have just asked the others if they like to come to school. Do you hear what they say, Candita?"

"Yes, Miss Singer," the class chanted together.

Candita nodded.

"Say it, too, Candita."

Candita nodded once more. "Yes, yes," she repeated in a whisper to herself. "Yes, Miss Singer."

Miss Singer walked to a closet and brought back a book for Candita.

"Now, let us open our books," said Miss Singer. "Linda, please begin. Page 9."

Candita, seeing the others open their books, opened hers. There was a picture on each page and there were many words under each picture. She looked intently at the words as if she could truly understand them.

Rafael leaned forward. He showed her the line Linda was reading aloud. She studied the line and tried to follow Linda, but it was as if she were trying to catch running water.

"Not so fast, Linda," said Miss Singer.

Linda came to the end of the page and turned it. Candita turned the page, too. On the next page there was a picture of a squirrel. Miss Singer talked about the squirrel.

Asquirrel. Candita repeated the sound to herself. It was a little like a Spanish word. *Asquirrel, asquirrel.* If Miss Singer would ask her, she could say this new word, too, but when Miss Singer told the class to say the new word aloud, Candita only whispered it again.

All morning she hoped Miss Singer would come and

sit beside her as she had done for a little while with
Alvaro. She could then begin to describe to Miss Singer
a few of the things of Mayagüez.

Almost at the end of the morning, Miss Singer did
come to sit beside her.

"Candita," Miss Singer said, drawing a chair up, "you
will never learn English if I speak to you in Spanish.
That is why I must speak English to you. Try to answer
in English, too. It doesn't matter if you do not speak perfectly at first."

Candita nodded.

"At first I will try to speak more slowly to you than to
the others. We will begin at once. From now on we speak
English. That is the way to learn English quickly, Candita."

Miss Singer had said they were going to be good
friends. But how could she speak to her friend in a language she, Candita, did not know?

"I will speak very slowly," Miss Singer repeated, but
it was as if she were saying, *You must not talk to me,
Candita, not unless you speak English.* It would be a long
time before she would learn enough English to talk to
Miss Singer, she thought.

Candita looked away from Miss Singer and down at
her desk, giving all her attention to listening, as Papa had
said. She tried very hard to listen to each word and to
understand. She tried so hard, her ears ached with trying. It was no use. She did not begin to understand.

How had it happened? A little while ago everything

had seemed right and good. Now everything was changed. How can I ever learn English quickly? she thought. How can I *begin* to learn?

The children, one after the other, read from the book. Candita looked out of the window at the cool blue sky. She was alone in a strange, new, cold land where people talked an unknown language. At this moment in Mayagüez the sun was hot and the air warm and the trees and bushes bright with flowers. The beach was wide and the waves made a soft crashing sound.

She could see it as if she were truly there. She and Paquita Reyes used to play all day and talk. That had been the best of all, the talks with Paquita while Paquita watched her make little figures out of damp sand and clay.

In the hall a gong rang loud and deep. Its echoing sound hung in the air.

Everyone in the classroom began to talk.

Linda leaned toward her. "Now we can talk Spanish. Where did you come from? What day was it when you arrived? Was it raining? When I came it rained. We were wet and we were cold."

"I came from Mayagüez," Candita said, "the neighborhood of Buena Vista."

"And I, too, but from the neighborhood of Dulces Lavios."

It was like home. Listening to Linda was like Mayagüez and like home.

"Sit with me," the girl named Carmen said. "Eat your lunch here beside me, Linda. We can all sit together. You, too, Candita. I have been in this class two months."

"And I four months," said Barnabe. "When I came I could not speak. I was like you."

"She is a little shy," said Carmen. "You were not so shy."

"She is a shy one, you are right," said Barnabe, laughing again.

"Where are you going, Candita?" Linda asked. "All of us stay in school for our lunch."

Candita shook her head. Mama and Margarita and the children would be waiting for her as they had agreed. She hurried downstairs.

Instead of Margarita and Mama and the children, Fernanda had come.

"There was not enough work for a whole day in the factory so I came to walk home with you. Margarita has taken the little ones to the park." Fernanda put her arm around Candita's shoulders. "Well, how is this school?"

"They speak English."

"It is strange," said Fernanda, "when one does not understand, no?"

"Yes," said Candita, "it is strange."

"I went to school for a few evenings but I could not learn. It was as if the English words escaped from me. I have no ear for words. But children learn quickly," Fernanda said, looking anxiously at Candita. "Do not worry."

The English words escape from me, also, Candita thought. I, too, am one of those who have no ear for words. Fernanda knew how strange it was not to understand, but Fernanda did not have to go to school. Fernanda did not know that one was all alone in a classroom when one could not understand.

Perhaps Mama will feel as I do, she thought. Mama had already found it too cold here. She will want to return, too. Then we will all go back to Mayagüez. I hope so. I truly hope so.

She did not say this to Fernanda. Perhaps, when they reached the apartment, Mama would say it herself. Perhaps she would say it today. Candita began to walk more quickly.

But Mama did not talk of returning home.

They had been reading about the squirrel all week.

"Rafael," said Miss Singer, "what is the squirrel's name?"

"Bushy," said Rafael promptly, standing up.

"His whole name," said Miss Singer. "What is the squirrel's whole name? Like your whole name. Your whole name is Rafael Muñoz, isn't it?"

"That is my name," said Rafael. "And the squirrel's name is Bushy."

Alvaro raised his hand.

"Tell us, Alvaro," said Miss Singer.

"Bushy Tail," said Alvaro.

"That is right," said Miss Singer. "Very good, Alvaro." She turned to Candita and said slowly, "You see, Candita, Alvaro came only a few weeks before you to this class. Already he understands what we are saying. Alvaro learns quickly."

Candita looked at Alvaro. It seemed to her he had not understood either.

"Alvaro," said Miss Singer, "tell us how you came to New York."

Alvaro stood up and smiled but did not answer. He shook his head and lightly shrugged his shoulders.

"Alvaro, did you come from San Juan?"

"San Juan," repeated Alvaro.

"Where is San Juan?"

Alvaro looked over his shoulder.

"In Puerto Rico?" asked Miss Singer.

"Yes," said Alvaro. "Puerto Rico."

"How did you come?" said Miss Singer.

"I come here," said Alvaro.

"How?" said Miss Singer. "Did you walk?" Miss Singer walked the forefinger of each hand on her desk.

"Yes," said Alvaro, wishing to be agreeable. He smiled at the walking fingers.

All the children laughed. Alvaro laughed, too.

"On the water? You walked across the water from San Juan to New York?" asked Miss Singer, raising her eyebrows.

Candita held her breath and listened to each word. Why were they laughing? She, too, would say *Yes* to every one of Miss Singer's questions. The children would laugh at her just as they were laughing at Alvaro.

Alvaro was brave. She would not laugh, Candita thought. More likely she would cry. Yes, she would surely cry. She was very sorry for Alvaro.

Miss Singer began all over again. "Alvaro, did you come from San Juan to New York?"

"Yes," said Alvaro, still smiling.

"Did you come on a plane to New York?"

"Ah, yes," said Alvaro, understanding at last. "Plane."

"In a plane. You did not walk on the water."

"Ah, no," said Alvaro.

The children could not stop laughing.

Miss Singer held up her hand for silence and said to Alvaro, "Was it a big plane?"

"Big," said Alvaro.

"Yes," said Miss Singer patiently, "in a big plane. Sit down, Alvaro."

Alvaro dropped into his seat and drew a deep breath.

Miss Singer wrote in a book.

In the little silence, Candita made up her mind: she would not say a single word. She would listen and say nothing. Even when she understood Miss Singer's question and knew the answer, too. Only when she could talk like Miss Singer would she talk in school. Not a day before then. Not in English. Only if Miss Singer talked to her in Spanish would she answer her.

She would not talk like a small child. She would not say *big, plane, yes, no.* She would speak English when she could talk about the shining ocean and the skimming clouds and the airport and the baby crying because it was a strange, new, cold land.

She would wait. She would wait until she could talk well enough so they would all say, *Candita speaks well. She understands and speaks English very well. Was Candita born in New York?* She would wait until someone could say, *It seems to me Candita speaks as if she were born in New York. . . .*

"Come here, Candita," said Miss Singer. "Help me with these crayons, please."

Candita sat still. *Come here* were words she knew, but now she looked away from Miss Singer.

In her slow, careful, childish Spanish, Miss Singer said, "Come here, Candita. Stand beside my desk."

Candita stood up and came to Miss Singer's desk.

In Spanish, Candita said, "Here I am."

Miss Singer looked disappointed.

"Now, girls and boys," said Miss Singer turning to the others, "take three crayons each from Candita. Candita will come to you with the crayon box. Help yourselves from the box." She gave Candita a flat wide box full of crayons of all colors. "After you have chosen your crayons draw something that you saw yesterday. What day was yesterday, Luis?"

"Yesterday it was Sunday," said Luis, standing up and speaking in a loud voice.

"Yes, yesterday was Sunday. Where did you go, Luis?"

"I go to the zoo," said Luis.

"I *went* to the zoo," said Miss Singer.

"You, too?" said Luis, pointing at Miss Singer.

Everyone except Alvaro and Candita laughed.

"No, I did not go," said Miss Singer, "but you must say, 'I *went* to the zoo.'"

"O.K.," said Luis. "I went to the zoo."

"Did you understand, Candita?"

Candita said nothing.

Miss Singer said in Spanish, "Please go from one to another so they may choose the crayons. Then do as the others do, Candita. Draw a picture."

Candita went with the crayons from one to the other. When everyone had taken crayons out of the box, Candita chose for herself a blue, a red, and a yellow. They were new and bright in color and smelled pleasantly of wax in the warm room. Then she went to her own chair.

Alvaro had begun to draw rapidly. Candita watched him. He, too, had been recently at the zoo, Candita thought, for he was drawing a giraffe. She knew what the zoo was and what a giraffe was because Papa had taken her and Margarita's little girls to the zoo. They had all seen the giraffe the first Sunday Candita had been in New York.

Candita began to draw on her paper. Blue for the sky with white uneven spaces left for clouds. Among the clouds Candita drew an airplane. Beneath all of it she drew a dark blue sea.

When she had finished, she saw that Rafael was looking at her picture. He said in Spanish to her, "This is a good picture."

"It is a scene I remember," said Candita.

"I, too," said Rafael. "The picture you have made recalls it to me."

Candita said, "Far below our plane were a thousand little mirrors."

"I remember that also," said Rafael.

Miss Singer said, "Remember, we speak English in the classroom. Are you speaking English, Rafael?"

"She does not yet understand English," said Rafael.

Miss Singer shook her head slowly at Rafael.

Candita went on drawing. She put some tiny patches of yellow over the blue of the sea and these places began to look like sunlight on water. More and more it seemed to her to resemble the ocean she had flown over. She did not speak to Rafael. Rafael spoke, instead, to Barnabe and to Linda in English.

On another sheet Candita began to draw a dog, asleep, forelegs stretched out.

Miss Singer walked by and stopped to watch her drawing. She said, "We have clay, too, Candita."

Candita did not answer but she stopped drawing. Miss Singer went to the cupboard and took from it a box of green clay.

"Do you know what to do with this, Candita?"

Candita glanced at the box and almost forgot she had decided not to answer Miss Singer in English. "Yes, yes," she wanted to say. There were pictures of clay animals on the box cover. She knew at once what the clay was for. The clay was like the wet sand of Mayagüez beach but much, much better.

She modeled the sleeping dog out of the clay, giving him a mild, peaceful expression. Then she made a squirrel, looking watchful. She would have made many more animals but these two had used up the whole box of clay.

"Everyone can see them here," Miss Singer said, putting Candita's animals on the window sill, each beside a white-potted geranium.

It seemed to Candita that the whole room looked friendlier now that her animals were on the window sill.

Among Mina Lewiton's many books are Rachel, and Rachel and Herman, stories about children who learn the ways of their parents' adopted country. Both are published by Franklin Watts.

Bright April

BY MARGUERITE DE ANGELI

Illustrations by the author

> *April Bright is a Brownie Scout. Her skin is the color of coffee with good cream in it. "Why must we be different?" April asks her mother. "I don't feel different."*

THE trolley car swayed and bumped along German-town Avenue. Past the Market Square, down the hill, past the five-and-ten-cent store, across the wide street where the market stood and where there was a movie and several big stores. The car swung screeching around another bend and threw April against the back of the seat that ran crosswise. She bumped the place where the dentist had just fixed her tooth. It hurt a little. When she cried, "Ouch!" a curly head in a blue bonnet popped up over the seat back and two blue eyes looked gravely into April's. A tiny pink finger pointed at her, and the little girl said:

"You're brown!"

The child's mother looked startled, but April's mamma just smiled and said:

"Yes, she's brown, and you're pink. Isn't she a nice warm color?" But the little girl didn't answer, and she and her mother got off the car. April's smile faded, and she turned to ask:

"Am I brown, Mamma?"

"Yes, of course. You are just the color of coffee with good cream in it." Mamma squeezed April's gloved hand.

"And you are just like your name and the month you were born in; dark April one minute and bright April the next!" She pressed the button for the next stop.

April felt the place where the tooth had been fixed. It wasn't so bad going to the dentist after all. Besides, it was fun to see the store windows and to ride in the trolley, especially on the way back. How she had dreaded it! Now, it was all over and the broken corner was mended. Now she could laugh about it. She and Tom had run into each other near the stairs the other day, and somehow, April's tooth was broken. Probably it was Tom's drumstick that struck her. He was never without those drumsticks; never for a moment. Papa sometimes slipped them away from under Tom's pillow after he was asleep, but Tom always woke up and discovered his loss. He looked so forlorn in his sleepiness that Papa always gave them back to him.

"The trouble is," Papa scolded, "your mind is on those drumsticks when it ought to be on something else. If you had been looking where you were going instead of rattling the sticks on the railing you wouldn't have broken April's tooth. You can't even study your lessons without tapping on the books or on the desk, and you nearly drive your mother crazy with your eternal beating on something."

Tom tested the sound of everything he came near. He filled the house with "bong-a-di-bong-bong" on the bathtub; "clickety-click-click" on the talcum-powder can; "tap, tap-a-tap" on the edge of the stairs as he came down, then "rattle-tick-tattle" on the banister spindles. He came out to the kitchen, touching every piece of furniture on the way, keeping time to his steps. He ended with a loud banging on the pot lid where Mamma was cooking, till she held her ears and begged him to stop. But sometimes he played a rhythm that set everybody in tune. April whisked the dishes off the table in time to it; Chris, if she was home, pranced and gestured till Papa started clapping his hands in a pattern of sound, and even Mamma must stop whatever she was doing and sit down at the piano and fashion a tune to match. Ken would have loved it all, but Ken was in the Army.

It was bitter cold when Mamma and April stepped off the trolley car, but they had only a short way to walk, and though it was against the wind and the streets were icy, they were soon turning in at their own gate.

"I hope Papa is home and the house is warm," April said.

"Yes, and *I* hope there is a letter from Ken and that Christine comes home for the week end."

April was always glad to get inside the house, where it was pleasant and clean, even though some of the houses just a few doors down the street were tumble-down and ill-kept. Mr. Bright was home. He had finished his work and built a fire in the fireplace, which was the kind called a Baltimore heater. He sat before the fire reading and dozing, with his feet on a stool, as usual, to rest them, for his work took him on a fifteen-mile walk every day. He was a postman. Today was Saturday, so there had been only one mail delivery and the walk was shorter. But it was hard walking on the streets that were covered with layer on layer of ice and snow, and the heavy shoes and galoshes were tiring. It was the coldest winter for many years, and Papa said many of the people he served hadn't been out of the house for weeks.

"If I didn't bring them letters and papers," he said, "I guess they wouldn't know anything that's going on in the world." He enjoyed his work, carrying messages of help and good will to people. Even those that brought sad news made him feel close to them.

"Only this morning," he continued, "I delivered a letter to a mother whose boy is still in an Army hospital. I remember when that boy was little and when he first started to school. I remember when he went away," he finished sadly. Then he laughed. "I guess I'm kind of a heart-throb in the community. Sometimes I'm Cupid, sometimes I'm Santa Claus, sometimes I'm The Law." April hugged him.

"Next week," she reminded him, "you'll be Cupid. It's nearly Valentine's Day, remember?"

"Yes," said Mamma as she went to hang up her things, "and we'd better be sure to get Ken's letter off today or it won't reach him in time. April, you begin." April sat down to write.

There was always family news to tell. Homely things like what they had for supper, or that Tom was helping Mr. Meyer in the drugstore on Saturdays. Exciting things like Uncle James being appointed as teacher in that famous music school in New York, or Chris getting her nurse's cap. April knew how proud Ken was of her for being admitted to training when she was so young, barely seventeen. Mamma said Ken would be interested to hear that the leaky roof over the kitchen had been mended and that Papa put new boards in the back porch where they had rotted away. Just as she reached this point, she heard shrill whistling and a "rattle-rattle-stop-stop" on the iron railing, and "So long, Nick!" So she knew it was suppertime. Maybe Sis would come home tonight! She finished off her part of the family letter with a valentine drawing. Ken said he liked letters with her pictures best.

All through the evening, and until after church on Sunday, they looked for Sis. When she didn't come Mamma consoled April, saying:

"We know there aren't enough nurses to go around. Chrissy has just had to give up her free day again to help. It is hard for her, but she is young and strong."

April liked to have Sis come home. She brought

strange and interesting stories about the patients in the hospital, and since she had been living away from home, she seemed like company. She looked so neat and trim in her uniform that April thought she, herself, would like to be a nurse too. Then she remembered that she and Sophie had planned to be teachers like Miss Bell. Sophie lived on Germantown Avenue, where her papa kept a drugstore. She was in the same grade at school as April and belonged to the same Brownie Scout troop.

Monday, when April came home from school, there were letters from Sis and from Ken. Sure enough, Chris had stayed on duty because one of the other student nurses was away on leave.

Ken wrote, "I may get home soon, but don't count on it too much because some of us have to stay here. It seems like a waste of time now, and we are all so anxious to get started on our jobs at home. I don't mind doing my bit, but I'd like to be sure of what we are coming home to." April wondered what he meant. Here was home just as it had always been. What could he mean?

Mamma said, "He means he hopes there will be a place for him to use the training he has been getting in architecture at State College." April still didn't know what he meant. But she knew from Mamma's look that it meant something to be anxious about.

Wednesday of the next week was Valentine's Day. As usual, it was cold and sleety, so April carried the valentine she had made for Miss Bell under her coat. Some of the other children carried valentines too. April couldn't help wondering if any of them were for her. They put them all into a big box Miss Bell had ready.

"This afternoon we will play post office and deliver them," she promised. After lunch, when the reading lesson was finished, Miss Bell gave them each bright red paper and crayons to make more valentines. April

made one for Sophie and one for Mamma. It was fun
when the box was opened. James was the postman. His
valentine for Miss Bell was a picture of herself. It
showed the comb in her hair, the dimple in her chin,
and the little mole on her neck, and even the way she
wrinkled her forehead. He didn't mean it to be funny,
but it was, a little. Miss Bell said she felt very flattered.
She liked the valentine April made, too, with its paper
lace cut with Mamma's nail scissors. She read the verse
aloud.

> "There's some words I cannot spell
>   Why it is I cannot tell.
> This I think you know, Miss Bell,
>   (I know Love begins with L)
> Anyway I write this line
>   To tell you you're my valentine."

It had been hard to find things to rhyme with "Bell,"
but when April remembered "L" for love, it had sounded
pretty good, she thought. The words were a little
crowded at the end, and she had crased "valentine"
twice before she got it spelled right. The paste smeared
when she put on the paper lace, but Papa said it looked
just as it ought for a little girl to give to her teacher.

April's name was called twice for a valentine. One
said, "Guess who?" and April felt sure it was from

Sophie, for when she looked up, Sophie's eyes were smiling at her over her hands that covered her mouth. Then the box was empty, and the hands on the clock pointed to nearly closing time.

Miss Bell quieted the chatter in the room with a motion of her hands, then said, "This week we celebrated Lincoln's Birthday, and we have had Valentine's Day. Next week we have another birthday. Do you know whose—Edith?" She nodded at Edith, who raised her hand.

"It's Danny's birthday next week. He'll be a year old." The boys shouted with laughter, and Edith sat down in confusion.

"No, dear." Miss Bell smiled at her. "I didn't mean Danny or anyone in our families. I mean someone we all know about and honor." Hands went flying up all over the room. April knew. She waved her hand wildly. Papa had said only last night that he would have a holiday on the twenty-second. "It's——" But before she could get the teacher's attention it came from half a dozen voices.

"Washington's Birthday! Washington's Birthday!" Everyone tried to make himself heard at once, saying it over and over till Miss Bell said, "SSHH! SSHH! Quiet, please!"

The closing bell sounded, and it was time to go home.

There was another letter from Ken. Papa read it at the supper table. In it, Ken said, "How I wish I could see you all. I'm still hoping but it will be some time before I get home. Lots of the fellows have gone, but it looks as if *I* will be here for a long while. If only there will be *real* peace when I do come home, this time spent so far away from you would not seem so endless."

April looked at Mamma anxiously, but Mamma kept her eyes down. The letter went on: "We heard the concert last night and I thought of you listening too. I could see Pop sitting there with his feet up, and you, Mother, in and out of the room, listening when you could. April, I suppose, was on the floor with the back page of the newspaper and Tom coming along from helping Mr. Meyer in the drugstore, whistling and rattling those everlasting drumsticks. . . ." He didn't write much more, but they all knew how much he wanted to come home. His room was all ready for him, and Mamma had washed the downstairs curtains, too, so the house would look welcoming.

Papa was the first to speak.

"Well," he said, trying to be cheerful, "we shall just hope and pray that he will be home soon for good, and we can at least be thankful that the work they are doing is helping to carry out the things we all believe are necessary for peace."

It was very disappointing.

"Chris will come home this week end, anyway," said April, hoping to make Mamma smile. And she did!

At four o'clock on Thursday it was time for Brownie meeting. April loved being a Brownie, but she was eager to be a real Scout when she was ten. Sophie was a Brownie, too, and the girls never separated without saying their secret password, D.Y.B. The girls could hardly wait for the day to come each week, for Mrs. Cole, their leader, always had something interesting for them to do. Usually it was something they could make, but sometimes she asked Flicker to come and talk to them and show them pictures. "Flicker" was her Scout name, and in summer she was a counselor at the Scout Camp. She told them about the trees and how to tell one kind from another.

"You can always tell from the seeds," she said, "so it is a good plan to learn about the seed first."

She told them about the birds, too, and how to recognize them. Already April had heard the cardinal singing, and she had seen the flash of red as he flew across the snow-filled yard. She had listened to the ridiculous chatter of the grackles that collected on the telephone wire outside the bedroom window too. The Brights' back yard was an ideal place for birds, for it was filled with old shrubbery and there were old trees all around. The neighborhood had once been good and the gardens well planted.

Flicker told the girls to watch for other birds that would come later as spring advanced, and cautioned them to be very still if they wanted to be wise in the ways of birds.

"Watch carefully," she warned, "and never make a sudden move. Birds are more easily startled by quick movement than by sound. Notice how the birds conceal their nests. While carrying building material or food for the young, they alight somewhere not too near the nest and wait to see if all is safe, then dart to the nest."

Flicker taught them to make a wren house too.

"Though wrens will build almost anywhere," she said. "Once they built a nest in the pocket of my father's trousers hung out to dry. They like to go under wood-piles or overturned boats and such places to find the spiders and bugs."

April thought she would remember to watch and see if the little birds went under the woodpile Papa kept for the Baltimore heater. Flicker promised a treat for the girls in the troop who could recognize the greatest number of birds. April noticed the trees, too, since Flicker had told them about the different kinds and how they grew. It made them seem like friends to know them by name.

Now Mrs. Cole was showing the girls how to make the most exciting things. "It will teach you to remember how necessary these things are to health and better

living if you make them and see what they are for," she said. But the girls liked to do them because they were fun, because they liked to be at Mrs. Cole's house, and because they liked to be together.

They were making two miniature tents like the ones used at the Scout Camp, and all the things needed to furnish them. Sophie's mamma, Mrs. Meyer, gave them a piece of unbleached muslin for one, and for the other,

Mrs. Bright gave them a piece of green denim left from the couch cover. The girls saved up ketchup-bottle caps for buckets, and smaller bottle tops for cooking pots. Wire from milk-bottle tops made good handles. The inside flat cap that is used for sealing the bottles was just right for plates; acorn tops would be fine for cups, and April found some in the little park near Greene Street.

Mrs. Cole allowed them to whittle out tiny wooden spoons, but no girl was allowed to use a knife until she had found a place to work large enough to stretch out her arms in all directions. Then, if the knife slipped, she wouldn't be likely to hurt anyone else. Small twigs and branches were fine for tent poles and uprights, and for legs for the table and stools. At first they made things too large, until Mrs. Cole reminded them:

"Just imagine that you are standing inside the tent by this little table we are making, and think how small these things would be."

April almost could feel herself growing small like Alice in Wonderland, and imagined that she was sitting on that tiny stool made of twigs and a bottle cap. That helped. She made the spoons so tiny that the first one broke, but after that they went better. She was so successful with them that Mrs. Cole asked her to show the other girls how she did it. The secret lay in using a single-edged razor blade that Papa had given her. April carried it in an aspirin box and used it to sharpen her pencils.

April explained, "You can take off such little bitsy shavings with it, and it's so thin it doesn't press too hard. The knife is stiff."

Sophie and Helen were working on the little chest of drawers to hold the spoons and other tableware. The drawers were small-size matchboxes glued together with paper pasted around to make them look like wood. For drawer handles they were using small glass beads put on with fine wire. The chest of drawers looked very real.

It was the day before Washington's Birthday. Papa had gone off long ago on his mail route, and Mamma stood at the door making sure that Tom and April wore their rubbers and were well buttoned up, for it was very cold again. She frowned at the littered street. Ashes and papers tumbled out of containers where they had been left for collection. It had rained, thawed, snowed, and frozen, layer on layer, until it was almost impossible to walk. Papa and several others in the neighborhood tried to keep the street clean and orderly, but even Papa couldn't do much with the thick layer of dirty ice that packed the walk. He and Tom did bring in the unemptied ashes to wait another week. But the men who gathered the trash were asking for more pay so they could live decently, and refused to work until they got it. Papa said he didn't blame them, but he did wish they would collect the trash. Some of the people in the block took no thought for the appearance of their houses inside or out. Some of them were not careful even of their own appearance. The children went to school in clothing that was not clean, with hair unbrushed and hands and faces unwashed. One of the children sat near April in school. She didn't like it.

"Maybe the teacher will think I'm like that!" she complained.

But Mamma reasoned with her.

"You will just have to be a little extra-careful and particular," she said, "and never fear! The teachers know which children are well cared for and the ones who are not. Perhaps if your daddy weren't so good at mending and fixing things we would find it harder to keep clean too. I know that most of these old houses along here have no heat except the one stove. The water freezes in

the pipes, and it takes a lot of water to keep a family
clean. Most of the roofs leak, too, and you know how
miserable that could be. Then, as the houses become
older and more run down, the neighborhood changes."
Mamma tucked April's collar in, and she ran to catch
up with Sophie.

One of the first things Miss Bell talked about that
morning was the disorder of the streets. She spoke in
assembly so all the children could hear.

"We are each one of us responsible for the cleanliness
of our neighborhood. If the wagons do not come to take
the trash away, then we must keep it put away neatly
until they do come. How many of you will promise to
go home this afternoon and do your part in cleaning up
the streets?" Almost every child put up his hand. Then
she talked for a while about the importance of cleanliness and neatness.

"If we are clean and neat about our homes and about
ourselves," she said, "we will be healthier and we will
respect ourselves. How can we expect others to respect
us if we don't respect ourselves?"

April was glad that Mamma was so particular about
keeping her clean and neat. She looked at Tom, who
sat on the other side of the assembly room. Yes, he looked
shining clean too.

There was a little play about George Washington,
with one of the boys dressed in knee breeches and a
cocked hat. One of the girls wore a cap and a fichu to
represent Martha Washington. When the classes went
back to their rooms, Miss Bell talked more about Washington. Then she spoke of other men and women in our
nation's history who had given their time, their fortunes,
and sometimes their lives, in order that we might have
a more perfect union. She reminded the class that this
country is for *all*, and that to be unfair or unkind to

anyone because of his race or religion is neither Christian nor American.

April remembered hearing Papa say the same thing only the night before. He had been reading an article aloud to Mamma, which said that some of the soldiers were not allowed to go to the regular canteens but had to go off by themselves. She knew, too, that Miss Bell was thinking of the quarrel among some of the boys in the schoolyard the other day.

Now, standing in front of the class, Miss Bell stopped looking so sober as she asked, "Who can tell us something about Washington?"

Many hands went up. She called on David, who stood up and said, "He was a surveyor." And sat down.

"Yes, he was a surveyor," Miss Bell nodded. "What else?"

One after another told about his being in the French and Indian War, about his home in Virginia, and about the terrible winter with the troops at Valley Forge.

"How many of you realize that Valley Forge is just a few miles from Germantown?" Miss Bell asked. Some of the children raised their hands. She looked at April. "My mother used to tell of a woman she knew whose great-grandmother was a little girl who lived at Valley Forge. She was just about your age, April, and she was commended by Washington for carrying water for his men." Then she called on Hallie, who had raised her hand. "Hallie?"

Hallie had lately moved to Philadelphia from the South. She still spoke in her soft Southern voice. "We used to live right near Wakefield," she said.

"Tell the boys and girls what Wakefield is. I don't think they know." Miss Bell encouraged Hallie to go on.

"Wakefield is the home where Washington lived as a boy," said Hallie.

Then she told about the sturdy brick house that had been built to look much like the one that had burned down. She said the front lawn went down clear to the James River and was kept trim by a flock of white sheep. She told about the beautiful gardens there and how many of the plants were still growing from the very ones that had been there in Washington's time. There were herbs as well as flowers: tansy and dill, rosemary and summer savory, bleeding heart and primrose. She said there was a large dovecote in the center of the garden, with doves flying in and out, and there was an old, old man who tended the garden and loved it. Sometimes he gave her mother herbs for cooking.

"That is fine, Hallie!" said Miss Bell. "That sort of story makes Washington seem like a real person."

Then the others were eager to tell things they remembered. Several told of ancestors who had fought in the Revolution, or had lived right there in Germantown while the Battle of Germantown was being fought. One boy still lived in the house where his great-great-grandfather had lived. It was just around the corner from the famous Chew mansion, which had stood in the thick of the battle.

April wished she knew something to tell.

Just then Miss Bell spoke to her. "April, why don't you tell us about the first man to be killed in the Boston Massacre?" But April said she didn't know about that.

"You don't? Why, he was one of your people, and his name was Crispus Attucks. Another was Peter Salem, who was killed in the Battle of Bunker Hill. And there were many others who helped to fight the battle of liberty. Aren't you proud?" April *was* proud. She looked over at Edith, and they smiled at each other.

Miss Bell went on talking.

"It's time we got on with our other work," she said, "but there is another name I wanted to mention. There was one man who did more, perhaps, than any other to provide funds for the Revolution. He gave his time and fortune to support the cause of liberty, not knowing whether the money would ever be returned. You know it takes a great deal of money to carry on a war. Sophie, I wonder if you know whom I mean?" But Sophie did not know and had nothing to say. Not one of the children knew, not even Bernie, who sometimes knew things that the others didn't. "Well, Sophie, his name was Haym Solomon. You ask your father to tell you about him. Now, we shall get on with spelling."

Just before school closed that afternoon Miss Bell reminded them about cleaning up the trash in the streets.

"You will have a holiday tomorrow to honor Washington. Just imagine that he is coming to Germantown, and try to make your streets fit for him to walk in. He used to walk in these streets, as you know. He came to Germantown in the summer to escape the heat of the city, for this was a country town then. He used to live in the Morris house right here on the Market Square. If you pretend Washington is coming to Germantown perhaps it will help you see things to do to make the streets look better. If you work steadily and happily together, it won't take so long. Remember now! *Clean streets!*"

It sounded quite fine when Miss Bell talked about it, but when April and Sophie came out of the schoolyard and saw the street as it might look to a stranger, it was pretty discouraging. Even the sidewalks were covered to a depth of three or four inches with dirty ice and frozen snow in which ashes had been strewn to make walking safe. Here and there along the way, boxes of empty cans and papers stood, overflowing onto the walks. They had stood there so long that rain had melted the cartons and all the trash lay in heaps. It was not a pretty sight, and April wished that the men would come along to collect it. She didn't know where to begin. It

was thawing a little, and a gurgle of water showed where ice had worn away near the gutter. April wished she could put off getting to work. She wished she could be on the safety patrol like Tom. There he stood down the street in his white patrol belt, helping the little children across Germantown Avenue. He held his drumsticks in one hand, using them as a signal to call the children, or held them up and rattled them for cars to stop. He looked very important.

April left Sophie at the corner and turned toward home.

"D.Y.B.," she called.

"D.Y.B.!" answered Sophie, and for some reason, remembering that secret sign made it easier to set to work.

April could see her father already busy in front of the house. He looked up when she came through the gate. "We must work on this ice while it is thawing," he said. "Get me a pail of water, that's a good girl."

April went in to get it. Mamma was in the kitchen coaxing the fire so the water would be hot. Together they carried water and broom and helped get the steps and the walk cleared. Then suddenly it began to freeze again. Little crinkles formed in the clean water, and a thin coating of glary ice covered the place they had just done.

"Oh, well," Papa sighed as he straightened his tired back, "at least it is cleaner looking, and tomorrow it may thaw again."

The next morning there were several of the neighbors out to help the girls and boys fulfill their promise. Sometimes long-lost articles were found in the trash. Tom found a piece of wire that he could use for the radio. April found a perfectly good magazine with fashion pictures that she could use for her paper dolls, and some baby-food cans that were just right for the miniature camp they were making at Brownie meetings.

The boys carted the trash to a vacant lot, and Mr. Bright was able to get some large cans from the Park Guard to hold it till it could be collected. Just when she was getting very tired of working April found a quarter! It was frozen in the ice where a box had been standing, but she dug it out with Tom's help. He tried to tell her that part of it belonged to him because he helped to get it out, but he was only fooling. A lot could be done with a quarter. What should it be?

At Brownie meeting that afternoon, Mrs. Cole gave the girls a surprise. She had asked Flicker to come and show them magic-lantern pictures of old trees that had

been growing since Washington's time. Some of them were right here in Germantown. Mrs. Cole promised that one day soon, when the weather improved, they would take a long hike up the Wissahickon Creek and perhaps find some of those old trees. They would take sandwiches and stay all day.

"Perhaps Flicker can go with us," she suggested. She was clearing a place on the table as she spoke and setting out the materials to work with. April brought out the baby-food tins she had found, and Mrs. Cole found a lid that fitted one of them. She set April to work whittling a tiny wooden knob for a handle. Then they fastened it on with a piece of wire and a bead to hold it underneath. It looked just like a real trash can! Felicia Marcolina hadn't finished hemming the tent, but some of the other girls helped her to set it up, anyway, just to see how it would look. April loved it. She wished she were really small enough to get inside the little tent; it looked so real. Mrs. Cole came in from the kitchen with a tray full of baskets.

"Since this is Washington's Birthday, I thought we would celebrate," she said. The baskets were filled with candies, and on the handle of each was a small American flag and a slip of paper with each girl's name and the secret sign of the troop.

"These are to remind us that we are all Americans," Mrs. Cole explained as she set the other baskets around the tent. "I hope you will keep the flag where you can see it every day, and that it will remind you to be real Americans and good Brownie Scouts."

Then she spoke of how much better the street looked and how proud she was of the Brownies. She began to sing the Brownie song, and the girls joined in:

> "We're the Brownies, here's our aim—
> Lend a hand and play the game,
> Where the Brownies live and play,
> That is where I love to stay."

They fastened the flags to their Brownie dresses and began to chatter and eat, all talking at once, comparing the number of candies in their baskets and counting the different colors.

Felicia held her basket up and said, "My brother Tony says he'll bring me a *real* basket from the South Pacific when he comes home. We had a letter from him today. It took two weeks for it to come!"

"Two weeks is a very short time to come so far," said Mrs. Cole. "It is wonderful the way the mail is carried during this time. It used to take months for a letter to come that distance."

"My daddy says it used to take weeks for a letter to go from here to Boston," April offered.

"I'm sure your daddy knows some interesting things about how people have communicated with each other," Mrs. Cole said. "April, why don't you ask him to tell you? Then we can talk about it the next time we meet."

April agreed. She was sure Papa would know lots about the way messages had been carried. He was always reading and said there seemed to be no end to the things you could learn about the development of post office service.

When it was time to go home, April walked the long way round with Sophie, and when Sophie coaxed her, "Come in just a minute and see my new paper dolls," she went in. It was such fun to try on the dresses made from crepe paper that she stayed longer than she meant to. Sophie's mamma was setting the table when she left, and it was beginning to get dark.

Mamma always said, "Home is the place for boys and

girls when night comes." Even Tom was expected to come home straight from school before going anywhere else, and to be home well before nightfall. April ran all the way home.

"Is that you, April?" Papa called from the living room, and almost before she could answer, Mamma called from the kitchen. "What kept you, dear?" It was all right when she told them where she had been, but she was reminded to come home directly after the Brownie meeting next time.

"And where is Tom?" Mamma wondered. "It is high time he was here. Supper is all ready and will spoil if we don't eat soon. Why doesn't he come?" Mamma looked anxious.

Finally she asked April to help put the food on the table, and they sat down to eat. Still there was no shrill whistle and no "rat-tat-tat" of drumsticks to tell them that Tom was on his way home.

There was so much discussion at the table concerning Tom and the need for children to obey their parents and come home at certain times that April forgot all about what she was going to ask Papa. They were nearly through eating when they heard someone at the door. April recognized Tom's voice, but he was not whistling, and someone seemed to be with him. Papa got up to see who it was. He was gone only a few moments and came back with Tom, who looked very subdued. Even Mamma didn't say anything about where he had been, but she and Papa talked quietly in the hall. She only told Tom to eat his supper, and then, while she and April washed the dishes, Papa talked to him in the living room. It was all very mysterious to April. Besides, Mamma looked solemn and scarcely spoke as she went about the kitchen work. It made April feel as if something dreadful had happened. At last she could bear it no longer.

"What is it, Mamma? What has happened? Is anything wrong?"

Mamma thought for a moment, then, resting her hands on the edge of the sink, she answered, "There could have been something terribly wrong. If it weren't for the fact that nearly everybody knows your father and knows what a fine man he is, Tom's name would be on the police record. Tom and Nick have been playing with some boys in that vacant building down the street. Today, just after they went into the building, the police came. It seems that these other boys have been taking fixtures from the building and selling them. Tom and Nick had nothing to do with that and didn't know anything about it, but the police took them all to the station house. Luckily, they know Papa. When Tom stood up for Nick they listened to him too. They called the school principal, and he told them that both boys have always been good citizens in school. So they didn't put Tom or Nick's name on the police record. If they had, it would stand against them all their lives, perhaps. It just doesn't pay to get into bad company. I think we shall have to move. If only Ken were home and working, perhaps he could plan a new home for us." Mamma looked sad.

"Move?" thought April. "And leave Sophie? Leave the Brownie troop?"

Papa kept Tom in the living room for a long time, and not once that evening did they hear the tapping of Tom's drumsticks.

In the morning there was a letter from Sis saying she would be home on Saturday. Mama began to plan for her weekly marketing. To April it seemed as if they always had good things to eat, but when Sis came home, Mamma tried to have the things she especially liked. They began to look for her after lunch on Saturday, but it was nearly dinnertime before she came.

"At the last minute," she complained, "I had to go and

help move a patient to another room. Had to scrub the bed and make it up fresh and even wash the window! I wouldn't mind so much, only that supervisor is such an old crank! Nothing ever pleases her, and she never says we do good work." Sis shook her head in disgust as she jerked her coat off and threw her hat onto the table.

"Take it easy, take it easy," Papa reminded her. "The crosser she is, the nicer you must be. Finally she will be ashamed to treat you less well than you treat her. You'll see."

"Well," Sis replied, "I suppose so, but sometimes it seems too hard to bear." Then she brightened at the sight of Ken's letter lying on the books beside Papa's chair. April watched Chris as she read through the letter. But all she said was, "OH-o-oh," and looked at his picture standing on the mantel.

Soon young people began to arrive to see Sis while she was home. Some of them stayed only a few moments, and some of them sat down to supper when Mamma made a place for them. April was allowed to stay up later than usual and watch while they danced to the rhythm of Tom's drumsticks. Mamma caught the spirit of fun and sat down at the piano, where she played tunes to suit. Things half remembered and half made up. Faster and faster flew Tom's beating, first on a chair back, then on the edge of the stone mantel, then on a book, next the lamp shade, the window blind, an ash tray, a crockery jar. Each different thing made a different sound and created laughter. Tom's antics were so funny that Mamma finally couldn't keep up with him for laughing, and everyone was exhausted from the furious motion and fun. April wished it could go on forever; she wished that always people could be happy and that everyone would like everyone else.

Next morning April surprised Sis by taking her breakfast for her to eat in bed. She had learned how to set a breakfast tray at Brownie meetings since Sis was home the last time. She knew how to put all the necessary things in their right places, on a fresh cloth, and how much more attractive it would look with a flower. She took a sprig of begonia from the plant on the window sill and put it in an empty salt cellar. Sis was pleased. April helped her get ready for church. She always sang in the choir when she was at home. When they started out together, Sis look so pretty, April couldn't decide whether she looked nicer in her nurse's uniform or in her regular clothes.

Evening came almost before they knew it, and it was time for Sis to get back to the hospital.

"Back to books and classes; back to carrying water for fussy old men and rubbing backs for cranky old women," she said, laughing. But April knew she loved every bit of it, even the hard part.

All that week and the next, there was no word from Ken. April knew from the way Mamma watched out the window for Mr. Benson that she was anxious to hear from Ken and to know where he was stationed. Mr. Benson served the Brights' mail. Papa's route was in another part of town. Mr. Benson had known Ken since he was a little boy. He knew how Mamma longed for a letter from him. Yes, it was like Papa said, "The postman is a kind of heart-throb in the community."

"Never mind," he comforted. "You'll be hearing one of these days soon. It's like that. When they get their orders, you don't hear for several weeks, then one day you get a letter and you know where he is, then you forget all about how long you waited for it. You'll see! You know there is no better mail service in the world than we have!"

Mr. Benson was proud of his work, just like Papa was. Mamma would laugh and feel a little better because

she knew how many anxious mothers there were besides herself, but she couldn't help wishing for the letter.

It wasn't till the night before Brownie meeting that April remembered to ask Papa about the Postal Service and how it all began. But it was too late then, and Papa said it would have to wait for next time. So when Mrs. Cole spoke of the talk they were to have, April begged for another week.

A few nights later Papa told her many things about his work and how important it was to have the mail de-

livered regularly, no matter what the weather or how
difficult it was to get it through to its destination. He
showed her the two red stars on his sleeve showing he
had carried the mail for twenty years. Then April
couldn't wait to see Mr. Benson the next morning to see
if he had stars on his sleeve. He had two black ones.

Papa said, when she asked him about it that night,
"That means he has served for ten years. He is younger
than I am." Then he told April how the words "post
office," "post road," and "postman" came to be used. He
said it all went back to the days of the ancient Romans,
whose language was Latin. One of their words was
"positus," meaning "placed," or "set up." Sometimes the
word was shortened to "postus" and was used to indicate
the markers set up at one-mile intervals along a road.

"So," Papa went on, "when the government of this
country set up its regular mail service, it marked the
roads with posts just as it was done in ancient times. The
mail was carried over these roads, and they were called
post roads. Then when there came to be offices set up
where the mail was taken care of, they were called post
offices. You've heard people say they want things done
posthaste, haven't you?" April nodded. "Well, that means
as fast as possible, because always the post has been a
symbol for fast and faithful performance. You know that
I always go to my work if I am at all able to go, and no
kind of weather hinders me. It has always been so. Ever
since those early days when Benjamin Franklin was Postmaster General, 'Haste, posthaste' has been the motto
of the postal force.

"In those days, of course, the mail was carried on horse-
back or by mail coach, in which passengers were also
carried. A mail coach was harnessed to the fastest horses,
and sometimes it was held up by highwaymen. You'd
better go to the library and ask Miss Shuck to find a book
that would tell about mail coaches and about the pony

express," he said. "I could tell you, but if you find it for yourself, you will remember it better. Besides, I think it a good idea for you to realize how helpful it is to be able to go to the library for information."

April knew Miss Shuck, for she had been getting books to read for a long time. During the summer before, Sophie had won a prize for the best written report on her summer reading, and April had been second. Miss Shuck read aloud to them every Friday morning and helped them to find books that were interesting. The library was not far away, just down the street and around the corner in the little park. Of course it was sometimes hard to remember to wash hands before going in, and Mr. Davis, the Park Guard, didn't like it when some of the children washed their hands at the drinking fountain. In summer it was pleasant to sit and read under the shade trees, or to watch the pigeons strutting about and thrusting their breasts out in silly postures. So when April went next day to the library, she asked Sophie to go with her. Miss Shuck was glad to help them, as always, and brought out a number of books that told of different ways in which the mail was carried. April began to see why Papa said there was a lot to be learned about the business of being a postman.

Before going home the girls went down to look in the windows of one of the large stores where new spring styles were displayed. April was fascinated with the hats and was sure she could design one for her paper doll like the one in the window.

When Thursday came, April had lots to tell the other Brownies and Mrs. Cole about the post. She remembered about the ancient Latin word "postus" because Papa had insisted that she learn it. Besides, it explained about those stone mileposts that were on Germantown Avenue.

The Brownies were still working on the two little tents

and the things to put in them. Felicia was hemming the edge of the second tent and talking busily, now that April had finished her story.

Felicia sat with her head on one side, putting the needle in and out of the stiff cloth.

"I thought I'd be a dressmaker when I grow up," she said, as Mrs. Cole leaned over to examine the work.

"Not unless you take smaller stitches, my little lady!" Mrs. Cole laughed and pinched her cheek. "Suppose we take out these few stitches and do them over. Shall we?"

Felicia grinned and said she would try to do better next time. They all began to talk of what they would do when they were grown up.

"I'm going to be a typewriter and work in an office," said Edith, who was rubbing smooth the table top they were making.

"Don't you mean typist? The typewriter is the machine you use," Mrs. Cole offered.

The girls giggled, and Sophie said she was going to be a druggist and help her daddy in the store.

April said, "I thought I'd like to be a nurse like Sis, but now I think I'll be a hat designer and be the boss of a big store on Chestnut Street." She airily sat up and tossed her head.

One of the girls laughed and said, "You? Why, they never let——" But she got no farther, for Mrs. Cole quickly slipped her hand over the child's mouth and, while she smoothed her cheeks and kept her from talking, went on to speak herself. She looked kind, but very grave.

"Suppose all of you learn to do the things you have to do *now* as well as you possibly can, then you will be ready to do whatever comes along. It is all very well to be at the head of things, but homely work is important too. Don't think you are too good to do any kind of work that seems necessary. You are respected for *the way* you do your work, any work. Remember, many people cannot do the things they want to do." The girls looked at one another, but they did not laugh.

When it was time to stop work and put the things away and the girls had left one by one, April was the last to go. She helped Mrs. Cole put the things in the large box in the shed and was putting on her coat when Mrs. Cole drew her close and said:

"April, dear, you are very good at planning things and clever with your hands. There are many things you will be able to do when you are grown. Be sure that you choose well. Then be sure you are so well trained that you will be able to take your place in the world. You may find you will have to go somewhere you don't want to go in order to be of the greatest service. Perhaps by the time you are grown up you can go anywhere you want to go." Then she added slowly, "I hope so." She looked very serious and unsmiling.

April felt very sad, though she didn't quite know why. Then she asked timidly, "You mean—you mean there are some places we can't go? You mean they might not *let* me be the boss in a big store?"

Mrs. Cole didn't speak but nodded her head slowly up and down, looking deep into April's eyes, which clouded over though no tears fell.

April felt as if something had struck her. Something made her remember the time when someone else was appointed postmaster instead of Papa, although he was qualified to serve. Maybe that was what Ken meant in his letter! She didn't say any more but clasped her unbuttoned coat around her and ran out of the door and down the steps at a bound. She slipped on the icy walk but righted herself and sped up the street. She passed several of the girls but didn't notice when they spoke to her. She passed Sophie as if she had never seen her; passed Tom, who stood on a heap of snow tossing his drumsticks into the air and catching them.

"April!" he called.

But she didn't answer, only flew on up the street, through the gate, up the steps, and into the house like a tempest, in search of Mamma. Papa was there in the living room with the big book he was always reading, but April wanted only her mother. She managed to keep down the sobs rising in her throat, while she listened, hoping to hear a sound that would tell where Mamma was. Then she heard the whir of the sewing machine upstairs. Mamma was there. She paid no attention to Papa's question, "Here! Here! What's the matter?" but dashed up the stairs and to the back room where Mamma sewed. She was there and seemed to know already that April needed her. She turned from the machine and looked at April questioningly. April threw herself at her mother's feet and broke into a storm of weeping. Mamma soothed her with soft sounds and with stroking her hair but could get no word from April, who only turned her head from side to side and continued to sob as if her heart would break.

Finally, when April had quieted a little, she said sadly, "So—it's come. Someone has hurt you. Who?"

April shook her head. She couldn't say that Mrs. Cole had hurt her. She loved Mrs. Cole. Besides, she hardly knew what had hurt her. When she could speak she asked, "Mamma, is it true that there are some places we can't go?"

"Well," Mamma began, "there are some people who think we are different from them. They don't understand what scientists have taught us, that all the peoples of the world are one family and that all human blood is the same. They don't realize that we all have the same Heavenly Father, and they forget that this country is for all people to have an equal chance. Now, tell me, what has happened?"

April looked at Mamma, trying to say what really had happened. She hardly knew, yet the feeling of deep hurt was still there. She began to tell how they had talked at Brownie meeting of the things they would do when they were grown up, and how April had said she wanted to be a designer and the head of a shop on Chestnut Street, and how one of the girls laughed at her. Then she told Mamma what Mrs. Cole had said, and the awful feeling she had inside.

"Why must we be different?" she begged. "I don't *feel* different."

"You aren't different, really," Mamma comforted, "except in the way one flower differs from another. Come here to the window," she said, drawing April into the circle of her arm. "Look out. I know it is beginning to get dark, but you remember where the flower beds are. You know how the tulips and hyacinths come up in the spring. Remember how I always try to find the dark purple hyacinths to set in among the lighter ones?" April nodded, and Mamma went on:

"Today I saw the points of daffodils coming up where the snow melted in the sun. It won't be long till they bloom. After that come the tulips. Remember the dark browny ones we love so much and how lovely they look among the bright ones? We really need those dark ones to make the bouquet rich and beautiful. You're my dark April. Dark April Bright! You're a Brownie too! Isn't that funny?" April sniffed, then giggled, while Mamma continued: "And you are going to learn how to do what you want to do so well that you will find a place for yourself wherever you want to go. And you must be so pleasant a person that you will make friends wherever you go.

"Come. Take off your dress and try this on." Mamma loosened April's arms from about her waist and helped her slip out of her sweater and skirt. April couldn't help being excited at the thought of a new dress. It would seem new even if Mamma did say, "It is made from those two wool dresses that Auntie gave me. The material in the skirts was perfectly good. I washed and pressed it, and it is enough for a jumper and a jacket, and I think there are enough pieces for a little hat, if you will show me how you want it."

Mamma put the jumper over April's head and smoothed it down. The jumper was of plain material trimmed with plaid, and the jacket was of plaid trimmed with plain. It was just like new and a perfect fit! Oh, Mamma was a wonder at making things! She always taught the girls to be very particular about their sewing. "When you sew anything it must look as if it grew there," she said. She made things for Christine and sometimes for her friends. April felt sorry for Tom because he was a boy and all that Mamma could make for him were pajamas.

"Do you like it?" she teased now, for April's smile showed how pleased she was.

"Oh, it's lovely," sighed April. "And I know just how I'd like the hat made!"

There was still a catch in her voice, but the storm was over. Mamma hugged her, and they went down to get supper. Papa was at the foot of the stairs as they came down, but he didn't say anything, just touched April's hair as she passed. Tom beat a tattoo along the railing of the porch and came rattling in the door.

April faces many problems in Bright April. *This author has also given us the story of a little Polish-American girl in* Up the Hill *and of a little French-Canadian girl in* Petite Suzanne. *All are published by Doubleday.*

The Fair

BY ELIZABETH ENRIGHT

Illustrations by the author

Garnet's wonderful summer began when she found the thimble in the dried-up creek bed. Her brother, Jay, her friend, Citronella, and even Eric—the stranger who had no family—all found the hot Wisconsin summer one to remember.

ON the ninth of September the sun came up with a special glory. The air was deep and clear and full of blue light the way it often is in September, and now and then the wind moved a little. There was a huge feeling about this wind though it moved so slightly; it was as if it came from far away, through a door that was open into another space.

Garnet woke up early. Before she was quite awake she lay with her eyes closed, half afraid to look for fear it might be raining. But even with them closed she knew it was going to be all right because the color behind her lids was clear and rosy and she knew the sunlight lay upon them. And she heard crickets in the meadow, and a fly buzzing against the screen, and somebody whistling outside. So it *was* all right and she opened her eyes. Oh what a day! She held up her arm in the sunlight; all the little hairs on it glittered like fine gold, and her closed fingers were ember-colored as if there were a light inside them.

She kicked off the blankets and pointed her foot into the sunlight, and her toes were ember-colored too, though not so much as her fingers.

She yawned and stretched and gave a sudden leap that brought her out of bed. Without waiting to put on a bathrobe she ran out of the room and down the stairs which were uncarpeted and hollow sounding, like drums.

Bang! went the screen door at the bottom, and Garnet was halfway across the lawn; racing towards a small pen that stood by itself. Eric had built it especially for Timmy.

"Timmy!" called Garnet, "Lazy Timmy, it's time to get up!" But Timmy had been awake for ages and came lolloping over to the fence rail looking interested and hungry. He was quite big now, and his coat was very stiff and fine; he stood well and looked as if he could take care of himself no matter what happened. Every day for several weeks Garnet had been training him to walk and stand like a prize hog. Mr. Freebody had showed her how to steer him along with two little boards, and how to make him stand neatly with his two front hoofs together.

Garnet scratched Timmy's back with a twig, and he leaned against the fence with his little eyes half closed, grunting softly with pleasure.

"Today you must remember everything I've taught

you," Garnet told him. "You are going for a long ride in a little crate that you won't like much. And then you'll be taken into a big sort of shed and put into a pen by yourself; but there'll be lots of other pens there with pigs in them too. So you can make friends and not be lonesome. Then by-and-by some men will come and look at you and you must walk right and stand right just the way I showed you, and maybe you'll win a lovely blue ribbon."

Timmy twitched his little tail that was all curled up like a pretzel; then he rolled over on his back so that she could scratch his stomach.

"Garnet!" called Mrs. Linden from the house. "You come in and get dressed this minute!"

It *was* rather chilly with nothing on but a nightgown. Garnet wrapped her arms around her cold self and hurried to the house.

"Will he win a prize, mother, do you think?" she asked.

"I shouldn't wonder, darling," said her mother, "he's a changed pig since you took him in hand."

Garnet went up to her room and dressed with care. She put on the blue dress and shoes. (But not the strapped ones; those she would never wear again!) She braided her pigtails so tight they hurt her, and scrubbed her face till it had a shine like shellac. Then she went down to the kitchen where she could hear bacon hissing and sputtering in the frying pan.

The whole family was going to the fair, and they were all dressed up for the occasion. Jay and Eric both had straight hair for once; they had used so much water on it that there were little trickles at the back of their necks; and Conniston solely for Timmy's convenience. The Lindens aprons so that he would be sure to leave the table without oatmeal decorations. Garnet thought her mother looked wonderful; she had on a flowered dress, and her hair was different. Mr. Linden looked fine too, in a dark suit and a collar that hurt him.

Garnet's stomach felt as if there were a pinwheel inside of it turning and spinning in a shower of sparks. She said so to her mother.

"It's excitement," said Mrs. Linden calmly, "excitement and emptiness. Eat your cereal." "Oh *mother!*" groaned Garnet, "I *can't.*" "Yes you can, darling," insisted her mother heartlessly. "You can't leave the house till you've finished every spoonful." Garnet ploughed through the cereal grimly.

"It's like eating Boulder Dam," she grumbled, but she finished it. Then she leapt from her chair and started for the door; and came slowly, sadly back.

"The dishes," she said. "Oh, let them stand for once!" cried Mrs. Linden grandly, "we can do them when we come home. This is an important day."

"You're nice," said Garnet, and gave her mother a hug.

Eric called through the window, "Come on Garnet, Mr. Freebody's here with his truck, let's get Timmy in his box."

"Poor pig!" said Garnet to Timmy, who struggled and rolled his eyes and squealed when they put him in the crate. "But just think if you win a prize!"

"That little hog don't care nothing about blue ribbons, I bet," said Mr. Freebody, "a couple of square feet of mud and a full trough and he'd be a durn sight more contented." Mr. Freebody laughed. "He sure looks pretty as a peach though, don't he? Smells good, too. How did that happen?"

"Oh, I washed him," said Garnet. "The soap smelled like that."

"My my what a fancy little hog!" chuckled Mr. Freebody. "With all them clean bristles and that fine smell of perfumery I'm going to be mighty disappointed in the Fair Authorities if he don't get a prize!"

Mr. Freebody had offered to drive his truck to New Conniston solely for Timmy's convenience. The Lindens didn't have a truck and there wasn't enough room in the Ford for both the family and Timmy's crate.

"But I'm going to ride in the truck with you, Mr. Freebody," Garnet told him.

"Just so's you can keep an eye on that pig, I bet," said Mr. Freebody, "well get in then. It's time we started."

Garnet watched the precious crate safely installed on the back of the truck; then she got in herself. She called good-bye to her family who were busily getting themselves sorted out and into the Ford. This was particularly difficult as Mrs. Hauser, her daughter Citronella and her son Hugo had just arrived and wanted to go with them.

"It's a good thing you decided to come with me," remarked Mr. Freebody, "otherwise I don't know how you *would* have got to the fair, or Timmy either. Them Hausers are a mighty fleshy family."

Garnet watched Mrs. Hauser get into the car. Did she imagine it, or did she really see the Ford sink down a little on its springs, as if it sighed under a great weight. My goodness, thought Garnet, Mother, Father, Jay, Donald, Eric, *and* Mrs. Hauser, *and* Hugo, *and*—

"Citronella!" shouted Garnet, "you come ride with us. There's lots of room, isn't there Mr. Freebody?"

"*Always* room for one more," said Mr. Freebody gallantly, leaning across Garnet to open the door for Citronella.

Garnet squirmed around to peer through the window at Timmy in his box.

"He looks as if he had hurt feelings," she said. "He'll probably never forgive me for this."

"Just try giving him something to eat and see how he'll come around," said Mr. Freebody. "Hogs are only sensitive between meals."

By this time the truck was halfway down the side road.

"My, I was awful scared I wasn't going to get to go to the fair at all," said Citronella. "Merle took the car to

Hanson to get the springs fixed, and Cicero and Dad and Uncle Ed took our Holstein bull to the fair in the stake truck. Wasn't anything left for us but the team till Mama thought of asking you folks."

"It's a good day for a fair," remarked Mr. Freebody, " 't ain't cold, 't ain't hot, and not a cloud in sight."

"Do you think he's warm enough?" asked Garnet.

"Who?" said Mr. Freebody, "Timmy? He's warm, don't you worry."

When they came to Hodgeville, Mr. Freebody stopped the truck.

"How about some ice-cream cones?" he asked.

"It's a fine idea," said Garnet.

"It's a marvelous idea," said Citronella.

So Mr. Freebody went into a drugstore and got a maple-nut ice-cream cone for Citronella, and a chocolate ice-cream cone for Garnet, and a plain vanilla one for himself. But for Timmy he bought a strawberry one and let Garnet poke it between the laths of the crate. Timmy's snout trembled all around the edges with joy, and in a second he had gobbled every crumb. He looked less miserable.

"He knows you ain't betrayed him anyhow," Mr. Freebody told Garnet.

Citronella just stood looking at them.

"Giving ice cream to a pig," she said, and gave her cone a long, thoughtful lick. "To a *pig!*" she repeated and gave it another lick. "My land, what a waste!" she said.

"I'm doing lots of awful things today," said Garnet complacently. "Leaving the dishes, feeding ice-cream cones to pigs, and eating one myself at nine o'clock in the morning!"

"Won't hurt you once in a while," said Mr. Freebody and they all got back in the truck and slammed the doors.

On they drove through the burning blue day. There was no haze on the hills, no mist on the river. Everything was clear as crystal. They passed Melody, and Garnet remembered the people on the bus, and the wonderful ride after the people got off, and how she'd bounced around on the seat and tried not to scream.

She looked back at Timmy. He was lying down.

"Do you think he's all right?" she asked.

"Who?" said Mr. Freebody, "Timmy? He's fine, never felt better."

Garnet looked at Mr. Freebody out of the corners of her eyes and laughed.

"You understand pigs pretty well, don't you Mr. Freebody?" she remarked.

"Sure do," said he. "Ought to. Raised enough of 'em!"

Now they could see New Conniston on its hill. Garnet felt the pinwheel in her stomach again.

They drove past the little shabby homes, and on through the main street with its big important stores and the dime store where Garnet had bought her presents; past the park with the fountain and on to the outskirts of the city where the fairgrounds were.

Then they drove through the wide gates into the new, gay world of the fair, which, like a magic city in a story, had sprung up over night.

It was a whirling, jingling, bewildering collection of noise and color and smell. Everything seemed to be spinning and turning; merry-go-rounds, the Ferris wheel, the whip cars. There were dozens of tents with peaked tops and scalloped edges, and little colored flags flying from them. Citronella grabbed Garnet and Garnet grabbed Citronella, and they bounced up and down shrieking with excitement. Mr. Freebody was calmer. "I always like a fair," he said.

They drove directly to the stock pavilions and stopped in front of the one that was labeled SWINE in big black letters.

The man in charge of it was fat and kind looking. His

name was Fred Lembke. He and Mr. Freebody carried the crate in, opened it, and put Timmy in a nice clean pen with hay on the floor. "He doesn't feel at home yet," said Garnet apologetically to Mr. Lembke, because Timmy just stood where he had been set down, looking insulted and loathing everything.

"He's a mighty fine little boar, just the same," said Mr. Lembke with real admiration in his voice (not just the nice-to-children sort). "Who's showing him?"

"I am," replied Garnet, feeling very motherly towards Timmy.

Mr. Lembke took a notebook from his pocket and a pencil from behind his ear and asked Garnet her name, and all about Timmy. Then he put a sign above Timmy's pen that said:

Class 36: Boar under 6 months.

Breed: Hampshire.

Owner: Garnet Linden.

Garnet read the sign over three or four times to herself. Then she turned to Mr. Freebody. "Am I supposed to stay and watch him?" she asked.

"No, no," replied Mr. Freebody, "you two little girls go on out and enjoy yourselves. You've got hours before the judges come. Three o'clock they'll be here, and see that you get back in time!"

"I don't know how I'll ever wait till three o'clock," sighed Garnet, but in the next minute she had forgotten all about time and waiting. There were dozens, hundreds of things to see and do.

First they looked at all the other pigs in the shed. There were several others in Timmy's class, some bigger than he, and some more important looking. Garnet and Citronella examined each one with anxiety.

"Well anyway," said Garnet, "I bet Timmy's got the nicest nature." "He's the handsomest, too," said Citronella stoutly.

The place was full of pigs. There were many different

breeds with high sounding names like Poland-China, Chester White, and Duroc-Jersey. There were grumpy looking hogs, and sows with litters of pigs all different sizes. In one pen there was a whole group of baby ones fast asleep; white as thistledown, they were, with pale pink ears and little turned-up snouts. It didn't seem possible that they would someday grow up to be boisterous, bellowing, bad mannered pigs. In another pen, near the front of the shed, there was a prize hog, black and thundery, and big as a grand piano. On the sign above him were pinned the ribbons from past fairs, all blue!

The whole shed resounded with the snorts, grunts, squeals and grumblings of pigs conversing.

"How rude they sound," said Garnet, "as if they never said nice things to each other, but just scolded, and snatched, and told each other to get out of the way."

The cattle pavilion seemed very quiet and respectable after that. There was almost no noise. Cows stood in stalls on either side of the shed, with soft, dull eyes, and jaws moving patiently. There were little calves with pink noses, and magnificent, dangerous looking bulls.

Garnet and Citronella stopped in front of the Hausers' Holstein, staring admiringly. He was massive and beautiful, with his shining black-and-white coat.

Mr. Hauser came and stood beside them with his hands in his pockets.

"Looks pretty good, don't he?" he remarked.

"He chased me once," said Garnet rather proudly. "I was pretty scared."

"Yes, and who saved you *that* time?" asked someone, giving one of her pigtails a jerk. Garnet turned around. Of course it was Mr. Freebody.

"You won't ever have to do it again," she promised.

"Looks like you couldn't lose, Herman," said Mr. Freebody to Mr. Hauser, and the two girls went on to look at the horses.

There were stallions in big stalls there, roan, and

dapple-grey and black. They had huge arched necks and dark fiery eyes. Their hoofs made heavy, restless noise upon the floorboards. And there was a little colt that was hard to leave. He had a satiny coat, and long unreliable legs that he could fold up like jack-knives. He looked delicate and mischievous standing by the strong protecting shape of his mother.

"If he was mine I'd name him Ariel," said Garnet stroking his nose. Oh, how soft his nose was! Like moss, like velvet, like the palm of a baby's hand.

"Of course it might not suit him when he grew up," she added thoughtfully. "Ariel's a funny name anyway. Like on a radio. I don't see what it's got to do with a horse," said Citronella. "If he was mine I'd name him Black Beauty like the book."

"But he's not black," objected Garnet. "Well, it's a good name for a horse," said Citronella.

Finally they tore themselves away, and left the dim sheds where the air had a heavy smell of hay and animals, and went out into the blaze and flourish of the fair.

They crossed a smooth dirt track that lay in a large oval enclosing the central section of the fair. Later in the day there would be trotting races on this track, and there would be crowds of excited people at either side, but now it was just a kind of road to be crossed.

They simply wandered for a while, pausing to look at the shies, and the shooting gallery, and the screaming people in the whip cars. They bought two ice-cream cones and poked along, stopping to read the signs outside of the tents that you had to pay to go into. There were a lot of them, all interesting. Aurora the Mystic Mind Reader. Professor Hedwitz, World Famous Phrenologist. Hercules Junior, the Samson of the Century. Dagmar, the Female Sword Swallower. Zara, the Jungle Dancer. Below the last name, Zara, there was a little notice saying: persons under 16 not admitted. Both Gar-

net and Citronella were dying to know why not. There were many other tents and sideshows but it was still too early in the day for them to be open, and those loud-voiced men who usually shout outside and take the money, had not yet appeared.

The flaps of the tent announcing Dagmar, the Female Sword Swallower, were open, and inside Garnet and Citronella saw a woman in a kimona sitting on a chair and darning a sock. She was chewing gum.

"Do you think it's her?" whispered Citronella as they went on.

"It *can't* be!" said Garnet. "I'm sure a sword swallower would look, you know, *different*. Not so much like other people. Wilder."

"I bet it is though!" persisted Citronella. "Maybe she *has* to chew gum," she added, "to keep her jaws limber or something. In order to swallow swords."

They went back to take another peek but this time

the woman noticed them, and though she smiled, she closed the tent flaps.

"I bet it's her all right," said Citronella excitedly. This was something to have seen, a real lady sword swallower darning socks just like anyone!

The merry-go-round looked wonderful. It was the kind that has only horses, not wild animals; but they were strange beautiful horses with flaring scarlet nostrils and broad grins. Garnet and Citronella each paid a nickel and got on. After a while the music commenced and the merry-go-round began turning. Up went the horses, high, swooping in the air as they glided, and then down like winged horses following the wind.

"I'm kind of old for this," remarked Citronella, who was eleven. "But I still like it."

"I'm never going to be too old for it," said Garnet. "All my life whenever I see a merry-go-round I'm going to ride on it, and when I have children I'm going to ride with them."

They had two more rides and then they got off, and continued their exploring. They got some popcorn, too, and then they had a ride on the whip cars. It was perfect. Their necks were nearly snapped in half, and all the little bones in their spinal columns kept feeling as if they were flying apart and then settling back in place again like something in a movie of Micky Mouse.

"Oh, gee!" squealed Citronella as they rounded a curve with a particularly terrifying wallop. "Isn't this awful?"

"But fun!" squealed Garnet in reply, and clutched Citronella as they rounded another curve.

They got off feeling very light and peculiar in their feet and rather whirly in their heads, and they went straight to a hot dog stand where they each bought and ate two hot dogs and a bottle of root beer.

"How about the Ferris wheel, now?" enquired Garnet, ready for anything.

"Let's wait a little bit," urged Citronella in a careful voice. She looked rather green around the mouth. "I don't feel so good," she said.

"Just don't think about it and you'll be all right," advised Garnet airily, not having a stomach ache herself.

They decided to go and see the cooking and needle-work exhibits in the big barnlike building at the far end of the fair. Hundreds of people had arrived by this time and Garnet caught a glimpse of her mother and Mrs. Hauser with Donald and Hugo.

"Don't say anything about feeling sick," Garnet cautioned Citronella. "They might think you should go home!"

"I feel better now, anyway," said Citronella, breathing a great sigh of relief. It was wonderful to know that she wasn't going to be sick after all; the fair took on a new color and beauty because of it.

"Oh I feel swell!" she cried joyously and gave a sudden skip.

They went into the barnlike building and looked at everything. There were hundreds of jars of jelly and pickles on the shelves, there were cut flowers in vases and growing plants in pots. In one of the glass cases there were dozens of different kinds of cake; golden cake, and marble, and fruit cake and orange; angel food and devil.

food and sponge! Each had a little card beside it with the name of the lady who'd made it.

"Oh how delicious they look," moaned Garnet." Oh how my mouth is watering!"

"Mine isn't," said Citronella. "I still don't feel so good when I look at those cakes."

So they went on to the needlework section. Here they saw rag rugs and braid, and hook rugs, and baby clothes, and children's clothes, and crocheted afghans, and quilts, and sofa cushions embroidered with flowers and big dog's heads and other beautiful things.

Garnet heard someone say, "Why there's that little hitchhiker we picked up over to Esau's Valley!"

She turned around, and sure enough, there was Mrs. Zangl in a big lavender dress and a hat with a rose on it; and behind her with his hand on her shoulder stood Mr. Zangl, that nice, nice man. Garnet was glad to see them. They shook hands all around and said what a fine fair it was, and Citronella was introduced.

"Are you exhibiting a quilt today?" Garnet asked Mrs. Zangl.

"Look at that," said Mr. Zangl, waving his outstretched hand towards a quilt hanging on the wall. "Just take a good look at that. See what the judges thought of it."

Garnet looked at Mrs. Zangl's quilt; so did Citronella. It was every color in the world almost; all made of patches put together like flowers in a garden. It was the gayest, most brilliant coverlet you could ever hope to sleep under. There was a big blue ribbon pinned to the card with Mrs. Zangl's name on it.

"Beautiful!" said Garnet.

"Just beautiful!" said Citronella.

"Just the colors alone would keep you warm," said Garnet.

Mrs. Zangl's gold tooth glittered.

"It's real nice of you to say so," she smiled. "I always

did like plenty of color. My, I felt bad when I got too fleshy to wear red dresses! I guess I take it out of my system by making my quilts so bright and all."

"How about ice-cream cones for you three girls?" asked Mr. Zangl heartily.

"Well—" said Garnet looking at Citronella—

"Well—" said Citronella looking at Garnet. "I don't believe just *one* more would hurt me if I ate it real slow. I feel fine now," she added in a whisper.

So they all had ice-cream cones. And Citronella ate every crumb of hers; she was entirely cured.

Then they thanked Mr. and Mrs. Zangl and promised to come and call if they ever came over to Deepwater; and Mr. Zangl said that he would come and take a look at Timmy later on.

As the two girls walked back among the tents and sideshows they noticed some people coming out of the one belonging to Zara, the Jungle Dancer (persons under 16 not admitted). Among them was a boy. It was Eric.

"*Well!*" said Garnet going up to him and hooking onto his arm so he couldn't get away.

"Yes, *well!*" echoed Citronella.

"When did you have your sixteenth birthday, Eric *darling!*" mocked Garnet.

"Maybe he can't read yet," taunted Citronella. "Maybe he's too young!"

Eric was unruffled. He just grinned and licked the long black licorice stick he was carrying.

"Oh I just took a big breath and stretched myself up and out. Then I looked straight ahead and gave my money to the man in that pulpit-thing and in I went. Anyway lots of kids are young looking for their age."

"Yes, but Eric, what was *inside?*" asked Garnet prancing along beside him.

"Something scary, I bet," said Citronella hopefully.

"Aw, it wasn't worth ten cents at all," said Eric disappointedly. "It was just kind of a stout lady in a grass skirt. She had long hair and a lot of bracelets, and she did a sort of dance. You know, like this—" He tried, with much wiggling, to imitate the jungle dancer. Garnet and Citronella were delighted.

They walked on looking at things and talking. Suddenly Eric began to laugh at something he was remembering.

"You know what?" said he. "That lady, that Zara, the jungle dancer; she had a pair of glasses on, the kind that pinch to the bridge of your nose; she must have forgotten to take 'em off. Did she ever look funny!"

They found Mrs. Linden and Donald sitting in the shade of one of the tents. They looked exhausted.

"Donald's been on everything he could ride on in this whole fair," said Mrs. Linden. "All except the whip cars and the Ferris wheel, and I won't let him go on those."

"Ponies—" bragged Donald, "I rode on real live ponies around a ring, and I was on the big merry-go-round and the little merry-go-round and that thing like a train." He looked at his mother. "But I *want* to go on the whip cars, and I *want* to go on the Ferris wheel."

"No," said Mrs. Linden automatically. She had been saying it for hours about those two particular things.

"Come with me, Donald," said Eric, "we'll go and see the little pigs, and the fine horses, and maybe we can find a balloon for you, someplace." He took Donald's hand and led him away.

"I don't know how we ever got along without Eric," sighed Mrs. Linden fanning herself with her pocketbook.

"Where are Jay and father?" asked Garnet.

"Your father's still looking at the farm machinery," Mrs. Linden said, "and Jay's been in the shies throwing tennis balls at china teapots for hours."

Mrs. Hauser came towards them puffing like a locomotive. She was very hot; there were dew drops on her upper lip and her big nice face was the color of the rising sun. Under her arm she carried two huge pink Kewpie dolls; one with a red ballet skirt and one with green.

"I won 'em," said Mrs. Hauser, grunting as she let herself carefully and gradually sink to the ground. "One at the cocoanut shy and one at the weight-lifting thing. You'd think they'd have better prizes than Kewpie dolls! Garnet, you can have the green one, and Citronella can keep the red. My, how my arches pain me."

"It's almost time for the stock judging, Garnet," warned Mrs. Linden, "you have about a half an hour."

"I know what let's do, we just have time," said Garnet. "How do you feel about the Ferris wheel now, Citronella?"

"I feel fine about it now," said Citronella.

So they went to the little booth by the Ferris wheel and paid their money, and when it stopped they got on and sat side by side in a little hanging seat with a bar in front to keep them from falling out.

The operator pulled a big lever and the wheel gave a lurch and a creak, and up they went backwards, with the earth and the fair dropping away from them like a vanishing world. It was rather terrifying but exciting too. When they came to the top they could see the tents and surrounding fields and houses of New Conniston all spread out and flat and strange. And then they went down again like going over Niagara Falls in a barrel, and then up again like being shot out of a gun.

The third time around just as they reached the top the wheel stopped, and all the little suspended seats rocked to and fro sickeningly.

"They're just letting some more people on probably," said Citronella reassuringly, and they leaned over the bar and looked down, down. But nobody was getting on. They saw the operator's bent-over back below them. He pulled the lever and the wheel gave a quiver but didn't move. They watched him jerk the lever back and forth angrily, push his hat to the back of his head and wipe his forehead. Then he looked up.

"Nothing to worry about, folks," he called, "just a temporary delay."

"He means it's stuck," groaned Citronella. "Oh, gee!"

"And it's almost time for Timmy and the judges. Oh dear!" said Garnet.

Looking down like that gave you an awful feeling. Garnet held onto the side of the seat and raised her eyes. Below and on all sides lay the fair, whirling and jingling and unconcerned. She had never seen a ladder high enough to reach to the top of the Ferris wheel. It made her feel queer to think of that.

"We get stuck in the worst places," grumbled Citronella, "libraries and Ferris wheels!"

"Oh, well they'll get it fixed soon," said Garnet hopefully.

But the Ferris wheel was stuck for more than half an hour.

There they were at the top of the world, or so it felt, and nothing could be done. The sun beat down unmercifully, and now and then the cool, wide, September air moved about them like cold currents at the bottom of a stream.

"There's Jay," said Citronella.

And sure enough, looking small and unimportant down there on the ground, stood Jay with his hands cupped to his mouth.

"Hey!" he yelled. "It's three o'clock! Hurry up!" They could barely hear him but guessed at his meaning when he pointed repeatedly at the watch in his hand.

"We haven't any *para*chutes!" Garnet yelled back.

"Maybe he thinks we should just spread our wings and fly," said Citronella acidly. She was thirsty.

Jay stared up at them helplessly, and then went over

to talk to the operator of the wheel. After he had spoken with him he looked up at the girls again and hunched his shoulders. "Nothing doing yet awhile," he shouted. "We'll send your dinner up by carrier pigeons." Then he laughed heartily and went away. He walked fast with his legs opening and shutting like a pair of scissors. Lucky Jay, thought Garnet. Lucky Jay, with two legs walking firmly on the firm earth.

"Awful funny, isn't he?" said Citronella sulkily.

"Oh we'll be down soon, don't you worry," comforted Garnet. She looked about her at the people in the other seats. In back of them was a man all by himself, reading a newspaper which he had thoughtfully provided. And in front a man and girl were writing notes on bits of paper and tossing them down to friends below, amid screams of laughter. Nobody seemed worried.

Just then the wheel shuddered and moved forward. Everyone had had enough of it by this time, and Garnet and Citronella had to wait while it stopped five times to let the people off who were ahead of them.

"Hurry!" commanded Garnet grabbing Citronella by the hand and running, "we've got to get to Timmy!"

"Oh land!" groaned Citronella, loping along and whacking into people. "I'm just about dying for a drink of water!"

"Afterwards," promised Garnet, "barrels of water afterwards. Come on, *do* hurry!"

But when they got to the track crossing there was a bar in front of the gate and an important looking guard beside it.

"Take it easy, now," he said to the girls as they pushed their way through the crowd to the rail. "There's a race going on. You'll have to wait till it's over."

Dust rose from the track as horses trotted past; sunlight glittered on the spokes of wheels.

"I never knew a race to be so slow!" complained Garnet,

hopping up and down and wringing her hands. "Oh *dear,* I can't bear it."

"Never mind," said Citronella. It was her turn to be comforting. "I'm real glad of a rest, we'll get there pretty soon."

Finally it was over. The guard lifted the bar and they went through. They never knew what horse won the race, nor did they care. They were running a kind of race themselves.

They dashed into the pavilion and Garnet pushed her way past people to Mr. Freebody whom she saw standing by Timmy's pen.

"Are we too late?" she gasped almost in tears.

Mr. Freebody motioned with his broad hand towards Timmy's card above the pen.

"The judges have been and went," he said solemnly.

"Oh dear—!" began Garnet, and then she saw what he was pointing at. A blue ribbon it was. A *blue* ribbon! Pinned to Timmy's card.

"Oh," said Garnet, for a moment speechless. Then she began leaping up and down. "Oh wonderful!" she shouted. "Oh, Mr. Freebody, how *wonderful!*" And she climbed right over the railing into Timmy's pen and gave him a good squeeze around the middle.

"Darling Timmy, aren't you proud of yourself?" she said. Timmy let out a stifled grunt.

"He's got his vanity same's the rest of us," commented Mr. Freebody leaning his arms on the railing. "Don't you go spoiling him now, or you'll have one of them temperamental hogs on your hands. He's had plenty of attention for one day, come on out of that pen and let's all go and celebrate."

Garnet climbed reluctantly over the railing. Timmy didn't care; he lay down comfortably on his side with his hoofs crossed, sighed deeply, and fell asleep.

Mr. and Mrs. Linden came towards them through the

crowd; they had been searching everywhere for Garnet.
Behind them came Mrs. Hauser. She had two balloons;
one shaped like Micky Mouse. and one shaped like a
Zeppelin. She also carried a cut glass bowl and half a
dozen wax fruit to put into it which she had won in
a bingo game.

"Did you see what happened to Timmy?" cried Garnet
hurling herself upon her parents.

"We were there when the judges came, darling," replied
her mother. "We watched him being shown."

"My goodness," said Garnet abruptly, "who did show
him?" She hadn't thought of that before.

"Who do you think?" said someone behind her giving
one of her pigtails a jerk. Garnet didn't need to turn
around to know who it was. Of course it was Mr. Freebody again. Naturally.

"Oh dear," said Garnet, "poor Mr. Freebody, always
saving my life."

Mr. Freebody laughed.

"Well you couldn't help it this time," he comforted her.
"I saw you settin' up there in that little basket with Citronella, and I says to myself, we'll just have to do without
her. I said so to the little hog too, and he told me 'Okay.' "

"You've done a fine job with Timmy," said her father
putting his arm around her shoulders, "maybe you'll grow
up to be the farmer in this family. Jay doesn't seem to
have much taste for it, and I think Donald's going to be
a G-man."

"How about Eric?" asked Garnet.

"Eric may not want to stay with us always," answered
her father. "But I wish he would."

"I do too," agreed Garnet. Eric was part of the family
now, a brother. It would be awful if he ever left.

"There he is now," said her father.

Eric had Donald on his shoulders, and Hugo Hauser at
his side. Donald had a balloon and a tin horn, and Hugo

had a bag of peanuts and a flag. They all looked dirty but pleased.

Garnet told Eric about Timmy and he had to go and see the blue ribbon for himself.

"Do they have prizes for hens?" he enquired. "Next year I think I'll show Brünnhilde!"

"Where's Jay?" asked Garnet. Where was Jay? She did want him to see Timmy in all his glory. She couldn't enjoy her triumph fully without him.

"Well doggone if I didn't almost forget," said Mr. Freebody suddenly. "Here it is Garnet." He fished in his pocket, "your prize money. Three brand new dollar bills *and* a fifty cent piece."

Garnet was dazzled by such wealth. She folded the crisp bills thoughtfully and put them into her pocketbook.

"Whatever will you do with it all?" asked Citronella rather enviously.

"First," said Garnet, "I will have a party. Tonight I'm going to buy everybody's supper. And after that—well, I haven't decided."

But she thought to herself; I will just keep it for a while, sometime I'll want it for something really important. Maybe at Christmas time; or maybe the next time I find bills in the mailbox. Or I wonder how much a second-hand accordion would cost?

"I'm going to look for Jay," Garnet told her family and her friends, and slipped out of the shed into the mellowing sunlight of the late afternoon.

She almost bumped into him a few minutes later; he had a box under his arm and was hurrying.

"Jay!" said Garnet. "Timmy got first prize!"

"I know," said Jay. "I saw him get it. Look, I won something for you. A present, because of Timmy."

Oh Jay was wonderful, Garnet thought, ripping the string and paper from the box with eager fingers. She

decided definitely to find out about accordions as soon
as possible. She opened the box.

There resting elegantly on a watermelon-pink rayon
lining were a comb, brush and looking glass all made of
pearly lavender stuff. Garnet was overwhelmed by their
beauty.

"Oh Jay!" she said. It was all she could say.

"Okay, forget it," said Jay in embarrassment. "I just
thought you could use 'em. Come on, let's go into some
of these tents and see what they've got."

They went into one tent after another. They saw
Aurora, the Mystic Mind Reader, but didn't think much
of her. "That's an old trick," scoffed Jay. "I could do that
when I was nine years old." They saw Hercules Junior
who was a chubby weight-lifter in a leopard skin and
knee-high sandals. They saw Dagmar, the Sword Swallower, and she was wonderful and she *was* the same
woman whom Garnet and Citronella had seen darning
socks earlier in the day. They saw the Jewel Girls and
Bruno, who were also perfect, and they listened to the
orchestra of Hank Hazzard and his Hayseeds. "My eardrums feel black and blue," Jay said afterwards.

By that time it was getting dark and they went to
gather their party together for supper. They had some
difficulty in locating Mrs. Hauser, but finally found her
at the shooting gallery taking aim at a teacup with one
eye closed. They watched her demolish a whole row of
teacups and some small statues, and receive with dignity
the prize, which was an oil painting of an Indian girl in
a canoe. It had a frame made of real birchbark.

"Grandma Eberhardt will love this," said Mrs. Hauser.
"She remembers Indians in Esau's Valley, and she's real
fond of pictures anyway."

They all had supper together at a counter. It was Garnet's own party, and everyone had a good time. As they
ate, the Great Zorander walked along his tightrope above

the fair ground; a spotlight followed him and made his spangles glitter. He seemed a radiant and enchanted being as he moved with accurate grace so far above their heads.

Afterwards Garnet went to say good-bye to Timmy. The shed was full of flickering light and shadow cast by the oil lamps hung from the ceiling. Timmy staggered to his feet and sniffed at the palm of her hand. But there was nothing in it for him so he lay down again.

"Good night, Timmy," said Garnet. "In three days I will come and take you home."

Driving away in Mr. Freebody's truck Garnet turned and looked out of the window. The Ferris wheel was a ring of light, and all the tents were lanterns full of light. Among the dark, surrounding fields the whole magical and temporary world of the fair glowed like phosporus on a dark sea.

Citronella yawned.

"I don't think I'm going to want an ice-cream cone for a long, long time," she said.

Other good family stories by Elizabeth En-right are The Saturdays, *published by Holt, Rinehart & Winston and* Gone-Away Lake, *published by Harcourt, Brace & World.*

Henry and the Paper Route

BY BEVERLY CLEARY

Illustrations by Louis Darling

There's a lot more to having a paper route than most people realize. Mr. Copper told Henry that he couldn't have one until he was eleven years old.

NEWS of Byron Murphy, genius, quickly spread throughout the neighborhood. All the boys and girls for blocks around walked, roller-skated, or bicycled past Murph's house several times a day, hoping to catch a glimpse of the new boy and his mechanical man. If they saw him working in the garage they gathered on the driveway a respectful distance away, to watch. As arms made out of pipes were added to the tin body, and the tin-can head was topped with an antenna, some were sure the robot would work when Murph finished it. Others scoffed at the whole idea.

There was one member of the neighborhood who did not stay a respectful distance from Murph. That was Ramona. She was not one bit awed by a genius. Clonking in her high-heeled shoes, she tagged around the garage after him. Of all the boys and girls, she was the only one who thought Tiger was a good name for a dog. She said that if she ever had a dog she was going to name it Tiger, after Murph's dog. Murph ignored Ramona, but this did not bother her at all.

Henry could see that Beezus was ashamed to have a little sister who was such a nuisance to a genius at work. He felt like telling Ramona not to be such a pest, but he decided he had better keep still. He was as eager as the others to watch the progress of Thorvo, but at the same time he did not want to call attention to himself and perhaps start Murph thinking about a paper route.

Then one afternoon, when Henry had finished delivering Scooter's papers, he went to the barbershop for a haircut. On the way home he saw Murph riding toward him on a bicycle, with Tiger puffing along half a block behind. Over Murph's shoulders Henry was astonished to see an empty *Journal* bag. At the sight of that bag, Henry suddenly felt more cheerful than he had felt since Murph had moved into the neighborhood.

"Hi there, Murph," Henry called out, with sudden enthusiasm. "I didn't know you had a paper route. I've never seen you around Mr. Capper's garage with the rest of the fellows."

"My route is in my old neighborhood," Murph explained.

"Oh," was all Henry said, because he was busy thinking that he no longer had to worry about having a genius take a paper route away from him. Now he and Murph could be friends. Maybe Murph would even let him help work on Thorvo—not doing the hard parts, that took a lot of brains, but things like handing him wrenches and tightening screws. He could probably save Murph plenty of time. Henry Huggins, assistant to a genius—that's what he would be.

And so on Saturday, when all the boys and girls in the neighborhood except Scooter—who was still confined to his house with chicken pox—gathered at Murph's garage to watch the progress of Thorvo, Henry no longer felt that he had to be quiet. "What are you going to make his legs out of?" Henry asked.

"Pipe," answered Murph. "Thick pipe, when I can find some."

"Maybe I can find some for you," said Henry eagerly.

"If you put a funnel on him for a hat, he would look like the Tin—" one of the girls started to suggest.

Henry interrupted to keep her from annoying Murph with what she was about to say. "There's a plumber over by the supermarket," he said quickly. "He might have some pieces of pipe you could have."

Murph did not answer; he was too busy hunting for something in a box.

Beezus and Ramona came running up the driveway to join the rest of Murph's audience. This time Ramona was not clonking along in high-heeled shoes. Instead, she had perched on her nose the frames of a pair of old sunglasses. They were much too big for her, and to keep them from falling off, the sidepieces were tied together at the back of her head with a piece of string.

I sure am glad she's not my sister, thought Henry.

"I'm wearing glasses, like Murph," announced Ramona happily.

"She kept asking and asking for a pair of glasses so she would look like Murph," Beezus explained apologetic-ally, "until Mother finally found an old pair and took the glass out for her."

Murph paid no attention to his admirer. He found part of a string of old Christmas-tree lights and fitted two of them into sockets in the robot's head.

"Are his eyes going to light up?" asked Robert, with a touch of awe in his voice.

"Of course," answered Murph.

"Oh, Murph!" exclaimed Beezus. "You can put in blue Christmas-tree bulbs, and he'll have blue eyes!"

"Thorvo's eyes are going to be red," stated Murph def-initely.

Beezus looked embarrassed, as if she should have realized how silly she was to think a robot should have blue eyes.

"I think red eyes are pretty," said Ramona, moving closer to Murph. As she stood by his elbow she began to practice whistling. She puckered up her mouth and blew, but no whistle came out. Then she tried sucking in through her puckered lips and succeeded in produc-ing a hollow whistling sound, as if she were blowing across the mouth of a bottle. It was not a pleasant sound, but she liked it, and she repeated it over and over.

"Sh-h, Ramona!" whispered Beezus. "You might bother Murph."

"Yes," agreed Henry, not wanting to see genius dis-turbed. "You better keep quiet."

But Ramona went right on with her whistling.

Between delivering Scooter's papers and watching Murph's progress on Thorvo, Henry found the time passed quickly. Finally the day arrived when Scooter was able to take over his route once more. On that day Henry went along with Scooter, who was once more his friend, to Mr. Capper's garage. "Say, Mr. Capper," he said, satisfied that he had done a good job on Scooter's route, "I do get to take Chuck's route, don't I?"

Mr. Capper looked sympathetic—so sympathetic that Henry braced himself for a terrible disappointment. "Well, Henry, I'm afraid not," Mr. Capper said kindly.

"You—you mean I don't get the route after all?" stammered Henry, hoping that he had not understood Mr. Capper.

"I'm sorry, Henry," answered Mr. Capper.

Miserable with disappointment, Henry stared at Mr. Capper. He was too overcome to say anything. He had been so sure, even though Mr. Capper had not made any promises, that this time he was going to get the route.

"Aw, Mr. Capper," protested Scooter.

Henry felt encouraged at having Scooter stand up for

him, instead of scoffing, as he usually did. "I—I thought you needed someone to take Chuck's route," he ventured.

"I did," answered Mr. Capper. "But one of the other district managers phoned me about a boy in his district who wanted to shift to this neighborhood."

"Oh," said Henry miserably. So that was why some other boy was going to have the route. It was not anything he had done wrong. All the same, Henry felt embarrassed. Everyone who knew how much he wanted a route would think it was pretty funny when someone else started delivering *Journals*. Everyone would think Mr. Capper didn't want him to have the route.

Henry felt especially embarrassed to have the other carriers see his humiliation. If only he had come early and talked to Mr. Capper alone. Henry kicked miserably at the bag Scooter was filling with *Journals*.

All at once a terrible suspicion leaped into Henry's mind. "Say, Mr. Capper, would you mind telling me the name of the new carrier?" he asked.

"Let's see." Mr. Capper frowned thoughtfully. "It was Bryan—no, that wasn't it."

"Byron Murphy?" prompted Henry.

"Yes. Yes, that's the name," agreed Mr. Capper.

So it was Murph, thought Henry bitterly. And after I offered to help him find some pipe for his robot's legs, too. A fine friend he turned out to be.

"Is he someone you know?" Mr. Capper asked.

"Sort of," muttered Henry. Well, Murph had the route and he did not, and there was nothing Henry could do about it. That in itself was enough to make him want to avoid the new boy. It wasn't that Henry had done anything wrong; it was just that Murph had experience, and a district manager to speak for him. Naturally, thought Henry. A genius can do anything, anything at all.

After that Henry wished Murph had not moved into

the neighborhood. The old genius, Henry thought cross-
ly. It did not seem fair for Murph to have a paper route
and be a genius, too. Every afternoon when Murph finished his route, Henry saw him ride down Klickitat
Street with the empty *Journal* bag over his shoulders
and Tiger puffing along behind. This made Henry feel
worse. Once he rode past Murph's house and yelled, "I
hope your old robot doesn't work!" No one heard him,
but he felt better for having relieved his feelings.

Then one day when Henry was returning from a swim
at the Y., he turned a corner near Beezus' house and
saw Ramona, with her arms full of *Journals*, skipping
along the sidewalk. Murph was nowhere in sight.

That's funny, thought Henry.

"Hey!" yelled Murph, appearing around the corner on
his bicycle. "You come back with my papers!" When Ramona ran on down the street, Murph pursued her.

Well, what do you know, thought Henry, as he
stopped his bicycle and sat with one foot against the
curb to watch this interesting scene.

When Murph caught up with Ramona, he jumped off
his bicycle and yelled, "You give me those papers!"

"No!" shrieked Ramona. "I want to deliver them. I'm
a paper boy!"

Murph grabbed the papers. Ramona hung on and screamed. Faces began to appear in windows. Front doors opened, and the neighbors stepped outside to see what was happening. Tiger arrived on the scene, but he only lay down on the sidewalk and looked tired.

Henry rode a little closer to have a better view of the struggle. He could see that Murph was pretty embarrassed to have the whole neighborhood watch him tussling with a four-year-old with empty sunglass frames tied around her head. He did look pretty foolish—not a bit like a genius.

Murph jerked the papers away from Ramona. Kicking and howling, she threw herself on the sidewalk. "You give me back my papers!" she screamed.

"They aren't your papers," said Murph, his face and

ears so crimson with embarrassment that Henry almost felt sorry for him, because he knew how exasperating Ramona could be. This time Murph did not yell, because he was trying to look dignified in front of the neighbors.

When Ramona beat her fists on the sidewalk, Henry could not help grinning. He could see that she was working up to a really good tantrum and that Murph, who was not used to her tantrums, wished he was a million miles away.

Then Beezus came running around the corner. "Ramona Quimby!" she said sternly. "You know you aren't supposed to run off! Get up this very instant!"

Ramona screamed and kicked her heels on the cement, exactly the way Henry knew she would. "I'm sorry, Murph," Beezus apologized. "I don't know how she got away."

Murph looked a little scared, as if somehow he were to blame for the scene. Hunching his shoulders as if he hoped to become invisible, Murph climbed on his bicycle with the papers, while Beezus grabbed her sister by the hand and tried to drag her to her feet. Ramona went so limp that she appeared to have no more bones than a rag doll. Beezus put her hands under Ramona's arms and started dragging her toward home. Wearily Tiger rose to his feet and trotted after Murph.

When the girls were far enough away so that he would not have to speak to Murph, Henry rode up to Beezus. "Hi," he said, above Ramona's howls. "Need any help?"

"I don't know what would do any good," said Beezus, and Ramona stopped howling to listen. "Ramona insists she is going to deliver papers."

"I'm a paper boy," said Ramona. "I have to deliver papers."

"You keep quiet," snapped Beezus.

"She sure gave old Murph a bad time," said Henry, try- ing not to show how entertained he had been.

Beezus sighed. "You know how Ramona is when she gets to pretending."

"I know," answered Henry, remembering the trouble he had had with Ramona during the paper drive, when she pretended she was a monkey. Oh, well, thought Henry, Murph will figure out a way to handle Ramona. Murph could do anything. That was the handy thing about being a genius.

The days that followed were difficult ones for Henry. He played with Nosy, brushed Ribsy, went swimming at the Y.—all the things he usually did—but something was wrong. Somehow he could not get interested in any- thing. If he were smart like Murph, he could invent a robot of his own to keep him busy, but the trouble was, he was not smart like Murph.

Then one afternoon when Henry was putting his bi- cycle in the garage, he was surprised to see Murph, with the empty *Journal* bag over his shoulders, riding up the driveway toward him. Now what can he want, Henry wondered, and cautiously decided to let Murph have the first word.

Murph came to the point at once. "You can have the route," he said.

Henry was too surprised to speak.

Murph looked extremely uncomfortable. "I said you can have the route," he repeated.

"You mean you don't want it?" Henry asked incredu- lously.

"Nope," said Murph, as Tiger caught up with him and collapsed on the driveway, panting.

"How come?" asked Henry, finding it hard to believe that a boy who had a paper route would be willing to give it up.

"Ramona," answered Murph.

"Ramona!" exclaimed Henry in disbelief. "She's just a little kid!" A genius licked by a four-year-old! If he hadn't been so surprised, Henry would have laughed out loud.

"I know," said Murph miserably, "but she sure can make a lot of trouble."

To keep from answering, Henry pretended to find something wrong with the chain on his bicycle. He wanted the route, all right. He had wanted it for weeks, and no matter how much trouble Ramona caused Murph, Henry did not intend to let any four-year-old girl stand in his way. It was not the thought of Ramona that kept him from answering. It was Mr. Capper. Henry was not sure the district manager would let him have the route.

Murph must have guessed what Henry was thinking, because he looked down at the driveway and said, "It's all right with Mr. Capper." Murph hesitated before he went on. "I asked him, and he said he would be glad to have you take the route."

The route is mine, thought Henry in a daze. Mr. Capper said so.

Murph looked thoroughly miserable as he continued. "I guess I shouldn't have taken the route when I knew you wanted it, but I just had to have it. Dad said my other route was too far away from home. I needed the money to buy parts for Thorvo. Dad thinks Thorvo is a waste of time, so I have to earn the money for parts myself and . . . well, I just had to have the route. But I've been having so much trouble I probably would have lost the route, and anyway, I don't want it. It takes all my time trying to straighten things out, and I don't have any time left to work on Thorvo. . . ." Murph's voice trailed away, and he looked unhappily at Henry through his glasses.

Henry found himself feeling sorry for Murph, whether

he wanted to or not. It must be hard to have a father who thought building a robot was a waste of time, and to have to wear glasses, and not be a good ballplayer. Why, Murph didn't even have a good dog like Ribsy. He only had tired old Tiger. And then Henry realized the importance of what Murph had said. The route was really his. "Sure, Murph," he managed to say at last. "I'll take the route."

"Swell." Murph was visibly relieved. He removed the *Journal* bag, pulled the route book out of his hip pocket, and handed both to Henry. Then he began to speak eagerly, as if he wanted to make up for what he had done. "I'll have to put Thorvo away for a while until I figure out how to earn some money for parts, and if you still want to go ahead with that private telephone I have most of the stuff we would need. And we wouldn't even have to go to the library to find out how to do it, because I already know how to build one."

"You do!" exclaimed Henry. "Hey, that's swell!" A genius was going to be a pretty good person to have around the neighborhood after all.

"Maybe we can get started Saturday," said Murph, as he started to leave. "You'll be pretty busy with the route after school."

"That's right. My route will take up a lot of my time," agreed Henry. "So long. See you Saturday." Stunned by his sudden good fortune, Henry continued to stand on the driveway in a daze. He had a paper route, and all because of Ramona, but somehow he could not quite believe it. In spite of the bag and the route book in his hands, his good luck did not seem real.

The next day at school, in order to convince himself that his route was real, Henry mentioned it every time he got a chance. When school was finally out, he went straight to Mr. Capper's garage, where he enjoyed being one of the gang at last. Even more he enjoyed starting out with a heavy bag of papers over his shoulders. The route was real, all right.

Henry had not gone far, however, when he saw something that made him pause. Ramona was sitting on the curb, with her feet in the gutter and her hands folded in her lap. She was no longer wearing the sunglasses, and Beezus was nowhere in sight. "Hello there, Ramona," said Henry. In a roundabout way he had her to thank for the route.

"Hello, Henry," said Ramona demurely.

I don't see what Murph was so bothered about, Henry told himself, and went on delivering papers. Ramona continued to sit on the curb like a good girl. She just wants to watch, thought Henry, feeling grown-up and businesslike. Since she wasn't wearing her sunglass frames, she had probably forgotten all about pretending she was a paper boy. He grinned at the thought of Murph's being intimidated by a little girl who sat on the curb with her hands folded in her lap.

Cheerfully Henry rode into the next street, but as he tossed papers he began to have an uneasy feeling that something was wrong. Ramona had been too good. It was not natural. She must be up to something.

Just to be on the safe side, Henry circled the block so that he was riding up Ramona's street once more. And there was Ramona skipping along the sidewalk, with her arms full of the papers he had just delivered. She was tossing them wherever she felt like letting them fall.

That Ramona! I might have known, Henry told himself. "Hey, cut that out!" he yelled furiously.

Ramona tossed a paper onto a lawn—the wrong lawn. Henry took off after her. When he reached her he let his bicycle fall to the sidewalk while he grabbed at the papers Ramona was clutching. "You give me those," Henry said fiercely.

"No!" screamed Ramona. "I'm going to deliver them!"

Henry knew what was going to happen next. He had seen it all before, only the first time he had thought it funny. Where was Beezus, anyway? She might know what to do. Henry jerked the papers away from Ramona, who threw herself on the sidewalk exactly as he had expected. This is where I came in, thought Henry grimly.

Ramona shrieked and grabbed his ankle with both hands. Henry tried to shake her loose, but she hung on.

"Beezus!" Henry yelled. "Beezus, come here!" Faces began to appear at the windows, and Henry felt extremely foolish and not at all businesslike to be standing there yelling for a girl to come and help him. Ribsy, who had been left at home so that he would not get into fights with dogs along the route, came running down the street at the sound of Henry's voice.

Beezus ran out of her house. "Ramona Geraldine Quimby!" She sounded completely exasperated. "You're supposed to be in the house. You know Mother said you had to stay in your room."

Ribsy barked furiously.

"I'm a paper boy," said Ramona stubbornly.

"Get her off my ankle, will you?" said Henry. Tackled oy a four-year-old, with the whole neighborhood watching! Henry felt a flash of sympathy for Murph.

Ribsy grabbed Ramona's coveralls in his teeth. There was a sound of tearing cloth. Ramona screamed.

"Ribsy, cut that out!" Henry ordered. Now people would probably think Ribsy was a ferocious dog attacking Ramona, and there was no telling what trouble that could lead to.

Beezus pried Ramona's fingers from Henry's ankle and started dragging her sister toward home.

"Quiet, Ribsy!" Henry said to his barking dog. "It's all right, fellow. She wasn't really hurting me."

"I'm sorry, Henry," Beezus apologized above her sister's howls. 'I don't know what we can do. (Ramona, be *quiet!*) Mother says she has to stay in her room until the papers are delivered, but if she doesn't get out one day, she gets out the next."

"We've got to do something," said Henry desperately. "I can't have people phoning complaints about not getting their papers all the time. I'll lose my route. Can't you think of something?"

"I've tried," answered Beezus. "The trouble is, when Ramona knows we don't want her to do something, that just makes her want to do it all the more. Mother says she is just plain contrary."

'Yeah, I know," said Henry gloomily as he looked at Ramona, who had stopped screaming and was listening with interest. Suddenly the sight of Ramona looking so pleased to be the center of attention made Henry angry. Who did she think she was, anyway? She wasn't so important. She was just a girl who went to nursery school and played in a sand pile; that was all. She wasn't going to get him into trouble. He was eleven years old and she was only four. If he couldn't figure out a way to keep her from bothering him, he wasn't very smart. Maybe he wasn't a genius, but he was still smarter than a four-year-old. If she continued her game, and of course she would unless he did something about it, he would get into as much trouble as Murph had. And Henry had no intention of going to Mr. Capper the first thing and saying he couldn't deliver the papers because of a girl who went to nursery school. No, sir!

Henry glared at Ramona and thought hard. The thing to do was to outwit her. But how? He had done it once when she had pretended she was a monkey and he would have to do it again. He could get some old papers and fold them and let her deliver them. No, that wouldn't work. People would pick them up and think he had delivered old papers. Somehow, he had to keep

her from pretending she was a paper boy. He could
. . . What *could* he do? And all at once Henry had an
inspiration. If only he had enough time. . . .

Henry looked at his watch. The papers did not have
to be delivered until six o'clock. That would give him
just about half an hour to see if his idea would work
before he finished his route. All he needed was a box,
some wire, a pair of scissors, and some red paint—no,
his mother's lipstick would be quicker—and a few other
things.

"Beezus, you hang onto Ramona," he directed. "I'll be
back in half an hour. No matter what happens, don't let
her get away."

Ramona looked fascinated. She could hardly wait to
see what was going to happen.

"Henry, what are you going to do?" Beezus called after
him.

"You'll see," answered Henry mysteriously. "Come on,
Ribsy!"

Henry rode home as fast as he could, and when he
got there he worked fast. He had to, if he was going to
finish his idea in time to deliver his papers. Scraps of
cardboard and bits of Scotch tape fell to the floor, but
Henry did not bother to pick them up. There wasn't
time. At last, and not a moment too soon, his creation
was finished.

Henry's creation consisted of a cardboard hatbox with
a wire coat hanger fastened upside down to the top. In
one side of the box he had cut holes for eyes and a
mouth. These he had outlined with lipstick, because Ramona said she liked red eyes. Henry set the hatbox over
his head and looked into the mirror. Not bad, he thought,
not bad at all. Really gruesome. Of course it was pretty
crude, but a girl who could pretend that a jumping rope
was a monkey's tail would not be too particular.

"Goodness, Henry!" exclaimed Mrs. Huggins, as Henry dashed through the living room. "You scared me!"

Henry did not stop to talk. He rode as fast as he could to the Quimbys' house, where Beezus and Ramona were waiting on the front steps.

"Henry!" exclaimed Beezus, when she saw his cardboard head. "Are you getting ready for Halloween?"

"Nope," said Henry as he lifted off his head and held it out to Ramona. "How would you like to be a mechanical man like Thorvo?" he asked, and held his breath as he waited to see if Ramona liked his suggestion.

Ramona beamed. There was nothing she liked better than pretending.

Henry relaxed and set the head on her shoulders. "Now remember," he cautioned. "A mechanical man can't move very fast, and he jerks along when he walks." That was to keep her from getting any ideas about being a robot who delivered papers.

"Clank, clank," answered Ramona, jerking down the steps.

"A mechanical man can't bend at the waist, because he doesn't have any," Henry added.

"Clank," answered Ramona.

Henry and Beezus exchanged a look of relief. His route was safe! Henry could see that Beezus was impressed with his idea. And it was pretty smart of him to think of it, Henry thought modestly. Maybe he wasn't a genius like Murph, but he wasn't so dumb, either. In some ways he was even smarter than Murph. Henry

found himself pleased with the thought of being smarter than a genius.

"Henry, what a wonderful idea!" Beezus sounded truly grateful. "Now she will be lots easier to chase."

Henry grinned. "Well, so long," he said, and mounted his bicycle. "I've got to get on with my route." *His route.* Henry felt like shouting the words so the whole world could hear them, because at last he was doing what he wanted to do—something important. And on Saturday he and Murph would start building their own private telephone line. Good old Murph! It was lucky he had moved into the neighborhood. Life, Henry discovered, was suddenly so full of interesting things to do that he rode his bicycle through a pile of autumn leaves in the gutter just for the joy of hearing them crackle.

"Clank, clank!" Ramona yelled after him.

"Clank, clank!" answered Henry.

Other good books about Henry and his pals include Henry Huggins, Henry and Beezus, *and* Henry and Ribsy, *published by William Morrow.*

Jane and the Chief of Police

BY ELEANOR ESTES

Illustrations by Louis Slobodkin

> *Exactly halfway down New Dollar Street in Cranbury, Conn., was the yellow house where the Moffats lived. Times were bad and there was a "For Sale" sign on the house, but the Moffat children—especially nine-year-old Jane—tried to forget the sign, hoping that no one would buy their home.*

AT one end of New Dollar Street were the railroad tracks. At the other end where the trolley ran was the house of Chief Mulligan, Chief of Police. The yellow house where the Moffats lived was sandwiched between these two exciting points. The lawn in front of Chief Mulligan's house was always the best tended on the street and the two small mulberry trees on each side of the stoop were always well-trimmed. They were two soldiers, chests thrust out sternly, on guard day and night for the Chief of Police.

When Jane went past this house, she was careful not to step off the sidewalk onto the lawn even one little inch. She tried to remember always to walk, never to run, lest the Chief of Police take her for a thief running from the scene of her latest crime. But she never walked *too* slowly lest she be arrested for loitering. If Joe and Rufus were with her she made them do the same. She warned Joe not to ride his bicycle on the sidewalk at that end of the street and not to ring his bell within several feet of the Mulligans' house. The Chief of Police might not like it.

Rufus had made a scooter out of an old roller skate and a soap box. Jane told him not to ride it on Chief Mulligan's sidewalk on warm days when the tar was soft and he might leave tracks. Once when Chief Mulligan's new sidewalk had just been laid, she had been horrified to see Rufus just swirling around and around on his heel, making a deep hole in it. Chief Mulligan's new sidewalk! She had packed it down the best she could. Then she had run home for a little flour to sprinkle

on it in order to hide all traces. Yes—and she had tried to show Rufus what a great risk he was running, doing such a thing.

If she saw Chief Mulligan himself come striding up the street, shoulders back, stomach out, stick swinging to the rhythm of his firm steps, she trembled and wondered what she should do. Should she walk past him in silence, stepping politely aside for him? Or should she just nod her head in a casual, friendly way? Or perhaps it would be better still to give him a polite "How-do, Chief Mulligan."

To tell the truth, Jane was rather reluctant to speak to him out and out. For although *she* knew very well who *he* was, it was not at all likely that *he* knew who

she was and he might arrest her for being bold. If she did not speak at all, however, might he not think she was pretending she did not know him? That she was attempting to slip past him unseen because of a guilty conscience for some past crime?

At last, however, she decided that the best and safest course to pursue was the casual, friendly little nod of the head. She'd seen Mama do this occasionally to people she did not know very well. But this little nod did not come naturally to Jane and required some practice before the mirror. Unfortunately one day when she had experimented on Chief Mulligan with the pleasant little nod, Rufus, coming up the street from the other direction, had asked her why for goodness' sakes she was bobbing her head around in that foolish fashion and making faces at the Chief of Police? Happily Chief Mulligan had seemed not to notice her at all.

But one day, a few weeks after the For Sale sign was nailed on the yellow house, something happened that brought this whole business about the policeman to a head. Janey was trying to balance herself on Joey's stilts. She was leaning against the house, eating a handful of sunflower seeds. She spat the shells as far as she could, trying to better her distance with each shell. At the same time she experienced a slight feeling of satisfaction in realizing that on Joey's stilts she was tall enough to blot out the For Sale sign. So far two people had already come to look at the yellow house. But they were very strange people. One had objected to living next door to a Brick Lot! The other had said that the whole place was too run down.

Now, as Janey put the last sunflower seed into her mouth, her attention was attracted by a new and totally unfamiliar figure walking up New Dollar Street. Obviously he was a person of great dignity. The gentleman held his head, which seemed extremely small in comparison with his stomach, tipped very far back. He wore a derby hat and he carried a cane. Never had such a person been seen on New Dollar Street. Unquestionably he was a person of the highest importance. Who knows? A mayor perhaps? A millionaire? He must have a lot of money in his pocket. He must be coming to buy the yellow house.

Jane spat out the last sunflower seed shell viciously. She spread her arms straight out across the For Sale sign. She was sure not one bit of the lettering still showed.

But she held her breath as this elegant person came marching along the picket fence.

"How do you do, little girl?" he said. He tipped his derby hat and nodded his head with much courtesy. Janey was too amazed to return his greeting. He must know her and he must be coming to the yellow house. But no. He reached the gate and marched right past it. And Janey noticed that he spoke in the same way to Mrs. Squire who was weeding her garden, and to Chet Pudge who was spinning his top on the Pudges' white sidewalk.

Jane jumped off the stilts and ran after the man. She felt a sudden surge of happiness to know that this stranger had not come to New Dollar Street to buy the yellow house. She thought it very funny the way he nodded to left and to right. She strutted up the street

right behind him. She stuck out her stomach and held up her head. She tried to copy his courteous air of friendly interest in all the houses and people as he glanced blandly from side to side. Janey had sneakers on her feet so she made no noise. The fine gentleman was totally unaware of the abbreviated shadow of himself that followed him up the street. Jane had mastered his step pretty well, she thought. This consisted of a slight rocking motion from heel to toe. How it would delight the rest of the Moffats when she got home! Imagine while they were all waiting for supper that

evening! In she would come, Mr. Importance! However, this jolly idea came to an abrupt end. As they were
passing Mrs. Shoemaker's house, Peter Frost came along
on his bicycle. He stopped beside Jane and hissed in
her ear:

"You can be arrested for that."

Horrified, Jane stood still on the heel of her left foot
and the toe of her right. She drew in her stomach and
removed the expression of bland interest from her face.

"I'm just on my way to Chief Mulligan's now. I'll see
that he hears about this," said Peter Frost in a stern
voice. "You see, this gentleman happens to be Mr. Pennypepper, the new Superintendent of Schools!"

With these ominous words Peter Frost sounded his
siren right in her ear. He rode off making a great noise
all the way up the street so that Mr. Pennypepper had
to stand still in his tracks and place two plump fore-
fingers in his ears to shut out the noise. Then, shaking
his head and rattling the coins in his pocket, he continued on his dignified way. But with no Jane behind
him. Heavens no! Jane had returned home in the greatest misery.

Of what use now were all the precautions she had
taken to treat the Chief of Police with the right degree
of respect? What use keeping Rufus and Joe quiet at
that end of New Dollar Street and filling in the holes in
the Mulligans' sidewalk? What would her punishment
be, she wondered. Jail, obviously. How dreadful that
would be, she thought mournfully as she disappeared
in the enormous lilac bush on the side of the house. Here
at least she felt she would have temporary security.
This was no ordinary lilac bush. It was a most unusual
one. You can't step inside most lilac bushes. But you
could this one because its many trunks grew in a circle
around a patch of hard, bare ground. Once inside the
lilac bush you were certainly well hidden from the rest

of the world. Sitting on one of the curling roots that thrust its elbow above the earth was splendid for thinking.

Jane thought and thought, but every thought led to jail. It certainly would have been nice to go in the yellow house and tell Mama about it. "I'm going to jail, Mama." And Mama would say, "Whatever for, Janey?" "For mimicking Mr. Pennypepper, Mama." And Mama would stroke her hair and perhaps even see that she didn't have to go to jail.

But Mama was working hard, cutting out a dress for Mrs. Shoemaker. When Mama was cutting out they must not disturb her unless it was something terribly important like Rufus falling out of the cherry tree. This business about Mr. Pennypepper was probably not quite important enough since she was not yet actually in jail. At this moment her gloomy thoughts were interrupted by Joe who thrust his head through the branches and said:

"Oh, here you are. Mama wants you to go to the store and get some sugar. She says hurry. Here's the quarter."

"Why don't you go? How much sugar?"

"I'm goin' bikin' out Mount Carmel way with Chet Pudge. Five pounds."

He put the quarter on a branch, sprang into his bicycle seat, rang his bell six times, and was off.

Well, of course there was nothing to do but go. Jane put the quarter in her pocket. She left the soft shadows of the lilac bush for the brilliant glare of the midday sun. Her heart pounded. She looked up the street and down the street. She saw no sign of Chief Mulligan, Mr. Pennypepper, or Peter Frost. Safe apparently! She breathed more freely and started for Brooney's delicatessen store. This was at the railroad end of New Dollar Street. It was as far from Mr. Mulligan's house as you could possibly go and still be on New Dollar Street.

Jane became quite carefree. The day was so bright. Impossible to think gloomy thoughts forever. She forgot all about the police, Peter Frost, jail, in fact all unpleasant things. She skipped up the street in the special way she had of flinging one leg across the other. She arrived panting at Mr. Brooney's and sniffed. She recognized the smells of potato salad, baked ham, dill pickles, sauerkraut, cheese, and coffee. It was very pleasant there. Mr. Brooney was just putting the finishing touches on his bowl of fresh potato salad.

"It smells good, Mr. Brooney," said Jane. "Perhaps you would give me the recipe." She said this as politely as she had heard many a grown person do.

"Give you the recipe? Not on your life. My recipes are my secrets. I'll give you a lollipop, yes. But my recipes, no." He cocked his head on one side and looked at her owlishly over his glasses as he handed her the sugar and a lollipop.

"Thank you, Mr. Brooney. I guess we'll just have to buy your potato salad if we want any of it."

"Yes, yes," he beamed.

Jane peeled the paper off her lollipop with keen anticipation. She stepped out of the store as she took the first lick. Butterscotch! But—oh, my goodness—sakes alive—who was that? Not . . . ? Yes, walking right towards her, not two doors away, was Chief Mulligan himself. He was walking very briskly. No doubt he would snatch her up in a second! So far he had not seen her. His attention was temporarily distracted by Mr. Brooney's little yellow dog, Jup, who kept nipping at his heels.

Jane looked around swiftly. In front of Mr. Brooney's delicatessen store was a large, square box. This was where the baker left his bread early in the morning. Quick as a flash Jane lifted the lid, jumped in, and crouched in a dark corner. She let the lid down gently and listened.

Tramp, tramp, tramp!

"Here he comes," thought Jane, heart in throat.

Closer the steps came and closer. Tramp, tramp, tramp! "Did he see me jump into the bread-box?" So near now that particles of sand kicked up by his feet spattered the bread-box. Tramp, tramp, and they stopped.

"Hello, Brooney," said Chief Mulligan.

"Hello, Chief. Rounding up all the criminals?" Mr. Brooney called out cheerfully from the store.

"That's right," boomed Chief Mulligan. "I'm after one of 'em that disappeared down by the railroad tracks."

"Oh-h-h," gasped Jane. "I suppose that's me."

"Well, good luck to you," said Mr. Brooney.

"So long," said the Chief of Police.

Tramp, tramp, tramp! The heavy steps went on up

the street. Jane gave a great sigh of relief. Fainter the steps sounded and fainter. At last she heard nothing but a stillness that hurt. Phew! But it was some time before she could get the echo of those feet out of her mind. When she was convinced that he must be several blocks away, probably at least as far as the railroad station, she cautiously raised the lid of the box a crack and surveyed the scene. How good the sunshine felt! She blinked for a second or two.

"Now the coast is clear," she thought and raised the lid higher.

Unfortunately just at this moment Mr. Brooney came out of the store with his broom and started to sweep the sidewalk. Jane lowered the lid and thought. Should she come out or should she stay in? She liked Mr. Brooney. He was jolly and always gave her a lollipop or a caramel, but the question was how would he like someone hiding in his bread-box? Probably not at all. She stayed in.

Mr. Brooney hummed a little song as he swept. It was one he had learned in the old country. He sang the same lines over and over, stopping only to speak a greeting to all who passed.

Jane began to feel annoyed. Her muscles were cramped. How nice and sunny it was outside! Oh, if she could only get out. Get out and go home. Mama probably needed the sugar. She would say, "Jane, whatever has kept you so long? You dawdle too much."

But swish, swish, went the broom and Mr. Brooney went on humming his little song. He was certainly very thorough. Jane pushed the lid up a crack and watched him balefully. There now, thank goodness! He had nearly finished. If he only didn't feel he had to sweep the street too. Jane was sure she had been shut up in that old bread-box for hours. She was hungry.

"I'll count to fifty and then I'll come out," she said to herself with determination.

She counted. ". . . Forty-eight, forty-nine, fifty," she breathed, pushing the lid up again a crack. Sure enough, Mr. Brooney had finished. He turned towards the store, whacking his broom on the bread-box as he passed.

A second more and Jane could jump out. But what was this?

"Hello there, Mr. Brooney."

"Why, Mrs. Shoemaker, how's yourself?"

Mrs. Shoemaker! What could be worse! There was no one, no one on New Dollar Street, who could out-talk Mrs. Shoemaker. And for goodness' sakes! Here she was sitting right down on top of the bread-box.

"Oh," thought Jane. "Now when'll I ever get out of here? I must think of some plan. I wish I was a ventriloquist."

Mrs. Shoemaker swung her short legs and occasionally kicked a heel against the side of the box. Mr. Brooney whacked his broom on the side of the store. Then he leaned against the fence, happy at the thought of passing a dull hour in a bit of gossip.

Jane felt she had been in captivity forever. She had practically forgotten how under the sun she had ever gotten into this box in the first place. Her eyes grew heavy. The voices of Mrs. Shoemaker and Mr. Brooney became more and more indistinct to her.

"I am a princess locked in a gloomy cavern," she thought, trying to console herself. Then she fell asleep and the black horse that was hers to ride in all her dreams came prancing to her rescue, and she was off—off—long golden tresses flying in the wind.

A clean get-away. Of course there was pursuit. Mr. Brooney and Mrs. Shoemaker, mounted on sorry nags, soon fell so far behind that in discouragement they abandoned the race. The Chief of Police fared better on a stout red steed belching fire and smoke from his nostrils. But—could he take wing across the lake as could her own black mount? He could not! Hurray! Snorting and panting, the red steed must fight the brambles around the edge of the lake. So he must if the Chief of Police wished to continue the chase. Apparently he didn't though. For as Jane looked back she saw that Chief Mulligan had dismounted. He stood on the shore of the lake and shook his night club after her as she faded from sight. And the red steed sent sparks from his nostrils that disappeared like shooting stars into the still night air. Jane laughed triumphantly at having outwitted her pursuers. She dismounted in the middle of a beautiful clearing in the heart of the forest. Here she refreshed herself with a deep drink from a sparkling spring and sank down into the moss to await the White Prince.

"Have you seen Jane Moffat? She's been missing two—three hours."

Jane woke up, blinking her eyes, her heart pounding. That voice booming above her head seemed at once both near and far away! The voice of Chief Mulligan, of course! Black horse and White Prince faded away. She was Jane Moffat in a bread-box. She heard Mr. Brooney say:

"Jane Moffat? Why, let me see now. Yes, she was here this noon after sugar."

"Well, she never came home with the sugar. Her mother's pretty worried. Now just what time was she here?"

"Let me see now," replied Mr. Brooney, trying to collect his thoughts. "Yes, she was here. When was it? When was it? Eleven o'clock? Twelve o'clock? But just a minute, Chief. Just a minute. Here's the baker and I have a bone to pick with him. He left me only fourteen loaves of bread this morning and he charged me for fifteen. Hey there, what do you mean?" he asked the baker.

The baker insisted Mr. Brooney must have counted incorrectly. The two started to argue. The Chief of Police stood by with an air of disapproval.

"I tell you," said Mr. Brooney, pounding his fist on the bread-box, "I tell you that I took only fourteen loaves of bread from this box this morning."

"And I tell you I put fifteen in," said the baker, pounding *his* fist on the box.

"Fourteen!"

"Fifteen!"

"Might be you overlooked one," put in the Chief of Police in a masterly fashion.

"Nonsense," growled Mr. Brooney. "However could I do that in broad daylight and all? Still, look in yourself if you think . . ."

Chief Mulligan had become very interested in the discussion. He got out his flashlight so they could see into the corners. Mr. Brooney raised the lid with a grand gesture. The three men peered in. There was Jane! She looked up at them, blinking. The three men gasped in astonishment.

"I'll be blowed," said Mr. Brooney.

"I'm dodder-blasted," said the baker.

The Chief of Police said nothing. With admirable composure he switched off his flashlight, put it in his pocket, and lifted Jane out. She felt for an instant the icy coldness of his badge upon her hot cheek. She tried to make herself a featherweight and held her breath. For a moment no one said anything. Chief Mulligan gave Mr.

Brooney a look which seemed to say, "This is the dispatch with which I am accustomed to discharge my commissions."

Mr. Brooney looked at the baker and said sarcastically, "Is that your loaf of bread?"

The baker sat down on the bread-box and mopped the flour off his eyebrows in great bewilderment.

Then Chief Mulligan started up the street with Jane still in his arms, his night stick bobbing at his side. Jane stole a look at the Chief's face. He was looking at her. Quickly she lowered her eyes and as quickly raised them again, so he would not think her dishonest and shifty-eyed. She noticed that he was smiling.

"What were you doing in that box?" he asked curiously.

"Hidin'."

"Hidin' from whom?"

A long silence and then very faintly, "You."

"Me!" Even Jane could see he was truly amazed. Could it be he had not been told about Mr. Pennypepper?

"Whatever for?" he asked.

"'Cause I . . ." and swiftly Jane told him about Mr. Pennypepper, jail, Mrs. Shoemaker sitting on the box. Suddenly Chief Mulligan broke into laughter. It started with a chuckle but turned into a loud, hearty laugh. Then into great guffaws. His stomach shook. Tears rolled down his cheeks. He had to put Jane down. He had to sit down on the curb and laugh some more.

Jane watched him in fascination.

"Why, he's nice," she thought.

His face grew redder and redder and the tears coursed down his round cheeks. Jane felt in her pocket for her handkerchief. She offered it to him gravely.

"There are tears in your whiskers," she said.

"Oh-oh-oh," gasped the Chief of Police. He mopped his face and blew his nose very loudly. Suddenly he stopped laughing.

"Little girl," he said, "don't you be afraid of a policeman any more or of anything. Remember this. A policeman is for your protection. He's nothing to be scared of."

Gathering himself together, Chief Mulligan stood up. He smoothed down his uniform, took Jane by the hand. In silence and great dignity they marched up the block. At the yellow house he shook hands with her.

"If I can ever be of any service, call on Chief Mulligan of the police force," he said.

Then he clicked his heels together and saluted.

All the Moffats were looking out of the window and saw him. Jane sauntered nonchalantly into the house.

From that day on, Jane and the Chief of Police were fast friends. She always left a May basket at his door and sent him a Valentine she'd made.

However, she still walked on tiptoe when she passed his house in order not to disturb him should he be napping. And she was still very careful not to step on his grass. Yes, and she was just as strict as ever about Rufus and Joe ringing their bicycle bells at that end of New Dollar Street.

For more stories of Jane Moffat, her sister, and her two brothers, read Middle Moffat *and* Rufus M., *by Eleanor Estes, published by Harcourt, Brace & World.*

INDEX of Authors and Titles

ACKNOWLEDGMENTS

The publishers wish to express their appreciation to the following publishers, agents, authors, and artists who have granted permission to use material appearing in this book. Any errors or omissions are unintentional and will be corrected in future printings if notice is sent to The Crowell-Collier Publishing Company.

THOMAS Y. CROWELL COMPANY ". . . And Now, Miguel," from . . . *And Now, Miguel,* by Joseph Krumgold, illustrated by Jean Charlot, copyright 1953 by Joseph Krumgold; Thomas Y. Crowell Company, publisher.

DOUBLEDAY & COMPANY, INC. "Bright April," from *Bright April,* written and illustrated by Marguerite de Angeli, copyright 1946 by Marguerite de Angeli; "The Yellow Shop," from *The Rachel Field Story Book,* by Rachel Field, illustrated by Adrienne Adams, copyright 1931 by Rachel Field, illustrations copyright 1958 by Adrienne Adams; reprinted by permission of Doubleday & Company, Inc.

FOLLETT PUBLISHING COMPANY "A Friend in Need," from *More All-of-a-Kind Family,* by Sydney Taylor, illustrated by Mary Stevens, copyright 1954 by Sydney Taylor; reprinted by permission of Follett Publishing Company, Chicago.

HARCOURT, BRACE & WORLD, INC. *The Hundred Dresses,* by Eleanor Estes, illustrated by Louis Slobodkin, is copyright 1944 by Harcourt, Brace & World; "Jane and the Chief of Police," from *The Moffats,* by Eleanor Estes, illustrated by Louis Slobodkin, copyright 1941 by Eleanor Estes; "The Girl in Pink," from *Plain Girl,* by Virginia Sorenson, illustrated by Charles Geer, copyright 1955 by Virginia Sorenson; used by permission of Harcourt, Brace & World, Inc.

HARPER & BROTHERS "A Different World," from *Candita's Choice,* by Mina Lewiton, illustrated by Howard Simon, copyright 1959 by Mina Lewiton; "The Wolf Pack," from *Little House on the Prairie,* by Laura Ingalls Wilder, illustrated by Garth Williams, copyright 1935 by Laura Ingalls Wilder; reprinted by permission of Harper & Brothers, publishers.

HOLT, RINEHART & WINSTON, INC. "The Fair," from *Thimble Summer,* written and illustrated by Elizabeth Enright, copyright 1938 by Elizabeth Enright Gillham; reprinted by permission of Holt, Rinehart & Winston, Inc.

THE MACMILLIAN COMPANY "Away Goes Sally," from *Away Goes Sally* by Elizabeth Coatsworth, illustrated by Helen Sewell, copyright 1934 by The Macmillan Company; "The Covered Bridge," from *The Covered Bridge,* by Cornelia Meigs, illustrated by Marguerite de Angeli, copyright 1936 by The Macmillan Company; used by permission of The Macmillan Company.

WILLIAM MORROW AND COMPANY, INC. "Henry and the Paper Route," from *Henry and the Paper Route,* by Beverly Cleary, illustrated by Louis Darling, copyright 1957 by Beverly Cleary; by permission of William Morrow and Company, Inc.

G. P. PUTNAM'S SONS "Waiting for Jeptha," from *The Trail of the Hunter's Horn,* by Billy C. Clark, illustrated by Veronica Reed, copyright 1957 by Billy C. Clark; reprinted by permission of G. P. Putnam's Sons, publishers.

RAND McNALLY & COMPANY "Pony Penning Day," from *Misty of Chincoteague,* by Marguerite Henry, illustrated by Wesley Dennis, copyright 1947 by Rand McNally & Company; Rand McNally & Company, publishers.

THE VIKING PRESS, INC. "Experiment 13," from *Centerberg Tales,* written and illustrated by Robert McCloskey, copyright 1951 by Robert McCloskey; "The Great Balloon Ascension" from *Henry Reed, Inc.* by Keith Robertson, illustrated by Robert McCloskey, copyright 1958 by Keith Robertson; "Little Navajo Bluebird," from *Little Navajo Bluebird,* by Ann Nolan Clark, illustrated by Paul Lantz, copyright 1943 by Ann Nolan Clark; reprinted by permission of The Viking Press, Inc.